This is a work of fiction. All characters and events are either a product of the author's imagination or used fictitiously, and any resemblance to real people or events is entirely coincidental.

PARAGON OF WATER

First Edition: November 2022

ISBN-13: 978-1-952145-23-0

PARAGON OF WATER

SPECTRUM LEGACY BOOK THREE

BETH ALVAREZ

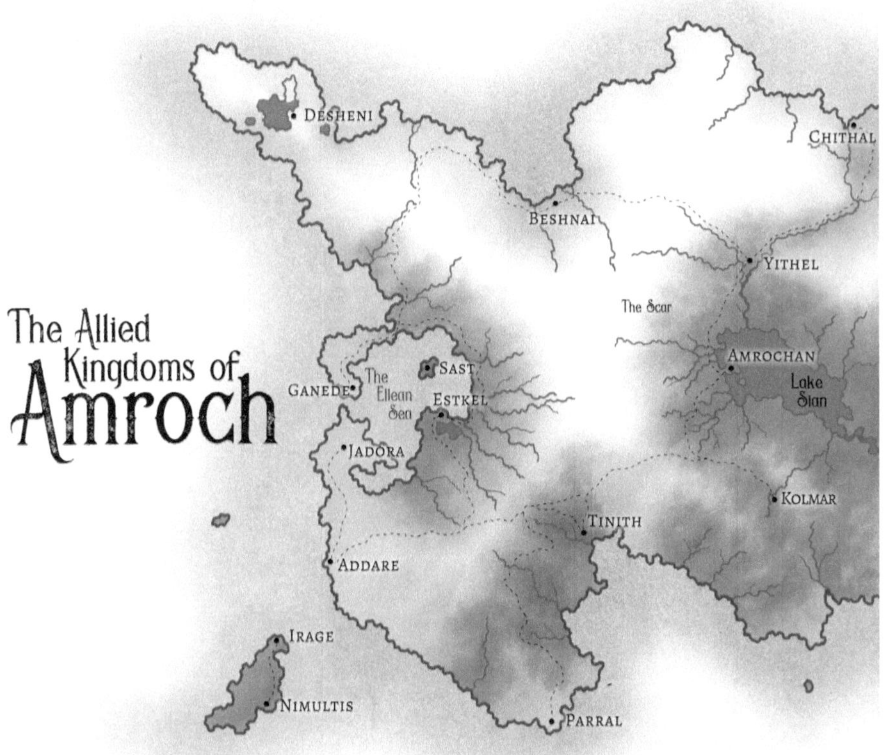

The Allied Kingdoms of Amroch
DESHENI
CHITHAL
BESHNAI
YITHEL
The Scar
AMROCHAN
Lake Sian
GANEDE
The Ellean Sea
SAST
ESTKEL
JADORA
KOLMAR
ADDARE
TINITH
IRAGE
NIMULTIS
PARRAL

CHAPTER ONE

THE PLATFORM ROCKED as Zaide sat down. "Ready." He shifted as he settled in the middle of the rough wooden square. The planks were scarred from years of transporting cargo, the gaps between each board wider than he'd expected. It looked rickety, but he'd seen what it could do and was sure it was sturdier than it looked.

Lark didn't seem to share that confidence. She inched closer to him and gripped his arm. The contact wasn't like her at all, and he blinked at her a moment before he thought to lay a hand atop both of hers. She trembled, but her jaw remained clamped tightly shut, her face etched with stony determination.

"Don't worry, Your Highness," the porter behind them called. "We ride the lifts all the time. No one's ever gone off."

"At least, not yet," Tula put in. She grinned, her green eyes sparkling with more than the afternoon sun.

Zaide shot her a stern frown. He'd never seen the princess scared, but it wasn't hard to imagine needling at her would make things worse. They still had to travel together, and he wouldn't invite more of her ire than necessary. "Just sit still."

"Aye. Here goes." The porter kicked something and the platform lurched.

A tiny squeak escaped the princess and she clung to Zaide's arm even harder.

A moment later, the platform began its descent. Tula laughed as the pulleys creaked and they sank toward the docks at the base of the cliff. The wind was strong and the lift swayed, but the ropes were sturdy and they kept a slow and steady pace. The whir and clank of the lift's gears faded away overhead.

Zaide scanned the horizon. To the west, the sea glittered without interruption. The ships hung close to land, and great numbers of them waited in the bay. Word that the city of Jadora had reopened its gates wouldn't reach the merchants until later that day. Metaphorically reopened them, he thought grimly. When they'd departed that morning, there were no gates left to speak of, and he doubted they'd be restored before word spread.

"Think we'll be able to find a ship?" He had to raise his voice to be heard over the rushing wind.

Tula shrugged. "Even if we didn't have such an influential party, there's bound to be somebody down there willing to run things to Ganede. What else can they do?"

"Stay and unload, now that the city's open?" But there was no way the merchants would know that yet. Zaide wondered whether it would be appropriate to tell them. No one would refuse the princess as a passenger. That Tula had become Magister of Jadora would have worked in their favor, too, but he suspected that was a secret they were expected to hold to themselves while her elder sister restored order. As far as anyone knew, Elsanna was Magister. Letting the truth spill would only cause trouble.

"We'll pick a small, fast boat. They won't be delayed much by one ride." Tula tapped her chin with one finger, as if reconsidering. "How long did you say it took to get across the bay before?"

"Just a few hours." It would have been nice if it were longer. He'd slept a little after the siege of Jadora, but Lark had insisted they needed to move on. Being rocked to sleep on a swaying ship sounded blissful.

"Well, no problem, then." She flashed him another grin, then returned her eyes to the sights around them. Tula had spent her whole life in Jadora, yet had never been granted the time to explore the docks that clung to the cliffs and granted passage to the Watcher's sister city of Ganede. They'd hurried up the cliffside when they'd disembarked on their way to Jadora before, driven by the smoke that warned what awaited them. Having time to wander meant this was a new adventure for her, as it was for Lark.

Of the two, Tula appeared to be having a better time.

Zaide patted the princess's hands and didn't try to extricate himself from her grasp. "We're almost down." He wasn't sure how else to offer comfort. Was comforting the princess appropriate? It wasn't as if anyone would recognize her, this far from Amrochan, but he still wondered. King Sendassian had already tried to strangle him once. Being seen with the princess clinging to him would surely invite a more successful attempt.

The lift lurched and the platform thudded to the dock. The ride had been less thrilling than expected, but it saved a considerable amount of time. Tula popped to her feet and shaded her eyes as she looked back the way they'd come, as if in echo of Zaide's thoughts.

He stood and pulled Lark up with him. "Here we go. Can you stand?"

"My knees are weak as water," Lark admitted. She kept her eyes screwed shut as he helped her stand, and she wobbled so badly that he grasped her by the shoulders to hold her steady.

"Afraid of heights, huh?" Tula asked.

"I've never been afraid of looking out from the palace ramparts." A defensive note crept into the princess's voice. "I'm not cowardly."

Zaide rubbed her arms soothingly before he realized such an action might be too familiar. He stopped, but held on to her until he was sure she wouldn't fall. "Nobody said you were. But you didn't have to ride with us, you know."

The look she shot him made it clear that separating was never an option, but she pulled away and spoke of it no more. "Let's keep moving. I'll secure transport for us. In the meantime, we need to compose a list of what we'll need for this part of the voyage."

"Voyage?" He almost laughed. "That's a little grander than I think the trip is going to be." He'd make a list, though. He'd outfitted himself well enough during his first expedition to Desheni, and there were only a few additional things he thought would be necessary for the trip this time around.

Tula all but pranced off the lift's platform. She bounced on her toes and pointed at the docks. "Oh, look at that boat with the patched-up sails! What kind of storms do you think it's been through?"

"We're not hiring a boat with patched sails," Zaide said, though he wasn't sure. If that was the fastest option and its captain agreed to transport them, Lark might not see fault with the boat's appearance.

The princess said nothing and marched down the nearest dock. She swayed on her feet once, but adjusted her bags and continued on her own.

Tula rubbed her mouth. "Hmm. I think she's mad at you."

"At me? Why? I didn't do anything!" He'd tried to ensure just the opposite, treating her kindly and offering reassurance. Why on earth had that backfired?

"I don't know, but I'll go help her find a boat. You should work on that list." She smiled, a bit of sparkle back in her eyes, then hurried after Lark.

Zaide lingered by the lift, gripping the straps of his bags and staring after them. The hot and cold attitude Lark took with him would be a source of consternation until the end of his days. "Princesses," he muttered. He heaved his things a little higher and trudged forward to find somewhere to sit.

A few empty crates beside one of the numbered docks provided a nice place to wait, and he settled there while Lark and Tula spoke to the sailors and porters that meandered up and down the sea-stained walkways. A few dock workers sent curious or suspicious glances his way, but he ignored them and instead gazed across the bay.

Traveling alone had been easy, but with the girls along, Desheni and its people would take a while to reach. Longer, if Lark tried to take the lead like she had between Kolmar and Amrochan. He couldn't help but grimace at the thought of the goborrins they'd encountered on that leg of the journey. At least this far north, they were unlikely to encounter them. He wouldn't rule out the possibility, not after the invasion of Jadora, but the monsters and their camps would be easier to avoid in the wilderness. The mountains had their own perils, instead.

"We'll need a good map," he muttered to himself as he dug in his bag for something to write on. All he found was the water-damaged songbook Resia had given him to accompany the Vale Hymnflute. He frowned as he ran a thumb over the edges of its warped pages. Reluctantly, he opened to the damaged endpapers at the back and fished a stick of graphite from elsewhere in his bag. He'd been meant to write notes for songs in the back of the book, not a shopping list. But this was what he had, and at the top of the list, he made a note to get a blank book and a good pen.

They'd need extra rope. A new pocket knife for him. He started to write down a need for a reliable fire starter, then reconsidered. They had Tula with them. Her latent magic had only just begun to awaken, but maybe her control over flame would spare them that expense. He scratched a question mark at the end of that line with a mental note to ask later. "And cold weather gear for all of us." That would be expensive, but necessary. Summer was approaching fast, but snow still capped the mountains, and that meant the risk of encountering tricen and tricewolves was still there.

"Plus not knowing what Desheni looks like this time of year." It was possible winter extended farther into the year than he was prepared for. Would Tula's magic give them an advantage over the ice monsters, too? He frowned deeper as he started a bulleted list of clothing each of them would need.

"Who are you grumbling to?" Lark asked as her shadow moved over his book.

Zaide hunched over the writing as if to protect it from her eyes. "Uh, myself?" He hadn't realized he was still muttering as he wrote. "I do that now. A lot, thanks to all the time I spent out here alone."

Inexplicably, her face brightened. "Well, you have us to talk to now, at least. I've found a sailor who's willing to take us. It's a little boat, just big enough for the three of us to fit while the captain and his assistant do the sailing."

"Assistant? The first mate?"

Her brows rose. "Coming from someone who doesn't know the anatomy of a ship. Referring to the man as an assistant is not incorrect. Come along, you can finish your muttering and mumbling on the boat."

Zaide was tempted to mutter and mumble some more right then.

Instead, he stuffed the songbook back into his bag and pushed himself from the crates. "That didn't take you very long."

"Money talks," was all Lark said.

She led the way to a tiny vessel tied to the very last dock in the row. Tula stood watching as the two sailors on board prepared for launch, her upraised hands curled to fists before her chest. She bounced on her toes as if set on springs.

"Welcome aboard," an older man with gray-shot hair called as Lark hopped the gap and landed in the little boat below. He had a worn look about him and moved slowly, but comfortably. The other man aboard was younger, but bore an unmistakable resemblance to his aging father. "We're glad to have you."

"Vosh is a family friend," Tula said when Zaide gave the boat a suspicious glance. "That's Osyn, his son. Osyn and Elsanna attended rudimentary together."

"Attended what, now?" Zaide asked.

The former librarian held tight to her robes as she jumped into the boat. It rocked hard enough that both sailors laughed, further cementing his distrust of the vessel.

"Rudimentary is what they call the first tier of education in Jadora." Lark made her way to a narrow set of steps that descended no more than knee-deep. A tiny door stood open to welcome them into what had to be the smallest cabin ever. "All children are required to attend, though further education beyond basic mathematics and reading skills is considered optional."

Oh. Zaide rubbed the back of his neck. Kolmar was so small, there was no formal education. The Elder had ensured all parents taught their children enough to get by in whatever profession they might pursue, but most knowledge was specialized to craft.

"Come on, lad. It's a small ship, but that makes her fast." Vosh grinned, his teeth stark white against his sun-browned skin. "There's a good wind today. We'll reach Ganede's docks in half the time a bigger ship would take."

Zaide stifled his doubts and slid into the boat with more care than either of the girls. He hadn't minded the bigger ships, but this looked like a decent wave would make it capsize. "What are you doing out here with such a little boat?"

"Shopping," Vosh laughed. "The boat's a pleasure my wife hates me for, but she'll be glad for it now, I think. When Jadora stopped letting merchants in, I worried my wife would run out of the herbs she takes for her health. I got the guards to let me out last week so I could try and find some in the merchant camps in the desert, but they said all the shipments are out on the boats still. I figured we could sail around them and find who's selling."

"And you're just getting to that now?" Zaide followed Tula

toward the cabin, unsure where else he could go. A row of seats rested along the back of the boat, but the shelter of the little cabin was more inviting.

Osyn was less enthusiastic. "We've been out here for days. Haven't found anyone yet. We dock up for meals, and that's about it. There are over a hundred boats out there, and nobody's willing to give a list of what freight they're hauling."

"Lots of smuggling, I'm sure," Tula said. She tossed her bags into the cabin without a care. Inside, Lark's startled yelp suggested she should have cared a little.

"Oh, no doubt. But if we have to wait for those herbs to make it to the city, I hate to think what it'll do to my poor wife." Vosh tightened something or another and went for the rope that bound them to the dock. "All ready?"

"Ready," Tula chirped.

"Ready," Zaide sighed.

Lark only grumbled inside the cabin.

The launch was unremarkable and easy, and Zaide ducked into the cabin to check on the princess. "You all right?"

She sat in the center of the floor, her bags and Tula's in a heap behind her back. "Fine. Just tired."

Tula peeked inside. "I'm going to watch the water for a bit. Keep an eye on my bags, okay?"

Lark patted the pile behind her with one hand and the librarian took it as confirmation. After Tula disappeared from the doorway, Zaide decided to shut the door.

"Kind of weird to run into people she knows out here, isn't it?" He kept his voice low, unsure all the tiny windows were fastened.

"Perhaps. But they were the ones that called to her. They were happy to see her at the docks and asked if she'd spoken with the rest of their family recently. That she had not and had no news for them seemed to be a disappointment." The princess leaned back against the bags, though they couldn't have been comfortable.

"You think they're really out here looking for herbs, or do you think they're part of the smuggling Tula mentioned?" His own skepticism came as a surprise. When had he grown so jaded?

"I don't think there's much they can do with a vessel so small. And Tula didn't tell them who we were, so I don't think there's any ulterior motive to their assistance. She said Elsanna has sent us to go shopping in Ganede for the Magister, which I suppose is truthful, and they offered their ship on their own."

"Hm." Zaide could think of no other response. It certainly didn't sound ominous, but after the false Magister and the tangle of politics left behind, caution struck him as wise. He settled on the floor, not beside her, but an arm's reach away.

For a time, the sound of waves and wind and cheerful voices just outside the cabin occupied the silence. Then Lark spoke, her voice subdued. "I apologize for my behavior on the lift. The height didn't bother me. It was the way it swayed with all of us on it."

He gave a soft snort of amusement. "It didn't bother me."

She started to say something, then shut her mouth and turned away with ruddy spots of color in her golden cheeks. Just when he began to wonder if he'd offended her, she gestured toward the low bunks that lined the cabin's walls. "Are you going to try and rest?"

Zaide considered it, then shook his head. The bunks were tiny, and the company wasn't proper. "I napped a bit this morning, remember? I think I'll sit with Tula, see if we can learn anything else about those ships out there." For all he knew, one of them could be carrying goborrins. Maybe that was how they'd reached Jadora to begin with.

"I think I'll stay here." Something odd colored her tone. Disappointment? He couldn't imagine why.

"Rest well, then. Mind if I leave my bags here?" He'd already slid the straps from his shoulder, but he still offered a smile of thanks when she gestured for him to suit himself. He left the bags where they were, but kept his blades. The Jadoran long knife at his left hip would take some getting used to, but he supposed the same could be said about the Spectrum Blade on the right. The sword had been silent since they'd left the city, but he already knew it was only a matter of time. His hand hovered over the blade's sheath a moment before he made himself move. "Call if you need anything."

Lark said nothing as he slipped out of the cabin. He stood with his stance wide and his back straight and gazed past the sailors. The city of Ganede was visible, but the bay was so crowded, Zaide didn't know how they'd get between all the boats.

"Zaide, come sit!" Tula called. She patted a space beside her at the back of the boat. "They're going to take turns steering and chatting with us. Once we're set on a good path, that is." She gave the trade ships a thoughtful frown.

He trudged over to take a seat beside her. "Think we'll really make it that fast?"

"I think most of the travel time is just weaving between all those big ships, there. The wind won't be as strong when we're down between them, but Vosh says he's got oars. We can all take turns rowing if need be." She pantomimed as she explained, every bit as excited and enthusiastic as a girl sent to run errands for the Magister might be.

"As long as we can do it with the four of us. I think Lark isn't feeling well." The color in her face indicated as much, anyway.

Tula blinked as if taken by surprise. "Really? I didn't think she was the type to get seasick."

"It's a bit different between big boats and ours," Vosh said, a good reminder that the boat was little enough for conversation to be overheard. "But it's just a short jaunt, pay it no mind. We're not like those big boats that cross back and forth between the ports. Once we're in a straightaway, you'll see how we can fly."

"He was a sailor for a fishing vessel when Elsanna and Osyn were young," Tula added. "When I was very small, before

Elsanna became one of the guardswomen, we used to come out in the summer months for Vosh to take us out to sea."

"I thought you'd never been to the docks?" Zaide asked.

Immediately, the librarian crossed her arms and looked withdrawn. "Well, no, not the docks, but..."

"Everything's supposed to go through the docks. That doesn't mean it does." Vosh chuckled. "Jadora has strict boating taxes, but if we stayed in the bay, well... It used to be a lot easier to launch unnoticed, and I'm sure you've seen how the land slopes down, nice and gentle."

Zaide glanced toward the shore, though it was obscured by boats. "You launched from the beaches? That's a long way from Jadora. It's all cliffs on this side."

"Not all cliffs," Tula said. "Just mostly. There's a little finger of the Ellean sea that curves around the Jadoran plateau, and there are beaches there. That was where we sailed. My grandparents used to live down there, before the Magister decided there shouldn't be any settlements in Jadoran territory beyond the docks and the plateau."

"A different time," Vosh sighed, and his son gave a solemn nod.

Tula's smile faltered. "A lot has changed since then."

Zaide understood all too well. "Maybe things will settle someday," he said, though as he scanned the countless ships in the bay once more, they gave him the distinct and unsettling sense that the worst changes were yet to come.

CHAPTER TWO

THEIR ARRIVAL at Ganede's docks was more unceremonious than Zaide's first visit. The three of them clambered out of Vosh's boat with little grace, and Osyn handed their bags up to them.

"Aren't you coming ashore?" Tula asked as she slid the straps over her shoulders.

Vosh shook his head. "We've yet to find any merchants with what we need. They're bound to be out there, and I'm going to find them before they decide to head back to Addare."

"Best of luck," Zaide said. He adjusted the blades at his sides, ensuring his bags wouldn't be in the way. He didn't expect trouble, but after the experience in Jadora, he wouldn't be caught off his guard. "If you see anything suspicious on those boats, though, be sure you send word to Elsanna."

The implication he might made Vosh raise his brows, but the man nodded. "Of course. Enjoy your trip, and if you see us on the water when you're ready to head back, feel free to flag us down and we'll get you home."

A shade of doubt crossed Tula's face, but Lark offered a courteous smile. "Thank you. Take care on the water." She steered Tula up the docks with a firm hand.

Zaide trailed along behind them. "We should get the clothing we need first. I remember where I got it before, the prices were good."

"Lead the way." The princess flicked a hand toward the city, where its low wooden buildings nestled against the evening landscape in a way that gave the impression they were settling for the night. A few lights had already begun to emerge in the city. Soon, Ganede would be lit up the way Zaide recalled, filled with a warm and sleepy glow.

He slipped past the girls on the dock and headed for the city's edge. The sand gave way to grasses that rippled in a mild breeze, and just beyond, the hard dirt paths waited.

"It's so lush over here," Tula whispered as they passed the first of dozens of planters. They overflowed with growth, flowers trailing down their sides in sprays of color.

"Wait until we pass the vineyards," Zaide said. "This way."

Their group received a few odd glances now and then, but it bothered him less than it had when he'd set off on his own before. They were an odd group. An Amrochan girl with her golden skin and hair, still garbed in Amrochan fashion. A Jadoran girl whose sandy complexion and flame-red hair might have fit in, save the fine robes she wore that were befitting of her new position as Magister. Those could have been explained away by claiming she was the Magister's assistant, he supposed, but that hardly explained the company she kept. Especially when he was the strangest of all, a broken-born youth in Jadoran clothing, with a Jadoran knife at one hip and a strange sword in a scabbard of Amrochan craftsmanship.

Being noticed didn't bother him, but he feared they would be memorable.

"What else is on your list, beyond clothing?" Lark asked as they trailed between buildings. She spared them little attention, focused on his back.

"A map. Supplies for things like notes."

"I have a notebook," Tula said.

"Yeah, I expected you would. I meant for me, though." He

hadn't considered whether he'd be able to find a pen or ink that would work well for travel. Would Resia accept a replacement songbook written in graphite? He doubted it.

Lark made a thoughtful sound. "We should get clothing first, as you said, then we should split up and get what we need for the rest of the trip. It'll go faster, and we'll be able to set out right away."

"Or we could find somewhere here to spend the night," Tula said with a sigh. "I'm exhausted."

The princess gave a stiff shrug. "You should have slept on the boat."

"How could I sleep on the boat? It was so exciting! Crossing the bay for the first time, seeing Ganede for the first time? I couldn't sleep. I've wanted to come here my whole life." Tula twirled and hopped ahead a few paces. "It's like a dream come true."

"It's also an important mission," Zaide said. "I wouldn't mind finding somewhere to rest, but we've still got daylight. It might be in our best interest to get things done fast and move on."

A hint of a smile curved Lark's lips. Approval? Easy to get, it seemed, as long as he agreed with her.

"Fine," Tula sighed, and her whole form slumped as if deflated. She trudged along like that for a moment, then straightened.

Just afterward, they rounded the corner and found the shop Zaide was looking for. Their stock of cold weather gear had diminished in the approach of summer, but there was enough they could gather what they needed in sizes that fit well enough.

Zaide was the only one who had ventured to Desheni before, and they looked to him for approval on their choices, but he'd grown distracted by a pen with bright brass nibs and vials of colored ink, all nestled in a velvet-lined wooden case. "I'm sure that's all fine," he murmured, not really hearing the question or who had asked.

Beside him, Lark crossed her arms. "A strange time to suddenly take a scholarly fascination."

He blinked, then scowled. "This is a responsibility." Magister Vorkaris had been generous in filling their purses. He snatched the box from the shelf. "Resia needs her songbook back, and I need to remake it before the old one winds up unreadable."

"Which would be your fault, of course." She nodded toward the door. "Tula and I are going to go get a map from the cartographer down the street. You pay for all this and we'll meet you near the food vendors."

"Stay together," he said, though he doubted she needed the protection. She carried herself with determination as she led Tula out the door, the librarian bounding along behind her with a skip and a jump.

Zaide stifled a sigh and scuffled toward the counter. The shop was empty, aside from him, and the shopkeeper watched with interest as he counted coins out of his new purse. "I need a book and some paper. Where can I find that?"

"There's a bookbinder three streets over." The shopkeeper pointed to indicate the direction. "But I don't know that they stay open late. You're headed north?"

They were memorable enough without letting people know where they were going. "Beshnai," he said, and it was only partially a lie. If all went well, they'd head that way eventually. "There are a lot of ships in the harbor, I thought maybe some of the merchants would try their luck along the north road and we might be able to hitch a ride."

"More ships every day," the shopkeeper agreed as he tallied everything piled on the counter. He gave Zaide's pen a thoughtful look before he added it to the list. "Most are giving up hope of getting things to Jadora. They're offloading here or near the marshes in Estkel. The money isn't as good as imports to Jadora, the desert pays high prices for everything to keep people bringing them supplies. But it's better than sitting in the harbor while your cargo rots."

"Doesn't Ganede export to Jadora, too?" Zaide stacked his coins on the counter. He'd been through this once before, knew the currency now and had kept count while the shopkeeper made his notes.

"We would if the gates were open. Not that it impacts my business much." The man plucked the coins from the countertop and ran his thumb over their edges to count. "Beshnai doesn't rely on our commerce for a lot. If a ride is what you're looking for, ask at the wineries to see if they're sending anything that way. Ganede might not have much to offer inland territories, but alcohol is treasured everywhere."

Zaide slid his pen case into one of his bags and gathered the folded clothing. It was too bulky to put away, so he kept it in his arms. "Thanks."

The man made a gesture of farewell, or maybe dismissal, and turned to put his money away.

It was only after Zaide slipped out of the shop that he realized the shopkeeper hadn't recognized him. It had only been a handful of weeks since his last expedition. Had he made that little of an impression before? Or had there been others of his people through that area? The thought made the back of his neck prickle and he squirmed, unable to spare a hand to scratch.

Aside from a fleeting glimpse in Tinith's market, he'd seen no sign of others like himself. When he'd first left Kolmar, he'd hoped he might encounter someone, anyone who could help connect him to his roots and the family he'd lost. His parents had fled the Shattered Lands, but there had to be others. Cousins, aunts. He'd never been under any illusion that broken-born were common in Amroch, but they'd been a thriving people once, and anyone he encountered in Amroch might hold some key to finding what he'd lost.

Or they could hold some connection to that which he fought against now. Much as he hated shouldering the burden of distrust his people had earned, he couldn't deny what he'd heard, either. He'd seen no people among the goborrin hordes outside Amrochan or within Jadora's walls, but if they were the leaders of those armies, they had to be somewhere.

Ships in the harbor. Goborrins in Jadora. Broken-born in Ganede. A hint of a headache spurred the space behind his eyes. It was all obvious, wasn't it? And maybe that was why the man asked where they were going. If they could send word to Beshnai ahead of whatever forces may be headed that way, the city stood a better chance of survival.

"Not everywhere has a dragon to protect it," he muttered as he made for the bookbinder's shop.

He reached the space just as the bookbinder was locking the door. An extra coin persuaded her to retrieve an empty journal and a stack of loose papers from her store, and with those jammed into his bags, Zaide turned to follow his nose.

The scents of Ganede's food were just as tantalizing as he remembered. They guided him through the streets, and it wasn't long before he found Lark and Tula sitting on the edge of a large planter, a map spread between their laps. Each held some sort of bread stuffed with meats and cheese, the aroma enough to make his stomach growl.

"Clothes," he announced as he dropped the pile on top of their map, earning a deep glower from both of them.

"Yours are in that pile, too. Why should I carry them?" Lark shoved the heap off the map and smoothed the wrinkles left behind. It wasn't paper; it was drawn on deer hide with rich black ink, guaranteed to be waterproof. A good decision, given what had befallen his last map.

"Because I just carried all yours over here. Where did you get your food?" His eyes darted to the bun in Tula's hand. Thick wedges of chicken protruded from its top. His mouth watered at the sight.

The princess pointed vaguely toward one of the vendors. "Let us study in peace, would you?"

"My pleasure." He left their new cold weather gear on the ground by their feet and retrieved a meal for himself, then scanned the street for somewhere he might sit. Why Lark and Tula had chosen to sit on a planter when there was a bench nearby, he wouldn't pretend to know, but at least he had somewhere quiet he could settle by himself.

With one hand, he fed himself. With the other, he retrieved his pen case and a piece of paper from his bag. The bench provided a relatively even surface for writing, and the nib was so smooth, it made writing easy.

He had two paragraphs down by the time he stuffed the last of his food into his mouth and licked his fingers clean. The third was almost finished before Lark stepped between him and the lamplight he wrote by.

"Another shopping list?" She planted her hands on her hips.

"None of your business." He angled the pen case to obscure his writing.

Lark spared it a glance, then frowned. "Pack up. We need to get moving."

As if that were a cue, Tula dropped Zaide's new clothing on the bench beside him. "We're not sleeping here."

Of course not. "Give me a minute to finish this, then we'll go."

The princess tapped her toe and drew a breath to speak, but Zaide raised a hand to stop her.

"Don't talk, or I'll end up writing what you're saying." He scratched out the last few words, then wiped his pen on the cloth that had been stashed under the ink bottles. The paper would need a moment to dry, but that gave him time to gather his gear and shove it into his already-bulging bags. "It's good we're going, anyway. I have some questions."

"As do I." Lark stepped back to give him space to rise.

He fluttered the paper in hopes it would dry faster. "I need to find somewhere to mail this on our way out of town."

Tula clapped her hands to her mouth. "A letter? That's such a good idea! Oh, I should have written one to Elsanna."

"Next time," Lark said. "Move." She was often short-tempered, but there was a note of brusque urgency in her voice that put Zaide on edge. Had she seen something? Heard something? His own concerns surged to the forefront of his mind, but she was already walking, and Tula hurried after.

Zaide scanned the streets they passed, but nothing stood out. People milled about, finishing the day's usual business. Shops closed as night fell and people lined up beside the carts and stands of food vendors. Everything was ordinary, aside from there being more Jadorans in the streets than he'd seen before. By now, plenty would have fled Jadora and sought refuge in Ganede. Only now would news of the city's safety be reaching Ganede's shore.

"Are we running from something?" Zaide asked as they passed beyond the city's borders and followed the only road north.

"A certain sense of impending doom, perhaps." Lark glanced back once, but her face revealed nothing. She kept her pace brisk.

"Really? I don't feel doomed." Tula scuffed a foot against the road. It was dusty and dry, and her foot left a narrow stripe behind. She scuffed the other foot to make it a pair, then swept her pointed boot in an arc.

Lark crinkled her nose. "What are you doing?"

"Making a happy face." Tula hopped to land with her feet side by side.

Zaide paused and tilted his head. "Oh, I see it. It's got its arms up, like it's cheering."

The princess scoffed. "Can either of you take a single moment to behave properly for this mission's importance?"

"But Amrochan's so muddy," the librarian complained. "I just want to enjoy every place we go."

"I'll take you to Kolmar when everything is over," Zaide said. "It's not as muddy as Amrochan. And there are lots of trees."

Tula brightened and hurried along.

He took the opportunity to move closer to Lark. "The

shopkeeper didn't seem to notice me. I mean, he noticed I was buying things. He didn't notice I was—"

"Different," Lark concluded for him.

It was more polite than anything he'd come up with on his own. "I guess."

She nodded. "Where we sat, you could see down to the shore. The city's right on the water. There were boats drawing up on the sand instead of at the docks."

"Is that unusual?" Zaide knew little about boats and sailing. He knew even less about docking practices and regulations.

"The only reason to avoid the docks would be to avoid taxes," Tula said. She swung her arms as she walked, her big, exaggerated steps at odds with the serious subject at hand. "Or to avoid someone seeing what you're unloading."

Zaide's brows drew together. "Why'd they go ashore where someone could see them, then?"

"Because they wanted to be seen. And that's why we're on our way out." Lark turned back again, but didn't slow.

There was something else hovering between her words, something left unspoken. Zaide would have preferred she be forthright, but he sensed he was supposed to understand what the subject had to do with his concerns.

That understanding hit him. He stopped and looked back. "But if they're on the ships, they could be—" He stopped himself without finishing. He didn't know *how* to finish. The maritime traffic in the bay could have meant anything. They could be refugees, chased from their homeland and forced to seek a new life. They could be people like him, raised away from all their families had known, struggling to find a new place to belong.

Or they could be leading a swarm of goborrins onto Ganede's shores, cementing the reason so many looked at him askance.

He swallowed.

Lark took his arm and pulled him along. "It won't serve you, Zaide. We need to keep moving."

"But—"

"I understand your concerns. I know you understand mine, as well. You've worked hard to earn the trust of everyone around you. Don't give them a reason to doubt you now."

He resisted, staring back toward the city. The shore on the other side was out of sight.

The Shattered Lands were vast. He remembered little of what his mother had told him, but that part stuck fast in his memory. The chance some unknown broken-born in a place like this, a city near the edge of the known world, might have some answer as to what became of his father? It was so remote it might as well not exist.

"There will be a time for that," Lark said. Her voice came softer now, colored with sympathy, though he doubted she would ever understand. "Right now, it's a time for travel, and for you to tell us what you know about the Shaman."

Zaide exhaled and his shoulders sagged. The Shaman. Their mission. Nothing else mattered right now. "Right," he said as he gave in to her pulling and let her drag him onward, away from the chance to seek answers he'd always hoped for and toward the destiny he'd stumbled into, instead. "His name is Athradan. Andriun's father. If I'm being honest, I don't know if he'll help us."

"Nothing new," the princess murmured.

Though they walked, Zaide couldn't help looking back one more time. The sword, the war, drove them forward and bit at their heels all the while. Ganede would be no different, but as he gazed back across the slate roofs and the inviting glow of warm lamps between them, he hoped his instincts were wrong.

CHAPTER THREE

LONG AFTER THE SUN SET, they chose a place to the side of the road and settled to make camp. The same spot had been used as a campsite by others, a ring of stones marking a fire pit even before they saw the ashes and soot inside. The waxing moon provided enough light that they hadn't drawn lanterns, but now, as they stood around the empty fire pit and peered into the scrub, light would have been helpful.

"Of all the things to forget to pack," Lark muttered as she turned a slow circle, scanning the ground for anything they might use for firewood.

Zaide turned up a few branches and twigs from bushes, but they had not yet reached the part of the peninsula where trees grew in abundance, so there was little hope of turning up more. "Maybe they didn't forget. Maybe they just figured we'd use Tula as a lantern."

"Me?" Tula pointed at herself. "Why would—oh, because of the fire magic. I guess I could try." Aside from blessing the Spectrum Blade, she hadn't tried to touch magic again. At least, not that Zaide knew. He understood little about what her new talents might entail or what having her magic awakened would feel like, and he hadn't thought to ask if the dragon had taken the time to introduce her to her new gifts.

"It's probably the best option we've got. Maybe you should start by seeing if you can set those twigs on fire. Even a little light would help." He motioned toward the tiny pile he'd started in the center of the stone ring.

The librarian pursed her lips, then shuffled closer. She held her hands out first, then knelt, as if to warm her hands by a fire. A fire that would be, he hoped. "Give me a few minutes. I have to remember how this went."

Lark crouched beside her, twirling a piece of dry grass between her fingers. "You bore some capability with magic before becoming Magister, didn't you? I felt it in you, at least. Did you not use it often?"

"I had it, I guess, but that's normal for Jadorans. We don't really use it. It's just kind of there." Tula wiggled her fingers. The moonlight outlined the concentration on her face. "It helps us resist the sun and the heat, and protects us from the crater's gases. They come out through the tunnels, sometimes, when the volcano seems like it might wake. But nobody goes around blasting fireballs or anything like that."

"Don't you worry about living on top of a volcano?" Zaide asked as he scouted around a nearby bush. He saw well enough in the dark to make out a few tiny twigs and dried leaves, but nothing that would make a difference. He picked them up anyway. "It could erupt any time and destroy the city."

"I guess it could, but it won't. There are channels to let the magma out. They're walled up on the sides of the plateau, but the volcano would blow them wide open if it ever came to that. I don't think it's ever erupted, though. Not in any of Jadora's history." The librarian tilted her head to one side, as if to consider that oddity.

Lark sighed. "I guess having a dragon's magic protecting the city would ensure that. The plateau is an odd place for a volcano, though."

"Oh, the plateau was made by the dragons," Tula said. "Vorkaris is a fire dragon, of course, but I guess there were earth dragons once, too."

The nonchalant way she finished made Zaide turn his head. "Once? Not anymore?"

"Not according to Vorkaris. When the Spectrum Blade was forged, there were only five left."

"So he might be the only one." Lark tossed her grass into the would-be fire. "You're going to have to tell us a lot about what Magister Vorkaris told you, but that's changing the subject. Do you think you can light a fire?"

"Hm? Oh, sure. I was just remembering how to do it." Tula grinned as she leaned forward and stuck a finger down in the center of the pile of twigs. A moment later, a glow ignited at the bottom of the pile, and a lazy plume of smoke curled into the air.

"We're going to need a lot more sticks." Zaide dropped what he had around Tula's hand as the first tongue of flame licked up the side of her finger. "This won't last long at all."

Lark leaned back to gather a few dead leaves from the edge of the hard-packed dirt ring where they sat. "Magic is similar in Amrochan, if I'm to be honest. There are people who sense it, some who can manipulate it, but it's not as strong a force as it once was. Or at least, most of those who held power no longer know how to wield it." She rubbed her arms as if to ward off a chill, though Ganede's peninsula did not grow as cold as the desert did at night. "I had tutors who still bore power. I was supposed to be like them, but no matter what we tried, my magic never woke. I can feel it around me, sense its use and its potential, but..." Her eyes darkened with a shadow of sadness that was more than just a lament for power that had never come to be.

Zaide settled beside her and put a hand on her shoulder. "Magic runs rich in Kolmar. Just about everyone I knew had some useful ability they could use to better lives in the village.

But it never mattered to them that I didn't, and it shouldn't matter to you, either. Magic's not the only useful skill there is."

"No," the princess agreed with a sigh. "But I can't help but think things would be going better if I could do what I'm supposed to. Maybe if I'd managed to wake my power, I could have..." She glanced his way and trailed off. She averted her eyes a moment later, but he already knew what she was looking at.

He sat with his legs crossed and put a hand to the Spectrum Blade. It sent a small hum up his arm and he made a face. "How come you never say anything when I need it?" he muttered.

Lark and Tula both cast him curious looks.

Slowly, Zaide drew the sword and laid it across his knees. It glowed softly in the dark, not enough to offer any illumination to their camp, but enough to make itself noticeable. "Sorry. I know it's weird. I'm trying not to talk to it so much. It's not like it answers, anyway."

"What do you mean by that?" Tula produced a few handfuls of leaves and dry grass from somewhere and fed them to the fire, one piece at a time. "Why would it answer?"

They'd all seen the way the sword affected him when he'd used it against the false Magister's guards in Jadora, but that had only been a day or two before. Without regular sleep, he'd lost track of time, and he certainly hadn't had a chance to explain himself. "I don't know. It reacts to me sometimes. Or reacts to things around it, maybe. Sometimes it just feels warm, or like a vibration. Sometimes it's like that little lightning crackle you get with wool in the dark."

"I hate those little shocks," Tula grumbled.

"I think we all do." Zaide trailed a finger down the length of the sword. He'd taken the time to properly clean it since their battles ended, but he wondered if the blade was still unhappy with him. "But it's like that. And it feels like things, sometimes. Like it's excited, or eager. Or angry."

Lark drew her knees up. "I think we can all agree we don't want to make the sword angry."

"That doesn't make sense, though." Tula rounded the fire to sit beside him and study the sword. "I'm kind of like Her Highness. I can feel when there's magic in things. I could feel the Molten Dagger every time I touched it. But I touched the Spectrum Blade yesterday when you had me restore power to it, and I didn't feel anything."

The princess drew her knees up farther and hugged her legs to her chest. "Even after you put power in it?"

"Yeah. It was like it swallowed it all." A curious frown worked its way onto Tula's face and she reached a finger toward the sword before she thought better of it. "Maybe Zaide's the only one who can feel it, because he's the one who got picked to use it."

He moved the blade a little farther away from the librarian, purely out of caution. "Maybe." He started to return it to its sheath, then paused with his thumb atop the embossed Z. "But... wait. I wasn't. Or, I'm not."

"Of course you are," Lark said. "You're the one carrying it right now, aren't you? It chose you."

"No. I mean, yes." Zaide shook his head, as if that would untangle his words. "I mean, the blacksmith in Amrochan. The one who helped me make the sheath. He felt it, too."

"He touched it?" Lark asked, surprised.

The memory of the smith's hand hovering over the blade came to mind. "No, but he put his hand out like it was hot. Like..." He illustrated by passing his hand over the top of Tula's tiny fire. "He said he sensed it. That it was powerful."

A new shadow flitted over the princess's face. "Why would a blacksmith sense the sword's power when I can't?"

"I don't know." And that he had no clue brought little comfort. He slipped the blade back into its sheath and tried not to worry about it now. There were answers somewhere. Sooner or later, he'd find them.

Tula gave a broad shrug and leaned back to prop herself on her hands. "Well, I guess we'll just have to show the sword to a bunch of people and see what they think. Maybe we can figure it out that way. The Shaman will be the next one, right? Maybe it only likes boys."

"It didn't seem to like King Sendassian," Zaide said.

Lark snorted. "Nobody likes my father."

Tula leaned forward to squint at her. "Not even you?"

The princess opened her mouth, then shut it tight. Tula stifled a gasp behind her fingers.

"What Lark likes is people not asking questions about her. And books, and study, big libraries, and making progress on this quest." Zaide leaned back to recline against his hands, the same way Tula had done. He stretched out his legs and crossed his ankles to warm his feet beside the puny fire. "So let's focus on those things for a bit."

"Yes." Lark leaped on the chance to change the subject, sat straighter and grew more collected. "Tula and I had the opportunity to review the map and plot a course. We'll break away from the road after the river bridge and follow the coast from there. The going should be easier, since it will allow us to avoid the mountain passes."

"And the bugraks," Zaide added.

"And... yes. Those. Of course." As if she knew what they were.

It was the same plan he'd been meant to follow in the first place, if he recalled correctly. It hadn't gone well at all. He pushed himself up with a grunt and returned to hunting for sticks for the fire. "Well, I'll let the two of you plan that, then. Warm up some food while you're at it, would you? I think I saw a tree over there, so I'll go look for wood."

"I could come with you. Tula can tend the fire and the food better than I can." Lark started to rise, but Tula put an arm in front of her.

"Don't follow boys to lonely trees in the dark while camping," the librarian said flatly. "Don't go to the tree afterward, either."

Zaide rolled his eyes. "That is not why I'm going to the tree."

"I don't know that! You could."

"Well, I'm not, and if I was, I wouldn't want to talk about it. Just stay here, all right? I'll be back." He turned away with the heat of awkward embarrassment in his ears.

As he left, he caught what sounded like a reprimand from Lark and a small giggle from Tula. Traveling with the two of them might prove more of an adventure than he was ready for. With fortune, things would change; when they reached the Desheni, he'd have Andriun to balance things out. At least for a time. He hadn't known what might befall the hunter when they parted ways, but the Shaman was Andriun's father. Surely that would protect him from the worst of his clan's ire.

The tree he'd seen on the slope proved small, but there were still a few branches around its base. He gathered them, along with as many dry leaves as he could carry, grateful for a moment of silence to think on his own.

No hint of emotion or magic came from the blade at his side, but he thought about it anyway. Or, he thought at it. As if his thoughts alone could provoke something in the sword, stir some secret connection he hadn't yet figured out. But no matter how he handled it, thinking at it or of it, nothing changed. The blade was silent and his thoughts were loud, tangled with worry and new confusion.

It had to mean something that the sword was dormant in the senses of some and not others. He'd found it strange enough that he could feel it, given his lack of power. But maybe the sword's choosiness was an answer of its own. It couldn't be drawn to magic, but maybe it was drawn to some other quality.

"As if I have any of those," he muttered as he scooped one last stick from the dirt.

He could fight, but that wasn't it. Sendassian was famed for his prowess in combat. If that was all the sword desired, it should have allowed the king to feel something, too.

Or maybe it had, and Zaide simply hadn't known. He didn't

know what to look for, didn't know what signs there may be that someone sensed magic or reacted to it. With Lark and Tula, he had their word to rely on. The same could be said of Portran, the smith in Amrochan. Sendassian hadn't mentioned it, but maybe he had felt something.

"Or at least, something beyond you not liking him." Talking to the sword was foolish, but for once, a sense of something washed over him in response.

Smugness.

A shudder coursed down Zaide's spine and he hurried back to the tiny camp.

Lark and Tula were already eating. They'd elected to take cold cuts of meat with them, and even reheated, the scent made his mouth water. He left his sticks and leaves beside the fire pit and knelt to add them to the tiny cluster of flames, one piece at a time. "Did you warm any for me?"

"Not yet. We thought you'd want it fresh." Tula brought out the wrapped package of meat and cupped it in both hands. A moment later, steam rose from beneath the dark paper.

"Her power comes naturally," Lark said. "It'll be quite an asset as we continue."

"I'm sure." Zaide took his share of the food and sat back on his heels to eat. He'd grown to miss cutlery, but his pack contained only a spoon and knife. Anything that could be done with a fork, he could do with his fingers. The sliver of dark poultry meat was hot, though, and he sucked in a breath through his teeth as he dropped it back into the paper packet and shook his hand.

Lark pointed at the deer hide map spread out on the ground as if she hadn't noticed his injury. "Based on what I'm seeing here, we should reach the river in a few days. Does that sound correct?"

"I guess. I didn't really keep track of time when I was out here before." This time, he blew on his food before he tried to pick it up. It didn't scorch his fingertips when he tapped it, so he popped a piece into his mouth. The herbs were salty and rich, satisfying in a way travel rations never could be.

"We need to move faster than that, though. We'll rise early and stop late each day, but we're going to need to push hard." The reason she desired speed remained unstated. Zaide considered asking, then decided it didn't matter. There were goborrins beating down Amrochan's doors, and for all he knew, they could be moving on Ganede that very moment. Their mission was almost done, and the last blessing would turn the tide of war.

Zaide stuck a handful of leaves into the fire to keep the new sticks from overwhelming it. "Well, we're on the road. If we're lucky, we'll encounter merchants headed for Beshnai when we're due for rest, and we'll be able to hitch a ride."

"And if we're not lucky?" Tula asked.

"Then we're going to have to learn to run for a long time." He smiled, but the flat look the princess gave him said she didn't appreciate his humor. What else was new? He fought back a sigh, but sobered, just the same.

Lark wiped her fingers clean on a cloth as she finished her food. Where she'd found a napkin, he wasn't sure. Had she packed it, or had someone packed it for her? He hadn't seen anything like it in the bags prepared for him. "Regardless of how we get there, we're going to have to push to reach the second river soon. The sooner, the better."

"Why does it matter?" The map showed no bridge across the second river in their path. They'd have to swim across no matter what.

Lark gave him a hard look and let nature answer his question.

Somewhere in the distance, lightning flashed.

CHAPTER FOUR

THE STORM HELD off until they'd slept a few hours, but the next several days were tarnished by a downpour. The rain was frigid and cloaked the landscape with dense fog, making it hard to keep their bearings.

All of them had elected to change clothes; the cold weather gear they'd purchased was water-resistant and better than being soaked to the skin, but after hours in the rain, they still ended up saturated. Finding somewhere to sleep became an ordeal, and even Tula's magic couldn't get a fire going in the storm. The going became easier when they reached the first stand of trees, but the road was still churned to mud.

Now and then, they encountered merchants on the road who'd gotten stuck in the mire and besought help. Zaide earned himself a vicious glower from the princess every time he obliged, but he couldn't bring himself to leave anyone trapped.

Four days later, with all of them dripping and exhausted, the storm relented.

The cessation of rain should have been a relief, but it introduced concerns that weren't likely to go away. All of them thought it when they crossed the bridge and ventured down the coast, but it wasn't until they reached the second river on another drizzly morning that their concerns were proven reasonable.

Zaide adjusted his hood to better block the cool breeze and gazed across the water. "Well, do we try it here, or do we go farther up?"

Where the map had indicated a shallow ford, they found an angry river that churned and frothed.

Lark came to a stop beside him, her lips pursed in thought. "The current is strong, but we could walk if we found somewhere it isn't so deep."

"With how high the water is here, I don't think trying it is a good idea. We could hope the delta is more shallow and head toward the sea." He wasn't sure about that suggestion. He'd been lucky the river he'd crossed to the north had sported a sluggish current and a wide mouth, split with rocks and patches of land. This side of the Desheni mountains was different.

The princess made a soft, thoughtful sound. "Where did you cross before?"

"Nowhere near here. It would take us days to get there, and even if we did, there would be the bugraks to deal with." He shivered at the thought of the ugly little creatures, with their gray skin and gangly limbs.

Tula said nothing, but wrung the strap of a bag between her hands as she stared at the rushing water.

For a while, they considered the river in silence. Then Lark sighed and looked upstream. "It's all hills in that direction. I fear the river will be deeper where it's cut into the hillsides. Let's move closer to the coast."

It seemed the best solution, so Zaide nodded and turned to follow the river's edge. "If you notice anywhere that's shallow enough to see the bottom, let me know." He doubted they'd find anything of the like, but there was always a chance. The rain runoff was murky and darkened what might otherwise have been clear waters.

They conversed little, all of them disheartened and weary,

but a hint of hope came when the river widened and flattened out after a handful of miles.

"Promising," Lark said.

"Yeah. Now I need a stick." Zaide turned in place to search the nearby trees. The woods weren't thick around them yet, so finding a branch that was both long and sturdy enough took some effort.

Tula watched with interest as he experimented with a few and eliminated those that wouldn't work. "What's that for?"

"For crossing the river. You don't want to walk out there blind, you have to scout ahead with something to make sure you don't misstep. You should get one, too. And Lark. We should probably walk separately. What's good footing for me might be too deep for someone else." He cast the princess a knowing look.

She met his eye and lifted her chin in defiance.

Tula, on the other hand, appeared to appreciate his advice. She scouted around the trees in search of her own branch, finally settling for one that was close to her height and as thick around as her wrist.

"Good." Zaide nodded in approval and headed back to the water's edge. His was a less impressive walking stick, but it was good enough.

Lark crossed her arms and watched him adjust his bags so they rode high against his back. "Is this what you did when you fell in?"

"No. The first time, I was on a bridge, and the goborrin I was fighting went through the rotten boards and took me with it. The second time, there were rocks above water all the way across the river, but the bugraks were chasing me, so I slipped." He knew she was trying to nettle him. She wouldn't get a rise this time. He'd done nothing wrong. "If I'd had time to prepare to cross, I don't think either time would have gone bad."

The princess had no retort, so he finished tying his bags, removed something from one of them, and hefted his stick.

He'd lost a book to the water once already and he wasn't

going to do it again. "Will you hold this?" He offered the old songbook, the empty journal, and the stack of papers to Lark.

Her eyebrows climbed, but she accepted the handful of belongings without complaint.

"I'll go first," Zaide said. "Once I'm across, you two follow together."

"Shouldn't all three of us go together?" Tula asked.

"If it were a familiar river, I'd say yes. I can come back for you if you want, though. Once I'm on the other side, I'll drop my bags." He contemplated the river's edge for a moment, then removed his curl-toed boots and socks and stuffed them into the top of one bag. They protruded strangely from beneath its flap. Then, with his stick in hand, he waded into the water and began to probe the depths. Silt stirred with each prod and made the water even murkier than before. "The mud's pretty slick, so be careful. Just watch for right now."

Most of his water-crossing experience was for the creeks around Kolmar; he'd never crossed the river. But one body of water was like another, and the creeks and streams were just as dangerous when the water ran high. He inched across the river bed with one bare foot at a time, seeking rocky footing and avoiding trenches and sucking mud. As he advanced, it grew deeper, until he was waist-deep. The ice-cold water rushed past him, threatening his footing and promising to numb his toes, but he found a meandering trail of stones and ridges that let him plant his weight and keep from being swept off.

By the time he reached the high bank on the other side, his teeth chattered, but his things remained dry. He untied his bags and left them near the base of a tree, where the raised roots that thrust through the topsoil kept them from the mud.

"Your turn," he called. "Want me to come back?"

Lark had already tied their bags high, like his. "I don't think that's necessary."

Zaide shrugged and waited as they followed.

One step at a time, Tula led the princess into the water, her arm linked with Lark's. They murmured between themselves as they shuffled across the riverbed in a wider zig-zag than what Zaide had found, but he watched from the bank and let them work through it on their own.

Eventually, they reached the other side. Tula beamed up at him. "That was easy! I was so worried when it got real deep, I thought it was going to be harder than that."

He grinned back. "Not everything has to be hard. The worst part is just being cold and wet." He offered a hand to the princess first, half expecting her to shove it away or ignore him completely. Instead, Lark clasped his hand and let him pull her up the bank. Her lip trembled with cold, but her eyes were bright and her bare toes were a bright red, indicating good circulation. Zaide clapped a congratulatory hand to her shoulder as he helped her up, only realizing after he'd done it that it might have been inappropriate.

Lark didn't seem to notice. She shuddered and hopped up to the roots, where she sat and sloughed her bags off to the ground to dig through them. Searching for dry clothing, no doubt.

"That was the only river we have to cross, right? We don't have to go through any others until we're on the way back?" Tula asked.

"As far as I know." He turned to offer his hand and help her up, too.

She reached for his hand as she took a step forward, misstepped, and crashed into the river.

"Tula!" Lark cried.

Zaide spat a curse and leaped in after her.

The current hit him hard when he landed in the pool that claimed her. Ahead, she tumbled in the water, her hair flashing on the surface each time she tried to right herself.

Urgency put warmth in his limbs. Zaide pushed after her, aided by the current that threatened to carry her out to sea. He was faster than her tumbling and a moment later, he caught something cloth. Tula flailed in the water and gasped when her head broke the surface.

"Calm down!" He tried to find her arms and still their lashing. He sought the bottom of the river with his feet and found nothing, though Tula kicked his legs more than once. Eventually, he found her hands. He latched onto one with both of his and reeled her close to hook an arm around her ribs. Staying upright was hard. Moving both of them would be harder. "Kick with me. Push toward the bank."

She wobbled and flopped uselessly a moment before she found a rhythm. One hand clutched his shoulder, while she tried to mimic him with the other. Instead of a strong stroke, it was more of a child's paddling, but it was the best he could hope for. Why had he assumed a girl from the desert would be able to swim? Foolish.

A wrong movement dunked him underwater. He spat when he came up. Grit clung to his tongue. "Kick," he urged again. "One, two, one, two!"

She fell into the rhythm after that and they flowed toward the bank, carried by the water.

Something brushed his foot. Mud. The river bed. Zaide kicked harder and his feet found the bottom. A moment later, Tula's feet caught, too. They struggled into the shallows and clawed at the bank to keep the water from claiming them again. Zaide found the better handhold, and he used it to push Tula up onto dry land. By the time he clambered up after her, he shook with exhaustion.

Tula upended her bags. Dirty water poured from their mouths and she gave a small, sad whine.

"Okay," Zaide panted. "Next time, we all go together." He stuck out his tongue and swiped a hand across it to remove the silt and sand and whatever vile things still lurked in his mouth. Dark flecks of something he didn't recognize and didn't want to stuck to his palm.

Another small whine escaped Tula's throat. She squeezed

water from her hair and looked down at her saturated clothes. Wet as they both were, the cool wind now felt frigid, but she voiced no complaints. Instead, she raised her head and scanned the trees around them. "Where are we?"

Zaide glanced up the river, back the way they'd come. One guess was as good as any. The brush along the river bank was thick, and he saw no sign of Lark. "I don't know. I guess it carried us pretty far."

Her hands lifted to cover her mouth, her eyes wide. "Are we lost?"

"I mean, we were kind of lost the whole time. It's not like I knew where we were to begin with." He stood and oriented himself, his hands unconsciously drifting to the blades sheathed at either hip. Both were still present. He drew them and upended the scabbards, one at a time, to let the water out. "We just follow the river back upstream, though. Lark will be headed this way." He assumed she would be, anyway.

"Lark," Tula repeated as she dragged herself to her feet. The patter of water droplets cascading from her onto dead leaves filled the air. "Do you think I should stop calling her Dasienna?"

"I don't know. Maybe you should ask her." The inside of the scabbards were both still wet. He frowned, then opted to carry his knife and the Spectrum Blade instead of sheathing them again. "Can you walk? Let's see if we can find her. We'll make camp and dry out for a bit."

"I'm sorry," she said in a small voice.

Zaide shot her a quizzical look. "For what?"

"Falling in." She gulped. "Not being able to swim."

He stared at her a moment, then shrugged. A foolish assumption, he reminded himself again. A few summers spent on boats or along beaches didn't mean someone could swim. "You didn't do anything wrong." Neither had he, either time he went in. "But I think we'd better avoid rivers as much as possible from now on." Three foul experiences was more than enough for him.

Tula said nothing, and it may as well have been agreement.

There were no game trails to follow in this part of the woods. Zaide struggled to pick out a path that would be easy to follow and gentle on their bare feet at the same time. Their passing was noisy and slow, but they hadn't gone far before Lark's voice rose among the trees.

"Tula?"

"Well, we can see who her favorite is," Zaide muttered. He used the Spectrum Blade to hold a branch out of the way while the librarian ducked underneath it.

"It's because I'm n-nice." Tula's jaw clattered and she rubbed her arms.

"I can be nice."

"Sometimes."

Zaide peered at her over his shoulder. "I just saved you from drowning. That's nice, isn't it?"

"Not if you c-complain about having to do it or r-rub it in." Tula leaned to one side, as if it would help her see past the trees. "We're here, Your Highness."

A hint of color moved in the undergrowth ahead.

"Right," Zaide called. "There's a trail there, we can get on it and meet you."

Tula went right.

He caught her shoulder and turned her the other direction. "Her right."

A hint of red that wasn't from the cold colored her cheeks.

The trail was narrow, but the ground was bare, speckled with the heart-shaped hoofprints of deer. They walked a little easier, the muddy ground soothingly firm after the squishing riverbed and swampy bank. Lark came into view a moment later.

"There you are," the princess breathed. She jogged to meet them and wrapped Tula in a hug. "Are you all right?"

"I'm c-cold." Tula clenched her fists and hunched her shoulders, as if it would stifle a chill.

"We're fine," Zaide added, though Lark hadn't looked his

way. That she was unconcerned about his well-being chafed, but he elected to ignore it and move on.

Lark glanced to their feet and apology sprang to her face. "I left the bags behind. I forgot your boots."

"Well, mine are wet, so he's not alone. We'll just go slower. And watch out for thorns." Tula mustered a smile, though her eyes were pinched and sad.

The princess held her arm and guided her through the trees. "We'll find a clearing. There's plenty of wood here, so we can build a better fire and get the two of you dried out."

Tula nodded her appreciation, but a troubled look wreathed itself across her features a moment later. "I don't have to write this down in the history of our adventures, do I?"

Zaide held back a laugh.

"Of course not," Lark said. "History is written by the survivors. Only they get a say."

Though she meant it as a comfort, Tula blanched.

He changed the subject. "Come on. I think I can see our crossing point." Instead of waiting, he pushed onward by himself to retrieve his things, grateful for the warmth of good boots he knew waited ahead. He wanted to find the statement funny, but after everything they'd encountered in Jadora, he wondered how much truth it still held.

Survivors wrote the history, but who among the living worked to see it erased?

Night fell and clothes were still not dry. Zaide checked his fur-lined gear a dozen times over before he concluded they'd be staying put for the night.

It wasn't a problem; they'd pushed hard through miserable conditions since their departure from Ganede. One day spent at rest would benefit them all, and while Tula insisted she was all right, she'd grown unusually subdued. Even now she sat beside the fire, her hands extended toward its warmth, her face solemn. She'd spoken little after they found a safe place to set up camp. He'd changed into his Jadoran garb, but her extra clothing had been in her bags and was just as soaked as the rest of her. She wore Lark's cold weather gear now, her own clothes hung over branches and spread across bushes so everything could dry.

Lark hadn't pushed for them to move, either. Tula's silence was bad enough. Lark's was enough to change his concern into dread.

Had Tula said something to the princess to make her worry? Had she breathed in water or swallowed something she shouldn't? Was water even safe for someone imbued with fire magic? He'd tried to ask, but each time he began to speak, Lark pinned him with such a dark glare that his words fled.

Instead, he milled around the camp, turning over the objects from Tula's bags that had been laid out to dry, gathering extra wood for the fire, hunting for familiar spring and summer plants that might be added to their rations for a better meal. The more he circled the campsite, the more a sense of uneasiness kept him moving.

At last, Lark couldn't take it any more. "If you're going to pace, go pace where we can't see you. You're driving both of us up the wall."

Zaide hadn't heard any commentary from Tula to indicate she was bothered. Even now, she kept her head down and her hands toward the fire.

He considered arguing, then put the thought aside. There was no point. All it would do was make the trip more miserable than it already had been. Instead, all he said was, "Fine." He rested his hands on the hilts of his blades. If nothing else, he could go practice sword forms. That was something he'd sorely neglected since they'd disembarked from the ship that carried them to Jadora's port.

Lark's eyes weighed heavy on his back as he wandered farther into the woods.

It was only after he passed beyond sight of the camp that he realized they were all on edge. The river incident had been unpleasant, but the uneasiness that prickled up and down his spine wasn't from their unexpected swim—and whatever it was, it made Lark prickly, too. In more of an outward way.

"Something wrong?" he asked himself in a murmur. Or maybe he asked his sword. He drew the blade, as if to redirect the question to it, or question whether or not he'd been talking to it in the first place. "It would be helpful if you answered sometimes, you know."

No response came. He gave the Spectrum Blade a gentle swish and the swirls of color on its surface whirled a little faster. Did it like that? Or was it just his eyes, fooling him into thinking the movement of the blade was a stirring of the colors?

He frowned and drew the blade back, easing into a battle-ready stance he'd started in often, back when he trained against the Kolmari.

Peaceful as the forest village was, it boasted competent fighters. More than one of the men in the forest had served at the garrison. More than one had seen battle. It wasn't spoken of often, but they'd taken great care to ensure their skill was passed on. Looking back, it made sense. Kolmar had always felt safe, but the people there—the older generation—had always known that peace was fleeting and uncertain. They'd known an attack would someday come, and they held the Spring Choosing as a way to prepare for it. The new insight changed so much of his perspective.

He spun with the blade to practice a swing and gave a shout when the strike was intercepted by a spear.

The Spectrum Blade bounced off the pole and the unexpected adversary twirled to stab for his head.

Zaide ducked to the side and brought his sword up, aiming for the gap in defense left by his attacker's lunge, but the other figure was too fast and spun away before it could make contact.

Where had he come from? The stranger's cloak fluttered

behind him as he brought his spear around in a spinning strike. Zaide barely caught it. The sword flashed when the spear made contact, and proximity worked in his favor.

He drove a kick toward his assailant's stomach. His boot connected hard and a deep grunt answered the blow, but the attacker didn't stop. The spear spun low and the haft hit Zaide's knee before his other leg was down.

Zaide collapsed and tried to roll aside, but a tree was too close, and he only made it halfway before the butt end of the spear drove his raised shoulder back to the ground and a foot slammed down on his chest. He wheezed and froze as the spear's point leveled with his throat.

Only then did his attacker pause. "Zaide?"

The familiarity of the voice stole a laugh from the last of his breath. "Andriun!"

"Why did you attack me?"

"You attacked me!"

"I did not." The Desheni hunter sounded offended. "All I did was step out to see who you were, and you came at me with that... that..." His spear drifted toward the Spectrum Blade. "That very strange sword."

The boot against his chest eased back and Zaide pushed himself halfway up from the muddy ground. "What are you doing out here at night? It's late for hunting, isn't it?" They hadn't been far from the river the first time he'd encountered Andriun, so their distance from the Desheni settlement now wasn't a surprise. Zaide searched the trees with his eyes, but he saw no others.

"Deer are more active at night." Andriun stepped back and offered a mittened hand. "But I am not hunting, no. I saw a fire. I came to investigate."

Zaide accepted the assistance in getting back to his feet. He'd be a little bruised in the morning, but he'd suffered worse. "Sorry, just us. No bugraks this time."

"You travel with women." It was more an observation than a

question, and Andriun paused to inspect Zaide's appearance. "And you are not dressed as Kolmari. I am sorry, I did not recognize you."

"Is that why you attacked me?"

"I did not attack anyone," Andriun said crossly. "But I would not blame myself if I had. There have been strange things in the forest. Strange people." His eyes drifted to the top of Zaide's head. The inference was enough.

"Lark said there were broken-born disembarking from ships in Ganede. I think she expects trouble." It hadn't been an accusation, so swallowing the distrust toward his appearance came easier this time.

"Lark? You have mentioned that name before, when we traveled together. She is one you travel with?"

As if summoned by the question, Lark emerged from the trees with her knives in hand. "Zaide? What's happened?"

Zaide jerked his head toward her. "She's the princess."

Andriun's mouth pressed thin. "I do not believe you have mentioned that." He regarded Lark thoughtfully, then looked behind her and stood straighter.

Just behind the princess stood Tula, blinking curiously at the two of them. A bit of light had returned to her eyes. Good.

"Zaide, who is this?" Lark lowered her blades, but moved toward them with a cautious step.

"This is Andriun. My friend." He motioned toward the Desheni hunter, grateful they hadn't been there to see the short skirmish. They could explain the brawl more easily without witnesses. Or else omit it from conversation completely.

Andriun flattened a mittened hand over his heart and bowed. "It is an honor to meet you, Your Highness. I must admit I did not expect that our paths would ever cross."

"Likewise, until recently," Lark said slowly. "What are you doing out here?"

Zaide answered for him. "The Desheni hunt all over these

mountains. He saw our fire and was on his way to see who was here."

"I hope our presence in your territory isn't seen as trespassing." Lark offered a polite smile, but it didn't touch her eyes. She was being careful, making her own judgment of the young Desheni man before them. Zaide's familiarity with him wasn't enough, it seemed.

If Andriun noticed her reservation, he didn't show it. The smile he answered with was warm and genuine. "It is not, Your Highness. You are welcome anywhere you may wish to go. But..." His eyes flicked skyward. "The pressure in the air has changed and it will rain soon. My camp is set up within shelter near to here. Perhaps we could go there? I will prepare a meal for your group and you might tell me how I can help whatever has brought you to this part of the world?"

"He's blue," Tula whispered conspicuously.

Lark waved her away. "I noticed the change in the air, myself. Do you think we should move camp?" She directed the question to Zaide, her face revealing nothing of her feelings on the matter.

He nodded. "I think it would be a good idea. Our things still aren't dry."

A faint crinkle formed between Andriun's brows. "Dry from what? It has not rained for days."

"I'll tell you later," Zaide muttered.

It made no difference to Andriun, for he shrugged and moved to follow Lark back to their camp the moment the princess turned. "As you wish it. Come, let us gather your things."

"Let's," Lark agreed, the single word punctuated by a distant rumble of thunder.

CHAPTER FIVE

ANDRIUN'S CAVE was quiet and warm. The embers of a recently-smothered fire waited in the front area, where the slope of the roof guided smoke out into the night instead of letting it pool in the cavern. The deeper part of the cave was blocked off by a coarse fabric curtain. He had hung it himself, one of his more clever additions, as it kept out drafts and protected the provisions hidden behind it from smoke.

"The front area is small, but the back is large enough that we all may sleep here," he announced as he led the group into the cave's shelter. The first raindrops had already started to fall, and all of them were eager to be somewhere dry.

"Am I correct in the assumption your hunters rely on natural shelters like this when traveling to hunt, instead of building cabins or waypoints?" The princess had been full of questions from the moment they had returned to their camp in the clearing to gather things. Andriun did not mind, but he could not help wondering if the probing was supposed to reveal something about him instead of the mundane things she inquired about.

"Yes, that is correct." He had already decided to humor her. There was something tense about her demeanor and distrust shone in her eyes. "The less we disturb the natural landscape, the more readily the wildlife approach our camps."

"We never stopped anywhere like this when you and your hunting party tied me up and dragged me back to Desheni," Zaide said.

Andriun flashed him a grin. "I believe when that happened, my party decided you were the quarry. We had been camping in our caves and alcoves before then. But we did not want you to see them, in case there were more of your kind." His smile faltered when the last two words escaped. It left his tongue poorly; those were words that brought offense. He sobered and decided to roll into a compliment to make up for it. "The hunters I traveled with at the time were impressed by how you fared against the bugraks you faced at the river and considered you a threatening opponent, so they did not want to present you with knowledge of where we might be found unprepared to fight. We did not speak of them much, you and I, but the bugraks are an inconvenience our hunters face often. We try to avoid them whenever possible. When they catch someone alone, it does not often end well."

Zaide laughed, indication the cover was well received. "I wouldn't say I fared well. They almost drowned me."

"But they did not, so our assessment stands correct." Andriun held out a hand in offer to take the princess's bags. She gave him a frown and did not release them, so he turned to extend the offer to Tula, instead. "You did not encounter bugraks at the river this time, I trust?"

"No, and that's probably good," Tula sighed as she handed over her things. "I was enough of a problem at the river."

He studied her face a moment, unsure if he should take it as a joke. He had interacted so seldom with Jadorans, and it had been some years since his last trip to pursue trade. He chose to focus on the first part of her statement, instead. "I am glad you did not encounter difficulty. They have been numerous along the river these days. Worse than the last time I ventured this way." There was a ridge of stone that sat above the cave's floor, just beside the curtain. He deposited her belongings there.

Zaide left his things there, too. "Somehow, that doesn't surprise me. We've seen some things since leaving Kolmar."

"You traveled back to your home, then?" They had not yet had time to discuss his friend or their quest or what had come after Zaide's departure, only the conditions of their travel and what they might like to eat.

"It feels like I've been all over Amroch at this point." Zaide glanced out the mouth of the cave, to where a steady rain had begun to fall. "Where's the rest of your hunting party?"

"Ah..." The first of the questions Andriun did not want to answer. "I am here alone. Which is why I scout the woods."

"Oh. Guess that explains why there's room for all of us." Zaide settled beside the ring of stones where the fire had been. "Tula, want to start this?"

"There is firewood there, behind the princess." Andriun turned to point, but immediately regretted looking Lark's way. She stared at him with a gaze so intense, it could have bored through stone. How had she determined so quickly that he was hiding something? His skin itched beneath her stare as if he were covered in sand.

The Jadoran girl slid between them without noticing the silent exchange. She moved two logs to the fire and pressed a fingertip to one. Flames sprang up around it and he did a double-take.

"You are a talented mage!" He had sensed simmering magic, but he had assumed it had been from the princess, or perhaps one of the artifacts he knew they must carry.

The artifacts would be another problem, but he would figure out how to broach that subject in time.

"She's Jadora's new Magister," Zaide said.

Andriun felt his jaw go slack, but he caught it before he made a fool of himself. "The princess of Amroch and the Magister of Jadora, both in my cave." He laid a mittened hand over his heart.

"I have been done an unjust honor. Please, sit. I will prepare a meal. Tell me, what has brought such guests to Desheni territory?"

"We've come to speak to the Shaman." Lark wasted no time, her words clipped and sharp-edged. "I'm told he is your father."

Beneath his hand, Andriun's heart beat harder. He bowed his head and removed his mittens. "Yes, that is so."

"He leads your people from a seat of power farther north, does he not?"

Already, he did not like where this was going. "Yes, that is also so."

"Then you will escort our party to meet with your father." A simple, solid command that left no room for argument. No room for discussion of his plight.

"Ah..." Andriun hesitated. He flexed his fingers and stuffed his mittens into a pocket of his coat. "That may be difficult for me to do."

The princess's eyes stayed on him, hard and unforgiving.

The look Zaide gave him was more compassionate. Or perhaps concerned. "What do you mean?"

Andriun held up his hands, palms out, fingers spread to expose the webbing between them. A sign of earnest vulnerability that may be lost on them, he thought, but it was worth showing them the best of his people's customs. "I will explain. Please, give me time. I will cook first. I must ask, Zaide. Is the rest of your mission complete? Has the Captured Spring aided you?"

"One mission turned into another. That's sort of what led us here. But it did help. With the spring, we got this." The broken-born turned to indicate the sword at his side in an unthreatening fashion. Andriun was not sure he would have felt threatened if the blade had been drawn. Zaide was pleasant, spirited and friendly. For all that he resembled the broken-born who had troubled Andriun's people in recent days, he was unlike them in every way.

"A truly unusual sword, from what little I have seen," Andriun said as he pushed back the curtain enough to slip behind it and retrieve a pan and some of his provisions. The hunting had been good since he had arrived at this cave. He chose pork from the boar shoat he killed the week before and packed in salt, then collected a few root vegetables from a basket.

"It is called the Spectrum Blade," Lark said, "and we require your father's assistance with it."

"With a blade?" Andriun allowed his surprise into his words. "My people know little of swords. We do not use them. They are cumbersome in the water."

"You're not in the water, though," Tula put in from where she sat beside the crackling fire.

He glanced at her, troubled. "No. We are not. Or, I am not."

The tiniest statement was still enough for the princess to understand. "Your people are?"

Perhaps he had let that slip too soon. "Well, some are. My home, our outpost by the lake, we are land-adapted Desheni. My brethren live in the sea."

Her eyes narrowed. "We aren't speaking of them."

Zaide settled beside the fire and held out a hand in offer to help with the cooking. "Your people live alongside a lake. I've seen it. Now that the weather's getting warmer and the ice will be thawed, do they move into the lake?"

"They used to. But the ice has not thawed for many years. If it has thawed in the absence of the creature we have destroyed, I do not know." Andriun passed his friend a skillet, then pulled a knife from his belt.

The princess flinched.

A mistake. A threatening gesture. He knelt slowly and bowed his head as he sliced the vegetables, a careful display to show he meant no harm. The princess did not frighten him, but it was not hard to tell he walked a precarious line between finding her favor or finding her scorn. If he wanted her help, scorn was not an option.

"Have you been out here hunting for that long?" Tula leaned forward to catch his attention. She was a pretty girl, bright-eyed and sweet-faced. He found himself looking at her for a moment longer than was appropriate.

"I have been out here since Zaide departed with the Captured Spring," he said slowly.

Again, too much said. Lark caught what was left unsaid. "But not hunting."

And that was enough for Zaide to understand, too, for his head snapped up and a look of uncertainty painted his face.

"I..." Andriun hesitated. What harm was there in telling them? It was only his pride hurt by the situation, and confessing sooner, rather than later, would make it easier for them to understand how little help he could offer. "I have been exiled from my clan."

"What?" Zaide cried.

Lark crossed her arms.

"I am not bothered." Andriun offered a smile to show his sincerity, though he felt himself wither under the princess's stare. How had Zaide managed to travel with this woman without crumpling beneath her disapproval at every turn? The look she gave him made him want to sink into a swamp and never be seen again. "After your departure, Zaide, I was taken home to be questioned. I told my father everything, and the elders of my clan chose my punishment. I was banished as a consequence of defying my father's orders and aiding you. But I do not regret what I have done. I have my own reasons and beliefs for making this choice, and I will accept their judgment."

"But you didn't do anything wrong," Zaide protested. "Even your father has to see that. If anything, they should be angry at me, or at Lark. The princess gave an order. It wasn't your place to defy that."

"I agree, but the elders of my people did not. They are

entitled to their own decision and their own rules. By their judgment, I have wronged my people, and so I am punished. I do not fault them for their choice." He spread his fingers again, another show of vulnerability.

Across the fire, Tula stared at his hands.

Suddenly self-conscious, he lowered them and returned his attention to the task of preparing a meal.

Zaide moved a pair of rocks close to the fire and placed the pan atop them so it straddled the flames, and Andriun put in the pork and the vegetables he had already sliced. Herbs would make a good addition, too, but stepping away at this point of the conversation might be seen as an attempt to escape criticism. He stayed put for now, welcoming whatever he had earned.

"Your problems with your father and your people are not our concern," Lark said.

Zaide shot her an incredulous look. "His problems with his father and his people are a direct result of what you sent me to do. We asked this of him. We need to fix it."

"What we need to do is focus on the task at hand." The princess's eyes hardened until they glinted like the stormy sapphires they resembled. "We require the Shaman's blessing for the sword, and that's what we will do. It wasn't our aim to interfere in Jadoran politics, either."

"But you still got involved." Tula had been so quiet that her interjection came as a surprise. Her face was soft, earnest, and—Andriun dared say—hopeful. "You got the false Magister arrested, saw Magister Vorkaris awakened, and new leadership installed over the city. Helping someone reconcile with his family seems pretty small compared to that, don't you think?"

Andriun rested his hands on his thighs and bowed his head until his shoulders curved, too. "I do not ask you to involve yourselves. I confess you may be able to help, and I may ask for some aid in resolving my problem, but it is not your duty. It is mine. You speak of a blessing, though. What is it you mean?"

His father was responsible for many things, but that was not one he had heard of.

Zaide looked to the princess as if to seek permission, but Lark's mouth took a sour twist. She did not want to tell him. Because he had not offered help? Or because she thought he was powerless to do so? Neither was accurate, but he remained unsure how much he was willing to risk this time. That he did not regret what was already done did not mean he was eager to make things worse.

Eventually, she uncrossed her arms and allowed them to drop to her sides, though she remained where she was, leaning against the stony wall. "You've seen Zaide's sword." It was not a question; the blade had been out when she found them in the woods after their unexpected spat.

"Yes," Andriun answered anyway, an invitation for her to continue.

Zaide shifted to draw the sword from its scabbard. "This was what the Captured Spring kept locked away. It and the other artifacts. It was hidden inside Kolmar's temple. Kind of funny, because I never knew." His smile was nervous, his pale eyes anxious. Did he fear retaliation from the princess, should he reveal too much? He had no reason to be concerned. Already, Andriun had begun to piece the story together on his own.

"The sword has lost its power," he concluded before his friend could go on.

The princess straightened, while Tula stared at him with her mouth in a round O.

A hint of worry creased his forehead. Andriun touched the space between his brows and stroked upward, as if to chase it away. "This is the blessing of which you speak, is it not? Why you carry the sword here now, instead of facing the shadow in the east. It does not have the power to turn back the darkness just yet."

"Why do you know that?" Lark asked, tone flat.

Andriun stared back at her, unsure what to say. "Why would

I not know this? This is the sword of legend, the blade forged to slay Gadranus and delay his Rise, is it not?"

"Nobody knows that," Tula murmured.

Even Zaide looked at him with surprise. That made his skin crawl worst of all. He fumbled for something to say, but his friend spoke first.

"Your records still bear information about the Spectrum Blade?" A familiar light touched the broken-born's eyes. Curiosity and optimism.

"The Desheni do not keep written records." Almost as an afterthought, Andriun used his knife to stir the things that sizzled in the skillet so they would not burn. "Our histories are an oral tradition, passed down between each generation in great clarity. We write little. The water is not favorable to such things. My clan is land-adapted, but our ways have not changed much since we departed the sea."

The three of them all stared without speaking. An uncomfortable urge to fill the silence prodded him, so he continued. "I was meant to be Shaman after my father. My magic is strongest in our clan. From the moment it showed sign it would awaken, they taught me the history of our people and the duty of our Shaman. What our people have done, and what we must do."

The light faded from Zaide's eyes until only wariness remained. "You never mentioned any of this."

"I did not think it was needed of me." He had no reason to feel defensive. Why did it creep up on him anyway? He stared at the food and willed his posture to remain relaxed. "When you told me the Captured Spring was needed, I thought this may be the case. But it is not my place to question the crown princess of Amrochan. Although I admit..." He trailed off, unsure the thought that sprang to mind was appropriate to say.

"Admit what?" Lark crossed her arms again, her stare sharp enough to cut the words right out of him.

"That I thought the sword was for your father."

Zaide and Tula exchanged looks.

Andriun observed them with a frown. "What?"

"In the Great Library in Jadora, one of the librarians said something about King Sendassian when he heard I was the Bladebearer." Zaide touched the Spectrum Blade as if he expected something ill to come from the contact, yet he could not seem to help the desire to touch it. "We were in a hurry, and he never mentioned it again. I didn't have a chance to ask what he meant, but..."

No amount of willpower would have kept the frown from Andriun's face. "Her Highness did not tell you?"

The princess's eyes narrowed with suspicion. Or maybe concern.

"Tell me what?" Zaide asked uneasily.

Andriun hesitated.

Tula bore no such caution. She turned where she sat and peered up at Lark. "You know, don't you?"

Lark stared back for so long, Andriun expected her to change the subject. Instead, her resolve slowly crumbled, and she sighed and let her gaze sweep toward the mouth of the cave.

The situation was disarmed. Now he could speak.

"The wielder of the Spectrum Blade is preordained." Andriun breathed deep and let his exhale carry some of his concern with it. "The identity of the Bladebearer to be is foretold by the Oracle who resides on an island in the southwestern sea. The Maker provides the Golden Lady of Nimultis with knowledge of each seat of power, and the Lady provides each seat of power with knowledge of who they must protect. When my magic began to manifest, my father was told the Maker had chosen me to be the next Shaman." He paused there and chanced a smile in Tula's direction. "She told him also that the next Magister would be a girl."

The Jadoran girl beamed back.

Lark tightened her arms around her middle, less a position of defense and more one of self-comfort. "And my father was ordained to be the Bladebearer. The Spectrum Blade was supposed to be his."

Zaide looked up at her, a whirl of confusion and thought splayed across his face. "But you wanted the blade for yourself."

"My father didn't believe it existed. I thought..." Her shoulders bunched and she tucked in her chin, her cold irritation morphing into a mask of sorrow. "I thought maybe I would be the next best thing."

"You knew it was supposed to be your father?" The hint of heat that entered Zaide's voice was unlike him.

Lark did not look his way.

"His role was foretold by the Oracle before I was born," Andriun said, unsure if the clarification would help or make things worse.

Zaide's jaw clenched tight. He stared at the princess for a moment longer, then thrust himself up with the sword in hand and stormed out into the night. The princess tucked in her chin and closed her eyes, her hurt clear.

Andriun and Tula remained by the fire and exchanged uncomfortable glances.

"I should not have said these things," he concluded softly.

"No. He needed to know. I just..." Lark did not finish the thought, her brows knit, her eyes squeezed so tightly shut that her nose crinkled.

Tula spread her hands to the fire, taking in the warmth. "He'll be all right. Zaide's a strong person."

Andriun stood. "I will speak to him."

"I'll cook," the Jadoran girl offered.

He mustered a smile and strode into the cold rain.

CHAPTER SIX

THE WATER that coursed down his face and the back of his neck was frigid, but Zaide couldn't make himself stir. He sat atop a rock on a ridge overlooking the dark woods, the Spectrum Blade laid across his knees. It glowed softly in the shadow of the night, ripples of color flowing from each point where raindrops struck its surface. He'd never seen it react to contact that way before, but he couldn't bring himself to care.

He shut his eyes and tried to breathe.

Footsteps behind him crunched on dead branches and squished in the mud. He didn't want company, and he readied himself to snap at whichever one of the girls had chosen to follow him.

Instead, Andriun emerged from the dark and sat on a lower outcropping of stone an arm's reach away. He said nothing, just pulled the hood of his fur-lined cape up a little farther to shelter him from the rain.

"I thought you'd like water," Zaide said.

Andriun considered for a moment before he spoke. "I do, but on my own terms. I do not like muddy water that clogs the gills, and I do not like cold rain."

Zaide snorted. He trailed a finger down the central ridge of the blade on his lap. It didn't react to him the way it reacted to the rain. For some reason, that irritated him worse than the icy water that slithered beneath the collar of his Jadoran coat to trickle down his spine.

"I am sorry," Andriun said after a time. "I have spoken carelessly. I do not mean to trivialize what you have done, nor question what you have worked for. That you have been chosen as Bladebearer is a remarkable honor and a great burden. I admire your strength, for I am not certain I could withstand the same if it were asked of me."

That wasn't what bothered him, but his friend's gentle delivery was still a balm to the sharp edges of his feelings. He'd never thought twice about drawing the Spectrum Blade from its resting place, and he hadn't stopped to consider what he might have done if the blade rejected him, either. Let Lark draw it, he supposed; they'd been there to claim it for her, and he'd tried to give it to her before, too.

The night's earlier conversation sprang to mind and Zaide grasped the sword by its hilt and slid it toward the Desheni hunter. "Don't touch it, it reacts badly if people try to do that. But see if you can feel anything in it."

"In it?" Andriun asked.

"You know, like magic. I don't know how it works. I'm not a mage, I don't know what magic feels like."

Andriun studied the sword for a time, then raised one webbed hand to let it hover over the blade. "I sense nothing. Why do you ask?"

Some part of him had hoped for something different. He drew the blade back onto his lap, clasped his hands together, and rested them atop the sword. "It'd be easier to accept I'm not special if I wasn't special."

His friend studied him for a time. Eventually, Andriun squared his shoulders and stared out across the forest. "I suspect this is not about the sword. Am I correct?"

"I don't know. Maybe. I don't know what it's about." A flash of lightning illuminated the trees and left an impression that lingered in Zaide's vision. "I just... I don't know. The longer I'm outside of Kolmar, the more it feels like my life is just one big question mark. When the sword rejected everyone else, I thought maybe it picked me on purpose, though I don't know why it would. Then I was told it can and will pick a new bearer if necessary. It didn't bother me to think it would choose someone else if something happened to me, but if it was supposed to choose Sendassian and chose me instead..."

"You wonder if the blade will change its mind." Andriun drew his legs up to cross his ankles. He rested one elbow atop his knee and stroked his chin with two fingers. "I do not know what to tell you, my friend. I am confused, as well."

"Does the Oracle you were talking about know when the sword chooses someone new? Or when it will choose someone new?"

"That, I do not know. If a new Bladebearer was chosen, or was to be chosen, I think that the Oracle would have sent word to the Shaman. And it is possible she has. I am sorry, I have not been among my people to know if word has come."

That the blade's decision could have been made at the last minute hadn't occurred to him. Zaide tilted his head and frowned down at the sword. "But you weren't told beforehand?"

"Does this threaten your sense of security?" Andriun's words were soft and judgment-free, but instead of bringing reassurance, they only made the confusion worse.

It wasn't security or a lack of it that hurt. It was old wounds that made less sense than ever. "I don't know how to explain this," Zaide murmured. He rubbed his temples and tried to sort out the thoughts. "You said the Oracle shares this information so the Paragons know who needs to be protected? So they can stay alive long enough to fulfill their destiny?"

"Yes, that is how it was explained to me."

It was all so close to making sense, yet farther off than ever before. Zaide heaved a sigh. "The Kolmari Elder kept me from going to the garrison in my Spring Choosing. It was what I wanted, what I spent my whole life practicing for, and he stopped me. I'm not a mage, taking me as an apprentice made no sense. But he was the Paragon. If he knew Resia would be the next Elder, it makes sense for him to take her as an apprentice. But why me? If I was chosen for this, if I was supposed to be the one to wield the sword, then maybe—"

"Maybe all the questions that have plagued you since then would be answered," Andriun finished for him. "I see."

"But you weren't told it was going to be me. It wouldn't have been a new thing, not something that cropped up the moment I set foot in that chamber beneath Kolmar's temple. My Spring Choosing was more than a year ago. Whatever reason he had to pull me aside, he had it then."

The Desheni hunter tilted his head to one side, then the other, then rested his chin against his fist. "Hmm. This gives me new concerns."

Zaide almost didn't ask, afraid his moment to wallow in self-pity would be stolen for something else, but he couldn't help wanting to know. "About what? The Oracle?"

"My father."

That was not the response Zaide expected. The first thing that sprang to mind was the possibility she hadn't been able to notify everyone. Maybe harm had befallen the Oracle before word could spread, and only a message to the Elder had escaped.

Then again, that was wishful thinking. A selfish notion that sought to make him feel important again. Zaide shook it away. "Your father?"

"He is... well. It is not my place to say what I wish. I am his son, and the man I know is not the one others see. But I have been concerned about his choices in the past. Choices he makes as a leader, I mean. Sometimes I feel his interests conflict with his duties, if that makes sense?"

"Like he's not fulfilling his role as Shaman the way he should?" Jadora's Magister came to mind. The false Magister had wormed his way into the palace somehow, and Tula had never been protected or told of her destiny. If her rise to the role of Magister had been preordained, shouldn't the previous Magister have made an effort to draw her beneath his wing before the time came?

But that Magister had no power either, Zaide reminded himself. Who knew how long it had been since the last true Magister had ruled over the desert city. If that was the man who received word of Tula's imminent power, maybe refusing to acknowledge her had been his choice of tactics for defending his role.

"Yes. That is to say, the role of Shaman has three prongs, and this is represented in the tridents sometimes used by those of my people who remain in the sea. My father keeps a trident mounted in his home to remind him of this. The first prong is the role of Shaman as Shaman, the chosen protector of the Captured Spring and representative of water magic. The Shaman is the most powerful water mage that is known. The second prong is the role of Shaman as Paragon, one of the balancing forces of power that serves to keep the rebirth of evil at bay. And the third is the role of Shaman as leader of the Desheni. Not just those of us who are land-adapted, but our people as a whole, though we have become estranged from our sea-dwelling kin." Andriun ticked off his fingers as he explained.

"So you're saying he's focused on the last one, even though he should be focused on the others."

"To say he pays them no mind would be untrue. He takes his roles very seriously and always has. He has always been Shaman first, a man and a hunter and a father second." Andriun shrugged. "But between the three there is to be a certain balance, and the center prong—the second prong, the role of Shaman as Paragon—is the longest for a reason. This is not the way I feel my father has lived his life."

Which didn't bode well for their mission. Zaide lowered his eyes to the glowing sword. The rain was not so heavy now, and its surface swirled in more colorful patterns. "He's not going to help us, is he?"

"I cannot say. But I will say it is likely for the best if I am not present when you approach him to seek help." It was a simple statement, free of resignation or disappointment.

"You've been out here since I left, haven't you?"

A smile cracked across the Desheni hunter's face. "It is not a bad way to be. I am free of responsibilities here. I fend for myself and explore as I please, and I no longer face pressure from my village's elders to accept a mate and ensure the next generation. I am not opposed to marriage, mind you. But I am young, and I fear I am not prepared for the work of keeping a wife happy. Or building a house in which to keep her." His smile melted into a grimace.

Zaide couldn't help but snort a laugh. "Building a house is one step of the Kolmari rite of passage into adulthood. The first step is fixing an old cottage and learning to live by yourself, but then you have to choose a permanent role in the village, learn to provide for a family, and build a home. I never made it past step one."

"Ah, but I can picture you as a craftsman," Andriun said. "You are good with a sword, but I do not feel you have a soldier's spirit. I do not think you are one who is meant to destroy. I think you are meant to create."

"I'm about as creative as a rock."

"Well, even a rock can be a useful tool in creation. Perhaps not one of these." Andriun indicated the rock they sat on. "But a rock can be shaped into something more. My people rely on stone for many tools, as the ability to forge metal underwater is understandably lacking, and the salt water is cruel to most metals. Many of our spears are stone, but so are our hammers. Our axes. And sometimes, even our toys."

"Toys, huh. You'll have to forgive me if I don't feel like being played with right now." Zaide contemplated his sword a moment longer, then wiped excess water from its surface with the palm of his hand and slid the blade into its sheath.

Andriun shrugged. "All I am saying is that you do not have to be a spear. You do not have to be a weapon that is wielded by fate, either. The sword has chosen you, and I trust you will fulfill your role to the best of your ability. But you are more than that, too, and what you are chosen for sometimes does not matter as much as what you choose for yourself."

Coming from Andriun, those words bore weight. He'd given up a great deal to aid them, by his own choice. Zaide looked his way, though without the Spectrum Blade's soft light, it was hard to see anything in the dark.

Slowly, Andriun stood. "I will take you to my people," he announced. "I cannot make my father assist you, but this is the path I have chosen for myself. I will aid you as I can."

Zaide rose, too. "Thank you." He felt as if there should be more to say, but right now, the task of convincing Athradan to assist them spun to the forefront of his mind and consumed all his thoughts.

"It will not be easy," Andriun said, as if reading his mind.

"No," Zaide agreed.

Nothing had been.

CHAPTER SEVEN

"You don't feel anything at all? Did you try to touch it?" Lark sent a glance back Zaide's direction as she interrogated their guide.

He met her gaze and put a hand on the Spectrum Blade, as if to protect it. A tingle brushed his fingertips, something light and different. Humor? That was one feeling he hadn't expected. The idea of the sword shocking people for fun had never crossed his mind. He dropped his eyes from the princess and gave the blade's hilt a suspicious glance instead.

"I understand it is unwise to try," Andriun said. Aside from the few moments spent observing it the night before, he had been uninterested in the sword. Probably for the best.

They walked single-file along a rocky trail, a mountain to one side and a sheer drop to the other. Zaide hadn't thought they were that close to the hills, but with the density of the trees, it was easy to miss the way the land sloped.

Andriun led them with a sure and certain step. Lark walked behind him, then Tula, and Zaide brought up the rear. The chances of them being attacked this far into the mountains were slim, but impossible to discount. When they'd first set off, there had been strange tracks near the mouth of the trail. Bugraks, according to Andriun. Zaide hadn't spent enough time studying their feet to know.

"It stings." Lark rubbed her hand at the memory of how the sword had sparked against her touch. "But it was just a snap when I tried. I understand the bite it gave my father was much more severe."

Andriun did not stop, but he turned sideways and slowed so he could look her in the face. "Sendassian tried to take it? And it rejected him?"

Zaide brushed a thumb over the pommel. The sword purred beneath his touch as if it were a cat. Unsettled, he removed his hand. "We tried to warn him."

"I do not accuse you of otherwise. Merely, I am intrigued by the idea that the sword could change its bearer so fully. Especially when it had been made clear that the Spectrum Blade belonged in his hand."

"Yeah, about that," Zaide began. "I can't help but wonder why you never mentioned the sword when I came to get the spring before."

"Why would I have mentioned it? You came seeking one of the keys. You already had the other two. I assumed if the princess sent you, you knew what she was after. Or perhaps that she knew what she was after. I am just a hunter. It is not my place to question princesses." Andriun flattened his hand against his chest. He'd put on his mittens again, shielding his hands from the unseasonably chilly air.

Tula glanced back and forth between them, scribbling furiously in her notebook.

"How do you write and walk at the same time?" Zaide asked.

"Hm? Oh. Practice, I guess? I walk into stuff sometimes, though." She flashed him a smile and returned to writing.

He frowned at her back. How much of what she wrote was observations based on what was said, and how much was verbatim?

"From the sound of things, Andriun, your people's verbal records are quite extensive. Maybe you can help us determine what went wrong in Jadora." Lark's tone shifted toward persuasiveness. "We believe the Magister who ruled the city bore no real power. We don't know how long the line had been broken after the dragon Vorkaris chose to sleep. Do your people know anything about this?"

"No. And yes." Andriun gave a broad shrug. "We were not told of the situation. But we also received no word from the Oracle about the identities of the Magister for some time. At least, that is what has been passed down."

Zaide suspected Andriun was only a little older than the rest of them. The previous Magister would have taken his position of power long before the hunter's birth. "Who was Paragon before your father?"

"My grandfather. And his mother before him. And her father before that. This on its own is an interesting story. The Paragon is not always chosen from one bloodline, you see. This is why the Oracle's power is vital. She provides clues for the identities, not often names, but enough information that they can be found. At least, with the three elements."

"At least?" Lark asked.

Andriun nodded as if there was nothing more to say.

"What do you mean by that? At least with the three elements. What else is there to know? The identity of the Bladebearer?" Zaide fought to keep his hand from twitching back to the sword.

"That and the identity of Gadranus when it comes time for the Rise. His name is more of a mantle, you see, something that he must claim once he becomes aware of his power and who he is. One hundred years between his death and rebirth seems a long time, but it is not so long that one would forget what has happened and name their child something so foul."

Lark made a thoughtful sound. "What of the Oracle? Hers is a role that must be passed down too, is it not?"

"Oh, yes. There are many such roles. But I will not bore you,

Your Highness." Andriun grinned. "I am sure there is little left for me to teach one with access to such knowledge as you have."

"You'd be surprised," Tula put in. "I thought we'd have a lot of information in Jadora, since we have the Great Library, but it turns out our records have been tampered with. There was all sorts of information missing. Things about the Magister's power, things about the Molten Dagger, everything about Magister Vorkaris being a dragon."

He considered that a moment, then nodded. "This is the problem with knowledge. When it is held in one place, it is easy to censor that which you do not wish to be known. This is why our oral histories are for everyone among our people. Not only for the Shaman's son." A hint of wistfulness touched his face.

"But the more voices that repeat the information, the more likely it is for incorrect information to be included in what you pass on." Lark tossed her head the way she always did when something irritated her. Tula squeaked when the princess's golden hair snagged on her pencil.

"We do not face this problem," Andriun said. "Communication is key in preserving the truth. We all speak it, so we all hear the stories and compare them. Information that is found in only one place is not considered to be valid. This preserves the core part of our history without corruption, and without risk of information being lost."

Something moved in the trees below. Zaide watched it from the corner of his eye. It could have been a deer, or it could have been something worse. "Does your history contain information that might fill in the holes in Jadora's history?"

"Perhaps. But that is a question for the elders among my people, those who are steeped in this knowledge and will not forget small things." Andriun's head turned, almost imperceptibly. He was watching, too.

Zaide lowered his voice. "What's down there?"

"Desheni." Andriun spoke as if he didn't care whether they were heard. "They know we come."

"Is that good or bad?" Lark asked in a murmur.

"Ah," the hunter sighed. "That is not for me to say."

The trees disguised their numbers, but Zaide estimated it was a party similar in size to the one that had taken him captive. "Why are they out here?" That a whole party would be sent to supervise one exiled Desheni was unlikely.

"Our territory is not fiercely guarded, but not all are welcome. We have had trouble in recent days. Or, they have." Andriun nodded to the group below as they slid through the trees. The distance between their parties was great enough that there was nothing to be heard but the usual sounds of the forest. "I have spoken to some of the hunters as they walk the woods. They do not like me, but they do not wish for harm to befall me, so they tell me what they know."

Lark watched them, too, her expression unreadable. "Have there been goborrins in the north?"

"No. But as I told Zaide, ah..." The hunter trailed off as if unsure what he was about to say was proper.

Zaide pushed his personal reservations aside. "How many broken-born has it been? What are the groups like? And what do they want?"

"It is a mix." Andriun slid a hand beneath the hood of his cloak to rub the back of his neck. "Most we find in the mountains are small bands of men. They claim they are scouts for larger groups, but we do not see these groups and we do not believe it. One time, at the tip of the continent, they did find families. There were women and children. But the men were with them, and all of them were frightened. We believe they traveled from the northernmost parts of the Shattered Lands by ship and were forced ashore by storms."

Something in Zaide's chest pulled tight. "Refugees?"

"The war intensifies at the border as Gadranus pushes his armies through," Lark said softly. "There are many who would choose to flee, rather than have their homes along Amroch's edge be consumed by violence."

He nodded. His parents had done the same. "But if they came by ship, where were they going?" He couldn't picture them weighing anchor in the bay between Jadora and Ganede. There were other settlements in that region, but they were small. Not the sort of place someone might seek refuge. Even his family had planned to travel to Amrochan. But travel had been difficult with a baby, and Kolmar had been the best they could do.

"We do not know. And they are why my people hesitate to simply drive out those who we find in the mountains. We do not wish ill upon refugees. But if they lead our enemies to our heart, what else can we do? When we find them, we urge them to leave. Often they are escorted to the coast, or to the road that runs to Beshnai." Andriun pointed the tip of his spear over his shoulder to indicate the south.

Tula paused her scribbling. "And if they come back?"

The Desheni hunter's smile turned grim. "I do not know, for I have not spoken to my people often. If they have encountered the same group twice, I have not heard."

Zaide doubted it would mean anything good. "So is me being here going to be a problem when we cross paths with these guys?"

"Perhaps. If we are lucky, the fact you travel with the Magister and the princess will protect you. Oh, and also the Spectrum Blade, but perhaps do not draw it. I do not think that would be taken as anything other than an affront."

The Shaman had accused Zaide of bringing violence and war before, just because he carried the Molten Dagger. The Spectrum Blade could only be seen as worse. "I'll try to keep it put away, then. Unless we run into bugraks or goborrins, we don't really need it until Athradan agrees to give it his blessing."

Andriun made a thoughtful sound. "You are optimistic, Zaide. But I like that, because I am an optimist too." Yet that was the most negative thing the hunter had likely ever said. It shifted the mood of the whole group, and for the rest of the afternoon, they walked in silence.

The Desheni hunting party followed them for days, then changed course. They closed the distance between their two groups, their weapons ready in hand as they approached.

Andriun put up a hand in silent order for the rest of them to stop. As they grew still behind him, Zaide deliberately settled his hand on his Jadoran knife instead of the Spectrum Blade. He half regretted that his hood was down, but he supposed there was little point in trying to hide now. The hunting party had pursued them long enough to know the color of his hair.

A man from the other party moved forward, demanding something in a language Zaide didn't understand, but recognized from his previous visit.

Andriun shook his head. "I travel in the company of Her Highness, Princess Dasienna. With her are her Bladebearer and Her Excellency, Magister Tula of Jadora. You will speak in the Amrochan common tongue out of respect for their station."

The way the man's lip drew back from his teeth showed what he thought of that. "We don't care about them, Andriun. You are the one who is unwelcome in our settlement."

Andriun rested his spear against the ground and let it fall back against his shoulder so he could hold both hands up, palms out. "I do not question the terms of my exile, but I will see they reach my father."

"We can take them without your assistance," the man said.

Lark sniffed. "I am certain you can, but he is our chosen guide. You may accompany us if you desire, or run ahead to notify your Shaman we are coming, but he will be the one to take us to your village."

The Desheni man's stare wasn't intense enough to be a glower, but it was close. He muttered something in his own tongue, then pointed his spear at Andriun's face and said something else.

Zaide started to reach for his weapon.

Andriun did not stir. His stillness stayed Zaide's hand.

The hunting party retreated a few steps, then turned to depart when their leader barked an order. A few shot hateful looks over their shoulders, though one of the men merely looked troubled.

Tula tapped the end of her pencil against her lips, then made a few notes. "I take it we're close to the village, then?"

"Close enough that they can be certain we are headed that way." Andriun smoothed one mitten over the top of his head. His black hair was sleek and orderly, which lent the motion something of an air of hesitance.

"Well, at least Athradan will be ready for us." Lark touched his shoulder to urge him on, but something shifted in the hunter's demeanor. When he took his spear again and their walking resumed, his pace was more subdued.

A sense of uneasiness radiated from the sword at Zaide's hip. "Yeah, me too," he mumbled.

Andriun didn't notice, but Tula cast him a thoughtful frown.

The path they took climbed into the mountains, then descended toward the village in a familiar slope. It was the same route they'd taken the first time, before Zaide had known who Andriun was. Before they'd stolen away in the night to fulfill the princess's quest.

Across the village, people stopped to stare. Some shuffled away in a hurry, sensing the same threat of trouble that pricked at Zaide and put him on edge.

Andriun kept his head up and ignored the spectators as he led them to the settlement's edge. A nearby woman snapped something at him, then spat.

Tula's note-taking slowed to a more deliberate pace.

They'd not reached the first building before a group of Desheni men wielding spears marched toward them. They spread out and blocked the way, spears leveled toward them.

"Go no further," one said, his words in the common tongue but his eyes fixed on Andriun.

"They are here to speak to my father," Andriun said calmly.

"The Shaman will not see them."

A muscle twitched in Lark's jaw. She stepped forward, unintimidated by the spears.

Zaide still put his hand on his Jadoran knife, ready to defend her if need be. Would the Spectrum Blade react to the spilling of Desheni blood the same way it did to the blood of humans? He didn't want to find out.

"I am Dasienna, crown princess of Amrochan and your future queen. The Shaman will meet with me, or he will face the fury of the crown." Lark took another step forward, as if there were no spears present.

A hint of uncertainty crossed the leader's face.

She caught his gaze and held it in challenge. "If Shaman Athradan requires time to prepare, then so be it, but I will not be denied. Tell him I have come, and I have brought my Bladebearer. Athradan's role as Paragon of Water will be fulfilled, or this Rise shall be recorded as the Rise in which Gadranus won."

A question from one of the other men made the Desheni leader tilt his head. They whispered back and forth for a time before the leader straightened and shifted. "The Shaman will be told, but you will not enter the city. You, least of all." His eyes flicked Andriun's way. He did not lower his spear.

"I am here only to escort the princess," Andriun said placidly.

"You will leave the premises at once."

Andriun pointed his spear back the way they'd come. "We will make camp on the mountain path. When my father is ready to speak with Her Highness, you will come to us."

The leader said nothing.

Lark took it as acceptance and spun on her heel.

Instead of letting them walk by themselves, the group of armed Desheni escorted them up the slope.

Zaide positioned himself between Lark and the men, though

their spears were all directed toward Andriun. He'd thought he'd be the one the Desheni distrusted. He never imagined something like exile would be taken so seriously.

When the group decided they were far enough away, one of the men stepped forward and took Andriun's spear. "*Kantasosh*," he snarled.

Andriun let him take the weapon, his head bowed and his hands raised.

Another spat at his feet before they departed.

"What did that mean? What he said?" Tula asked in a whisper.

Andriun's face had grown stony. "Child-killer."

CHAPTER EIGHT

THERE WAS nothing at their waiting point but rocks. Lark chose a large stone at the base of a cliff to sit upon. She said nothing, but the expectant way she looked at Andriun would have made anyone squirm. He bowed his head and braced himself for the sort of questions that were sure to come.

Zaide was the one who spoke first. "That doesn't make any sense. All you did was help me get the spring."

"Yes, and helping you get the spring is why they call me that." Andriun had hoped to explain as little as possible. In retrospect, that had been foolish. They would need a full explanation, and they deserved it, too. Especially if he wanted their help.

"This has to do with the spring?" Lark asked. Her gaze was intense. The longer she stared at him, the more Andriun understood why someone with as much spirit as Zaide bowed readily to her demands. She bore a forceful intensity, an air that made it clear she would be obeyed. Even with his desire to tell as little as possible, Andriun found himself nodding.

"Yes, and why allowing Zaide to take it has harmed my people." The weight of her eyes made him feel as if he might buckle. He tried not to meet her gaze for more than a moment, though he knew he could not avoid it forever. If he wished for her to think him earnest, they would have to lock eyes.

Tula sat cross-legged on the ground with her notebook poised.

Andriun sat, too, but hesitated. "Please, do not write down what I am going to tell you."

The Magister's brows lifted, but she said nothing. He could not make her put her notes aside, nor could he censor history. But his people had kept their ways private for a reason, and the least he could do was ask.

"I know we are not yet friends and you do not have any reason to heed me, but I do not want my people to be judged for this." He touched his chest. "The judgment should rest on me, for I am the one whose choices have led our ways to become a terrible risk."

A thoughtful haze clouded her eyes, but she still held her pencil. A tiny part of him hoped the princess might back him up, but Lark remained silent, too.

Andriun sighed. He had tried. "What they say is not wrong. Because of me, because of what I have done, our children will die. I do not ask for sympathy, but I would ask for your help, Your Highness." He forced his hands to his lap, where he clasped his mittens together. It would have been easier to stare at his hands as he spoke, but to keep his head bowed would signal shame. He was not ashamed of his actions, only saddened by what they brought. So he straightened his spine and met the princess's stare with a calm face.

"Speak your piece, then," the princess said. "I cannot confirm or deny assistance until you tell me what it is you wish."

Diplomatic and non-committal. He had expected nothing less. "For this situation to make sense, you must first understand how our people have changed. We are fish. We are meant to be in the water." He hooked a thumb in the collar of his cape and coat and pulled down both to display his upper gills. "We still reside near the water, because we need it to thrive. But my clan is not like the rest of the Desheni. We are the appointed guardians of the Captured Spring, and so we have changed. Through many years, our form has changed. The sea-bound Desheni are a large, beautiful people, with bodies suited to life in the water. We no longer are."

Lark's chin rose as he spoke. Her gaze became more calculating, appraising. Zaide hovered beside her, listening, but his feet were restless.

Andriun went on. "We remain here in the mountains because we must. We have no choice. The source of the first gift of water magic is here, in these lands, and this is where the Paragon must stay. It is our sacrifice to serve the Maker, the king, and to serve you as well, Your Highness. The lake here, where the land-adapted Desheni have settled, is cold all year round. There is ice on the mountains all year. And for half the year, perhaps more, our home bears ice and snow."

Still, the princess said nothing. What he would have given for some small confirmation his words meant anything.

"We are thin," he said. "Compared to our sea-bound kin, we are but sardines next to healthy trout. Our bodies lack the insulation to protect us here. Parted from the water for so long, our fat deposits have dwindled. So we are in constant danger of frostbite, of dead and rotting flesh that will kill us if it is not removed. You understand this risk?"

"Yes." The single word of confirmation told him next to nothing. Lark remained still, but her rich eyes took a guarded sheen. In the silence that followed, the soft scratch of Tula's pencils as she took her notes made his stomach threaten to revolt.

Andriun swallowed back the sour taste in his throat. "To an extent, the Captured Spring protected us from this, as it can heal many things. But its greater protection came in what it allowed us to do. We are fish, you see." And oh, he hoped she did. "But to shelter ourselves from this harm, so that we might serve in the role we are given, we have crippled ourselves. When our children are born, to protect them from cold, we sever the most delicate part of their bodies. We cut off their tails."

At last, the princess's face twisted with emotion. Pain and disgust wrestled to dominate her expression. "That's barbaric."

Beside her, disbelief and horror mingled in the way Zaide looked at him. Andriun had known the information would not be well received, but he had hoped to spare himself this judgment. Or, to spare his people from it, at least.

Tula's pencil grew still. Instead of disgust or disapproval, her face was shaded with sorrow and sympathy. Her fingers twitched against her book as if she warred with herself. Then she folded her notebook closed, the passage left unfinished.

Andriun swallowed. He would thank her for that, later. "Understand," he said slowly, "this is not a choice we make lightly. None of us wish to part ourselves from the water in this way. But to fulfill our duties, it must be done. The Captured Spring is what makes this possible. It is both a blessing and burden for our people. Because of it, we sever our tails. But with it, the practice brings us no lasting harm. The spring's healing powers ensure we are healed fully and that no children are lost when the amputation is performed."

"But the spring was hidden away in a cave," Zaide said.

"Yes, for its protection. But it replenishes itself, and its waters are not diminished by being parted from the spring. Once each year, my father would visit the cavern to drain the spring. He carries its liquid in a silver vial he wears around his neck, to be used through the rest of the year while the spring recovers."

Zaide's face grew paler, something Andriun hadn't thought possible. "The spring was full when we retrieved it."

Again, Andriun swallowed. "Yes. My father's pilgrimage had not yet taken place. Now, his stores have run dry. There is nothing left, and so my people are left with a terrible choice to make. Few children will survive the amputation. But if their tails are not cut, then in the coming years, few will survive the winter.

This is an impossible challenge, one I have brought upon my people. That, Your Highness, is why I ask—"

Before he could finish, Lark yanked the silver chain over her head and extended the Captured Spring.

He squeezed his eyes closed. He had expected criticism. At the very least, he thought convincing her to relinquish the artifact would take more effort. "Thank you, Your Highness." He took the vial from her hand and curled both his hands around it. It was cool, even through his lined mittens. A comfort. Reassurance.

"So you'll take it back and they'll let you back in, right?" Zaide sounded confident about that conclusion, but he shifted on his feet, betraying his uneasiness.

"I do not think so." Andriun had come to terms with that long ago. Setting things right for his people was all that mattered; he had embraced the repercussions of his actions the moment he helped Zaide escape the ruined ice cavern with the Captured Spring in his possession. "I can give back the safety of my clan's children, but I cannot so easily restore their faith in me."

His friend shook his head hard, refusal of a fact that should have been simple. "But you're destined to be the Shaman. They can't just turn you away."

"It is true the Oracle foretold my place as Paragon of Water. But my father is yet young, and the day I will take his place is far off. When that day comes, I may still be chosen as Paragon. But I will never be Shaman. The leadership of my clan will be fractured, and the role of Shaman as both leader and Paragon will be destroyed." He shrugged. It did not matter. He was little more than a placeholder, a bridge between this Rise and the next. His exile would be little more than a sentence in the oral histories of his people, but he was unbothered by his lack of legacy. The fact it was a lack, and not a legacy of ruin and despair for what he had done, was all that mattered.

"It's not too late to fix it, right? For all the babies?" Tula asked quietly. Her concern struck him as endearing.

"I do not think so." Unsure what to do with the spring, he slid its chain over his head and freed his black braid from beneath it. How he would approach returning the artifact to his father was the next problem to solve. "It is done early, soon after birth, to minimize scarring. But there are only a few children who have been born since the spring was taken, and they are no more than a handful of weeks old. My father will know more. He is our medic, he performs all the tail cuttings." Had none of this happened, that responsibility would have fallen to him. Andriun wondered if it was better this way. He was not sure he had the stomach for such a procedure.

"Then let's hope he meets with us soon," Zaide said.

Andriun nodded, then bowed his head. Tucking the spring beneath his coat should have been a relief. Instead, he found himself more troubled than ever before. "I am sorry for involving you in this. I had hoped my father would listen to reason and understand why we must allow the princess to take the spring, but he was unwilling to hear any of my arguments. I fear it is my strong stand that will make him resistant to helping you now."

Lark's jaw tightened. "Well, let's hope he's more likely to listen to my reasoning than yours. It'll be hard for him to deny the role when the Spectrum Blade is right before his face."

He wished he could support her confidence. His nerves had grown rattled, instead. "I cannot say what will happen, but know that I have spoken to Zaide about my father's ways. I know him. He will put his people before all else."

His people. Andriun's brow furrowed. Not their people. Why had it come out that way? It was not what he intended.

"Perhaps," Lark said as she pushed herself from the stone and turned toward the village. "We'll see soon, won't we?"

Three Desheni hunters—men Andriun once considered friends—climbed the hill. The darkness in their faces when they saw him was enough to make him glad the Captured Spring was hidden beneath his coat. He had suffered enough for one day. There was no reason to invite more trouble.

When they came close, all three of the men held their spears ready as they faced Lark. "The Shaman will speak with you," one announced. "But only you."

"My Bladebearer will accompany me. His presence is not negotiable." She held herself regally, a proud and imposing figure who would not be disobeyed.

From the way the Desheni men shifted, they had not been prepared. They exchanged glances and murmured words in their own tongue, discussing whether Athradan would punish them for bringing more visitors than allowed. Eventually, they concluded the Shaman's orders were not worth a fight with the princess.

"Your Bladebearer may come, but the others will stay here," the leader of the group said.

Zaide turned with a question, but Tula grinned at him before he could ask. "I'll work on my notes while you're gone. I trust you'll remember everything said so I can write it down."

"I'm not going to promise that," Zaide said. His smile hid a hint of mischief.

Andriun stayed on the ground and resisted the urge to tell Zaide to be mindful when he spoke. It was no longer his place. He had fulfilled his promise, led them to the village and convinced the princess to return the spring. Right now, there was nothing more he could do.

That she had entrusted the Captured Spring to him when she knew she would see his father had not escaped him, but he already knew that gesture was in vain. He rested his hands on his thighs and watched as Lark and Zaide followed the three Desheni back toward the village.

"Andriun?" Tula asked, her voice hesitant, yet sweet to his ears. She inched closer to where he sat.

She would worry about her friends. About what might befall

them, and about what might not make its way into her notes. None of that was anything with which he could help, but he still tilted one fin-like ear her way to indicate he was paying attention. "Hm?"

"I, um…" She twirled her pencil between her fingers. "Nothing I've ever read about the Desheni says anything about tails."

That was not where he thought the conversation might go. His brow crinkled and he turned to face her. "Do you think I lie?"

"No! I mean, not at all, that's not it. It's just, uh, I guess the resources in the Great Library have a poor understanding of Desheni physiology, because none of the anatomical diagrams illustrate tails at all. So, the amputation scar. Could… could I see?" Her wide emerald eyes blinked at him, as sweet and innocent as her smile.

"The—you—you know where tails go," he stammered. Maker's mercy, why had she asked *that?*

"Well, yes. Why do you think I waited until we were alone to ask?" She grinned.

That was *definitely* not where he thought the conversation might go.

Her eyes brightened as heat stole up his neck and into his face, and when her face lit up too, he hated the sort of notes he knew she would take.

Beneath their blue skin, the Desheni blushed purple.

CHAPTER NINE

Zaide's stomach turned. It had begun with a lump of dread nights before, when Andriun had shared all that about tridents and the Paragon's role and the reluctance Athradan was sure to show when they asked him for aid. It had only grown worse since then. Realizing what sort of person they were going to speak to had made his stomach roll over so hard, it was a wonder he hadn't been sick then and there.

"I've got a bad feeling about all this," he murmured as they walked.

Athradan had been severe and unforgiving the first time Zaide crossed his path, and the man hadn't even had a reason to dislike him then. Now they approached the Shaman's cabin as thieves who had stolen the well-being of infants.

Infants Athradan was tasked with mortally wounding, Zaide reminded himself. That knowledge had made his stomach churn hardest of all. He understood the apparent necessity of it. The Desheni couldn't leave the cold while still attending their duties. But those duties had been neglected, even railed against. Athradan had refused to aid them before, and there was less chance he'd aid them now.

"Then allow me to handle the situation," Lark replied. "You

get tongue-tied when you're flustered. It'll only make things worse."

"I do not." Did he? He squinted at the ground, trying to remember.

Lark's face could have been that of a statue, for all the amusement she showed when she looked his way. "I will speak. You will stand there and draw the sword so it may be seen, should I decide it's necessary."

As they approached the stairs, one of the Desheni men who led the way raised a fist. "No weapons. You will leave them all here."

Lark shrugged and unsheathed the daggers strapped to her thighs. She passed them to one of the men, then nodded toward the Jadoran knife at Zaide's belt.

He removed it from its sheath and handed it over.

The man pointed at his sword.

Zaide hesitated.

"The Spectrum Blade does not leave his hands," Lark said.

"I said no weapons. If you wish to see the Shaman, you will abide by his rules."

Her eyes flashed, cold and stormy like an angry sea. "The Shaman's voice has no authority over mine."

The man's shoulders squared and his hand tightened on his spear, but his gaze was no match for Lark's. Finally, he relented with a shake of his head and something muttered that made Zaide wish Andriun were there to translate.

He led them to the door.

Lark did not wait to be let in. She shoved the door open and marched inside. The room beyond was dark, as Zaide remembered, but the shadow didn't bother her.

"A bold girl with no manners," a rasping voice mused.

Zaide followed close on Lark's heels. Behind them, the door remained open. The three Desheni guards stationed themselves beside it. Did they think the blade he still carried meant he would attack? A prickle of annoyance that wasn't wholly his own crawled through his shoulders.

"A woman you should kneel before," Lark replied. "But you know who I am."

Though winter no longer gripped the settlement, the Shaman was still swathed in dark furs. His face was more pinched than Zaide recalled, but his long, white mustaches bore more beads than before. "As well as you know me."

"I know you're a liar," Zaide grumbled.

The princess shot him a withering glare, but he returned it.

"He said there was no Shaman. That he had no magic." He didn't need to defend himself, yet he couldn't help it. Andriun had sacrificed a great deal to aid him, and all of it could have been avoided if the man before them had been honest.

Lark's lips twitched, but she peeled her gaze away and returned her attention to the Shaman. "I am here to call upon you to fulfill your responsibilities as Paragon of Water."

A wheezing laugh escaped the old man. "You are here to feed your father's ego, nothing more. To act where he wouldn't, so he might claim victory that shouldn't be his."

"It shouldn't matter who claims a victory now, as long as there is one," the princess said. "My father's failure to become the Bladebearer no longer matters. The sword has chosen a new wielder."

Zaide skimmed the Spectrum Blade's leather sheath with the fingers of his left hand. He wanted to chime in, but he'd irritated Lark enough for one day. They'd never had a chance to speak of Athradan's refusal to aid them in depth. In retrospect, that would have been wise to discuss while they were trapped on that ship.

"Yes," Athradan said slowly. "So the Oracle said." His dark eyes narrowed to slits as he regarded Zaide and his face twisted into a sneer.

Heat prickled beneath Zaide's hand. Indignation. "Mind

what choices you question," he said, chancing the princess's ire. "The sword takes offense at your disapproval."

That caught the man off guard, for his eyebrows lifted until they looked as if they might tip off his head. "You said you were here for me to fulfill a duty. The sword is already awake?"

Zaide still wasn't sure how to answer that. While he deliberated, Lark spoke.

"The nature of how the sword speaks to him is a mystery to anyone who cannot wield it. But while it speaks, its strength is depleted. You will restore your portion of its power, and we will continue on to fight the battle from which my father's forces shelter you."

Athradan's sneer returned. "No. I don't believe I shall."

The slight flare of Lark's nostrils was all that betrayed her anger. She stood straighter and stared at the Shaman, her silence demanding he explain.

He turned away. "What does it matter if you strike him down? What does it change? It's one more battle in a war that never ends. Your father has fought the forces of Gadranus since the moment he took the throne. His father fought before then. On and on it goes, a never-ending battle, a hollow victory that soon comes undone."

"One hundred years of peace is a blessed reward," the princess argued. "A chance to raise children without worrying whether or not we'll all be killed by goborrins in our sleep."

The Shaman ticked a finger. "One hundred years of peace is a concept that drives you all, but this is but the lifetime of one man. You speak of the safety of children, yet should you strike down Gadranus this very day, your own children will still live when the Rise begins anew. What does it matter, this endless fight to hold him at bay? What does it matter, whether you're ruled by one king or another?"

The resignation in the old man's words turned Zaide's already unsettled stomach. "You've given up."

"I will not fuel this battle," Athradan said. "For generations, we have sacrificed our well-being to answer what the Maker has asked of us. The Desheni are not a warlike people, yet we have fought and struggled against nature itself since we left the sea to answer this call. But no more. Our spirit is broken. This war has cost our way of life and the lives of our children. No more."

"Your children are no safer in a world where you refuse to fight." Lark stepped forward, her fists clenched at her sides. "You think you have suffered beneath the blessings of power the Maker has given you, but you don't know suffering yet. Look at my Bladebearer."

The Shaman's head turned, ever so slightly.

Lark spread a hand toward Zaide. "You know the fate of his people. The fate of those crushed when they couldn't—or wouldn't—fight back. This is the fate of the rest of Amroch, the rest of the world, if we do not fight!"

Athradan heaved a sigh. "You are an ignorant child."

Zaide couldn't hold his tongue any longer. "At least she's trying! Maybe you don't think a hundred years is worth it, but you're hidden up here in the mountains, where you don't even allow your people to visit Ganede anymore. My family is dead. Our history is gone. I've carried the scars of war since before I can remember." His hand flew to his left ear, though he didn't know why. It had been cut short in some incident he couldn't recall, an injury his mother had never explained, a secret she'd taken to her grave.

He forced his arm down and gripped the Spectrum Blade's hilt instead. "My whole life, I've prepared for this war. Prepared to defend the only place I've known as home, because every other place was taken from me. One hundred years is enough. And I deserve that peace."

Lark touched his arm. Not to still him, but in a gentle stroke of reassurance. Support. Something he'd needed without knowing it.

Athradan shifted. His feet were hidden by the long furs he wore, the sound of his footwear silenced, giving the illusion that he glided across the room instead of walking. "Mind your bladebearer," he said in a curious, sing-song way. "This boy you trust carries venom in his heart, and he will poison you, too."

"Bless the sword," Lark ordered.

"No." The Shaman raised a hand and said something to the men who waited just outside the door. The three of them stepped into the shadow of the cabin. They circled around and slid between the two of them and the Shaman, their spears pointed.

"You will leave," one of the men said.

A hum radiated up Zaide's arm, followed by heat. It twisted its way across his shoulders, up his neck, and down his other arm. Anger. Its claws raked against the back of his head and bloomed down the muscles of his back. He exhaled hard. "The sword will be blessed." It demanded it.

The Shaman snorted. "Not so long as I draw breath."

"Then maybe you won't for long," Zaide replied.

Lark's eyes widened, but his did, too.

He hadn't intended that. Hadn't even thought it. The heat and anger that poured from the sword eased back, like a snake having struck, and a sense of wrongness washed over him in its absence.

It took everything in him to hold back a shudder.

The spears inched closer, threatening his belly, and he raised his hands to signal surrender. The Desheni men forced the two of them out the door without another word from the Shaman.

The moment Lark's boots touched the ground, she spun to march back up the slope.

Zaide followed, his hands still aloft, lest the Desheni take his movement as a threat. Maker's mercy, why had he said that?

When they reached the bottom of the slope, their escort halted and returned their weapons, and they were allowed to continue on their own. Lark stormed up the trail with her back rigid and her fists balled at her sides. "I told you to let me do the talking." The words hissed strangely, spoken through clenched teeth.

"I'm sorry." He didn't know what else to say. "I don't know what happened. I don't know why I did that. I wasn't even thinking it, and the sword—"

"Oh, shut up." Her ponytail cracked behind her like a whip.

"I'm sorry," Zaide repeated weakly.

At the top of the hill, Andriun and Tula sat on the same rock where Lark had perched before, both of them hunched over her notebook.

Andriun saw them first, and when he saw the stormy look on the princess's face, he leaped to his feet. "It did not go well." He was disappointed, but unsurprised.

"No," Lark said. "We need a new plan."

The Desheni hunter nodded as thought clouded his gaze. "Then I have a suggestion." His hand went to his chest, where he'd tucked the Captured Spring out of sight, and Zaide only hoped this new suggestion didn't involve any caverns of ice.

CHAPTER TEN

 another way to replenish the sword's power."
Andriun walked a few paces ahead, their group returned to a
single-file order. The mountain paths here were narrow, the air
cold.

Zaide hugged his arms tight to his middle as he walked.
Weren't they near summer now? He no longer knew the day and
wasn't certain of the month, but the early spring days that
framed the Choosing were far behind them. "Which you're
choosing to tell us now instead of earlier for what reason,
exactly?" He regretted the way he spoke as soon as the words
were out. It was harsh, unlike him. It was unreasonable to take
out his frustration with the situation and the strangeness of the
sword's influence on his friend, but that hadn't kept his words
from being sharp.

Andriun didn't mind, though. All he did was offer a polite
smile over his shoulder. "Because I am not sure that it will work,
while I was sure my father's power would. It is better to try the
certain option first, no?"

"I guess." Zaide was not sure Athradan's power had ever
been a certainty. After what they'd found with the Magister in
Jadora, he considered the possibility the Shaman hadn't lied;

maybe he bore no magic. Andriun's power had been a surprise, and so there was nothing to say his parents had possessed such a gift.

"It was foolish of me to think I could force him to help." Lark was not given to such confessions, but she walked with her head bowed and a pensive look on her face, from what Zaide could see. She had changed the order of their procession and walked before him now, which he suspected was related to his outburst in the Shaman's home.

Did she question his trustworthiness now? Or was she angry that he'd disobeyed her order to remain silent? She hadn't asked what had come over him, nor had she given him time to bring it up again. The more distance they put between themselves and the Desheni settlement, the less sure he was he wanted to. It would be better to let it fade, a slip forgotten over the course of whatever still awaited them.

At least, that was how he hoped it would be remembered. The sword had been silent since it released him from its anger. No thoughts, no sensations. He hoped it would stay that way.

What if this was what the Shaman meant, when he asked if the sword had awakened? What if power wasn't the only thing that woke? The notion the blade could channel itself through Zaide was unsettling, and he hadn't a clue what to expect. The records mentioning the blade were incomplete, according to Tula, which meant nobody knew what the awakened blade might be like.

Or, next to nobody. Zaide fixed his eyes on Andriun's back. His friend's knowledge of the Paragons had proven more robust than anything they'd read. Maybe he knew more about the Spectrum Blade, too.

"Zaide?" Lark's voice snapped him out of thought and he looked at her blankly. Her brows knit with frustration. "I said, what do you think?"

He glanced past her. Tula and Andriun still walked with their backs to him. "About what?"

The princess tossed up her hands. "Weren't you listening at all?"

"I was..." He didn't know how to explain the thought process without inviting questions he wasn't ready for. He'd find time to talk to Andriun first, then broach that subject. "Sorry. I was just thinking."

"I promise it will not be that bad," Andriun said. "I do not even know if we can get in."

Zaide glanced between his friend and Lark. Whatever he'd missed was about their destination, then. "Um, I don't..."

"We'll try it," Lark said before he could finish. "We haven't got much else to work with right now."

"And if we get there and we can't get in, we'll just go back and try Athradan again. Maybe this time I can talk to him. Let the fires of Jadora convince him." Tula hooked her arms as if to flex her biceps, but her arms were slender and her coat billowed, making the gesture absurd.

"Please, let us not talk about burning my father," Andriun said.

"You never know." Zaide wasn't sure where they were headed, but at least the subject had changed, so he could try to lighten the mood and figure things out later. "Maybe Vorkaris would be an effective mind-changer."

Tula giggled and as they walked on, the afternoon sun seemed to brighten.

The landscape changed little during the course of the day's travels. They wound farther into the mountains, where the growth was lush and untouched. The density of the trees reminded Zaide of home, stirring an uncomfortable homesickness to life within him. The feeling persisted when the sun began to set and they settled to make camp.

"Let me borrow your knife," Andriun said after Tula made it clear she would start the campfire on her own.

Zaide produced the Jadoran weapon from its sheath and offered it hilt-first. "Decided to take up fighting with blades?"

The sound his friend made was one of mild distress. "They took my spear. They did not give it back." He pointed over his shoulder. "There is a sapling over there that will make a decent replacement, but I have nothing with which to cut it down."

Zaide spared a glance for the girls. They conversed quietly while Tula stacked wood in a hollow in the earth. "I'll come with you. Maybe I can help."

"Oh, good. Because I still need to find a good piece of flint, unless you are willing to let me strap your knife to the end of my stick."

"That knife was a present. I want it back."

Andriun chuckled to himself and stepped high over the brush. "I will teach you to shape flint into a good blade, if you wish to learn. Between a good piece of flint and a good sturdy tree, you will never lack for tools."

"Yeah? What about rope to tie it together?" Zaide followed. He was more in his element here than the desert; he slid past thorny brambles and beneath low branches with a practiced ease.

"That is woven from the bark of the sapling, which you strip from the wood. Do they teach you nothing in Kolmar?" The hunter stopped beside the nice, straight sapling he'd chosen and knelt to cut it off at the base. "I am sorry for robbing you of your work, little tree. Your roots are strong, so hopefully I only set you back a few years."

Zaide watched him chip away at the sapling's base for a moment, then drew the Spectrum Blade. "Back up."

Andriun shimmied backwards to give him room. He swung once and struck the little tree low, just above the cuts his friend made. The Spectrum Blade flashed on impact and sliced straight through.

The Desheni hunter gave a low whistle. He put out a hand to catch the sapling as it fell, then sat cross-legged to cut away the branches at its crown. "That is an impressive artifact."

"I just wish we knew more about it." Zaide sat, too. Instead of sheathing the blade or laying it down, he stuck it into the earth and let it stand on its own. The dirt didn't seem to offend the blade. If anything, its swirling colors grew sleepy.

"I'd say you are doing well, if my father is the last Paragon whose blessing you need." The Jadoran knife was sharp and it wasn't long before half the branches were stripped. Andriun paused to brush his thumb over the blade, studying it with an appreciative eye. "I do not know how you found the others."

Zaide cocked his head. "What do you mean?" Tula had been a surprise, but it wasn't as if finding her had been difficult. Vorkaris had identified her. Even if the dragon had chosen someone else, he would have been right there to reveal the new Magister's identity. Resia was even easier. That she would be the new Elder after their mentor had been a well-known fact.

"Well, that is the thing about the Oracle and what she sees. Sometimes, we are easy to identify. Other times..." Andriun leveled a hand, then rocked it back and forth to indicate a precarious balance. "Did she not tell you this herself?"

The question made no sense. Zaide's brow crinkled.

The hunter's did, too. "You have been to see her?"

Slowly, Zaide shook his head.

Andriun's face fell. "Oh. Oh, this... this is not good."

This wasn't the way their conversation was supposed to go. It was supposed to be a lead-in to Andriun explaining everything the Desheni knew about the sword, not exploring how little Zaide and the rest of them knew. How did every conversation of late leave him feeling more foolish? "I have no idea what you're talking about, but you're right. I can tell it's not good."

Andriun rocked forward to bury his face in his hands. "Oh, your people have lost more knowledge than I had imagined.

Where have you been? Who have you seen? Tell me, I have misunderstood what you have done."

"We saw Resia in Kolmar," Zaide said, ticking off a finger. "She's the Paragon of Forest. Then we came to Jadora, and Tula became the Paragon of Fire. Now we're here. That's all three, isn't it?"

"Three!" his friend groaned into his mittens. "Zaide, no! That is only—there are five, how can you not know this?"

The word hit like a punch in the gut. *"Five?"*

"The spectrum! The spectrum of magic! It is not only three elements, three colors. They mix, they combine, but there is more. There is light, and there is darkness. Maker's mercy, Zaide, there are still the hardest trials to go."

"Why do you know this?" Zaide cried. "Why didn't you say something sooner?"

"Because I assumed that you all knew! Were you not in the Great Library of Jadora? The library is supposed to know everything, from the histories of the Rise to—"

"But I don't know! Did you not figure that out when you were telling us about the Oracle before?"

"I told you so that *you* would know!" Andriun gripped his head with both hands. "You are at the princess's beck and call. She knew about Sendassian, that he was to be the Bladebearer. I thought she would have taken charge, that she would lead the expedition where it needed to go. To lead you. You are so poor at listening, I thought perhaps you did not grasp the depth of the Oracle's role."

Zaide stared back, so jarred he didn't even have the wherewithal to be offended. Did Lark know? Was there more she had kept from him?

Andriun exhaled slowly and slid his hands back over his head, smoothing his hair. "But I suppose this makes sense. I should not have assumed. At least, I did not think it would be so easy to reach..." He trailed off, then leaned forward to regard

Zaide with narrowed eyes. "Is it because you are not a mage that you do not understand the spectrum of magic?"

"Maybe?" Zaide tried to sound nonchalant, but his mouth had gone dry. Five Paragons. Not three. He'd thought they were close. He'd *wanted* to be close.

A tingle brushed the edge of his senses, another unfamiliar sensation.

Apology?

He slid a hand through his snowy hair and stared at the hesitance in the blade's shifting colors. "I guess the name makes sense now."

"Yes," Andriun said flatly. "And I will confess that I am relieved. It is rude of me to question your education, but I admit I had begun to wonder."

Zaide snorted. "Thanks."

Five Paragons. Not three. He heaved a sigh.

Lark's boots crunched in the undergrowth. "What are the two of you shouting about over here?"

Zaide twisted where he sat. "How many Paragons are there?"

The princess blinked.

"How many blessings does the sword need? How many are there?" Heat swelled in his chest and flowed into his voice. An anger that was his own, not the sword's. It still shimmered beside him, sleepy and subdued. Their connection fed him nothing more.

"Zaide..." She paused as if she didn't know how to continue —or didn't want to.

"So you knew that, too?"

When she said nothing, he scoffed, stood, and snatched his sword from the earth. The blade offered nothing as he stormed off into the thick of the woods.

The Oracle. Fates foretold. More Paragons. Sendassian, the chosen Bladebearer. It was enough to make him want to scream.

All this time they'd worked together, he'd trusted the princess knew best. How was he supposed to trust her when she kept secrets from him at every turn? The Elder had done the same thing. Hidden knowledge, kept him in the dark. He saw better what that meant, now; what they thought of him, what they desired. A tool to use. Nothing more.

He struck a branch as he passed it by. Resentment bubbled up inside him.

Dasienna just needed a weapon. An arm to wield the sword she couldn't. Someone to control, someone to order about. Someone to do her bidding with blind trust.

Maker's mercy, but he'd been worse than a fool.

He pushed farther into the darkening woods, letting his anger cool to more decipherable feelings. Betrayal, frustration, more complicated things he couldn't yet explain. He found a fallen log on which to sit, stuck the Spectrum Blade into the ground before him, planted his elbows against his knees, and let his head hang.

Shadows deepened around him. The blade's light stayed soft.

It expressed nothing.

"I wish you could talk," he muttered. "It feels like you're the only one who's thought anything of me."

But it couldn't, and with only the shifting colors on the blade to keep him company, loneliness took him like never before.

Even at the time of his mother's death, he'd had companionship and support, people who cared. He'd been taken in by his mother's friends, comforted by the friends he'd grown up with, raised by a second family that only wanted the best for him.

Zaide slid his fingers into his hair and gripped his head as he stared at the dirt. The forest was so like Kolmar, yet so different with its pines and unfamiliar undergrowth. His fingers tightened against his scalp. "What am I doing out here?"

The Spectrum Blade gave no reply.

Night deepened and his mind emptied, nothing but a hollow sense of discouragement left behind.

After a time, the sword's glow brightened and its colors shifted more toward red.

"Hello-o-o-o?" Tula called from somewhere between the trees.

It wasn't hard to find him. It was dark and his sword glowed. Zaide stayed where he was and let her tromp through the brush to reach him.

Her robe snagged on everything and she unsnared it each time. Eventually, she stopped a few paces away with her hands clasped in front of her, and they regarded each other in silence.

She cleared her throat. "They said you're mad at both of them, so I have to be the diplomat now. I told them that wouldn't work well and that you didn't like me, but they didn't want to listen."

"I don't not like you," Zaide said.

"You don't... Oh. It's confusing when you say it that way." She shuffled forward in the leaf litter and then sat on the ground with her knees drawn up to her chest and her hands resting on her ankles.

Diplomacy implied she'd been sent to smooth things over, but she just sat there, looking up at him with soft eyes and a pensive look on her delicate face. When she finally spoke, it was in a conspiratorial whisper. "Want to know a secret?"

Did he? He'd had enough of secrets to last him a lifetime.

She cupped a hand beside her mouth to shroud her words. "I'm mad at them, too."

"Yeah, but not for the same reasons. You're the Magister. You get to be someone important. The Oracle's first choice, and someone who gets to know everything. Nobody's trying to blindside you."

"Well, that's not true. I mean, yeah, I'm the Magister now. But I wasn't, and I didn't expect to be, and I was more surprised than anybody when I realized Vorkaris said the Magister was me." She patted her chest with a hand. "I never had any training with magic, or training in how to be a leader, or anything like that. I'm good at finding reference books, though, and using a card catalog, and looking for the exciting parts of boring things. Having adventures, you know?"

Zaide stared. "What's a card catalog?"

"It's a bunch of drawers full of information about books, sorted by things like title, author, subject, things like that. It helps you find where books are shelved, anywhere in the Great Library. Some people find them intimidating." Tula grinned, but her mirth was quick to fade. "Andriun told us what he told you. What he said... there isn't anything in the Great Library about it."

"But Lark knew," Zaide said. Her silence had been enough to make that clear.

"Because her father did. Because the Oracle's clues to the Bladebearer's identity were pretty obvious, and he was told the rest of what to expect, too. But she didn't know everything, because it's not in Amrochan's libraries, either. And she wasn't supposed to overhear some of the things she did." Again, she held a hand beside her mouth, as if that was enough to keep her words from carrying. There was no one nearby to hear them, even if they did.

It hardly justified all the princess had kept from him, but at least the reasons behind her knowing things made sense. Zaide turned his attention to the Spectrum Blade. "How much did you know?"

"Me? Not much. Not until I talked to Vorkaris, anyway. I think dragons must know everything, since they live so long." She smiled, her white teeth glittering in the sword's strange light. "I knew about the three artifacts, and the Paragons who were supposed to protect them. I didn't know anything about who the next Paragons were supposed to be, or that there were others."

"The dragon told you that part?"

Her smile now was fleeting, nervous. "Yeah. And he told me I would need to speak to someone who knew what this Age's Oracle had foretold to help me learn the rest of what I needed to know, since he'd been asleep. So I asked Dasienna, and she told me to keep it to myself. Because she thought if you knew everything, you'd end up doing something dangerous."

As if nothing he'd done so far had been dangerous. He thought of the battles, the travels, the number of times his life had been threatened.

Tula went on. "So yeah. There are supposed to be five Paragons, but the thing is, we aren't sure we need them all. According to what Vorkaris said, the Spectrum Blade doesn't utilize all its power equally, because they're all balanced differently, so they're consumed differently. He called them colors and shades."

"Because there's red, green, and blue," Zaide said. "And then..."

"Black and white. The balance between the colors shifts most often. The light and the dark are more stable, because they're always present together." She interlaced her fingers. "Where there's light, there's shadow. And Dasienna doesn't think those have been depleted." She opened her hands, palms up, and gestured toward the sword.

Zaide rubbed his face. "The glow."

"So the force of light is still in it. That's why she didn't want us to talk about it yet. If we don't need the Paragon of Light, we won't need the Paragon of Shadow, either, which is a good thing, because..." She trailed off and flinched. "Well, we think we know who that is."

"Who?" he asked.

Tula grimaced. "I'll let you think about it for a second."

Someone they knew. Maker's mercy, that could be Moros, for all he knew. "Tula, I've met so many people on this trip—"

"I didn't meet him. But you did. Just think real hard." She twisted her little finger, the corners of her eyes pinched.

Zaide sighed and rubbed his temples. Someone they'd met when Tula hadn't been present. Someone with power.

His stomach dropped. "No."

"Dasienna told me about him." She scanned the trees as she whispered, as if the darkness around them might contain what she spoke of and she didn't want it to hear. "About how he was made of shadows and flowed across the water. It sounds like he was terrifying."

"That doesn't make any sense!" Zaide slammed a fist against his thigh. "That power went into making that sword. Why would Gadranus help forge the only sword that can kill him?"

Tula made a patting motion with her hands, telling him to settle. "I don't know. There's a lot we don't know. But as long as the light magic hasn't been depleted, the shadow magic shouldn't be depleted, either. So water—blue—should be the last element we need."

Zaide rubbed the back of his neck. "I hope you're right." And if she wasn't, what hope was there that Gadranus himself would bless the blade?

A crash and shriek split the forest. He leaped to his feet as birds took wing from the nearby trees, chattering in distress. A heartbeat later, Andriun and Lark stumbled down the slope with crude torches in hand and everyone's bags strung on their arms.

"Move!" Andriun barked. "We must go!"

Zaide jerked the Spectrum Blade from the dirt and dragged Tula to her feet. "What's happened?"

Andriun all but threw Zaide's bags to him. He caught them and slid the straps up his shoulders, and the answer to his question burst over the edge of the hill a moment later.

Bugraks.

CHAPTER ELEVEN

"How many?" Zaide led the way through the underbrush, more familiar with the ways of the forest than any of the others. He darted under branches and dodged thorn bushes with grace, though he looked back several times. He'd counted half a dozen of the ugly little creatures, who appeared to be having trouble with a blackberry thicket. That was good; maybe they could outrun them.

"Too many," Andriun replied. "If there is one, there are too many, because they are never alone and there will be more. If there are ten, there are far too many, and you best start praying."

That mirrored Zaide's previous experience pretty well. The forest flattened out ahead, a gentle slope into a valley with a creek at the bottom. There was less growth here, the trees more mature, the dense canopy blocking out the sky. Their group spread out, the space letting the others run alongside Zaide instead of behind him.

"Where are we going?" Lark was already breathless from running.

Andriun stared straight ahead. "Across the water, up the hill, around the big stone, down the next—"

"You're just saying everything we can make out in the dark!" Tula cried.

"Yes, and when we have passed all of those things, we will keep running east until they grow tired!"

Judging by how hard they were breathing, Zaide wasn't sure they'd outlast the bugraks. A clatter against the tree he raced past marked the first attack. "Rocks!"

A barrage of thrown stones followed. For an instant, Zaide thought the monsters would miss them in the dark. Rocks thudded into trees and dirt, cracked against branches and battered leaves. One smacked the bag on his back and he couldn't help but duck.

A startled yelp from Tula said she hadn't been so lucky.

"Get to the creek!" Andriun called. "They cannot cross water so easily."

The hill grew steeper near the water. Lark slipped in the leaves and gave an unbecoming squawk. She caught herself against a tree before she went far, though her torch tumbled down the damp earth to extinguish in the water.

Zaide altered his path to intersect with hers. "No more falling into creeks," he said as he scooped her back onto her feet and held tight to her arm with his free hand. He still held the Spectrum Blade, its light welcome in the encroaching dark.

"Yes, we'll leave that sort of thing to you." She stumbled a step, then ran alongside him.

The creek was not as wide as it first looked, no more than ten feet across, but it was still too far to leap. Zaide jumped into the water first and turned to help Lark down.

A stone cracked against his forehead and for a second, he saw stars.

"Don't fall!" Lark cried, clinging to him as he rocked on his feet.

His equilibrium returned a second later, but blood coursed down his forehead and a wash of yellow-orange filled his vision.

A few feet away, Andriun hefted Tula across the creek and

onto the other bank. "Your Highness, you cannot stop," the hunter called.

Lark hissed something Zaide couldn't make out and tried to drag him across the creek bed. The bottom was thick with mud and they both sank ankle-deep.

Zaide staggered and pushed her ahead. "Go, we'll stave them off."

"But your face," the princess protested.

He made it a few more steps, then shoved her up the bank and turned to meet the bugraks in combat.

The instant he faced them, one launched a crude spear at his head. He ducked aside and caught the creature at the water's edge, the Spectrum Blade cutting through its bony body like a twig.

The blade flashed and the hum of battle coursed up his arm, but the water was up to his knees and the sucking mud kept him from moving with any sort of speed.

Beside him, Andriun flowed across the creek, unhindered. He twirled his torch in one hand and his unfinished spear in the other, and it was only when it glinted in the firelight that Zaide realized his Jadoran knife was tied in place of a spearhead.

"Sorry." Andriun offered a toothy grin, having caught the look on Zaide's face. "I will return it when we are done." The Jadoran blade was keen, and it cut down three bugraks with a single sweep.

Not to be shown up, Zaide lurched across the water to climb onto the bank. He deflected another primitive spear with his sword, then skewered two of the gray creatures with one stab.

The desire to show off faded immediately, when a dozen new flat faces appeared to replace the two he'd dispatched.

"We will not be able to beat them. We must retreat." Andriun moved backwards, his eyes on the enemy at all times.

Zaide tried to mimic him, but the mud was a hindrance and the blood dripping down his face a distraction.

Andriun swung the torch behind him. "Get out of the water."

Unsure if the motion was an invitation, Zaide stumbled up the far bank and plucked the torch from his friend's mittened hand.

With his hand freed, Andriun swept his arm wide across the creek. Water burst upward and solidified in jagged spears of ice, wounding more than one of the bugraks as they tried to cross.

"I can do that, too!" Tula cried from somewhere uphill.

"You are supposed to be running!" Andriun shouted back.

"You'd set the forest on fire," Zaide said, almost at the same time.

Andriun's eyes widened. Clearly, he hadn't considered that possibility. "We cannot hold them. We need to move." *Before Tula tries to help* was left unsaid, but obvious enough from the way his eyes flicked toward the librarian on the hillside.

Zaide turned to sprint toward her without a word. The Magister, he corrected himself as he ran. He couldn't keep thinking of her as a librarian.

Nor could he run fast or far, he discovered. Bleeding like he was, his vision was discolored and blurred, and his head pounded. It would only get worse from there.

Behind him, Andriun dragged a wall of ice up from the creek. It wouldn't hold the monsters back long, but forcing the bugraks to go around it would buy them a little time.

Lark waited for Zaide to catch up, her face pinched. He didn't dare look back, but the way her brows drew tighter and tighter together told him the ice wall was little help.

"Hurry," Andriun urged.

The angry squawking and squabbling of the creatures at their heels reminded Zaide of seagulls. *And now's not the time to be lost in fancy,* he told himself.

A note of anxiety pinged his arm. Worry? Zaide stumbled, but Lark kept him upright. Maker's mercy, but it was hard to keep his bearings with blood in his eyes and nothing but a torch and the sword to illuminate the way.

He must have frowned at the torch, for Lark took it from his hand as she dragged him along. Wasn't he the one who'd always done the dragging? He wasn't supposed to be slowing anyone down.

Abruptly, they breached the top of the hill. Another valley spread before them, another hill on the other side.

"We can't keep running," Lark said, though who she spoke to, Zaide wasn't sure. "He's bleeding a lot, we need—"

"We will heal him on the other side." Andriun caught Zaide's other arm and helped them move faster.

Tula was halfway down the hill already. "I can still burn them!"

"No!" the rest of them replied in unison.

She rolled her eyes so hard, her head rolled with them. Her pace slowed, and they caught up with her fast.

"Do not slow down," Andriun said.

Tula clapped a hand to her chest, offended. "I didn't have a light!"

He waved a hand to tell her to keep moving, though when he spoke again, it was to Zaide. "Beyond the hilltop, they should turn back. They will not like going there. We will heal you then."

"I'm fine," Zaide replied.

"But you're bleeding a lot, and you won't be fine for long," Lark said.

They struggled onward over uneven footing and steep inclines. Going uphill should have been hard, but the bugraks flowed over the terrain unhindered, closing the distance between them.

"Is that firelight?" Tula asked between breaths.

They crested the hill at a run. Below them lay a camp. Half a dozen men leaped to their feet around the campfire and Andriun spat something the rest of them couldn't understand.

Broken-born soldiers, all six.

They stared up the slope as Zaide and the others crashed down toward their camp. A moment later, a sharp squall from the top of the hill announced the arrival of the bugraks, and the men drew swords.

Zaide pulled away from his friends and braced himself for battle, but the men rushed past their ragged group to engage the gray-skinned creatures that poured over the hill.

"Keep going," Andriun whispered as he urged them on.

Leaving strangers to fight the swarm they'd inadvertently agitated felt wrong, but they didn't give Zaide a chance to argue. Lark grabbed one arm and Andriun grabbed the other, and they ran so fast he thought he'd be pulled off his feet.

The bugraks gave up their pursuit.

Just over the top of the next hill, rocks jutted from the hillside and offered shelter. Andriun herded all of them beneath the outcropping as he pulled the Captured Spring from beneath his coat. "We cannot stay here," he said as he shoved the vial against Zaide's mouth, forcing him to taste it.

It was cool and sweet, not unpleasant, but the forcefulness with which it was administered still made Zaide grimace and turn away.

Andriun kept the vial from spilling, and Zaide licked blue droplets from his lips. "I'm fine," he insisted. How many times had he repeated those words now? A dozen? It felt like it. But he wasn't fine. He was dizzy, and now that they'd stopped, he found himself sinking to the ground and gasping for breath.

"Head wounds bleed a lot." Lark pushed his hair back from his face to inspect the injury. "It's quite swollen."

"Wash it." Andriun extended his own water skin for the task. "If it is clean, the spring's remedy should keep it from forming a bad scar."

Before Zaide could protest, the princess thrust her torch into Tula's hands, dumped water over his face, and wiped the drying blood away with her thumb. He turned his head and spat.

"Hold on," Lark murmured as she alternated trickling water over the injury and cleaning the surrounding area. Tula shuffled over with a cloth from her bag, and the princess took it to finish the task.

Cold as the water was, it was still a relief to be clean, so he shut his eyes and let her continue. The gooey itch of blood subsided and as the spring's power took effect, the pain subsided, too.

Andriun stuffed the vial back under his coat. "We cannot rest long. They will come after us. They will want answers."

"I mean, I'd want answers too, if a bunch of teenagers went running by and dropped a bunch of ugly little monsters on us." Tula tilted the torch this way and that, watching the flames with a thoughtful frown. "I could have stopped them, I'm pretty sure."

"And burned half the mountain in the process." Andriun pointed to the trees overhead, his mitten turning his hand into an odd triangle. "There are many pines here. They burn easily, even when green."

Zaide deemed himself clean enough. He caught one of Lark's hands and pushed her back. "Let me up. We should put out the light and walk in the dark. Maybe we'll get away unnoticed." The noise of bugraks and battle echoed through the forest. If they could move while the campers were distracted, they might make it beyond where they could be tracked.

Any other time, he thought he'd be excited for the opportunity to speak to another like himself. Now, the possibility of the broken-born demanding an explanation for why they were in the forest made him want to run.

Lark started to protest, but Andriun stepped between them and helped Zaide to his feet. "We will keep moving. We will put out the lights. We are near to where I intend us to go, and I do not wish to be followed."

The moment he was standing, Zaide sheathed the Spectrum Blade. Tula gazed wistfully at the torch, but she didn't fight. Instead, she closed her eyes. As she did, the flame extinguished.

"Walk as quietly as possible. Stay close to the rocks."

Andriun pulled up the hood of his cape and turned to lead the way, just as a broken-born man stepped around the stone that hid them from the hillside.

Zaide's eyes went first to the sword in the man's hand. Blood dripped from the curved saber's edge. Then he glanced up. The stranger's face was hard and angular, his white hair grayed with dust and grit. His eyes locked with Zaide's and his brows drew together with concern. He asked something, his voice coarse but tone gentle, yet the words meant nothing.

Zaide didn't know what to say.

Another man appeared behind the first. He asked another question, his tone less kind, and the first man shook his head.

The second snorted. "Whole-lander," he muttered, his accent both thick and strange.

The first man's eyes flicked skyward, not quite a roll, but close enough.

"Sorry?" Zaide wasn't sure what else they wanted from him.

"You are injured?" the man asked.

Zaide shook his head, then nodded. "Not bad."

The answer seemed to satisfy. The man glanced to the others. "You're as mismatched as us against the land."

Lark straightened. "Scholars come from every walk of life."

"Scholars?" The man grinned, but the expression was far from reassuring. It looked out of place against his hard jaw, and several of his teeth were broken.

"We came seeking the Desheni, hoping to add their history to our libraries, but we were turned away. Our hired guide was taking us back to the road, but our camp was ambushed by those creatures. We thank you sincerely for your help." She folded her hands against her chest and dipped in a curtsy. Tula mimicked the gesture.

The man considered them for a time, then returned his attention to Zaide. "You're not from the ships?"

Which ships? Those in Ganede, or the ones forced aground in the north? Either way, the answer was no. Zaide shook his head.

"Do you speak Wemic?"

Zaide didn't even know what that was. He shook his head again.

"Katec?"

Languages from the Shattered Lands, he assumed, but which part? He knew nothing about his family's homeland. "Just Amrochan common."

"Ah," the man sighed, disappointed. "Born here?"

"No."

"Refugee?"

This time, Zaide nodded.

The man nodded back. "Us, too."

Zaide glanced toward the campsite. The others had not returned to the fire. "The six of you alone?"

"Mmm. Our families remain on the coast. We chose to scout ahead, look for someplace to settle. The people in these lands are unfriendly, but the mountains here are uninhabited. The Desheni are all down by the lake." The man nodded toward Andriun. "Plenty of space for both our people, eh?"

Andriun said nothing, his face still and unchanging. Beside him, Tula remained unusually quiet.

"Do you need rest? The others are almost done with the beasts. You are welcome to sit at our fire." The broken-born raised both brows, both question and invitation.

"We appreciate the offer," Lark said, "but I believe we would feel safer if we continue travel through this night. I don't think these mountains are any place for scholars."

The man grinned again. "True, they're not." Then his attention returned to Zaide. "We no longer have scholars among our people. The breaking of our land has all but stamped out our ways. But we will settle here, and we will save what we can. Come back when you are ready, eh? Maybe you can help preserve what's left."

"Thank you." Zaide refrained from saying anything else. When everything was over, he'd be free to do as he pleased, but the idea of returning to these mountains to seek the broken-born put an odd prickle between his shoulder blades.

The man gave them one last nod, then trudged back toward their camp, where the others had begun to return.

Andriun's hands tightened on his spear, his shoulders tense. "He is lying," he murmured once the man was out of earshot.

"What makes you say that?" Tula asked in a whisper.

"Because the language he first spoke was not Wemic, nor was it Katec. That was Torec." A shadowed storm brewed in his eyes. "The language of Gadranus."

CHAPTER TWELVE

"WE ARE CLOSE," Andriun announced as the forest grew light. The sky was hidden behind the branches of trees far overhead, a mixture of needles and leaves that blotted out the blue but let light filter into the forest below.

They had remained quiet through the night, but with dawn's arrival, they were too exhausted to speak. Zaide wasn't sure he had words, anyway.

His first encounter with his own people was supposed to yield answers. It was supposed to be a comfort, a connection, a clue to the parts of himself that had always been unknown. Where he might be from, where relatives might be.

He appreciated the aid those men had offered, but that they'd immediately hidden behind falsehoods left him knotted up inside. It didn't have to mean anything that they spoke the same tongue as their enemy. Countless people had to speak Torec, and not all of them had to agree with Gadranus and his actions. But he admitted it didn't look good.

He'd wondered how Andriun knew the difference, but Tula had inquired before he could. The Desheni had all learned to pick out the sounds of the different tongues, the hunter explained; with broken-born appearing along the coast and throughout the forest, it helped determine who could be left alone and who should be watched. Despite his exile, Andriun was still seen as more trustworthy than the white-haired strangers his people watched. In some ways, his perpetual presence in the forest had become an advantage. The rest of the Desheni wanted information. Often, he had it.

"You've been here before?" Lark's voice interrupted the dismal thoughts and Zaide lifted his head. The valley they were in looked little different than the rest of the mountains to him, but they'd reached a place that sat particularly low between hills.

"Yes. Though not often. That camp's proximity to this place is what makes me nervous." Andriun led them lower still, to the deepest point of the valley. There was no water here, though a rocky trail lay at a strange crease between the slopes. They followed it for some time.

"You think those broken-born are headed here?" Zaide's throat rasped uncomfortably after hours of silence. He swallowed hard and reached for his water skin. After the exertion of fleeing the bugraks and then walking all night, their water stores were low.

At the end of the rocky path, a smooth-faced cliff closed the end of the valley. Andriun led them toward it, though there was nothing to be seen. "I do, and it troubles me."

"I'm sure we have to worry a lot about some foreigners finding some rocks." Tula scuffed her boots against the pebbles. She no longer tried to draw smiling faces in the paths. Her mirth had dissipated some time ago. Any other time, Zaide might have stopped to ask what was wrong, but he could hardly sort out his own thoughts, never mind trying to work through someone else's troubles. When they settled, he'd encourage Lark to speak with her.

Andriun frowned, but continued on. "The place I am taking you is forbidden to outsiders. But, as I am already exiled, I do not think there is much else that is to be done to me for disobedience."

"They could kill you," Tula suggested.

He snorted. "My people are not killers. Our ways are gentle. They would do no such thing."

"I wish the same could be said for mine," Zaide murmured. The saber the man who'd spoken to them carried had been strange. Gently curved like a Jadoran blade, but longer and thinner. He'd gotten a good look, watching blood drip from its end.

"I understand your discomfort, Zaide, but they aren't different from you." Lark veered a little closer as she walked. She'd stayed close since washing his face, her worry over his injury clear, though she hadn't mentioned it. The wound had already closed, solved by the spring's refreshment. Her worry now was unfounded. "They were proficient with the bugraks, but you're an accomplished swordsman, yourself. You've slain hundreds of goborrins."

"But they're goborrins and bugraks," Zaide said. "How do we know that's all they've killed?"

"I am sure that is a great concern for you, but now is not the time for it." Andriun pointed his spear—still tipped with Zaide's knife—toward the wall. "Quickly. We will enter, and then I will close the way. I do not want to leave sign we have passed." As if to make a point, he paused to smooth out a rut Tula left in the gravel.

She harrumphed and marched ahead with her chin up. "This isn't a very good adventure. Not like the one in Jadora."

Zaide raised a brow. "What part of Jadora was a good adventure?"

"Well, there was lots of running back and forth, and there were monsters, but there were a lot of people on our side and we got to run around in the palace. Here, all we've got is..." She trailed off and opened a palm toward the cliff.

Lark tilted her head back, following the lines of the cliff to the sky. "Where exactly are we, Andriun?"

"I will tell you when we are inside."

Zaide trusted him, but the lack of clarity was still disconcerting.

Before long, they stood beside the stone wall with Andriun in the lead. The rock was solid, marred with a few odd shapes.

"Are those duck footprints?" Tula asked with delight.

"Very comical." Andriun peeled off his mittens and fitted his webbed hands to the imprints.

Zaide watched for cracks to form or for some door to reveal itself, but nothing happened.

Gradually, a soft glow enveloped Andriun's hands. It was cool blue, almost white, but it only lasted a moment. "There," he said as he removed his hands.

The ground fell open below Zaide's feet. Lark shouted and Tula yelped as the three of them dropped. They hit something cold a few feet down, and as they skidded down the ramp into darkness, Zaide couldn't help recalling the slope into the cavern below Kolmar's temple.

Hands found his arm in the dark and clung close. They bumped against the walls and the Spectrum Blade's scabbard caught against everything, turning them around more than once, slowing their descent. Unhindered by a sword or another person, Tula's shriek grew more distant as she slid ahead faster. It was Lark who held on to him, then. Zaide caught her and pulled her close, wrapping himself around her to shield her body from the fall.

"We're going faster!" Lark cried.

To where, Zaide didn't know. "Hang on." He tried to orient himself so they slid feet first. Once he got it, the ride was smoother. Unlike the slope in Kolmar's temple, this was slick and cold. His thick coat protected his back.

The princess held tight and he felt her tremble.

The angle changed. They slid out across a glass-smooth floor and eased to a stop. A little farther ahead, Tula groaned.

Zaide sat up with Lark in his arms. She still shook, clinging to him in the dark. Another tally mark went on the mental list of things he suspected King Sendassian would kill him for. "You both all right?" he asked.

"I think that would have been fun if I'd known where I was going," Tula said.

Lark said nothing at all.

Zaide slid the Spectrum Blade from its sheath and left it on the floor. Its light was a cool blue, illuminating dark, smooth walls that reached higher than the light carried.

A rasp caught his attention and he turned his better ear toward it.

Something sliding.

A bright glow appeared on the ramp they'd just descended, then Andriun slid into view. He held his spear in one hand and a brilliant light in the other, though Zaide didn't know where it had come from.

"Sorry," Andriun said as he put down his feet and stopped in an offensively controlled manner. "I forgot where the top of the slide would be."

Lark shoved herself away from Zaide so forcefully, she knocked him over. "You forgot."

"I would have suggested you step back." He pointed upward. "I have closed the hatch, but it is not impossible to force it open. I suggest we move deeper, toward the door."

Zaide grunted and pushed himself upright. "Wasn't that the door?"

"That was more like the gate at the front of a garden. Now we cross the garden, then we reach the door." Andriun stood and crossed to Tula to offer her a hand.

She squinted at the light. "What's that?"

"I made a lantern. It will not work ahead, the magic is too strong and will drown it out. But it will help us for now." He wriggled his fingers inside his mitten until she accepted the help.

Not wanting to be rude, Zaide stood and offered his hand to Lark. She slapped it aside and stood on her own.

"Oh, excuse me." He raised his hands in both defense and surrender.

The princess ignored him. "You still haven't told us where we are."

"As I have said, I believe there may be another way to restore power to the sword. That way is in here." Andriun moved his lantern—really, it was just a rock in his hand—to show the way. "We have passed beyond what is recognized as Desheni territory, although my people still see this place as ours."

Zaide's hands went to his bag. "What? I would have noticed if we'd gone that far. Lark, where's the map?" He'd held it at some point, but now that he searched his bags for it, he recalled it had never been put in with his things.

She produced the map from her own bags and crept closer to Andriun, where the light from his stone would illuminate it. "It does seem unlikely we could have gone that far, even with a guide. Where are we?"

Andriun rested the end of his spear on the ground and let the weapon lean against his shoulder. "Here." He touched the map between the two rivers shed from a high mountain peak. They'd crossed one of those rivers, and the road to Beshnai was on the other side.

"But we're in a valley. Those rivers shed from one of the highest mountains in the area, don't they?"

"Yes, but the mountain is crooked. It presents a steep front toward the road, but the back of it, where we are, is not so high. Of course, we are not on the mountain now. We are beneath it." The hunter grinned.

"Whatever for?" Lark asked.

Tula touched her chin and leaned closer. "The mountain between those two rivers. This is... oh. Oh!" She clapped a hand over her mouth.

Zaide fought back his annoyance. Of all the times to lose her words, why was it always when she'd figured out something they needed to know? "This is what?"

The Magister beamed. "You know what they call this mountain? Because of those two rivers? It's the birthplace of water!"

"So it's like the spring under Kolmar's temple?" Zaide slid a finger over the map. "A source of power?"

Andriun nodded. "This is where water magic came from. The waters buried deep beneath this mountain. The stories of our people say that the Maker pulled the Desheni themselves from these waters, then let the rivers carry them to the sea."

"The rivers formed by watersheds wouldn't be connected to an underground spring." Lark rolled the map and stuffed it back into her bag.

"If that is what you believe, you are free to do so. But it does not change that this source of water is where our magic originated. If there is any way to restore power to the Spectrum Blade without needing my father, it will be here. Come." He set off into the dark, the end of his spear clicking a steady cadence that echoed in the empty space.

Zaide positioned himself at the back, sandwiching their group with sources of light. The Spectrum Blade did not glow near as intensely as Andriun's lantern, but it was better than nothing. "I have some questions about that power." He delivered the statement as smoothly as he could. It still hurt that secrets had been kept, but responding with anger wouldn't yield the answers he wanted now.

"You are free to ask," Andriun said. The apparent entry hall they'd landed in narrowed until walls were visible to both sides, a blue-black corridor of shining, glinting stone. Or was it stone?

Tula put out a hand, evidently with the same thought. Her fingertips brushed the wall and she jerked back her hand. "Is this ice?"

"Perhaps. Or perhaps it is very cold and very shiny stone. I do not know for sure, for my senses are not as clear here as they are above ground." Andriun shrugged. The material of the walls made little difference to their mission.

"Neither are mine," Lark said. She reached out, but didn't touch the wall. Instead, she let her hand hover a few inches away. "Normally, I can at least sense magic. Everything here feels strange. Muddy."

Zaide poked the wall with the tip of his sword. It didn't react, nor did it leave a mark. He frowned, then shook off the distraction. "My questions, though. Andriun, maybe you know more. Before those bugraks showed up, we were talking about the Spectrum Blade and the Paragons." That was harder to speak of; that the very number of power sources had been kept from him was infuriating, whether or not one of them was nigh unreachable. "Why would only three types of power be drained from it? Why not the other two?"

"Ah. Hmm." Andriun tilted his head back and gazed at the ceiling as he walked. "The last Rise and the sealing of Gadranus that followed is less documented by my people, as we had withdrawn from the northern seas. His land holdings pushed to the northern coast during the last Rise, so the other Desheni fled to the west. So, the only knowledge my people have is of a secondhand nature."

"I thought your clan was land-bound?" Tula asked. Her notepad had come out and she held her pencil poised above the paper.

"Land-adapted. This does not mean that we do not communicate with our brethren in the sea." The tiniest touch of irritation showed on the hunter's face. Did Tula's questions have that effect on everyone? He cleared his throat a moment later and the irritation cleared from his countenance, too. "My understanding of the situation is simple, though. When Gadranus was sealed, it was with a seal that held four points. A three sided pyramid. The Spectrum Blade would have been the anchoring point, and then the three artifacts would serve as the other three points. These artifacts together became the keys to reach the blade again, did they not?"

Lark stopped. "Tula, let me see your notepad." She held out

her hand, and though Tula eyed her palm with anxiety, she passed over her writing implements.

Zaide and Andriun stopped, too.

The princess turned to a blank page and began to draw. "The sealing point was a circle with altars around it." A circle went down first, followed by squares to represent the altars. Zaide still thought of them as benches, though he supposed that was disrespectful of him now. Her borrowed pencil connected the altars.

"A triangle." Zaide's brow furrowed. "So if the Spectrum Blade was the other point, it would be—"

"Right in the middle," Lark finished for him. She drew a tiny circle in the center of the triangle.

"The room where we found the sword was a circle, too," Zaide said.

"And the stairs descending from the altar room were in a spiral." She added them to her sketch.

Andriun observed, then nodded his approval when she finished. "Yes, that is my understanding of how it worked. The seal would have depleted this power from the sword, with elements corresponding to the artifacts. The sword must be the focal point for this seal, for it is what held Gadranus's spirit captive until this Rise began."

That, Zaide admitted, made sense. "Have seals with all five parts of the sword's power been used before? Wouldn't they be stronger?"

"I am sure they have been used. I am also sure if I think long enough, I will recall a story about that happening before. But it does not matter, because it is the seal versus fate, and unfortunately, the Rise must be." Andriun pulled the notepad from Lark's hands to give it one more long, thoughtful look, then he passed it to Tula. "You may record all this information. I am sure your librarian heart is in agony, listening with no way to write this down."

The Magister all but swiped it back from his hands, then

retrieved her pencil from Lark. "This is important information. Not just for our records, but for us. If we're going to seal Gadranus away again until the next Rise, we need to know this. And plan."

"There will be a time for planning," the hunter agreed. "But for right now, we are here."

They stopped before a pair of doors made from the same material as the walls, dark and cold and carved in patterns that resembled frost. Andriun's lantern dimmed and began to flicker, but the Spectrum Blade's light remained steady. Zaide shifted so he could be the first to step through the doors—or at least, the second.

Andriun touched the seam where the doors joined and a soft light welled beneath his bare fingers. "I believe it is stone, but it is very cold."

"And sealed with magic?" Zaide glanced to the girls for some indication his guess was right, but their faces revealed nothing. Being able to see the effect of Andriun's work but not feel it had grown unnerving fast.

"Not sealed, that I can tell. But it is wise to check for traps, for my father was the last person to be here, and I do not know if he would have anticipated my visit."

Tula laid a hand over her heart. "Your own father would set a trap for you?"

"We are not on the best of terms. Even before my exile, we were not. I do not think he ever wished for me to become Shaman. But it is safe. Let us go." He pushed, and the doors swung open. The distant roar of water filled the air and the lantern's light vanished.

Zaide swept his arm forward, so the Spectrum Blade's flowing light could wash over the chamber ahead.

A small flight of stairs descended to a circular walkway. Transparent columns rose from its edge, reaching farther overhead than the weak light carried.

"Careful," Andriun cautioned as he took the lead. "We will

follow the walkway left, but avoid the center. It is a long fall to the waters below."

Zaide dutifully positioned himself between Lark and Tula and the railless walkway's edge, the Spectrum Blade between them creating a barrier to keep them at bay. As they walked, he let his right hand drift over the columns. They were perfectly clear, but frigid, and damp to the touch. "Ice?"

"Glass. It is not so cold here that ice would not melt."

The water on the surface was cold enough to make him think it was ice anyway. Zaide peered over the edge of the walkway, but it was too dark to see anything below. The roar of water came from somewhere down there, though it was distant enough that not even mist wafted on the air.

Andriun stopped and turned his spear sideways, blocking the path. Zaide almost walked into it.

"Huh," the hunter said.

Ahead, a wide section of the walkway was missing. No trace of it lingered at the curved side wall, and the end of the walkway was perfectly squared. No accident had removed it. "Your father's doing?" Zaide asked as he examined the wall and held out the sword. Something gleamed overhead and he squinted to make it out. A small glass orb set halfway into the ceiling on the other side. "Is that something?"

"Everything is something," Lark said.

"Especially when you make a girl mad," Tula added. "Then even nothing is something."

Andriun disregarded both their commentary. "It appears to be something. A switch, perhaps? It could be a drawbridge of sorts."

Zaide stepped back. "That's too far for your spear to reach." Even with his long knife strapped to the end. "Magic, maybe?"

"Perhaps." Andriun lifted a hand to try. A moment later, he made a sound of displeasure.

Lark glanced between his hand and the orb in the ceiling. "What's wrong?"

"My power will not manifest here. I am trying, but nothing is happening."

Tula swept back her sleeves and stepped forward with both hands out. Her mouth twisted. "Mine won't, either! I can feel it, I'm doing what Vorkaris taught me, but it just..."

Zaide couldn't fathom what that feeling might be. "Doesn't come out?"

"I have not experienced this before. This is not pleasant." Andriun flexed his hand and shook his head. He was still bare-fingered after opening the doors, but now he pulled on his mitten.

"Well, there are other ways of hitting things." Lark produced her tiny crossbow from her bag.

Tula cupped a hand around her mouth. "Illegal," she whispered.

Zaide rolled his eyes.

Whether or not she heard the comment, the princess gave no indication. She took aim and loosed one of the little bolts. It pinged against the orb, and a soft purple glow swelled inside it. When the orb filled with light, a low rumble shook the walkway beneath their feet. One by one, stone steps emerged from the wall beside them to fill the gap, with only tiny spaces in between.

Lark stepped back, satisfied. "Well, that was simple."

"A concern on its own, perhaps." Andriun went first. He walked with care, but the stone was solid enough. When he reached the other side, he waved for the rest of them to follow.

The girls hurried across and Zaide brought up the back. As his foot left the walkway's edge, the rumble returned, and the walkway retracted into the wall. He watched as it stopped, flush against the rest of the wall's stones. "Strange."

"At least it will be easy to reach from this side, eh?" Andriun poked his spear toward the orb, but didn't touch it.

"Don't forget you need to give that knife back." Zaide

resumed his place beside the walkway's edge, but he let Andriun lead.

Motifs like icicles and swirling waters etched the walls, revealed by the Spectrum Blade as they passed. Zaide paused to study one such relief a moment longer. "The water's flowing uphill."

"That's the opposite of what water does," Lark said.

"No, I mean, in the walls. The carvings. Look." He swung his sword closer to the wall after she and Tula passed. "The swirls show the motion. It's all going up."

The girls stopped to look. Andriun continued on. "As I have said, this is the birthplace of water. The water must emerge from the spring deep underground. To do this, the water travels up."

"Up a mountain?" The princess still sounded skeptical, but Zaide found himself eyeing the hole in the center of the walkway with a new wariness.

"Yes. Look. There is another gap in the way." Andriun halted at the edge of the gap and searched the nearby walls and ceiling for another switch.

Zaide spotted it first. "There." He pointed not across the gap, but to the other side of the cylindrical shaft. The edge of the walkway on the opposite side held an orb, not visible in the Spectrum Blade's light, but visible when he turned so the blade was hidden behind his body. Shrouded in darkness, the orb emitted the faintest purple glow.

Andriun cast him a thoughtful look. "You see well in the dark."

"From growing up in the forest, I think. It's pitch black in Kolmar at night." Candles and lanterns were never left to burn for long. Morning came early, and most of the village retired shortly after dusk fell. An unexpected pang of homesickness put a deep ache in his chest, so he put the thought out of mind and pointed across the chasm. "Can you hit that?"

Lark studied the distance and placement as she fitted a new

bolt to her crossbow. "I think so." She took aim, adjusted her footing, repositioned the crossbow, and braced herself.

The arc was perfect. The bolt pinged off the glass, and the orb lit up.

Tula bounced on her toes and clapped.

"How many more of these do you think there will be?" Lark asked as she lowered the crossbow and counted how many of the razor-tipped bolts remained.

"I cannot say. I did not know they existed to begin with." Andriun shrugged.

Zaide turned back to scan the floor. "Did we get the first bolt back?"

The princess shook her head and motioned for everyone to move. "It went down the shaft."

"Maybe we'll find it lower down," he suggested, though it seemed a vain hope. The bolts were little and the pit was deep. Never mind the water sure to be at the bottom.

Andriun's head snapped up, followed by his hand. He motioned for silence.

All of them grew still, and the low grumblings of water filled Zaide's ears, coupled with something else.

A rasp. A scrabble. The sound of scraping stone.

"What is that?" he asked in a whisper.

Andriun's face darkened. "We are not alone."

CHAPTER THIRTEEN

THEY CIRCLED the cylindrical drop twice more before they were greeted with options other than down. Zaide pointed the sword at each of the three hallways that branched off from where they stood. Andriun had grown so tense that he didn't dare speak, so he merely pointed again with the sword and then looked to the hunter for an answer.

Andriun didn't seem sure, himself. He looked back and forth between the three options, then lowered his hood and swept his hair back from his fin-like ears.

Zaide couldn't help staring. He'd grown accustomed to his friend's blue skin and webbed fingers, but he wore his hood up and his hair styled in such a way that his ears were often hidden. That the shape of them should catch his attention struck him as odd, until he realized Andriun tilted his head to listen.

Angling his ears to hear better, the way Zaide often did.

The subtle motion struck a new chord of kinship within him, and Zaide mirrored the action, listening for what his friend might hear.

The water was louder down the leftmost hallway. He pointed the sword that way and tilted his head in question.

Andriun nodded.

Everyone crept that direction. Whatever it was they'd heard, it put everyone on edge, and now even their footsteps seemed loud.

They filed into the chosen hallway. Once inside, Andriun stopped to search the entrance. Zaide guessed at what he might be looking for and waved for his friend's attention when he found an orb—smaller than those that controlled the walkway—embedded in the wall. At Andriun's silent order, he touched it. The orb was smooth, ordinary glass to his fingers. He expected something to show it worked, a tingle or a hum like what he often felt in the Spectrum Blade, but nothing came. He didn't know why he'd expected it at all. That he sensed the magic in the sword was unusual. If it was magic at all.

At first, nothing happened. He touched it again, and instead of just a tap, he pressed in. The orb sank into the wall and a hissing rasp flooded the hallway as a solid slab rose from the floor to seal the hall's mouth.

Everyone remained still, the Spectrum Blade's light washing over them like ripples of water.

"Won't that let whoever's up there know where we've gone?" Tula twisted the edge of her robe in both hands.

Compelled to comfort her, Zaide touched her shoulder. It did nothing to help her relax, but it earned a frown from Lark. Did she want poor Tula to be worried? Maybe she was worried, too, and enjoyed having someone else express it. Zaide didn't understand women well enough to know.

"It may. Or it may not. I am unsure if you noticed, but there were four doorways, and one of them was already closed." Andriun drew a circle in the air and indicated exits at the cardinal points. "So they may ignore them, as they are closed. Or they may be torn between two choices, as two are now closed."

Whatever the outcome, Zaide hoped it ended without them being pursued. "Do you know who's following us?" He thought of the broken-born men in the hills. If they were followers of Gadranus, would he have sent them to do something to the spring beneath the mountains? Andriun had been so confident they'd lied about their purpose in the wilds. But all they'd done was ask what language he spoke when he didn't understand the first.

His brow crinkled and he stared at the floor. Come to think of it, they'd spoken first in Torec, according to Andriun, but the rest of their questions had been Amrochan common. Had the man made an assumption, or had it been some sort of slip?

"Bring the light." Lark's order carried from farther down the hall.

Zaide looked up with a start. The rest of them had moved on. They stood at the edge of what he could see, the sword's light feeble against the oppressive dark.

"At least the air is fresh," Tula muttered as he came closer. She rubbed her arms as if chilled. "This is so different from the caves and tunnels under Jadora."

"Well, they are opposite places." Andriun smiled, a playful spark in his eyes. "As we are opposite people. You are red, I am blue."

"And together, it's purple," Zaide said, recalling his friend's awkward attempt to deliver a joke on their first expedition.

An inappropriate joke, he remembered the moment Andriun sputtered. Maker's mercy, he was turning purple on his *own*.

Tula clapped a hand over her mouth to stifle her laugh, while the hunter covered his face with his mittens and said something in his own tongue.

Only Lark was left unamused.

Of course she was. Zaide met her stare, but she didn't hold his gaze for long.

Instead, she crossed her arms and turned to Andriun as he regained composure. "What is the goal, here? Is this hallway to hide, or to get us closer to our destination?"

"Both." Andriun wiped his eyes and cleared his throat. "I hope it will slow down those who follow us. If they are following us, and not simply trying to reach the spring. At the bottom of this shaft, we will find the water. All we have to do is continue down."

"And hope there aren't any traps set in here," Zaide added.

The princess uncrossed her arms long enough to wave a hand. "I'm sure I'm not the only one feeling for traps. Everything has a certain buzz to it, but things did feel different when that door was closing, or when the walkways were moving."

"A buzz, huh." He flexed his fingers on the Spectrum Blade's hilt.

It did not respond.

You know, some guidance sometimes would be nice, he thought at it.

Still no response.

He sighed and pushed to the front, where he could lead with the sword's light. "So we're just looking for stairs."

"Or slopes," Andriun said. "Or more slides, like the one we took to enter this place. The slide was fun."

Tula harrumphed. "For you." She stayed close to Zaide's back.

He didn't look to see the order in which the others followed. It didn't matter; they were all going the same direction, and the only direction they could go was forward. "You've been here before, though, right? So you have a little bit of an idea of where we need to go?"

The length of Andriun's hesitance was not reassuring.

"You have been here?" Lark asked.

"Well yes, of course. With my father. But, ah..." Andriun rubbed the back of his neck.

"But you haven't gone all the way down to the spring," she concluded.

"Well, no. The spring itself is considered dangerous. My people visit this place from time to time. It is a holy place, somewhere we offer praise and thanks to the Maker, but our visitation is limited to the upper hall. At the foot of the slide." Andriun pointed upward.

"If the entrance is a slide, then how do you get back out?" Tula asked.

Zaide had been about to ask the same thing. "We don't have to climb back up that thing, do we?"

"Well, some do. Usually, we would tie a rope and leave it to dangle down the slide, so that the spirited youths may try their hand at climbing. It is a great sport. But it is not necessary, no. There is another exit, one easier to manage. Right now, however, getting to the spring is what we must concern ourselves with."

"How deep does it go?" It was too dark for Tula to write, or Zaide suspected they would have seen her notebook return.

"I do not know. Far."

Lark made a sound of discontentment, but nothing more. With the knowledge of people on their heels, the urge to chat about their surroundings dissipated, and they traveled downward in silence.

The halls twisted in graceful curves. Concentric circles, Zaide thought, based on the angle of the walls. Or else a spiral. The walkway's curve expanded and stairs appeared. It made the descent faster, but it wasn't long before the motion of descending made his thighs burn.

Not as bad as climbing, he reasoned. Hopefully there would be no urgency driving their return to the surface. He wasn't sure he could sprint up that many stairs.

After a time, the floor leveled out and they followed the corridor around a long curve. The motifs on the walls had never changed. Still waves and water hovered to either side, etched deep into the glass-smooth stone. This deep underground, the proximity struck him as threatening. Perhaps the walls had grown closer together; he didn't think they'd been so close before.

"There's something ahead," Lark said.

Zaide had been preoccupied with the walls. Now, what appeared to be one blocked their way. Nine small glass orbs decorated a smooth pane in the center, surrounded by a frame twisted with whirlpool shapes.

"A door?" he guessed.

Tula squinted at it. "I feel something here."

"Magic of some sort," Andriun agreed.

Lark stretched past them to let her palm hover before the orbs. "Some sort of protective ward. It's tied to the edges of the door. I think the orbs are to disarm it."

Zaide held the Spectrum Blade closer to the door—if that was what the apparent dead-end was—and searched the shapes around it for clues. "Can you tell what it does?"

"It's to prevent the door from being opened any other way. I'm not sure what the ramifications of doing it wrong may be, but this must be strong, if we're able to sense it above whatever that hum in the air may be." The princess lowered her hand. She, too, searched the door for some indication of what they were to do.

Tula nudged Andriun's shoulder. "Any guesses?"

He shook his head, but stepped forward anyway. "It could be anything. A pattern, a number, some sort of shape. I cannot recall hearing anything about this before. Nor do I remember seeing any patterns among my father's things that resemble this." He peeled off a mitten and let his finger hover over the orbs a moment before he mustered the will to act. In rapid succession, he tapped four of the orbs.

They lit up, held the light, then faded.

At first, nothing happened. Then he reached for the orbs again, and a white spark lanced out and popped against his hand. Andriun shouted and jerked back.

"Don't tell me that was our only try," Lark almost groaned.

Without regard for safety or sense, Zaide reached out. The princess grabbed his arm, but he planted his finger on the cool stone between the orbs, rather than touching any of them.

Nothing.

"Either we each get a try, or it just needed a minute to reset."

He withdrew his hand and made a soothing motion toward Lark, who scowled at him with such vehemence he suspected she wasn't soothed.

"Okay, then I'll try next." Tula wiggled past them to stand before the door. "Nine lights, three by three. There has to be some sort of pattern. Maybe something we've missed?"

"Or it's a numerical code and we have no hope of breaking it," Lark muttered.

"So negative, Your Highness," Zaide said. He scanned the door again. "Maybe something with these vortex marks."

Tula leaned back to view them by the sword's light. "There are too many. More than nine."

"Unless it's something mathematical, that won't work." Lark crossed her arms tight and tucked in her chin, thinking. "And I don't think it's related to the path we're on, because there were four paths. That doesn't seem to connect to a three-by-three grid."

"Perhaps we should activate the same number of orbs that we interacted with on the way down?" Andriun suggested.

Tula extended her hand, then paused. "That was only two, right? The bridges?"

Zaide shook his head. "Three. There was the one at the door, too."

"Oh, right." She grinned, almost apologetically, and touched all three on the top row.

Light bloomed inside each of the spheres, lingered, then faded.

Andriun sighed. "Nothing."

"Guess you're up next, Princess." Zaide tilted the sword closer to the door.

Lark frowned. "Why me?"

"Because I'm holding the light, and you're smarter than I am." He offered a smile, but it did nothing to soften the seriousness of her face.

Slowly, she moved forward. "I did have one thought. The

whirlpools around it, they're going different directions. Maybe the ones turning one direction are the ones meant to be counted." She pointed out several that twisted to the right, then some that twisted left.

Zaide hadn't looked closely enough to notice. "How do you know which ones, though?"

"I'm not sure. I suppose we ought to count them both."

He scanned the shapes. "Seven go left. Nine go right."

The princess winced. "Pressing all nine seems too obvious."

"The seven do not fit in," Andriun said.

They both paused to look at him.

He blinked at Zaide, then turned to the princess to continue. "The water current. If it is not affected by the shape of a basin or altered by its surroundings, whirlpools always rotate to the right. At least, in northern waters."

"It's worth trying, then. At least it seems tangentially related to the subject." Lark shrugged and activated seven of the orbs.

They faded.

"Still nothing," Tula sighed.

"Do we try the nine?" Zaide didn't see anything else that might serve as clues.

No one said anything.

He shrugged and swiped his whole hand over the grid. Every orb lit up, glowed, and went dark.

Lark bowed her head.

"So much for that." Tula scratched her neck. "Andriun, do you want to try again?"

"Not if it means being bitten by that magic again." He rubbed his hand, sullen.

Zaide lowered his sword. "The Spectrum Blade does the same thing to people when they try to touch it. Sparks a lot like that."

"I will make a note to never touch your weapon." Andriun returned to the door, though the corners of his eyes were pinched. "I do not know what I am to try."

Lark waved a hand. "Anything. Does it matter? We're out of ideas."

He looked as if he might say something, then shook his head and tried to poke an orb. A crackling white bolt snapped his hand again and he jerked it back with a hiss. "It seems we are out of tries, as well."

"No, we've got to make this work." Zaide pushed his friend aside and stabbed one of the orbs with a finger. The same bolt leaped out at him and he hissed at its sting, but persisted.

"Stop that," Lark snapped.

"What's our other choice? Going all the way back and taking a different path? Finding another door that's sealed off like this one?" He activated another series of lights.

Lark tossed up her hands and walked away. Andriun and Tula lingered, but neither tried to stop him.

After a while, his hand grew numb and the shocks no longer bothered him, though his fingers were red. His companions settled on the floor, and if Lark had stayed close enough to see, he couldn't tell. The one time he glanced over his shoulder, he couldn't see her in the dark, but the popping white bolts that lanced from the door still glowed in his vision.

He tried dozens of combinations. Patterns. Any series he could think of. Numbers relating to the artifacts, to the places they'd been, to how many Ages scholars had recorded. Nothing worked.

Frustrated, Zaide growled and punched the center orb. His knuckles split. The orb lit up, blinked, and a glow washed out across the rest of the door.

He stepped back. "Oh, come on!"

A low rumble shook the ground beneath them. Andriun and Tula popped to their feet as the door sank into the leftmost wall.

"What is it? What happened?" Lark reappeared from the shadow and watched as the last of the door slid out of sight. "What did you do?"

"He hit it." Tula adjusted her bags and leaned forward to

peer into the new corridor. Instead of continuing straight, it turned to the right and ran into the darkness, where the sound of water was loud. She bounced on her toes.

Andriun put a hand on her shoulder to keep her from running off on her own. "In hindsight, a single press of the center button should have been an obvious choice."

"Could've spared me a bit of suffering." Zaide shook his hand in hopes it might restore feeling to his fingers.

"Suffering you brought upon yourself." Lark pointed ahead, silent instruction for him to lead.

Tempted as he was to argue, he held the sword before him and made his way down the new hall. It bore a gentle downward slope, and a damp scent reached his nose. Not dank, but refreshing, like misting rain. He closed his eyes and breathed deep. It was invigorating, like a taste of the curative liquid in the Captured Spring. After their long travels, something so energizing was a blessed reprieve.

Tula hugged her robe tight to her body. "Oh, something here is strange."

"The water." Andriun's voice was soft, reverent. "You are Paragon of Fire, the element which opposes what we approach. You are, ah..."

"Unwelcome?" She sounded crestfallen.

"No. Not unwelcome. Just... oppositional." Andriun curled his hands to fists and bumped his knuckles together. "It is no surprise that it will make you feel ill at ease."

Zaide stopped and raised a hand, telling the others to stop.

Andriun collided with his back. "Oh, sorry."

"There's something ahead," Lark murmured.

Above the roar of water, the steady clap of footsteps filled the corridor. They echoed in the emptiness.

Zaide's fingers tightened around his sword. How had whoever was above them found their way down first? Maybe their path hadn't been blocked by a door. Or maybe they'd known the key to getting them open.

At the far end of the hall, a light swelled, and a handful of figures moved past. Zaide squinted, but the glare from the bolts of magic had muddied his vision, and his eyes had yet to clear.

"Oh, no," Andriun groaned.

"Broken-born?" Zaide suspected they might follow them, but he'd hoped not.

The hunter gripped his spear and twisted his mittened hands around it, more an action of dread than preparation for combat. "Worse."

Zaide's brows rose.

Andriun gave him a grim smile. "My father."

CHAPTER FOURTEEN

At the far end of the hallway, Zaide stopped and peered into the room ahead. He'd expected something different, and he stared up through the open center of the cylindrical room with a frown. They'd looped around in circles and gone back to the room where they started, but there was a wide gap between the walkway here and the one above. This had to be the only way down. Or at least, one branch of the only way down.

"Do you see them?" Tula leaned over his shoulder as if she'd be able to see.

Zaide grunted and pushed her back. "No." He didn't dare do more than whisper.

While he wrestled with Tula to regain personal space, Andriun slipped past them and crept to the edge of the walkway. He peered down, then retreated fast. "They have stopped below. We should wait."

"What are they doing down there?" Zaide watched the splash of light and moving shadows against the far side of the room. He'd sheathed the Spectrum Blade so they wouldn't be seen so easily, but he already missed its light. His eyes were good in the dark, but not so good that he'd be able to see when the party led by Andriun's father left the room.

Andriun motioned for them to retreat into the hall. Only once they'd moved a good distance from the exit did he speak, and then he held his voice to the same weak whisper Zaide and Tula had used. "They pursue the same thing we do, I believe. The spring where water was born."

Lark had lingered behind the rest of them. She made no move to come closer now. "Are they here to prevent us from reaching it?"

"I do not think so. I do not think they know we are here. But they must have set out soon after your meeting." Andriun turned back toward the exit. The light had grown weaker.

Zaide reached for his sword, then hesitated. Perhaps they should wait until things grew pitch black.

"Why are they here, though? We haven't figured that out, have we?" Tula squinted until her nose scrunched, then felt in the dark. Her outstretched arms found Andriun's coat. She clung to him like a grass burr. Puzzled, he shook his arm as if it might dislodge her. It didn't.

"The same reason we are here," he said as he gave up the attempt to remove the Magister. "This is the source of all water magic. It is the source of the Captured Spring's magic, as well."

"He seeks to replace the spring, then." Lark rubbed her chin. "Is there any possibility that could happen?"

Andriun shook his head. "It is a desperate attempt. The spring cannot be replaced, but I suspect he hopes some trace of the power that made it can still be harvested here."

"Why'd he wait until now to look for it, though?" Zaide checked the end of the hall again. It had grown so dark, he doubted the Spectrum Blade would be seen. He unsheathed a few inches of the blade, its cold light spilling across the hall.

Lark winced and looked away. Had she been looking directly at the blade? It wasn't that bright, but staring in the dark was sure to make even its soft glow intimidating. "Who can say? It's not like—"

Before she could finish, Andriun spat something in Desheni and shoved everyone toward the end of the hall. "Move!"

The Spectrum Blade clapped back into its sheath, and the sudden absence of light made the arrival of a new light source that much more visible. A purple glow illuminated the far end of the corridor, where the door had closed behind them. Booted steps clacked in the dark.

Zaide had a mind to share some choice words of his own. Those weren't Desheni. The Desheni didn't wear hard-soled shoes.

He hurried onward, toward the fading light of the Shaman's party.

"Wait!" Tula cried. She groped along the wall, trying to find her way.

Zaide backtracked to catch her hand. "Grab Lark," he whispered. The light had stopped retreating. He silently prayed whoever walked with Athradan hadn't heard her call.

Tula laced her fingers with Lark's and gave his hand a squeeze. He pulled them along, leading the way through the darkened cylindrical room. The water was loud; maybe their voices hadn't carried.

That hope was shattered by the sounds behind them. People running. Coming after them.

Andriun raced along behind them, herding the girls with the shaft of his spear.

"They're going to see us," Lark hissed.

"We've already been seen." Or heard, anyway. Zaide wasn't in the mood to argue semantics. "And we have to get down there anyway, seen or not."

The last traces of light faded and he slowed. Even with good eyes, he couldn't see in pitch black. Tula huddled against his back as he fumbled for his sword in the dark. The Spectrum Blade was bright by comparison, and it brightened as the footsteps behind them grew louder.

Oh no you don't, he thought at it with a scowl. *Those are people, remember?*

Or, he assumed they were. What if it was something like the salamanders in Jadora?

Then they wouldn't be wearing boots, genius, he told himself a second later. He pushed Tula and Lark behind him and turned to face the way they'd come.

Andriun turned, too.

Zaide eyed his spear. "You've still got my knife."

"And you have a sword."

One that screamed when it tasted human blood. Zaide opened his mouth, then remembered he had yet to share that information with Andriun. A story for another time, he decided as the first shadowy figure stepped out from the hall. A dark cloak shrouded the stranger, but Zaide caught the hint of gray-white under the hood. The broken-born had followed them. He'd known the possibility, but the sight still made his stomach sink.

Lark drew a knife.

He started to tell her to run, but instead of bracing to fight, she grabbed his empty hand and pressed the blade into his grasp.

"Be safe." She squeezed his fingers around the hilt and was slow to let go, but Tula pulled her away and hurried down to the doorway Athradan's party must have taken.

Zaide switched the Spectrum Blade from his left hand to his right. The princess's fine knife felt tiny for a primary weapon and he wondered if he'd be better adjusting to fighting with the Jadoran blade most often.

Andriun watched him with a quizzical expression, but there was no time for questions. The first two broken-born men descended on them in a whirl of dark cloaks. Andriun caught an axe beneath its head and flipped it back. When the man stumbled, he rammed the butt end of his spear into his attacker's ribs.

Zaide dared not feel relief when his opponent brandished a sword. He deflected the first strike with the knife and hated how fragile it felt in his hand. "We aren't here to fight you."

"Best get used to it, boy," the man snarled. His voice and face were both unfamiliar, but their garb was the same. He didn't know where their friendly leader had gone and for a moment, he wondered if that meant a problem.

Andriun thwacked Zaide's opponent in the side of the head.

Zaide spread his arms. "That one's mine!"

Instead of arguing, Andriun pointed his spear toward the door, where Lark and Tula looked back with anxious faces. "Go, I have an idea."

"I'm not leaving you to fight alone." Zaide knocked the sword from his attacker's hand. It flipped off the side of the walkway and vanished into the pit.

"What makes you think my idea involves staying here?" Already, Andriun hopped backwards, buying himself enough space to turn with his spear in hand. He sprinted down the slope and Zaide could either stay and fight, or follow.

He chose to follow, though he gritted his teeth as he ran. The broken-born men stumbled over themselves and over each other as they tried to chase after them.

Lark yanked Tula into the hallway to make room, but the broken-born were on them before they reached the door. Zaide knocked a strike aside with the Spectrum Blade, its iridescent colors whirling in excitement.

Not against people! He willed the sword to react appropriately, but it still hummed when he swung it to deflect another blow. *Why can't you be consistent?*

"Keep moving." Andriun's spear nudged Zaide's ankle, forcing him back a step.

Were they not in the middle of a fight, he would have objected to being herded around like a sheep, but it was all he could do to keep the man in front of him from drawing blood.

Their blades were heavy, but fast, and a hit from one could be crippling.

The knife in Zaide's left hand was too short to be useful, the Spectrum Blade in his right too... itself. His arm tingled and he silently cursed the artifact as he worked his way backwards.

The walkway was too narrow for more than two of the broken-born men to fight, but each time one stumbled, another slid in to take his place. The one Zaide had disarmed returned with a dagger. An equal match, at last. Zaide parried with the sword and lunged with Lark's knife, the silver blade biting deep and yielding a cry of both anger and pain.

Andriun's spear had caused several injuries by now and when he drove it forward with full force, all six men retreated.

Zaide started after them, but a hand snatched the back of his collar and threatened to choke him.

"Get in here!" Lark grunted as she hauled him backwards into the hall.

Andriun bounded after them and slammed a fist against the wall. A block of stone rose from the ground.

The orbs, of course. Had the broken-born figured out how to open the doorways, or had they merely followed the trail left behind by Zaide and his companions?

As the door clacked shut and drowned out angry voices on the other side, Zaide pried Lark's hand off his coat and allowed himself a cough. "Are you trying to kill me?"

"I might, when everything is said and done." She snatched her knife from his hand and wiped it clean on his sleeve. His lip curled at the dark streak left behind.

Tula crowded beside them. "The Shaman's men are coming back up. What do we do?"

"We go speak to him and hope that he is friendlier than the last time you tried." Andriun turned his spear at an angle and used the pole to shove all of them farther down the hallway.

All three stumbled, but righted themselves a moment later. The hall ended at a narrow, curved stairway. Zaide put himself at the front. A sword would be better than a spear in such spaces, though Lark's knives would have been best of all. Judging by the way she'd quickly returned her blade to its sheath, she didn't want to greet the Shaman with weapons out. Wise, but he had no choice. They still had no other source of light.

"I should go first," Andriun said as they neared the curve. Everyone flattened their backs against the wall to let him pass, and Zaide put himself at the back. Maybe if he had his sword out at the rear of the party, it would be less threatening. They had just fought the broken-born, after all. And the broken-born were sure to find a way in before long.

Ahead, the stairway widened, and a dozen Desheni—men and women—stood with lanterns in their hands. All of them stared at Andriun in surprise. He descended, unfazed. The last two stairs were underwater, but he waded in without removing his footwear.

Athradan shoved two lantern-bearers apart, fury burning in his eyes as his gaze snapped from his son's spear to the glowing sword in Zaide's hand. "You desecrate the sacred waters!"

"We come seeking the water's help." Andriun strode forward, his spear held above the water's surface. "If you will not help us, then what other choice do we have?"

"A choice to honor the last wishes of your clan," the Shaman snarled. "You are not welcome here."

Lark stepped down beside him. "He is welcome wherever I bid him go. I have demanded his help, and you are not free to deny me his aid."

Shouts echoed from above. The lantern-bearers looked past them, into the dark.

Zaide turned back with his sword ready.

"You lead ruffians and violence to my spring. You shed blood above the sacred water. Have you no shame? You pollute the one thing left that's pure." Athradan laid a hand against his chest, his face twisted with grief. "Do you truly wish your people such suffering? I see the blood on your garments, the blood on your weapons. I beg you, keep it away until we see what may be recovered."

Tula snorted. She remained on the stairs, her attention fixed on the water and her nose crinkled with displeasure. "You're only here because you thought you could come down and do something to seal the magic away."

"You know nothing, Jadoran," Athradan spat.

"How come you never came down sooner, then? How come you waited until Dasienna brought her Bladebearer to restore the sword's magic?"

The voices grew louder. Zaide climbed the stairs. "We've got company again." He braced at the mouth of the stairway's curve, ready to engage. He was mid-stride when water surged up around his legs and froze solid. His forward momentum made him lurch hard, his legs wrenched in the ice, and he caught himself against his fingertips. Behind him, cries of surprise from Lark and disgust from Tula announced their similar fates. More water flowed up the staircase, and if they'd been startled, the broken-born men on the stairs were scared out of their wits.

Try as he might, Zaide couldn't free his legs. He twisted as far as he could. Lark's ankles were similarly trapped, but Tula was encased up to her waist. She pounded her fists against the ice, then flattened her palms against it and bared her teeth. Fire blasted from beneath her hands and was rapidly extinguished, churning thick clouds of steam into the air.

Beyond her, Andriun remained free. He swept a hand outward and a ring of ice that had formed around him dissolved.

Athradan scoffed. "You've shamed your family, shamed yourself, betrayed your people. Can you not leave us be? Is this really the legacy you've chosen to leave behind?"

"I have not chosen my legacy." Andriun was calm, placid. He kept one hand flat, as if to press the water around him down. As he strode through it, his movement made no ripples. "It has chosen me. It was never my choice to be born in this time or with the powers that have all but forsaken my people. As it was never yours. But the difference between you and I is that my call has come, and I have answered it."

The Shaman's expression warped with anger. He spoke heatedly in his own tongue, the words lost on Zaide, but at least the man was distracted.

Zaide turned the Spectrum Blade to chip at the ice that surrounded his ankles, while Tula's efforts made the steam clouds around them ever thicker. His sword chopped through the ice with ease, but it reformed around his legs faster than he could break it away.

Nearby, Lark had the same struggle. No matter how many times she removed a section, it came back. She persisted, hacking pieces of ice free and tossing them aside without cease.

Tula whimpered and shook her hands, her fingertips bright red from the cold, and through it all, Andriun continued to argue with his father. The other Desheni remained silent, observing without so much as a shift to betray their thoughts.

Finally, Athradan raised a hand and Andriun fell silent. Zaide expected the Shaman to try and entrap Andriun the way he had the rest of them, but instead, he raised a solid sheet of ice between their groups.

Zaide growled and stabbed the ice harder. "Come help us."

Andriun stayed where he was. "You will have to wait."

"My feet are freezing."

"My father is Shaman. I am skilled, but I cannot hope to best his magic. You must wait until he releases you." Andriun twisted his hands around his spear.

Lark paused, her breath ragged from effort. "You mean we're trapped here?"

"That is essentially the situation, yes." He bowed his head, his shoulders slumped. "He will seek to sabotage our efforts. Whatever we seek to do when this wall of ice falls, we must do it quickly, for we will have little time."

"Can you be a little less spooky and ominous, please?" Tula

pushed against the ice that encircled her, but it did not budge. Why had she thought it might? She'd already blasted it with enough heat that the air was dense with fog.

Andriun sighed. "I cannot, because I do not know what to expect. When the ice falls, the spring may be ice, itself. Or worse."

Zaide didn't like the sound of that. "Worse how?"

"He may seal the exits, so that we may not leave, even if we are successful."

An angry cry from the hallway came at just the right moment to sound like a protest.

"Well," Zaide said, "at least we won't be stuck in here alone."

Lark sniffed and slipped her knives back into their sheaths. "Oh, of course. Perhaps this will present the perfect opportunity for you to ask your new friends for a history lesson. Maybe they can tell you a few things about what the Rise is like on the other side."

He shot her a glare.

"Please." Andriun motioned for both of them to settle. "Do not fight now. We must make a plan for what is to be done."

The princess produced something from her bag and flipped it in her hand. The Molten Dagger.

"I already tried magic," Tula said.

Zaide wished he'd thought to ask for it. "Yeah, but that thing broke magic ice once. Maybe it'll do it again." It had melted the ice giant that once held the Captured Spring within its body, then melted the entirety of an ice cavern's ceiling after it had fallen in. If anything could free them, it was the dagger.

Andriun raised a finger, signaling for her to wait. "Hold on. Do you feel that?"

All of them grew still. Zaide tilted his head this way and that, turning his better ear to search for things that might have escaped his notice before. He heard nothing and felt only the magic ice that encased his feet.

Tula and Lark, however, grew troubled.

"Whatever that was," the Magister said slowly, "I didn't like it at all."

Lark's eyes darkened. "If he's done something to the spring..."

"He would not harm it," Andriun said before she could finish. "But I do not doubt that we will be hindered."

Tula stiffened. "There it is again. What is that?"

The ground strained beneath Zaide's frozen feet. Ice creaked and popped.

Andriun looked down, suddenly realizing what the noise meant. "Oh, no," he groaned.

The Shaman's ice wall exploded, and a torrent of water burst through to sweep them off their feet.

CHAPTER FIFTEEN

THE TORRENT HIT with the force of a waterfall. Andriun leaped toward Tula to shelter her from the blast and choked as it stole the air from his lungs. A current stronger than anything he had ever felt sucked him off his feet a second later. He was not alone. Zaide and the princess found each other in the water as it carried them upward. Somehow, the Bladebearer held tight to his sword, to Lark, and still managed to catch a spire of glass to keep from being washed away.

Andriun was not so lucky. The current tore the spear from his grasp.

Tula flailed in the water and kicked him twice before he took hold of her and got her head above the surface. Foam stung his eyes and he struggled to support her. Maker's mercy, could the girl not swim at all?

"Be still!" The roar of the water was so great that he had to shout to be heard, but the Magister froze in his arms and stared at him in wild fear.

He had known the spring could carry them from its cavern. He had ridden it before—long ago, in his youth—but the water had never raged like this.

"I can't swim!" Tula cried.

He bit his tongue to keep it from betraying him. Telling her he had noticed would not help the situation. Instead, he repeated his instructions. "Be still."

She clutched his shoulders as he held her up, inadvertently mashing his face into her cleavage. The heat of embarrassment rushed to the tips of his ears and he squeezed his eyes shut. Why had she not put her cold weather gear on before they descended into the spring's cave?

They whirled upward until the waterway curved and light became visible. He had hoped his father might mean to deposit them at the entrance, but their luck was not so great. "Hold on," he cautioned, though her grip on his head and shoulders was so forceful, he did not know why he bothered. He tried to see Zaide and Lark in the water, but it was so turbulent, he saw nothing but the water itself. He tried to steer their movement, but he still wore his mittens and shoes, and neither were effective as rudders.

The light grew brighter and they spilled out into daylight. The water crashed down the side of the mountain, overflowing the banks of the watershed and sending them hurtling past trees and rocks that would surely kill them on impact. Andriun struggled to keep them centered in the water.

Something white caught his eye. Hair? He opened his mouth to call, but Tula lurched forward and plunged his head underwater. His gills flared in a natural response, promising air, but sucking in water would not help him speak. He gasped when his head broke the surface.

"Sorry!" Tula cried. She wiggled against him, freeing his face from its proximity to her chest. She ended up on his back, her legs wrapped around his waist and her arms about his shoulders with her hands flat on his chest. That was better.

He spat water before he could speak. "I think I see—" He stopped himself before he could finish. That was *not* his friend.

"Broken-born," Tula said with a hint of fear.

Her weight on his back made him bob under again, and he spat to clear his mouth once more. "Fish guts."

The farther downstream they traveled, the calmer the water grew, though the current remained strong. Finally, his feet reached the ground. He sought and failed to find footing several times before he was able to stand. The current almost swept him off the buried stones, but he braced himself and leaned into it. Inch by inch he shuffled toward the bank. "Where did they go?"

Tula craned her neck. "I don't see anyone."

Perhaps that was good. Being washed ashore with the broken-born and no weapons with which to defend themselves was sure to end poorly.

Andriun caught a nearby tree branch to help haul them out of the water. Tula tightened her legs around his middle and grabbed hold of the branch with both hands to help. Together, they dragged themselves ashore, where he allowed himself to collapse against the dry ground and gasp for breath.

The Magister peered at him with wide eyes. Or, not at him, precisely. She stared at his neck and he grew conscious of the way his gills flexed as he breathed.

He tried a smile, unsure if it was curiosity or distress that made her look at him so. "They do not help much when my head is above the surface."

"Huh? What?" She blinked and her attention transferred to his face, instead.

"You know. To breathe." He motioned from his neck to his chest.

Her delicate brows drew together. "Don't they let you breathe underwater?"

"Not if there is no water for them to filter." He paused. She was a scholar. Had he found a gap in her knowledge? "How do you suppose the water passes through?"

Rosy spots bloomed in her cheeks, pretty against her sandy complexion.

Andriun sat up and held out his hand. His mittens were

sopping, as was the rest of him, but he would take care of that after he had enjoyed a moment to regain his strength.

She reached for his hand, unsure. He clasped her fingers, pulled her hand close to the side of his neck, and exhaled hard. Most of the air in his lungs escaped through his nose, but the soft stirring of warm breath would grace her fingertips there, too.

Tula squeaked, jerked back, then laughed. "It goes through!"

"Which is why we must surface and clear our lungs when we wish to speak." He peeled off his mittens and wrung water from them. He would be better off wringing everything, he decided, regardless of how soon he caught his breath. He unfastened his coat, heavy with water, and let it slide off his shoulders. The rough-spun shirt he wore beneath had no sleeves, a contrast the Magister found interesting, given the way she stared.

After a moment, she followed his lead, removing her red and gold coat so she could squeeze out the excess water. Her billowing pants, so popular a style in Jadora, hung heavy around her legs. "Can I, um... can I write that down? About the gills?"

Andriun blinked. So it was not known. He had not thought his people *that* secretive. "I do not see any issue with you sharing how our gills work. But I hope you do not mean to write it down now, because we need to find Zaide and the princess."

A new voice broke in. "The princess, you say." A dripping figure in a dark cloak stepped around a tree, a rough sword in his hand. The broken-born man glared out from beneath his saturated hood, his hair stark white and plastered to his face after the unexpected washing.

Tula leaped backwards. Another man emerged from behind a tree at her back. He caught her arms before she could turn.

Andriun started to rise, but the chipped edge of the first man's sword angled against his neck before he could. Slowly, he lifted his hands to show he was unarmed.

"Where are they?" the man asked. His voice was harsh, gritty, devoid of the kindness it held when he had spoken with Zaide.

"We do not know. Please, lower your weapons. We are no

threat to you." Andriun gestured to his coat on the ground beside him. "You may look to see that we are unarmed."

The tightening of Tula's jaw told him that may have been a lie.

"Unarmed, eh? Then what's this?" The tip of the sword traveled downward, skimmed over Andriun's gills, and snagged the chain of the Captured Spring.

Did the broken-born know of the artifacts? Not even all the people of the Allied Kingdoms did. Andriun kept one hand up, signaling he meant no harm. He let the other travel to the chain so he could pull the spring out from underneath his shirt. "I practice medicine. A healer for my people." He tilted the vial to show the blue liquid that sloshed inside. "It is a tincture to aid them when they are ill." All truthful, but the man still frowned.

"Take it off."

"That, I cannot do. Ill luck." He stuffed the vial back under his shirt and raised his hands again. He was defenseless, should the men choose to strike, but there were only two of them now. Where were the rest? That they might have been smashed against the rocks was both too optimistic and too cruel to hope.

The broken-born grunted. "Stand up."

Andriun climbed to his feet. His footgear squished unpleasantly. He would have to pour out the water. Magic could have pulled the water out of everything he wore, but magic took strength and concentration, and he was lacking both after the spring's rude ejection. He had not known his father's sway over water was that strong—or that it had existed at all. "May I take my coat?"

The man kicked it toward him. It flopped like a stranded fish.

Andriun dared to scan the water nearby as he bent to pick it up and squeeze more water from the sleeves. He had hoped to see his spear. The knife on the end would surely glint in the sun. But he saw nothing, and when he straightened with his coat in his hands, the second man was tying Tula's wrists with a narrow cord.

"Hands behind your back," Andriun's captor ordered.

Unwilling to invite violence, he slid on his coat and put his hands behind him, as ordered. Tight cord cut into his wrists.

The two men conversed in their own tongue. Andriun had heard some of the language before, enough to identify it, but not enough to understand what was said. Still, he doubted it was anything good, and the solemn expression that had taken Tula's face was similar.

He lifted his chin. He would remain calm. Steady. Whatever the purpose of these men was, it was not likely to threaten them for long.

The sword returned to poke Andriun's back through his coat. "You will answer our questions once we reach our camp."

"Our answers will illuminate little. I am as confused about what happened in that cave as what you must be. But we will help how we can." Andriun did his best to sound unbothered. It worked a little too well, for Tula shot him a hateful look. He met her gaze and for a moment, he admired the fire in her eyes.

Once they had taken a few minutes to compose themselves and touch their magic, no mere cords would hold them. If Tula's might was half as strong as her temper, he would have to keep her from burning down the whole forest.

The sword jabbed again. "Walk."

Tula's captor spared her the jabbing and merely wrestled her around to follow the lead of Andriun and the man who had tied him. The leader, Andriun decided. The others had answered to him before, as well.

"Were the rest of your men injured by the eruption of the geyser?" He did not think that was the best term for the water, but it was certainly the best description of what they had experienced. "If they were, I may be able to offer aid. I am less skilled in the healing of humans, but I am willing to try." And he meant it, despite Tula's glower on his back. Whether or not the men holding them were enemies, they were still people, and he would not have their injuries on his conscience.

"They're fine," the man said, and the brusque delivery was enough for Andriun to know they either were not fine, or had not been found at all. Perhaps they had ended up in the same place as Lark and Zaide. With luck, his friend and the princess fared better.

They trudged through the woods in uncomfortably wet footgear. Not toward the entrance to the birthplace of water, like Andriun expected they might, but up a slope and away from the direction they'd come. Now and then, they passed through sunny patches, the warmth a blessing against their cold, wet clothing. They could do nothing but drip dry for now. Andriun suspected he could dry their clothes easily at this point, but he was not ready to reveal his magic. From the way Tula walked along with her chin tucked and her mouth in a sullen pout, he thought she felt the same.

He sensed her access to power, a simmering heat that need only be prodded to life, and he appreciated that she did not wield it yet. He mulled over how he might communicate with her before he concluded simply speaking was best. She did not know his language, nor would she recognize any of the gestures his people used while hunting. Not that he could perform many with his hands bound.

He cleared his throat. "If you find our companions, you will bring them to your camp as well, yes? The waters were fierce, I fear for their injuries and would like to tend to them." He posed the question to their captors, but hoped Tula would infer his plan from his words. If the broken-born might reunite them with the others, it could be better to wait.

"You'd better hope we don't find them," the leader replied.

In that case, it was probably better that they not wait. Andriun bit his lower lip in thought. He did not need gestures to direct his power, but from watching her poke fires to life and her efforts to melt the ice his father had trapped her with, he suspected Tula did. Before she could do anything, he had to get her hands free. Would that be easier now, or once they were settled somewhere in a camp? They could find themselves in a worse situation, tied together or tied to a tree, and he would have less freedom to use his power without concern for accidental injury.

As he considered striking out against the man who guided him, they crested a hill, and the thought they could merely cut their bonds and make their escape vanished like a snuffed flame.

In the valley below, dozens of tents stood in tidy rows, and hundreds of goborrins walked between them.

"Oh." He could not stop the single word before it slid free.

The sword jabbed between his shoulder blades, uncomfortably close to the ridge of his spine. "Don't stop."

Instead of stopping as the man feared, Andriun dropped below the sword's reach and kicked the man's legs out from under him. The broken-born went down hard.

The other man shouted something and came at him. Andriun was already back up on his feet. He flexed a hand and willed the water from his clothes into his grasp. It hardened into a razor-edged shard of ice between his hands and he dragged it through the rope that bound him.

Tula gasped and bounced on her feet, straining against her bonds. She could have burned through them if she focused. Or maybe the water hindered her ability? He knew so little about fire magic, and learning more would have to wait. The second broken-born was on him with a sword drawn. Andriun dodged and darted near to drive a knee into the man's groin. He toppled with a howl.

"Get me, get me!" Tula spun to present her tied wrists. Andriun snatched the sword from the ground and sliced the cords to turn her loose.

The moment he did, a vicious grin twisted her lips. Her hands snapped open and a flame ignited in either palm. Coils of light wrapped her arms, intriguing, but not something he could spare attention for now.

He grabbed her by the shoulder and pulled her along. "Run."

Her delight became confusion. "What? Why? We're free now, we can—"

"We can stay here and incite the wrath of an entire army, or we can run for now, help our friends, and warn my people. Which do you think is better?" He had not meant it to come out so hard, and when her expression melted into a mixture of disappointment and guilt, it put an uncomfortable weight in his chest.

"We must help the princess," he added. He had not fully deciphered the group's dynamics yet, but he suspected Lark was the Magister's closer friend. "She could be in danger."

The flames in her hands extinguished. "Right. Burn later."

Grateful there wouldn't be an argument, he grabbed her by the hand and started running.

She had long legs and kept pace with him easily, giving her time to point at the sword he still carried. "Can you use that?"

"We do train for combat, despite the peaceful ways of my people, but I cannot say my training includes swordsmanship."

Tula snorted. "You could have said no."

As they ran, a bugling call went up from the campsite. Andriun bit back a curse. "That is not good."

She pointed back the way they'd come. "Goborrins can't swim."

"Broken-born can."

"Yeah, but then we'd just be dealing with people, and not those ugly pig-things."

Andriun's nose scrunched. "You cannot swim, either."

"That just means it's a good time to learn, right?" The smile she flashed him was altogether too delighted for the precarious situation in which they had landed.

Yet he did not have an argument, so he focused on their escape. The return to the watershed was fast with both of them running at top speed, and when he had the presence of mind to let go of her, they both ran faster. The water had settled, the outburst from the underground spring having passed and allowed the waterway to return to its normal flow.

"That water is not deep," he said between breaths as it came into view. "It will not stop any goborrins."

"Then it won't stop us, either." Tula adjusted her stride and soon outpaced him. She leaped into the water without hesitation.

He shook his head. Had she no sense of self-preservation? He righted his bags before he jumped in after her. The water was now only waist-deep, and though she was clumsy, she waded ahead. "Slow down. The current could still take you." He extended a hand to help her balance. She gave it an odd look before she accepted. Where had his mittens gone? He frowned. Left behind on a hillside somewhere. He had liked those. They were comfortable.

"Do we head back to the spring first?" Tula looked up the mountain with a wrinkle in her forehead.

A glance backwards revealed no one was after them yet, but Andriun dared not slow. "We pass over that hill and follow the watershed. The water may have carried them farther than it carried us." And their companions could have washed out after them, too. There had been no sign of either one of them as he and Tula tumbled down the hillside in the blast. He recalled the handhold Zaide found as they were washed upward. His grasp might have put them several minutes behind, if they had been torn free at all.

"What if we don't find them?"

He did not want to entertain that possibility. "We will follow the watershed to the river, and the river until we see no signs of the spring's eruption. Then we will turn north. With luck, we will encounter a Desheni hunting party to warn." They reached the far side of the water and he boosted her out.

"And without luck?" She grasped his wrist with both hands to help pull him up.

"We will discuss that if we find we have none." The glitter of something not far downstream caught his eye. "Ah! But we do have some luck." He cast his stolen sword aside and hurried down the bank. His spear was wedged between stones and he pulled it free with little effort.

Tula took the cast-off sword. "My sister gave Zaide that knife, you know. I think he'd be real mad if you lost it."

"Then we shall not tell him that I almost did. Hurry. The bugles still sound." He pointed the way with his spear. He was coming to like how it felt with the long knife on the end. He had planned to replace it with a good piece of flint, but now he reconsidered. Perhaps he could find a metal blade to use instead.

The Magister tucked the sword under her belt and hurried on.

CHAPTER SIXTEEN

LARK COUGHED as the water receded. She coughed until she had
no air left in her and her body slumped. Zaide held her to keep
her from falling. Their perch at the edge of the walkway was
precarious, and though he didn't know how far the water had
carried them, he doubted anyone would survive the drop.

When her coughing didn't abate, he helped her onto her
hands and knees and gave her back a generous thumping. She
choked up water and swayed.

"I've got you." He rubbed her shoulder blades in silent
apology for the previous blows. Would striking the princess like
that get him in trouble, even if it was meant to help? He didn't
know, but with how pale she looked in the soft wash of light that
came from the Spectrum Blade as it lay on the floor, he decided
he was all right with risking it.

"I know." Her voice was tiny, weak, and all but strangled
between coughing fits.

He rubbed her again. He didn't know how he'd managed to
catch her in the water, much less hold fast to her, his sword, and
a column all at the same time. Looking back, he didn't know
where his hands had been or where the strength came from, but

in the midst of everything, he'd kept his head above water. He'd failed to offer Lark the same luxury.

"Sorry." He didn't understand the compulsion to apologize, but he didn't fight it, either. She didn't reply, but her coughing ceased. As she worked on catching her breath, he allowed himself to look up the cylindrical room's open shaft.

He'd seen Tula with Andriun. Knowing the Desheni hunter was with her freed him of concern. If Zaide had been able to save Lark from the surging water, there was no doubt Andriun would keep the Magister safe. The question was how far the water had taken them.

And, Zaide presumed, what they were supposed to do now.

The princess rocked back to sit. She wiped her mouth with the back of her wrist and peeled long strands of her golden hair from across her face. "Any sign of the others?"

"I saw them on the way up. Andriun will handle it." But where he'd be handling it, Zaide didn't know. He couldn't see far enough up to tell if they'd caught themselves at a higher level, or if the water had carried them elsewhere. Or maybe it had taken them back down? He glanced downward, but there was no sign of the lantern-bearers and no light to reveal the spring. Disappointed, he sat back. "What do we do now? Go up, or down?"

"Nowhere," Athradan answered.

They both jumped and turned where they sat.

The Shaman stepped from the shadowed doorway, his weathered face as craggy and serious as the mountain they sat beneath. "You are surprisingly capable."

"Somehow, I don't feel like that's a compliment." Zaide reached for the Spectrum Blade. He expected the Shaman to do something, but Athradan merely watched.

Lark drew herself to her feet. She was ragged and soaked, but managed to stand firm. "Your son said you would hinder us. And you have, every step of the way. I begin to question your allegiance."

Athradan's eyes narrowed. "My allegiance belongs to my people alone. I will serve no other."

She scoffed. "Then you align yourself as an enemy of the crown. My patience for your belligerence has expired."

Zaide stood and positioned himself beside her, sword ready. The blade was no different for having touched the water he could only assume was magic, but where it had hummed with readiness before, now a crawling sense of hesitation slipped up his arm. "We don't want to fight you," he said, not knowing if he spoke for himself and Lark, or himself and the blade. "We never did. We don't even ask you to be involved. Just help us awaken the blade and the Desheni will be asked for nothing else."

"You've already taken more from us than has ever been asked. Why should we grant you anything else?" The Shaman flicked his fingers. More Desheni—not the lantern-bearers, but armed men—slipped from the hallway behind him.

Zaide gripped his sword with both hands and took a step forward, but Lark caught his arm before he could take a second.

"Arrest them," Athradan ordered. "They will stand trial before our people for the wrongs they have committed."

Zaide lurched forward until the princess's grasp tightened. "We haven't done anything wrong!"

"Then you should have no concerns about standing trial." The Shaman smiled smugly.

Lark remained unthreatened. "We don't." The Desheni advanced on them with ropes, but she raised a hand to signal there was no need. "We will go with you. And when it is shown that nothing improper has been done, you will assist us in blessing the blade."

"You seek to bargain a great deal for a prisoner." Athradan switched to his own language to give orders, then stepped aside and let the armed Desheni escort the two of them into the hall.

"And you speak arrogantly for a man whose power is fleeting."

Zaide wanted to plant his feet and fight, but Lark didn't

release his arm. She pulled him along, her eyes darting from the Spectrum Blade in his hand to the scabbard at his side. His jaw tightened. So did her grasp. Frustrated, he shoved the sword into its sheath.

Athradan followed behind them. "You keep your so-called Bladebearer on a tight leash."

"On the contrary, I have no need to leash him. We work toward the same end. As you should work alongside us."

Zaide wasn't sure he agreed with the sentiment. With the sword put away, she released his arm and let him walk on his own, but she'd already made it clear she would be obeyed. Sometimes, he wondered why he bent to her will so easily. Then he remembered how close King Sendassian had come to strangling him already.

Sometimes, going along with things was just safer.

The Shaman said nothing more.

When they reached the slope they'd all skidded down, a long ladder lay against it, providing footholds all the way up. A few Desheni went first, then they nudged Zaide and the princess along until they began the climb. The nudging didn't stop, and by the time they reached the top of the slope and emerged into daylight, Zaide was tempted to snap their spears.

"Are we to travel all the way back to your settlement by foot, then?" Lark asked.

"The Desheni do not use horses, carts, or ships," one of their escorts said. "Our own limbs serve us well enough."

"Perhaps they'll serve well to carry us when we grow tired, then. Your Shaman's unwillingness to fulfill his duty to the crown has already led to my exhaustion." She sniffed, and her face became so haughty that Zaide had to choke back a laugh.

The Shaman did not share his amusement. Athradan herded the group to the north. "Our roads will make the way easy for your incapable legs."

Zaide didn't recall any roads, but he wouldn't give them more information about his adventures through Desheni territory than necessary. If there were roads, Andriun would have an explanation for why they were hidden and why they hadn't taken them before. Right now, there was little point in wondering about anything other than where the other half of their party might have gone. Instead, he turned his thoughts toward what they *had* encountered in the forest. "Where are the broken-born who followed us?" They certainly hadn't been arrested. Zaide saw no one else with pale hair.

Several Desheni gave him quizzical frowns, which made him frown, in turn. Hadn't they seen the other group? Athradan had to be aware of them. He'd sent water up the stairwell to trap them before they reached the spring.

"There were no others," the Shaman said simply.

Perhaps they'd all been washed away. Zaide thought of Andriun and Tula on their own with the less-than-friendly sextet of men and silently prayed the two of them had found better luck than he and Lark.

A strange new sound rose above the keening horns and trampling hooves of goborrins. Andriun had heard it before, but not often, and it took him a moment to grasp how much worse things had just become.

"Dogs?" Tula sounded incredulous. "Dogs don't even like goborrins!"

"Beasts will grow accustomed to anything, with the right exposure." It was a lot more eloquent than what thoughts first filled his mind, and a lot more suitable to the company of women, besides. He considered the tone of the canines' barks as they echoed through the hills, puzzled out how far away they had to be, and adapted his pace. The way he sped up spoke for itself, for Tula clamped her mouth shut and gripped her bags tighter as she matched his stride.

They had alternated running and walking, thinking it would

let them outpace the goborrins from the camp he knew they were not meant to see. Any other time, he suspected it would have been enough. But the broken-born they encountered in the woods had to be men of some importance, or else the fact they had been blown from the spring together held importance, or there would be no reason for a band to persist in pursuing them across the hills.

Clearly, whatever the reason, the camp had declared them a problem.

The dogs grew closer.

"We need help," Andriun said.

"If Zaide were here—" Tula began, though she cut herself short and exhaled hard. They both breathed heavily; the longer they fled, the harder it became to pick up the faster pace after each spell of walking. Abruptly, she stopped and turned.

Andriun jogged to a halt. "What are you doing?"

She turned toward their pursuers and set her feet wide, a defiant gleam in her eyes. The dogs crested the hill across which they had just come. "Maybe if we fight back, we'll scare them off."

His eyes shot to the dogs, four great gray-black beasts that looked nothing like the wolves in the wood. "The goborrins will catch up."

"I'd rather fight goborrins than spend forever running." The Magister swept her sleeves up her arms and spread them wide. A soft glow began under her skin and swelled to the surface. Dragons emerged as a pattern of light twisted around her arms.

He had seen the markings before, when his father had trapped them in ice. But that had been just a fleeting glimpse. Now, he admired the shimmering detail of each ridge and scale. The mark of her power was impressive. For a fleeting instant, he envied the display. Even had he not forfeited his destiny, the Shaman bore no such marks. Subdued, he returned to her side and braced with his spear ready. Magic might have been more effective, but they were a long way from the watershed.

"Too bad you can't just freeze them, huh?" Tula asked, as if sharing his thoughts.

Andriun tried to smile. "I suppose a roast is an acceptable alternative."

"Yeah, but hold your nose. Dog meat stinks." She spread her hands as the dogs neared. Flames sparked to life above her palms and she snapped her hands together, sending a burst of fire toward the beasts.

A chorus of yelps went up from the dogs as the stench of scorched hair scented the air. The dogs peeled away, two to either side, yipping and crying. Flames licked across their bodies as they ran.

Tula hopped in place and pumped her arm in victory.

Then the goborrins came over the hill.

"Oh," she squeaked.

At least twenty of the pig-faced brutes poured down the slope, a white-haired man among them. Andriun could not see if it was one of those who had captured them, but he did not care to stay and find out. He grasped Tula's arm. "Run."

"Good idea." She turned to flee, a little more vigor in her legs as they rushed over the crown of the next hill.

Each slope grew higher, and as the way became more steep, they were forced to slow. Andriun pointed up the hillside at a diagonal, then pulled her along. Changing the direction let them ascend more easily, but not as swiftly, and he silently prayed the dogs would not return. Even if they did not, they presented a new challenge. "We need to find water. We have to eliminate our scent trail."

"Oh, sure," Tula panted. "We'll just hop over the hill and find a creek, then jump right in."

Despite her sarcasm, she still looked pained when they crossed the next peak and there was no sign of water. The yips and howls had abated, which meant the dogs might have fled beyond hearing, but the stamping feet of goborrins never quieted.

Andriun steered her at a new angle, hoping it might give them an advantage. If they were not where the goborrins expected them to be when they made it across the ridge, maybe it would buy them time. "There will be another watershed," he said between breaths. "We have come far already. Up the next slope and to the right. We will make it." And if they were fortunate, it would be wet. Not all the mountain streams were.

Tula still ran hard, but her strength was flagging. "How do you know?"

"I can see it." He pointed. "In the shape of the land. The mark in the hillside." His finger traced downward at an angle, indicating how the water must flow from the snowcaps in the spring. They were all but thawed now, as summer took the mountains.

She followed his gesture, but did not appear relieved. She said nothing and struggled to run.

Andriun chanced a look back, just as the goborrins crossed into view. Their dogs were with them again. Or maybe new dogs. He could not see them well, but they struck him as distinctly unburnt. "Ah," he started.

"I hear them." The Magister stumbled on a loose patch in the rocky soil. He caught her arm before she fell.

The next peak came and Tula laughed in relief. Below, a glittering ribbon of silver cut through the trees. A creek.

Andriun blew out a sigh of relief on his own. It veered south, when they wanted to go north, but a trek along the coast would be easier than tromping through goborrin-filled woods, and running downhill was easier still. They both picked up speed as they ran. Each step landed hard, sending a jolt up Andriun's legs, but the creek was wide and welcoming. He released Tula's arm and pushed forward on his own.

The creek spread before him and he leaped in before he realized Tula would need help.

She skidded to a stop beside the water's edge and he hurried back to aid her.

"It is all right," he promised as he opened his arms in invitation. "I will help you. I will teach you."

After one fearful glance back, she slid over the bank and into the water. It was deeper than it looked. She went in up to her chin with panic on her face before he got hold of her.

"Easy." He pulled her near and guided her arms and legs to aid their float. "Stay like that. I will guide us." And once they were beyond the goborrins and the reach of their ugly blades and uglier dogs, he would try to teach her to swim.

The swift downhill current swept them along so fast, the party of monsters that followed gave a cry of dismay.

Andriun laughed as the goborrins slowed to a halt, but his delight was quick to flee when Tula sniffled. He held her at arm's length, bewildered. "What is wrong? We made it!"

Her lip trembled and her bold green eyes shone like glass. "But my notebook." She sniffed again. In the midst of everything, danger and adventure and risk, the one thing that broke through was the loss of her notes.

He held her by the arms and stared into her eyes, unsure what to say. In the end, a quiet "Oh," was all that escaped.

Scholars, he decided, were an unusual breed.

CHAPTER SEVENTEEN

Not long after the journey began, Athradan ordered his hunters to tie Zaide and the princess as captives, no matter how agreeable they'd been. Zaide swore the ropes were tighter this time than when he'd first encountered the Desheni. But Andriun had been the one to tie him then, and he'd begun to realize his friend was not as much like the rest of his people as he first believed.

No one spoke to them further, and Lark had little to say. She remained solemn and stoic as the Shaman led them to a stony outcropping that ringed the mountains. It was unlike the path they'd taken when Andriun first led him through the mountains, which had been reminiscent of the game trails in Kolmar's forest. The roads were narrow, but clear, paved with gravel and tidily maintained. They were also higher in the mountains than Zaide would have thought to go on his own, and the altitude proved both chilly and unpleasant for the lungs.

They did not stop for rest, nor did they make camp, and just when Zaide wasn't sure he could go a single step farther, they passed a ridge that had kept the Desheni settlement hidden from view. Relief washed over him in such a wave, it offered a second wind. But to his side, Lark swayed on her feet.

The Shaman pointed. Two of the men who led the princess by rope stepped back to grab her by the arms. They dragged her along when she stumbled.

"Be gentle with her," Zaide snapped.

Athradan shot him a scowl. "Perhaps you would like to carry her, then?"

He lifted his chin. "Untie me and I will."

Several of the Desheni laughed, but the Shaman said something that cut them short. One sullen man stepped forward to cut Zaide's bonds, then Athradan pointed at the princess. "Do it."

Zaide glowered back at him, even as he shuffled over to Lark's side. They hadn't cut her ropes, so he put her arms over his head and bent so she could climb onto his back. "Get on."

"Zaide—" she protested.

He hooked an arm behind him to catch her leg. Reluctantly, she clambered up, bags and all. He settled his arms under her knees and hefted her up a little higher. "I've got you," he murmured.

Her brow furrowed, but she nestled her face into the side of his neck and said nothing more.

Another word from the Shaman put them all back into motion. Desheni men surrounded them and for the first time, Zaide realized it was only men. There had been women among the Desheni in the birthplace of water. Where had they gone? Had they stayed behind? If so, why hadn't he noticed before now? He skimmed the faces of those who remained, as if they might hold some answer, but he gleaned nothing beyond the notion they despised him. Somehow, that information didn't come as a shock.

The descent from the mountains to the settled valley was difficult with Lark on his back, but Zaide was determined to make it down without incident. By the time they reached the foot of the slope, sweat was thick on his brow and made his shirt cling uncomfortably, but he didn't falter.

"Imprison them," Athradan said, and that he spoke the order in their language and not his own made it clear he wanted them to know precisely what awaited. "We will call a council and begin discussion of all that has transpired."

Lark's arms pressed against Zaide's shoulders as if seeking a hug. He shifted her a little before the hunters separated them from the Shaman's group. He knew where their holding cell was; he'd been there before. He headed for the lonely shack where the wooden bars of the empty cell awaited.

The men ushered them inside and once he set foot inside the cell, Zaide knelt so the princess could climb off.

Before she had both feet on the ground, one of the men cut the straps of Lark's bags to free them without unbinding her wrists. He started after Zaide's, but he held up a hand and removed both of his bags on his own. The man grunted and took them all.

Another stepped forward to remove Lark's knives from her thighs. Once he had them, he reached for the Spectrum Blade's hilt. A crackling hiss filled the air before he touched it and Zaide angled his hips to move the sword away. "Don't touch it," he warned.

The Desheni man disregarded him and lunged forward to take the blade. A snap and sizzle mingled with the man's cry of pain.

Zaide opened his mouth to explain and was backhanded across the face. His hands snapped up to his mouth and he stumbled back a step. Fury washed through him like heat radiating from his side. At the same time, Lark lurched forward to reach for his face.

"Don't," he said to the sword, but the princess froze, her brows drawn together.

She lowered her hands.

The Desheni man spat something he didn't understand and thrust a finger toward the corner.

Zaide gestured for him to settle. He licked his split lip, the harsh taste of iron enough to make him wince. Slowly, he unsheathed the sword at his side. He stepped from the cell to prop the blade up in the corner, then returned to Lark's side.

The man's face only grew darker, but he gave no orders. He didn't say anything. Maybe he didn't speak their language. Zaide had assumed all the Desheni could, but maybe only those who ventured outside the village did. He thought of asking, but the man slammed the cell shut and locked them in, then removed himself from the shack.

A few of the other Desheni looked to the sword and murmured between themselves. Ultimately, none of them decided to risk it, and they filed from the shack one by one. When the door closed, the only light that remained was the thin sliver that framed the door, and that which radiated from the Spectrum Blade.

They both gazed at the door for a time. Then Lark turned to take Zaide's jaw in her hands. "You're bleeding."

"It's not bad." In truth, he felt his heartbeat in his lips and teeth, and the scent of his own blood was strong enough that it turned his stomach. But he didn't want her to worry, so he removed himself from her touch and wiped his face with his sleeve. It hurt, but it was a minor injury. He'd suffered worse.

As such, the shadow of dismay that floated across her features struck him as excessive. Slowly, Lark sank to sit on the floor with her back against the wall.

Anger still flowed from the Spectrum Blade, but it was weaker now that the blade wasn't at his side. It had morphed, too. Hints of indignation swam through the emotion. "It's fine," he said, perhaps more crossly than he'd intended.

The princess's head lifted, her expression hurt.

Had he been physically able to kick himself, he would have. "Not you. It."

Her gaze slipped to the sword, then the floor.

The thought of apologizing had just surfaced in his mind when he heard Lark sniff. The sound was so bizarre, so out of place, that it wasn't until she tucked her chin in tight and drew her shoulders forward that he grasped what was happening.

Zaide slid forward and knelt. "Hey." He didn't know what else to say. He reached for her face, but she turned away.

"I'm sorry." Her shoulders trembled and she wiped at her eyes, though the rope on her wrists made it awkward. "I can't seem to stop, I—"

"It's okay, you don't have to." He sat beside her and pulled her into his arms. At first, she resisted, but her resolve was short-lived and a moment later, she turned her face to his chest and burrowed in.

Zaide was not well-practiced with comfort. Instead, he focused on practicality and sought her hands while she leaned against him. The knots in the rope were tight, but he picked at them until he got her hands free.

"I'm just tired. I'm so tired, and everything has gone wrong. Amrochan, Jadora, even here." The princess fought to hold back tears, but holding her breath and biting her lip only seemed to make them flow faster.

He wiped them away with his shirt. "I mean, it's not going great, but I wouldn't say it's gone wrong. We're here, and the sword's almost unlocked, or whatever it is that's supposed to happen."

"But we can't restore it, not without the Shaman's help."

"We don't know that. We didn't even make it all the way into the spring. We can try again when we get out of here." Zaide wasn't sure how they were going to do that yet, but leaving Desheni was the only option they had.

"Or maybe my father was right, and this whole expedition was a waste of time. The whole time, he's said it was pointless. No one even knows we're out here." She didn't resist when he dried more tears, but she turned so she wouldn't have to look at him.

"Not sure that's true. Don't forget the people who saw us. It changed a lot in Amrochan, seeing us cut through those goborrins to reach the city. That news spread fast." He glanced toward the Spectrum Blade in the corner. Its agitation had settled; he no longer felt anything, and its iridescent colors had calmed to a slow shift of sleepy tones.

Lark considered that for a time, then squeezed her eyes closed and nodded. "That's true." She scrubbed her cheeks with the side of her hand. "I'm sorry. I don't know what's gotten into me. I'm just..."

"Tired," Zaide finished for her. "I know. We all are. Everything gets dark when you don't think you can keep going." Against his better judgment, he threaded his fingers through her golden hair. His mother had stroked him that way when he was small. Later, when he was older and his frustrations grew to be more than he could bear, Sarma had soothed him the same way.

She leaned against him and he shifted to make it more comfortable for them both. When he slouched with his back propped against the wall, she rested her head on his stomach and stared past the wooden bars. Her eyes reflected the shifting light emitted by the sword, creating the illusion of churning storm clouds in her gaze. "How do you do it?"

"Do what?"

"Keep going all the time. You never stop. You've been going since we met in the woods and you've never slowed down. You're so strong, and I... I feel like I'm always about to break."

He studied the sword, too, to keep from looking at her as he petted her head and toyed with her hair. "So do I. I'm just better at hiding it, I guess."

"That's not good for you."

"Neither is running into peril all the time, or thinking I can hack and slash my way through a whole army, but you don't seem to have any problems with me doing that." He meant it in jest, but she shifted, her face contorted with distress. He went on before she could speak. "I don't mind. It's what I always wanted. Or, I thought it was. A chance to get out there and fight, to do what I was told my father did, to do something to stand up for the family I lost. Don't get me wrong, I love Resia's family. Verlin and Sarma are good parents. They gave me brothers and sisters, and I know they all love me as much as I love them. But the hurt stays. The heart's always big enough to add more family, but it never stops hurting for the ones you lose."

"And then I pulled you away from all of it," she murmured.

Zaide mustered a smile. "Nah. You made it interesting. Besides, if anything, you helped me get out of Kolmar. I'll never know why the Elder kept me from going to the garrison, but I guess looking back, I have to be glad he did. I was there to help when things got bad. If I'd had my way, maybe I wouldn't have been. My family's safe in Amrochan. Selfishly, I'd like to think that everything I've done had a part in keeping them safe."

"I'm sure it did." A weary smile graced her lips.

He smoothed back her hair. "You should rest."

Lark raised a hand to touch his face. Her fingertips were soft, gentle. "You're a good friend."

"I'm sure you'll change your mind about that before everything's over." He fixed his eyes on the sword and fell silent as she relaxed against him. He'd kept the Desheni from taking the Spectrum Blade, but they'd be back before long, and he didn't want to face them empty-handed.

CHAPTER EIGHTEEN

"We are being followed." Andriun had not been sure at first. The wide creek and the river it connected to carried them fast and far. The idea they could be pursued so easily after such an escape had been unpleasant to consider, but he could no longer deny what his senses revealed.

It was not the same party as before. They had no dogs, just the loud, trampling hooves of goborrins. If there were men with the monsters, he could not tell, but he doubted they would remain so focused on pursuit without something to drive them. Or someone, he thought with a grim smile.

After they climbed from the river, Andriun had forged up the coast with as much speed as he could muster. He knew every trail through the wild and every road that intersected them. He had taken care to avoid the road, where his father's patrols might be, and stayed on the narrow paths where the hunters they might encounter were more likely to be people Andriun knew and had befriended. There were some among the Desheni who were still kind to him, though his relationship with his people as a whole had changed. When they crossed paths, they regarded him with uncertainty, perhaps hoping he might explain his actions in a way they could understand. He regretted that he had not. No matter how he hoped he might cross paths with another hunter now, the trails remained empty, and he could not help but wonder if his own reticence had scared them off.

"Where?" Tula asked when he said nothing more. She turned this way and that, but they were deep in the wilds and there was nothing to see.

Andriun held up a fist. She stopped at his signal and when he turned his head to listen, she mirrored the action.

A steady, thumping cadence carried through the trees, muted some by the leaves but amplified by the silence of the woodland creatures.

"They march." He kept his voice low, though he supposed there was little point. He knew little of the skills such creatures might have, but tracking them had proven an easy task. Perhaps goborrins had the senses of normal pigs. He thought of them scouting and sniffing around for truffles and almost snorted. The skills of monsters mattered little at this point. As long as they stayed ahead of the group, no further trouble would come to them.

As if the goborrins were not trouble, themselves? Andriun shook his head as he continued through the underbrush. He had chosen a place where the forest was dense on purpose, but now he wondered if it had been wise. Their path would be difficult to follow and they would be hidden from sight, but branches and leaves would bear their scent.

Tula listened for a moment longer, then hastened to close the gap between them. "We're miles from their camp. Why are they still after us?"

Andriun wished he knew. He did not even know why the goborrins were there, or how long they had been there, or how close they had come to the Desheni settlement. The thought they meant his people harm put dread in his belly, the feeling simultaneously a cold weight that dragged him down and a fire that fueled determination.

If he could not protect his people, at least he could warn them.

The rest, unfortunately, was in his father's hands.

They broke through a dense point in the underbrush. Andriun hissed and retreated into the brush with an arm out to bar Tula's path.

She started to protest, but he pressed a finger to his lips and pointed.

"I hope you are ready to run," he whispered as she inched close enough to see into the clearing.

Another goborrin camp, smaller than the one they had seen before, lay nestled between the trees.

She grimaced and sank to a crouch behind the bush. "Maybe they aren't following us. Maybe we picked the worst possible path to take."

"Perhaps, but this is not good. We are close to my village. Why are they here?" He dreaded the possibilities. Worse than that, he dreaded how many more camps might be hidden in the mountains surrounding his home.

"How much farther?"

Andriun pointed in the direction of the settlement and searched the sky, as if it might offer clues.

"You don't know?" The Magister sounded incredulous.

"It is daytime. It is hard to tell where I am when I have nothing but trees as a point of reference." He gestured toward the canopy with his palm up. "But we are close. I am sure of that. So we move through the brush that way, and if we are spotted, then—"

A bugle sounded and a clatter arose from the camp.

"Run!" Tula bolted in the direction of the village, crashing through leaves and branches.

Andriun bit back an oath and ran after her.

Goborrins roared and seized weapons from the ground and from sheaths. They surged toward the two of them.

"I hope you are able to run faster than that!" Andriun caught her arm as he caught up and threatened to overtake her. Her robe snagged on everything as they ran. She jerked her arm away from him and gathered up the fabric of her robe to clutch it to her middle. It helped somewhat, but he readied his spear anyway.

Fleet as they were, it did not take long for the goborrins to catch up. Andriun split off on his own to jab with his spear, aiming for a monster's exposed legs and hoping it would slow it down. He had never fought goborrins before all this, had never even seen them, and the size of the beasts was enough to intimidate the most skilled of warriors.

Tula halted not far off. "Don't stop, you can't fight them alone!"

"I do not want to fight them at all," he replied as he swung his spear sideways. The long knife that served as a makeshift spearhead raked across a goborrin's knee and the monster toppled into the one beside it. When the two went down, the half-dozen behind them all but tripped over their bodies, presenting a perfect opportunity to run.

Andriun rejoined the Magister and they burst from the trees together to emerge onto the village's main road. They ran faster on the packed and rocky ground.

The village was full of people tending late afternoon chores. He waved his arms overhead and shouted for them in his own tongue. "Get the hunters! Find shelter!"

They stared at him as if his words made no sense. Then a goborrin crashed out of the trees beside him and their confusion was replaced by screams. Andriun spun to fight. Tula spread her hands and summoned her fire to help, and he prayed that was not the only help he got.

~

Zaide woke with a start when the door opened. For an instant, he saw the glow of snow and smelled the cold. Then he snapped free of the memory and touched Lark's shoulder to wake her. Judging by how fast she pushed herself away from him, she was just as disoriented as he'd been. Shadows moved into the doorway. The light beyond was rosy, tinted by sunset, and more shapes clustered beyond the silhouettes that came toward them.

"Rise," a man ordered. "Council has been called."

Zaide fought to keep from looking at the Spectrum Blade. He hadn't figured out how to get the sword into his hands, but he'd have no chance of getting it if he tipped off their captors before he even stood. He climbed to his feet and offered the princess a hand. She ignored him.

Slowly, his vision resolved and the figures in the small shack came into clear view. Only a few had stepped inside, but they carried both spears in their hands and strange knives at their belts. They didn't look like stone, but they weren't metal, either. Zaide found himself puzzling over the weapons far longer than he should have.

Lark combed through her hair with her fingers and strode toward the simple door as someone unlocked it. "I trust we shall settle this quickly."

They confirmed nothing. They didn't even acknowledge that she'd spoken. The man at the door opened it and pointed for both of them to exit.

Zaide followed the princess from the cell, but a pair of men with their spears ready stepped between him and where the Spectrum Blade rested against the wall.

His jaw tightened and he considered whether or not he should start a fight just to claim it now—and whether or not he'd get it back later if he didn't.

Voices rose outside. Shouting, then startled cries from children. The hair on the back of Zaide's neck stood as unpleasant memories washed through his mind. He knew those sounds, knew the surprise and fear that spurred them.

The hunters at the door turned away, murmuring questions.

Zaide shoved past the two men between himself and his sword. Neither seemed to notice.

"Zaide, what—" Lark started, but he cut her short with a look so sharp, even she drew back.

A word of alarm passed between the hunters and they abandoned the simple prison.

Uncertainty touched the princess's eyes.

"They're here," Zaide said.

No one remained outside to guard them. He blinked against the sunlight as he stepped out and turned to follow the flow of people. Families went one direction. Desheni with spears went another. The sword in his hand sent an agitated thrum up his arm.

No sooner than he'd rounded the corner of a building, the goborrins came into view. The sword's surface ignited with color, more intense than anything he'd seen from it yet. How bright would it grow when the last of its strength was restored?

Goborrins charged down the slope to meet the hunters, but two figures near the top of the slope caught his eye.

"Tula!" Lark exclaimed.

Zaide snorted. "I knew it. She is your favorite."

"What, are you jealous?"

"I have saved your hide several times since this adventure started. The least you could do is a thank you, you know." He sprinted ahead and met a goborrin head-on.

The Spectrum Blade flared as he drove it through the monster's gut. More than one cry of surprise went up from the Desheni around him, but it was soon replaced with sounds of awe. For an instant, he thought it was their reaction to the sword. Then a lance of ice burst from the monster just behind the one he'd felled. He twisted in place to find the source, expecting it might have been Andriun's work. Instead, Athradan strode up the main walkway of the village, his hands spread and his eyes hard.

Zaide caught his gaze. He didn't dare hold it for long, not

with more goborrins charging down the hill, but he held it long enough to will the Shaman to take notice.

See me. See whose side I'm on. Understand why you need to help.

If the Shaman thought anything, his face didn't betray it.

Zaide tore his eyes away and moved forward to slay the next beast.

"Zaide!" Andriun exclaimed. They worked in opposite directions, Zaide going up the hill, Andriun coming down. "You are alive. I am glad." The hunter stopped long enough to slice the back of a goborrin's knee, sending the monster crashing down the hillside. It tumbled past Tula, yielding an awkward squawk from the girl on her way to greet the princess.

"You, too." Zaide dispatched it the moment it landed.

Andriun motioned with his spear. "I have your knife."

"Thanks." They moved together toward another goborrin, but ice burst from its body before they reached it. It was fast, brutal, and he barely had time to turn before the Shaman summoned such power again.

One after another, the goborrins on the hillside fell. The hunters raised their spears to cheer. Zaide stopped, rooted to one place, unsure how he should react. He'd wanted to help, but he'd expected more, thoughts of the attack on Kolmar vivid in his mind.

No more than a dozen goborrins had emerged from the forest, and after a Desheni hunter put one last struggling beast out of its misery, none remained. Zaide scanned the ground to be sure.

Tula and Lark stood together at the foot of the hill. The Magister recounted something with an unnecessary amount of animation and as she spoke, Lark grew more solemn.

Andriun looked back up the hill, clearly expecting more. When nothing came, he turned to face the Shaman's approach. "Father, there—"

"How many times will you seek to shame me?" Athradan

interrupted. "To shame your people? Now you seek to bring violence upon them because you don't get your way?"

Andriun stiffened. "There are camps in the forest. Enough goborrins to—"

"And so you lead them to your people?"

Zaide started forward. Before he'd taken more than a step, the Shaman gave a flick of his fingers and hunters encircled the princess and Tula. More moved toward him. The sword in his hand sent pings of warning through his fingers.

"I came to warn my people." Andriun squared his shoulders and remained calm, though the set of his brows and the clench of his jaw betrayed his frustration.

Athradan scoffed and strode forward. He hovered eye to eye with his son, his lip curled in a sneer. "You've come to bring them ruin. You were born for such greatness, and now..." He trailed off as his eye was drawn downward, caught by a glint of silver.

Zaide's stomach sank.

Slowly, Athradan reached for the chain around his son's neck. Andriun stood resolute and unflinching. The Shaman lifted the Captured Spring from where it was hidden and his mouth fell open with disbelief.

"This..." Athradan curled a hand around the vial, his swollen knuckles growing pale. "How long have you had this?"

"Give me time to speak, and I will answer every question before our council," Andriun said.

A sense of alarm shot up Zaide's arm and he couldn't keep his shoulder from twitching. The hunters who guarded him pressed closer and grasped him by the arms. They couldn't touch the blade, but their grip made it clear they would keep him from using it.

Athradan jerked the spring so hard, the chain broke. "Before, I cast you from our village. Now, I cast you to the desert. Take them. All of them. They will not be allowed to set foot back in our territory."

"You can't do this!" Tula shouted. She pressed against the hunters who held her, a fire in her eyes to match her magic. "You can't keep fighting against your responsibilities! Can't you see how you're needed here? You were chosen to help protect this world. Why do you refuse that call?"

The Shaman looked her way, then disregarded her. He stepped back with the Captured Spring in his hand. "Do not leave them unattended. Give them what supplies are needed for their trip and then remove them from our territory. They will not be trusted to obey again."

Andriun set his jaw and stared at the ground.

Lark said nothing at all, her face smooth and unreadable as the hunters grasped her, too.

"You can't escape this." Zaide could hardly move with how his captors gripped him, but he pointed at one of the dead goborrins with his sword. "You can hide in the mountains as long as you want, but this war will reach you. Gadranus will reach you, unless we're given the power to stop him."

The Shaman turned a speculative frown his way. For a moment, Zaide thought the man might say something, but he just shook his head and clasped the Captured Spring to his chest.

Zaide gritted his teeth as the men turned him toward the path and forced him past the piglike corpses that littered the ground.

"It is no use, Zaide. He is in denial. Nothing will change his mind." Andriun walked without fighting, resigned to his fate.

Their escort stopped at the top of the hill. Zaide didn't know what they'd stopped for until a pair of women came, carrying their bags.

They held out the bags as they approached, but Lark pointed at the ground. "Leave them. Then leave us. There is no point in wasting time here any further. The north is no use to us."

The women put down the bags, but the hunters who surrounded them remained.

"At least let us walk alone," Tula grumbled. She tugged one arm free of her escort, then the other.

"You heard the Shaman as well as the rest of us," one of the hunters said. "You are to be escorted from Desheni territory. Some of us are not so eager to defy our leader." The man gave Andriun a pointed look, which Andriun returned with a grim smile.

Lark sniffed and gave her ponytail a swish. "Then you shall keep us company while we repair our bags. Something for you to consider, the next time you damage someone else's property." She dropped to sit in the middle of the path and rooted in her things. She produced a small packet from her belongings and opened it to reveal a sewing kit.

Zaide's eyebrows rose. Of all the things she might have packed to travel with, he hadn't imagined a princess would pack a needle and thread. "Let me help."

"Put away your weapon," one of the hunters ordered.

An odd, quivering sensation coursed through the Spectrum Blade. "You're the ones holding me. You're going to have to let go."

They exchanged worried glances, but released him. Zaide sheathed the sword and let his hand linger on the hilt. He sensed something, but it made little sense. Anticipation burned in every fingerprint, a hot tingle that warned him of something yet to come.

"Don't get any ideas," the Desheni said, misinterpreting his hesitance to release the blade.

Zaide peeled his hand from the hilt and settled on the ground beside the princess. "It's unhappy." The hunters wouldn't understand what he meant. From the way they looked back toward the village or off into the forest while they talked among themselves, he didn't think they cared to understand, either.

Lark made a small sound, little more than confirmation she'd heard him. She passed him the sewing kit before she set to work mending the strap of her bag.

The sun was setting. It wouldn't be long before light faded, and they'd be stuck traversing the forest in the dark. Zaide threaded a needle and tried to copy her handiwork and mend her other bag before it grew too dark to see what he was doing, wondering if that was why she worked so slowly. Her stitches were precise and tiny, obviously the work of an experienced seamstress, but her speed was unbefitting her skill.

He studied her face between spells of watching her hands. Now and then, she glanced back toward the village. He followed her line of sight.

"They're fast to clean up," she said when he frowned. "Even the soldiers outside of Amrochan aren't so efficient. The Desheni are hard workers."

Who diligently removed any sign the goborrins had been there. They even combed the gravel and dirt to disperse the stains left by the beasts' muddy brown blood.

"A strong people." Zaide watched as they dragged away the last corpse. Where were they taking it? He hadn't seen where the rest of them ended up. In Kolmar, the monsters had ultimately been burned. The same method was used in the battlefields outside Amrochan.

"Remarkable how fast they're able to recover from such an attack." Lark shook her head, either in disbelief or admiration. Or maybe it was disapproval, or skepticism.

Zaide puzzled over the options for a moment before he pieced together her point. How many times had the Desheni been attacked? How many times had they swept the event under the rug as if it didn't matter? Either they were willfully ignorant of the danger they were in, or there were more secrets the Shaman wasn't sharing. The latter seemed more likely. There was no mistaking the bewildered disgust that had been on Andriun's face as he looked over the dead goborrins. Zaide had seen the same look on the faces of the Kolmari on the day of the Spring Choosing, the first time many of them had encountered such monsters anywhere outside of books and folktales.

"Shall I check those straps for you?" the princess asked. She held out her hand to ask for her other bag, but her attention traveled back to the village below.

Stalling for something. Waiting for a sign, though Zaide couldn't fathom what. He passed over the bag. "I think I need more practice."

"I would agree with that assessment." She ran her fingers over the tangle of thread he'd made, as if contemplating removing everything he'd already done. Eventually, she stitched over the top of it and gave each strap a few tugs when she was finished. "There. That should do." She pushed the sewing kit back into her things and gathered both bags onto her shoulders. "We may leave now. With luck, this will hold well enough that I won't have to stop and mend things again." She stood and motioned for their escort to lead the way.

The hunters grumbled to themselves over the delay, but forged onward.

Andriun and Tula remained quiet, as they had been while the bags were mended, and Lark carried such solemnity that Zaide didn't feel he should try to break the silence.

They had not gone far before the night grew dark and they were forced to stop.

Andriun took in their surroundings and shook his head. "We should not stop here. We are too close to... things which I would like to not be close to."

"Articulate," Zaide said.

His friend gave him a flat look.

"He's right, though," Tula put in. "We weren't far off the road when—"

Lark cut her short. "But you're not alone now, and we have plenty of Desheni huntsmen to keep us safe, should we run into trouble."

"Hunters," Andriun said.

"What?"

"Hunters. Both men and women hunt, we do not distinguish them with the term huntsmen or huntswomen."

The hunters continued setting up their camp, uncaring of their being discussed.

Zaide snorted a laugh. "With that kind of pedantry, you're going to fit into this group real well."

Andriun frowned.

"You are coming with us, right?" Tula appeared at his side and took his arm in her hands.

One of the hunters snorted. "He has no choice. He travels with you, he leaves with you. He will not come back." From the way the young man shook his head, he didn't agree with that decision. A former friend of Andriun's, perhaps.

Or an ally for our group, Zaide thought.

"He's welcome among us." Lark lowered her bags to the ground someplace out of the way, but near enough to the fresh-kindled fire to be easily visible. "Excuse me for a moment."

The hunters started to stand with their spears in hand, but Tula pointed back at the ground. "What she *means* is to give her privacy for a moment. Honestly, have you no manners?"

Lark grimaced, but trudged into the woods anyway. The hunters watched, but when she stepped behind a tree some distance away and did not emerge to either side, they settled.

For a time, everyone busied themselves with sorting supplies, setting up the campsite, or preparing food. When Lark did not return in a timely fashion, the hunters began to murmur. Zaide didn't understand them, but their gestures gave him the gist. He pushed himself up from the ground. "I'll go check on her," he told no one in particular.

The hunters didn't like that suggestion. They gripped their spears and started to rise, but Zaide waved a hand at them and slid the Spectrum Blade from its sheath. He drove it into the ground beside the fire, a silent promise he'd be back.

"Probably saw a snake or something and is too proud to call for help," he muttered as he departed the ring of light that surrounded the campfire. He didn't believe it for a second, but the Desheni might. All they knew was Dasienna the princess, not Lark the capable fighter and independent adventurer. Though he supposed by now, they might at least know both names.

He crunched through the undergrowth, mindful not to sneak up on her. "Lark?" He kept his voice low, lest that startle her or whatever kept her from returning, just in case there was some truth to his sham. He lingered just behind the tree she'd ducked past, but she did not reply.

Zaide rested a hand against the trunk and tried again. "Your Highness?"

No reply.

He eased around the tree, preparing to shield his eyes and accept a tongue lashing, then blinked when there was no one there. Disruptions in the soil were hard to make out in the dark, but he had enough practice to determine what they meant.

She'd lowered herself to the ground and slid down to the next tree, then the next. He glanced over his shoulder, but no one was looking, so he followed the trail down the hill and out of view. Here, the trail changed. Shallow footprints in soft earth led the way and before long, the light of another campfire came into view. The camp was just beyond a rise. Lark crouched at the side of the hill.

Zaide did not crouch, but lowered himself as he crept through the trees. Years of experience in the forest made his passage all but soundless, but as he approached, he lowered a hand and rustled some leaves.

The princess started and did not relax when she saw him. Instead, she pressed a finger to her lips and pointed up, indicating they should crest the hill.

He followed her lead and they chose separate trees to crouch behind as the camp on the other side came into view.

Goborrins milled about, building fires and sharpening swords while broken-born gave orders and arranged formations.

In the middle of it all stood Athradan.

CHAPTER NINETEEN

WHEN ZAIDE and Lark returned from the woods, their faces were more solemn than ever before. Andriun considered a joke about poisonous leaves and itching, then promptly discarded the idea. He had not intended to share it with the princess, for whom such a joke would be wildly inappropriate, but even Zaide—who he thought might appreciate the humor, being that he was a man of the woods—did not appear as if jokes would be welcome.

Andriun chewed his dried berries and contemplated what the two of them might have discussed while away from the camp. A plan of action seemed unlikely; they had not been gone long enough to develop more than a few potential schemes. Their faces were more troubled than thoughtful, besides.

The princess settled beside her bags, while Zaide took the Spectrum Blade from where he had left it beside the fire. He scraped dirt from the sword and returned it to its scabbard before he sat. The Desheni Andriun's father had tasked with escorting them from the north did not seem to care where the two of them had been, and Tula did not seem to notice they had returned. She sat hunched over her notebook, muttering to herself as she pored over every page.

The book gave him an idea. Andriun moved closer and

leaned in to see the letters she traced and restored. The pages were crinkled and blotches of ink stained some, but most of the graphite marks seemed to have survived.

"Are you in need of help?" He held out a hand, both an offer of assistance and a request for one of her odd pencils.

Tula held her book to the side and pouted at him.

"She's protective of her notes," Zaide said.

Andriun had already determined that on his own. He persisted, offering the Magister his best pleading look. "Surely your hands need a rest. I can rewrite your pages on Desheni culture for you. I remember everything we discussed while we walked."

Her eyes narrowed, but she considered the suggestion. After a while, she grudgingly pushed the notebook and her pencil into his hands.

He offered a smile and turned to the first page he recognized as something she had written under his direction. A few of the lines were smudged, but no more than that. He traced them carefully, then added a note at the top of the page. *Something is wrong.*

Tula's brow furrowed and she reached for the pencil. "No, I think you misspelled that."

"I did not," he protested, though he let her take it.

Her own note replied. *With Dasienna/Z?*

Andriun nodded slowly. He cradled his chin with his forefinger and thumb. "Ah. Yes."

"And there was another line about this here." *Secret? How do we ask?*

The book was the obvious solution. "I do not think that was there. That was in a different section." He turned forward until he reached a blank page. "Here."

"It was not!" Tula protested.

The princess lifted her head and glowered at them both. "What inane thing are the two of you arguing over now?"

"He doesn't know where my notes were. He's moving

everything." Tula turned back a page and pointed at something unrelated. "That was over here. You remember, don't you, Your Highness?"

Lark rolled her eyes. "I have no idea what you're talking about. I can't see your book from here."

Tula huffed, pulled the notebook from Andriun's hand, and marched over to display it before the princess.

A moment passed before she frowned. "From what I recall, you're both wrong." She pushed the book back to the Magister.

Had she seen the notes? Was that her answer, a graceful way to tell them both to mind their own business, or had she misunderstood the point of the notebook's presentation? Andriun hesitated, then pointed toward Zaide. "I want a second opinion."

"I want you to leave me out of it," Zaide replied. "I don't care about your notes."

Andriun stood anyway. He rounded the fire to take the notebook and handed it to Zaide. "Does this placement make sense to you?" He tapped the notes with a fingernail that was perhaps a shade too long. The absence of the life comforts he had known among his people had manifested in peculiar ways.

Zaide glanced at the page, then looked again. His brow furrowed.

More of a reaction than the princess had given. Whether that was good or bad, Andriun did not know.

"On second thought," Zaide murmured, "give me that pencil. I think the princess was right."

Andriun pointed, instruction for Tula to bring the pencil. "See? He agrees with me. He was a scholar too, was he not?"

"Not a very good one," Lark grumbled.

Zaide ignored her and scratched something out. He held the book against his knee as he wrote, doing his best to keep the side of his hand from touching the paper. Andriun had never seen anyone left-handed write before. The whole process struck him as so awkward, he could not imagine Zaide at a desk at all.

When the note was finished, Zaide clapped the book shut on the pencil and passed it back. "If you're going to rewrite everything that happened on this trip, you're going to need to make sure you've got sources to support your claims."

"Analytical of you." Lark pulled some supplies from her bag and settled to eat.

Andriun opened the book to see what it said.

Escape first. Then we talk.

Uneasiness bubbled in his stomach like a taste of bad fish. This time, forcing a triumphant smile took more work. "See?" he said as he displayed the answer to Tula. "I was right, you did not have it in the right spot."

"And neither did you." Tula leaned close to squint at the page. She frowned, first at the writing, then at Andriun. The expression was more severe than a mere mistake deserved. He glanced toward his fellow Desheni, but they paid their squabbling little mind. Perhaps Tula's role as an academic had been played up enough to make her concern over notes believable.

Andriun made a soft, thoughtful sound in his throat, then closed the book and pushed it into her hands. He already knew they needed to escape their supervisors, and sooner than when they reached the border. With the number of goborrins in the forest, restoring power to the Spectrum Blade struck him as more urgent than ever before.

Perhaps that was an inappropriate sentiment. It had always been important; people had always been in danger. What did it mean of him that he was most concerned only when his own people were threatened?

But they were already at risk. The thought sprang forth unbidden, unwelcome and unpleasant enough that he squeezed his eyes closed. Perhaps the true problem was that he had waited too long to act.

"Well," he said when a morose silence had fallen across the camp, "we will have to wait until daylight to sort out the rest.

Some of those pages have grown difficult to read. In the meantime, allow me to forage nearby. I will find herbs for a good Desheni tea."

That caught the attention of one of their escorts. He pushed himself up with a smile. "I'll go with you."

Going alone would be faster, but involving one of the guards assigned to their group would make everything else easier. Andriun grinned at him. "Good, thank you. Her Highness has seen little of our hospitality. I believe there are berry bushes nearby, their leaves will make a good addition."

"If only we had honey," another complained.

"We will make do with berries." Andriun motioned up the slope he intended to climb. He had not gone far before the firelight grew too weak to see. He crouched to scoop a sliver of stone from the earth. It was cool in his bare fingertips, a reminder of the ice his father had wielded against them. He should have been prepared. The ice and water never should have taken him. He should have been ready to fight back, willing to do what he knew had to be done. Instead, he had clung to his ideals and his unwillingness to harm his people—his father, most of all.

Ironic, perhaps, that in trying to help them, he had wounded them more grievously than he ever imagined.

"Raspberries," his companion called in their own tongue.

Andriun nodded his approval as he curled his fingers around the stone and pushed power into it. He kept it soft and subtle, weaker than the Desheni lanterns his people used to carry to Ganede to sell. He needed little light. The calming white glow that filled it was more than enough. "I see a spicebark tree ahead. Have you a knife I could borrow?"

The hunter snorted. "We both know you wouldn't be trusted with a knife."

"By whom? Because it does not sound like you would not trust me." He pointed to the tree in question and waited for some of its bark to be added to the harvest.

Hesitance. The hunter glanced at him, then looked away. "Who I would choose to trust doesn't matter now."

"But it does." Something else caught Andriun's eye. He collected the herb and crammed it into his pocket while the hunter was distracted.

The warm scent of spicebark filled the air after just two cuts. The hunter paused with the tip of his knife resting against the tree. "We all know you won't abide by your father's orders." He spoke softly enough that his voice wouldn't carry. The camp wasn't far off. "None of us want that fight when the time comes."

"I do not ask for help."

"Good. Because I fear what Athradan may do if you get it." The hunter shaved a small piece of bark from the tree. Only the hardened, cracked exterior was taken; nothing deep enough to expose the green, growing layer underneath. "Spicebark is a good choice. It covers many flavors without being conspicuous."

Andriun raised a brow. "Help for the tannins in berry leaves. Only the finest for Her Highness to try. Bitter tea would not do."

His companion offered a wry smile and they completed the harvest in silence.

The herb in his pocket had not been seen, but Andriun already knew he was found out. They returned to the camp and laid out everything they had gathered so the princess and the other Desheni could examine it.

"Raspberry and blackberry leaves for health," Andriun announced as he pointed them out, once again speaking in the common tongue taught throughout most of Amroch. "Fresh raspberries for sweetness and flavor. White-star daisies to relax tired muscles, and spicebark shavings to add a warm taste."

The other Desheni nodded their approval.

The princess appeared intrigued. "A basic blend, but effective. What did you call this? White-star?" She picked up a small flower and turned it between her fingers.

"Chamomile," Zaide remarked.

"I have heard it called that, yes." Andriun grinned. "Our own words for some of these are different. I have translated them to the best of my ability."

"Well, I appreciate it. I look forward to tasting this blend." She placed the flower back with its fellows and made herself comfortable nearby, distracted with what appeared to be a book full of musical notes.

Andriun's smile faded as he jammed the herbs into a tiny travel pot one of the other Desheni had brought along. The hunter who had helped him gather herbs said nothing, but a sad look of resignation crossed his face.

Guilt dragged Andriun's heart down from where it ought to be, comfortable in knowing what he was doing was right.

Leaves, berries, and bark for taste, he thought as he poured liquid from his full water skin. White-star—chamomile, Zaide called it—as a relaxant.

And from his pocket, moth's tongue, for sleep.

CHAPTER TWENTY

ZAIDE JERKED AWAKE, puzzling over the whispered words he hadn't understood, though they'd roused him from sleep. His eyelids were like lead weights and protested against his efforts to pry them open. Everything was muddy, hazy, but something warm pressed into his hands cut through the fog.

A cup, he realized. Hands that weren't his own guided the cup to his mouth, where citrus-scented steam could tingle against his nose. He breathed deep, tried harder to open his eyes, and found himself squinting at Andriun.

His friend nodded in encouragement and pushed the cup more insistently.

Zaide drank.

On the other side of the fire, Tula and Lark drank, too. Behind them, their Desheni escort still lay sleeping.

Satisfied, Andriun patted his shoulder and left him to finish his drink on his own.

The princess watched as Andriun gathered everyone's bags and helped them with the straps. He carried one of the supply bags their escort had brought, along with his own things, and his spear rested on the ground beside the fire. Zaide hadn't noticed the Desheni bring it along, but he glanced at the knife serving as a spearhead and found himself grateful.

Andriun motioned for the girls to finish their drinks and rise, then looked toward Zaide. When he saw him watching, he raised his hand and gave two gestures. One to ask if he understood, and one to ask if he was all right.

Zaide nodded in response, though he was so groggy he could hardly think straight. The Desheni hunters still slumbered on the ground when he emptied his cup and pushed himself to his feet. He wasn't the only one who swayed, but Andriun appeared at his side to grip his elbow and help him balance. Lark and Tula clung to each other in a similar fashion. Neither said a word as they started down the road.

One step at a time, Zaide followed, grateful for his friend's support. They worked to keep their movement quiet as they stole away from the camp. After they'd stumbled half a mile, Zaide found his legs a little steadier and he walked on his own. By the time they reached what had to be the mile mark, they were all a little more alert.

Despite the distance between them and the camp, Andriun kept his voice low when he finally spoke. "I am sorry for the unpleasant awakening. The tea will help restore your senses faster."

Zaide grunted softly and rested a hand against the Spectrum Blade to keep it from bumping his leg as he walked. A sense of concern pinged against his skin. "I'm fine," he mumbled.

"You might be, but I feel like my head is full of wool," Lark said. She rubbed her eyes with the heels of her palms.

Andriun offered a nervous smile. "Yes. I am sorry."

The princess turned her head enough to give him a suspicious glower. "Why are you sorry?"

"That is the tea. The first tea." His expression faltered. "I did not partake so I would be able to rouse you."

Zaide's thoughts were still muddy, but not so muddy that he didn't grasp what was being said. "You drugged us?"

"I am sure I can think of a more polite way to say it, but for simplicity, yes. I do not think the hunters would have been willing to drink if all of you avoided consuming the tea. Since I was busy serving it, I do not think they noticed that I did not drink."

Tula squeezed her head between her hands. "I'm going to stop accepting drinks that people offer me. At least I can walk in a straight line now."

"And now we can figure out what we're supposed to do." Zaide shook his head as if that might help his grogginess. He was comfortable trudging along, but his thoughts weren't turning as fast as he felt they should. By now, he should have had ideas to lay out. "We've got to do something about those goborrins, and..." He trailed off and glanced Andriun's way.

"And your father," Lark added with a pinch of apology.

Andriun's brow furrowed. "My father?"

The princess did not elaborate. Instead, she cast Zaide an expectant look. He tried not to cringe. Why him? She was the self-appointed leader of this expedition.

"There was a camp just over the hill." Zaide pointed in the direction he meant, though they'd long since passed beyond that hill and the nest of goborrins that waited behind it. "Lark wanted to see it so she could determine their numbers, maybe try to send a letter to Jadora to ask for help, but when we crested the hill, Athradan was there."

Disappointment, then resignation crossed his friend's face. But not surprise. "Ah."

Tula raised her brows, but Lark was the one who spoke. "You knew?"

"No," Andriun said slowly. "But I... suspected. I have suspected for a long time."

A conversation from what felt like another time sprang from Zaide's memory. "When we first met, when we went to get the Captured Spring. You said you didn't trust your father."

"Yes." Andriun put his head down, as if admitting it shamed

him. "I did not have proof, but I... well, if this is what you say you have seen, I believe you. And my heart hurts for it." He put his palm flat against his chest.

For all that he remained solemn and stoic, Zaide recognized his hurt. Deception from one you were supposed to respect *did* hurt. The Elder came to mind and for the first time, Zaide wondered what proof there was that the old man's secrecy had been born of good intentions.

"I have a question," Tula put in.

Andriun kept his head bowed, but opened a hand in invitation.

"Your speech pattern is different from the other Desheni. Your accent is the same, but the rest of them speak with contractions, while you don't. Why is that?"

The question was so far detached from the situation at hand that Zaide grimaced hard enough his eyes shut. "What? What does that have to do with anything?"

The Magister gave a little pout and held up her notebook. "I'm just trying to fill out the section on the Desheni."

"Maker's mercy, Tula!" Lark cried. "Now is hardly the time."

"I can speak with contractions," Andriun said, unbothered. "You heard some of our language. It is sharp, a combination of sounds that click or whoosh, noises that derive from what is audible underwater. Our language doesn't use contractions because the blending makes it hard to understand. I feel the same about your language. All the it's and don'ts and won'ts, they sound muddy. So it's not that I can't. I just don't like them."

Zaide and Lark both stared at him.

Tula scratched furiously in her notes.

After a moment, Andriun cleared his throat. "But Her Highness is right. It is not the time for such conversations. We have gone perhaps two miles, and we must curve east if we are to return to the birthplace of water."

"We should get off the road," Zaide said. "I know your

people are good trackers, but staying on the road makes it even easier for us to be found."

Andriun scanned the slopes in the dark. "Between the two of us, I believe we may be able to mask our passing. There. We will cross through the brush and press east."

"Mask our trail?" Tula asked. "Like brushing it away with leaves?"

Andriun frowned. "How are you supposed to brush tracks out of mud?"

"We pass through the brush here, single file, then fan out. We want to be a few feet apart so we don't leave a single clear trail. Go slow, so you don't break any branches." Zaide pointed into the woods. "We'll need to find an area with less undergrowth after that. Maybe a game trail. Once we find it, we'll do something about our shoes."

Lark went first. She selected an area between shrubs that was thinner and checked the flexibility of their branches before she pressed through. "I suppose brushing tracks away works perfectly well in the desert."

"Well, yeah, it's just sand." Zaide motioned for Tula and Andriun to follow the princess's lead.

Andriun waved a hand to suggest Zaide should go first.

The two regarded each other for a time before Zaide raised his hands to request a game of hunter-elder-fox. They'd tapped fists against their palms twice before Lark scoffed. "Zaide, just come. Stop wasting time."

Chastised, he put his head down and slipped between the bushes with Andriun at his heels. He would have preferred to be in the back, where he could ensure their passage was hidden well enough to meet his standards. He'd learned a number of tricks through the years, forced to work harder at stealth travel to compensate for the disadvantage of his coloration, so he couldn't help looking back to be sure things were done right. Andriun rearranged a few branches to mask where they'd passed before he moved on. Reluctantly, Zaide admitted he'd done fine.

They spread out and pushed on in silence until they reached an older part of the forest, where the thick canopy kept the scrub from growing. There, Zaide showed them how to cover the soles of their boots with leaves to reduce the prevalence of their footprints. When they continued, they traveled in a tidy line. Andriun took the front to lead them toward the birthplace of water, while Zaide took the back and tasked himself with masking their trail. By the time the sun rose, all of them were ready for a rest.

"We cannot linger," Andriun said as they perched on stones and fallen logs, things that wouldn't show signs of their passing.

Lark rubbed her eyes and buried her face in her hands to stifle a groan. "We still don't even know if this plan is going to work."

"We could always make a new plan." Tula drew her feet up onto her rock and hugged her knees. Mud dulled the rich red of her coat, and numerous clinging leaves and burrs threatened to damage the fabric when it came time for removal.

"She's right." Zaide ran his fingers through his hair, feeling across his scalp with each swipe of his hand. "We don't have to go back and retry at that spring. We never knew if it would work in the first place."

The princess snorted. "What other options do we have?"

Tula rocked backwards and pointed her toes to the sky. "We can always go back, catch Athradan while he's up to no good, then tell him he can either help us with the sword or have us expose his nefarious deeds to all the Desheni and the whole rest of the world."

"Nefarious deeds," Lark repeated.

"It is not any worse an idea than others that have been put forward," Andriun said. "I do not know if my presence would help in that case, though."

"But what if it did?" Zaide asked. "What if you being the one to tell the Desheni what he's done helps you regain their favor? At some point, they have to come to understand that everything you've done has been out of a desire to help." He paused to probe something a second time. A fleck of bark came away between his fingers.

Lark's nose crinkled. "What are you doing?"

"Checking for ticks." He resumed the effort with his head tilted at a funny angle.

Andriun rubbed his chin. "It is a possibility, I suppose."

"Ticks?" Tula blinked.

"No. Well, yes." Andriun frowned. "But we are not discussing the ticks."

Zaide finished his task and sighed as he picked dirt from his fingernails. "What do we lose by going back? Time?"

"Mental capacity?" Lark grumbled.

Andriun ignored her. "We risk capture. Perhaps worse. My people are not violent, but to continue to provoke them cannot end well." A crease of worry formed between his brows, but he drew a breath and put visible effort into smoothing his expression. It had to be difficult, facing a situation like this with equanimity. Not for the first time, the fleeting thought it was a shame Andriun was not yet Shaman crossed Zaide's mind. He would make a skilled diplomat.

"Then there are the goborrins," Tula added solemnly. "There are only four of us. We can't fight an army."

"We don't have to fight an army," Zaide said. "Just its leaders. Remember Jadora. Without a clear leader, the goborrins fled. The same thing happened in Kolmar." By now, the barrier to keep those monsters out had to be restored. He couldn't help but wonder about Aren and Resia and the state of things in his ruined home village, but worrying about Kolmar now wouldn't help anything.

Lark shook her head and pushed herself up from her seat. She paced like an anxious cat, her arms folded across her chest. "But this isn't like Kolmar. The leaders here are broken-born and the Shaman himself. For us to reclaim Jadora, the acting Magister died. Are you really willing to accept the same loss here?"

The fact the Magister had either killed himself or had been killed by his own side sprang to Zaide's mind, but something else struck him before he spoke. He narrowed his eyes. "Why does the death of the Shaman worry you more than the deaths of the broken-born?" They were all people, but her concern for the Paragon over the others was clear.

The princess gave an exasperated sigh. "Zaide—"

"Peace," Andriun interrupted, making a soothing motion with both hands. "We gain nothing from fighting each other. This argument will get us nowhere. I do not wish to see any death, but they have chosen their side and my father has, too. We will vote. Do we return to the birthplace of water, or go back and fight?"

"Fight," Zaide said without hesitation.

"The birthplace of water," Lark said, almost at the same time.

They locked eyes in a moment of silence. Irritation glowed in her eyes, which made him wonder at how quickly he'd decided. He knew the risks. The costs. But he wasn't sure he agreed with Lark's assessment, either. The false Magister had still been alive when the tide of battle turned. If they could imprison the leaders of the goborrin army here, perhaps it would have the same effect.

"Fight," Tula said a moment later. "That water place was uncomfortable, anyway." She rubbed her arms as if to ward off a chill.

Andriun gave a single nod. "Then the decision is made."

Lark dropped her arms. "What? You didn't vote."

"I am the one who asked. I abstain." He rested a hand against his chest in that earnest gesture he used so often. "Besides, the three of you are my superiors."

"What?" Tula dropped her feet to the ground. "None of us think that, Andriun. We're all equals here. If you think we should avoid your father, I'll change my vote."

He gave his head a firm shake. "No. My father made his decision. Now I must make mine."

"And that is...?" Zaide already knew his friend wouldn't change his mind, but there was a difference between moving forward in silence and giving him a chance to speak.

"I have been passive for far too long." Andriun bowed his head and exhaled, but when he looked up, his dark eyes were hard with resolve. "We fight."

CHAPTER TWENTY-ONE

"Here is the plan." Andriun hoped his voice sounded more confident than he felt as he unrolled the hide map and touched a finger to the tiny point that marked his home village. The space around that point held nothing but lakes, rivers, and vague indications of mountains. Some of those were not accurate in the least, but he would not fault the people of Ganede for trying their best. Their information was limited to what his people had shared. In the years since his people ventured to the city to trade, a lot of that information had become lost or muddied.

The others leaned close over the map as he gathered his thoughts. It was arrogant to call his scatterbrained notions a plan, but what else could he do? He had been the one to decide they should stand and oppose his father. There were rational ways to do that, and as the one once meant to take his father's place, he should have grown into an effective strategist by now. Part of him disagreed; the Desheni avoided conflict when possible. To seek it out now went against his nature, not only as a person, but as a member of his kind.

Andriun trailed a finger down to approximate the location of the goborrin camp he and Tula had encountered while fleeing the broken-born. "We will pinpoint the location of the goborrin camps first. We have encountered at least three, and we must be prepared to find more."

"The one where I saw your father was here." Lark touched a spot on the map that was uncomfortably close to his village.

Tula produced a pen from somewhere, as well as a bottle of ink. It should have come as no surprise that the scholar would be prepared to write things, but he had only seen her graphite pencil before now. "Should we number the camps, or name them? Something like that?"

"Numbers will do," Andriun said. Naming things gave them permanence. If he had his way, the camps would cease to exist before the week was out. He winced at his own hastiness as he moved his hand and let the Magister mark the campsites. How did he plan to eliminate entire camps? Even with every Desheni hunter behind him, they could not hope to destroy so many.

Zaide twisted a hand around the hilt of his sword in a steady, repetitive motion. He had nothing to add, but the eagerness in the restless way he moved told Andriun they would need to be cautious. He did not doubt his friend's capability in combat. He had seen enough firsthand, had dueled him and called a draw when he felt they risked real harm. Zaide had relented then, but Andriun found himself unsure. His friend was rash and bordered on reckless. How would he handle accepting orders from someone other than the princess? He had not taken well to instruction in the ice cavern.

"We will scout this far from the village." Andriun traced around the mark with a fingertip. It was a broad circle, but if they split up, they would cover the whole space in a day's time. "We need to know how many goborrins are in this space. They do not move quickly. If any are beyond this area, they will not reach us the day we begin things in the village."

"When we begin things, huh? So we're just gonna show up and stir up trouble?" Tula drew circles in the air with the tip of her pen.

"I do not like that choice of words, but yes. We will estimate the number of goborrins, speak to any hunters we encounter while we are scouting, and plan to meet at the edge of the village before dawn tomorrow morning."

An uneasy frown touched Zaide's face. "Meet at the village? So we're going to split up?"

Andriun nodded. "We will be unable to scout this much territory if we do not. First, we must know how many goborrins are near enough to attack when I confront my father."

The princess gave her fingers a flick. "That will be fine. We are all capable enough to defend ourselves if we run into trouble. Although I suggest we plan to meet at the north end of the lake and travel to the village together. That way, if any of us encounter trouble, we know where to go to wait for the others."

He nodded again. "Then that is what we shall do."

Tula cleaned her pen before she put it away. She had already marked the scant few camps they had found. "So when you say you're going to confront your father, does that mean more arguing? Or are we talking about another kind of confrontation?" She curled her hands to fists and raised them to signal a fight.

Andriun wished that was not what he meant. "I will speak with him first, as is our way. But I do not anticipate the conversation will go well. If he is working with the forces of Gadranus, as Zaide and the princess have seen, then I anticipate he will call on them to dispose of me for making myself a persistent pest."

"I have a proposal, then," Zaide said.

Andriun and the others all cast him expectant looks.

"We should head to the first camp together, then split up after we've established what sort of information we need to make note of at each campsite. Things may come to mind as we look, and we won't have any way to ensure the others get that information if we don't establish that we need it ahead of time." Zaide's hand returned to the Spectrum Blade and for a moment, his eyes unfocused.

The way the sword communicated with him was a curious thing. Andriun still sensed nothing from the blade, but whenever he looked at it, he sometimes took the strange notion it was looking back. Such as now. Uneasiness made his spine prickle and Andriun returned his eyes to the map. "I would prefer if we separate early, but I understand your concerns. Perhaps instead of searching for a new camp, we should return here, to the one nearest the village. We have doubled back a good way since escaping our escort. It should not be far."

"Does that take us too close to the village?" Lark looked to him in concern.

"It is close, but if we approach from the western side, we should avoid attention." In truth, he was not confident of that, but he put on a brave face. What else was there to do?

"Does it matter?" Zaide asked with a hint of that impatience that drove so many of his actions. "Do we even need these numbers? A lot can change in the span of a day. We can count all the goborrins we want and it won't change that we're going to have to fight them off."

Andriun sat on his heels, considering. To an extent, he wondered the same thing. Did it matter? What was the point? Perhaps all he was doing was stalling, keeping himself from having to challenge his father in the way he most dreaded. They would not understand. Perhaps they could not, without knowing what challenging the Shaman in the way he intended would mean for his people. That was something they did not need to know. Duels were not unheard of among other cultures, but these were his people, his ways. A duel between Desheni was not to be taken lightly.

"I understand this concern," Andriun said slowly, "but I still believe it is best if I know what to expect. If the village is attacked during my confrontation with my father, the two of us will be unable to aid its defense. Would you walk blindly into battle, not knowing what awaited you?"

He regretted the question almost as soon as it left his mouth, for Zaide shrugged.

"We do seem to have done that often enough," Lark admitted.

Andriun glanced between them. "I apologize, Your Highness, but you do not strike me as that impulsive."

"Oh, she's very impulsive," Zaide muttered.

Tula raised her fists before her chest in excitement. "Me, too!"

Now Andriun regarded her, too. "You do realize that none of this is reassuring?"

Zaide rubbed the back of his neck. "We're working on it."

"Well, it sounds like having a reasonable adult in your group will be good for all of us," Andriun grumbled. He rolled the map and handed it back to the princess.

"Are you an adult?" Tula peered at him thoughtfully. "Your face is all smooth, I thought you were a beardless baby like Zaide."

"Hey," Zaide growled.

Andriun was not offended. "Desheni men do not begin to grow beards until they are well into adulthood. Perhaps when they are sixty years of age or so, their beards will grow. But I lack my father's hard jawline. My face is more like that of my mother. I am unsure if I will let mine grow, when the time comes." He rubbed his chin thoughtfully. "But that is still some time off."

"For most of us, sixty would make one an elder," Lark said as she put away the map. "I have heard the Desheni have longer lifespans, but I did not realize it was that much greater."

"According to our records, limited as though they may be, the typical life expectancy for one of the Desheni is around a hundred and twenty years," Tula said.

Zaide stood and offered Lark a hand. She ignored it and he curled his fingers into his palm. "So not too much longer than the rest of us. I think Kolmar's Elder was like ninety years old."

The princess frowned at him. "The last I knew, you said he was eighty."

"Did I? I don't really know." Zaide flashed her a grin. "I do know he was old, though. Besides, it feels like it's been ten years since we set out from Kolmar." Something dark touched his eyes. A burden, Andriun thought; he had seen that shadow in the eyes of elders, those who had lived through more troubled times than he. Something for them to speak of at another time, he decided.

"The days do blur together and stretch, but we are not served by dallying, no matter how long a time it feels we have. If we could linger, I would make spears. Come. Let us round to the west side of the goborrin camp and take count while the daylight is good."

Tula sighed and pushed herself up from the dirt. Clear imprints from her knees stayed behind. "So I guess we won't have time for a nap, huh?"

"If I still held the Captured Spring, I would offer you a taste of its tincture," Andriun said. "Unfortunately, for this task, we will have to rely on grit alone."

"Good thing we've got plenty of that." Zaide dusted his hands against his thighs and turned to the west, though he could not hide his dismay.

Andriun did not know what else to say, so he took the lead, and the others followed without complaint.

They trekked westward in single file, still mindful of the tracks they left behind. The Desheni hunters they'd escaped were sure to be looking for them; after Lark and Zaide had confirmed his suspicions about his father, Andriun doubted the man would be kind in the wake of their failure.

He knew the forests well enough to be sure of their location as they curved south of the village and around the west side of where the camp would be, crossing over the road they had escaped from just the night before.

By the time they reached a point he thought they could veer back toward the camp, though, all of them flagged. Tula, in particular, he thought looked unwell. Perhaps her time as a librarian had not required much endurance. But the princess fared little better, her eyes as heavy as her step. Reluctantly, Andriun scanned the forest. They were far enough from where they started, and far enough into territory he doubted anyone would think to look for them after their escape.

"We will rest," he announced, though he did not want to stop. The sooner he knew what they were up against, the better. But they were of no use to anyone if they encountered trouble while exhausted, and it was safer to sleep in a group.

"Thank the Maker," Tula sighed as she sank to the leaf-covered earth where she stood. She tipped over with her eyes shut so fast, he almost thought she had fallen asleep before she reached the ground.

"Can we afford the pause?" Zaide alone looked as if he could keep going. Was it strength or determination that kept him moving? That was one thing Andriun would acknowledge with respect; Zaide's determination knew no bounds.

"We can't afford not to pause." Lark settled beside Tula and reached to smooth the other girl's hair. Tula made a sound of annoyance and batted at her hand like an agitated cat. She was not asleep yet, then. Perhaps the princess had disturbed her as she drifted off.

Zaide wore a frown, but he sat. For a time, the group was quiet, and he tilted his pointed ear to the trees.

Silence ruled there, more unsettling than any army they could have heard.

"The birds don't like goborrins," Zaide murmured, as if that explained everything.

Andriun hoped it did. He had little experience with the creatures. "Are they close enough for concern?" He mimicked his friend's volume. They should have been far enough from the camp that they could rest without worry, but he did not know how far or how often goborrins scouted.

For a time, Zaide said nothing. He scanned the forest, his eyes a colder blue than Andriun remembered. Evidently, he saw nothing of concern. His shoulders relaxed first, but his eyes remained hard, sharp, like honed ice. "Should be fine."

Andriun considered scouting toward the camp while the others rested, then thought better of it. They were all tired, including him. There was no sense looking for trouble. It would find them on its own soon enough.

He gave himself the first watch; after an hour, Zaide woke and volunteered to take a shift. Sleep did not come easy, despite the fatigue that made Andriun's bones feel heavy, but he drifted off at some point, for he startled when someone shook him awake.

Andriun blinked away his weariness and frowned up at Tula in confusion. He had expected Zaide. Instead, the Magister hovered close with a finger pressed to her lips.

A moment later, his grogginess cleared enough to let him hear the steady pulse of drumbeats echoing throughout the woods.

"Goborrins," Lark whispered nearby. "Drumbirds aren't quite so deep."

They also did not range so far north. Andriun had never heard such a call and could not fathom what a drumbird might be. Would the village elders recognize the noise? Would they be suspicious of something so out of place? Some of them had traveled far, ventured as far as the landing point where his people had first come ashore to answer the Maker's call to defend the birthplace of water. That was farther south than even Zaide's home, where he assumed the creatures were familiar.

Andriun gripped his spear. He still missed his gloves. "We will get a look at their camp now." Were they moving? The drum calls had to mean something. Did they plan to attack his people? No, that made no sense. His father's involvement should have promised some sort of protection. At least, that was what he told himself. It made it easier to understand the betrayal when he assumed it had been committed as a way to shelter the rest of the Desheni.

The others nodded and gathered their bags. Zaide already carried his. The broken-born crept through the trees, inching closer to the camp as if called.

For one brief moment, Andriun considered calling him back. But Zaide was experienced, well-armed, and knew what to expect from the beasts in the camp. He made as good a leader in this moment as Andriun himself could. When Zaide looked back, as if to ask for instruction, all he did was nod.

Tula and the princess fell in at Andriun's back, and he followed Zaide up a slope and down its other side. The next crest was higher, if barely, and the underbrush made it difficult to pass without noise. Zaide's movement was all but silent, practiced and confident. Between the two of them, they should have marked an easy path. Somehow, Tula still rustled every branch she encountered.

Hopefully, goborrins had bad ears.

As he crested the hill next to the camp, Zaide dropped low and raised an arm to obscure the stark white of his hair. His face twisted and he turned back, breath drawn to speak. He thought better of it, for he beckoned Andriun closer with one hand.

Frowning, Andriun crouched and slid through the brush to see what lay ahead. He had expected an ugly campsite, haphazardly thrown together, strewn with weapons and grumbling monsters.

Instead, he was greeted with a handful of cages in orderly rows. Beyond them, pale canvas tents stood out against the vivid green of the landscape, but it was a different color that drew his eye downward, to the cages.

Blue.

His own people, taken captive.

CHAPTER TWENTY-TWO

ZAIDE WASN'T sure what the word that escaped his friend's mouth meant, but he understood the tone. Judging by the state of their garb, the Desheni in the cages below were hunters who had been captured some time ago. Each of the five hunters sat in their own cage, isolated from the others. A few cages were empty, but all of them were set far enough apart that the captives would not have been able to reach each other.

Lark crept up by his side. They were still a good number of yards from the camp's edge, but the stillness of the camp was unnerving enough that when she spoke, it was scarcely more than a whisper. "Why capture them? Why not kill them?"

Their captivity was unexpected for a number of reasons, but the strangest part was the lack of guards. No one watched the captives. Sitting as they were, with their heads down and limbs still, perhaps the goborrins had decided guards weren't necessary.

"They are dangerous," Andriun murmured. "We will speak with them. We will set them free and we will ask them what they know."

"It could be a trap." Zaide couldn't fathom it being anything else. How did they know they were even truly captives? They were dirty, but maybe it was all a ruse.

Andriun shrugged. "I will go."

"No," Lark said, putting an arm out before him so he couldn't move. "I will."

Zaide's eyes snapped to her face. "What?"

She met him with a level stare. "If it's a trap, it's better that it spring on just one of us. Andriun will be the next Paragon of Water. Tula's the Magister, and you're the Bladebearer. I will go. Of everyone here, I'm the least valuable."

"*What?*" Zaide's voice cracked, even in a whisper.

To his left, Tula crouched on the other side of Andriun. "What are we doing? Oh, prisoners. How'd they get there?"

Before any further argument could be made, Lark drew her knives and crept forward. Zaide tried to grab her, but Andriun gripped his shoulder and held him back.

"Let her," the Desheni hunter whispered.

"But—"

"We will protect her if something goes wrong," Andriun said. "Give her this opportunity to prove herself, if it is what she desires."

Zaide would have preferred to charge in ahead of her, put himself between her and the goborrin camp. Andriun's hand tightened until he relented, though he couldn't tear his eyes from Lark's back as she crept down the hill.

At last, she reached the first of the Desheni in cages and knelt to whisper to the captive hunter. Bright, genuine hope lit the woman's face and she reached through the bars to grip Lark's hands as they spoke.

"I know her," Andriun whispered.

"I mean, you should know all of them if they live in your village," Tula said.

Any other time, Zaide might have replied with a snappy comment of his own, but a prickle of discomfort crawled through his side and writhed its way up his spine. The sensation clawed at the back of his head and made him shudder. He moved a hand to the Spectrum Blade at his hip. *I don't like it, either,* he thought at the sword.

It sent a more anxious prickle in response, and he hated to admit it was right. He wasn't just the hand that wielded the Spectrum Blade. He was Lark's appointed Bladebearer. She'd introduced him as such. His place was there, in the hollow beside the winding camp that nestled between hills.

What was the point of that, anyway? Camps were meant to be on hilltops, the high ground easier to defend.

Unless that's the point. His eyes flicked up, toward the trees, and his heart skipped.

He leaped to his feet.

"Zaide," Andriun prompted, but he saw them a moment later. Goborrins between the trees, lining both sides of the camp.

That was the trap. The goborrins did have the high ground, and placing the Desheni captives in the valley meant Lark was open, vulnerable, and disadvantaged.

The Spectrum Blade hummed as Zaide drew it from its sheath. Its surface whirled with colors, agitated, eager for battle, but dread filled his veins. They weren't supposed to be seen. Not so soon. He couldn't cut through an entire camp, could he?

Lark had two Desheni free. Zaide hadn't seen how she did it, but she moved on to a third before one of them cried something and pointed up the hill.

Once spotted, the goborrins abandoned any pretense of stealth. They bellowed and roared as they flowed down the hill. It wasn't a full army—not enough to populate a camp that size—but enough to overwhelm anyone who came to aid their captives.

The Desheni woman Lark had freed first grabbed her by the shoulders and spun her toward the slope, shouting something. Zaide didn't hear. He was already on his way down, cutting across the hill at an angle to meet the goborrins.

Somehow, they didn't see him coming until it was too late.

He swept his sword up into one's side and the beast went down hard, light searing in its wound. The lack of proper armor had always been a blessing, yet it was such a disadvantage that Zaide didn't understand why they hadn't changed their state of dress. They'd come from somewhere, crossed into Amroch through Kolmar's forests. Surely they knew about him by now.

Instead of joining the fight, Lark moved to the next cage. Three of the Desheni were loose; they crowded around her in battle-ready stances, though they bore no weapons. Zaide couldn't look at them long, but that glance was enough to convince him they meant her no harm. As he lunged forward to catch a second goborrin with a stab to the back, steel flashed beside his head.

Andriun's spear—still tipped with his Jadoran knife—whirled in and took another goborrin in the shoulder before it could bring its club down on Zaide's head. Maker's mercy, where had that one come from? Before he could turn to look, a fireball streaked past them and Tula let out a whoop when it struck its intended target.

"Be careful with that!" Andriun shouted, sharing Zaide's exact sentiments.

The goborrins from the opposite hill were closing in on the cages. Lark glanced up a dozen times as she tried to open the latch on the fourth cage. She hacked at a lock with her knives, each strike growing more desperate. She couldn't try much longer.

Zaide bolted down the slope and flung himself into their path, just as a sword flashed for the princess's head. The Spectrum Blade sparked, but the force of the goborrin's swing cast him off balance.

"Get them out of here!" Lark shouted.

"Little busy right now." Zaide gritted his teeth and turned his stumble into a spin. Instead of striking a goborrin, the Spectrum Blade tore through the uppermost part of the wooden cage. He hadn't planned it, but the blade cut through the bars as easily as goborrin flesh, and he reoriented himself to meet the next attack.

The Desheni knocked over the cage behind him, helping their companion free. One prisoner left, then they could run. He scanned the woods ahead and grimaced. One prisoner, and at least thirty goborrins.

Andriun and Tula tore into the left flank, so he focused on the right.

Fifteen. He only had to kill fifteen more. His strike went wide and his sword missed its mark. By some miracle, an axe that should have cleaved him in two missed, and the breadth of its swing gave him time to reevaluate the situation.

He'd dealt with more than this. He'd carved his way through an entire army outside of Amrochan. Yet now, with a band of only thirty goborrins—no, fewer, the others had felled three more—he couldn't stave them off. His body ached, his muscles burned.

He'd hit his limit, and adrenaline was no longer enough.

In that instant, his priorities shifted. Release the last Desheni. Escape.

The goborrins came at him like a wall of too-pink flesh and his stomach dropped. The space between the cages was tight. He had nowhere to go and not enough room to fight. He deflected one sword after another, but the goborrins drove him back until he stumbled against Lark.

Andriun cut and sliced, but the Jadoran knife on his spear was less effective against beast flesh than the Spectrum Blade. He should have traded that for something else, something that could cut through armor with ease. If they could find the Molten Dagger in their things, then...

Idiot, Zaide snarled at himself. Artifacts. Where were the artifacts? He dropped to one knee, letting a goborrin's blade pass over his head as he swung his bag around and plunged a hand into it. He was too tired to think straight, too tired to remember the tools at his disposal.

He tore the Hymnflute and its holster from his bag, where he'd tucked it with the intent to practice and rewrite songs from Resia's ruined songbook.

Zaide raised the pipes to his lips and blew hard. Wind lashed outward with the shrieking notes, knocking goborrins backwards. They stumbled over each other and fell, squalling and covering their ears.

He couldn't play and fight at the same time, so he shifted into the song they'd used to spin a barrier before, the invisible shield of air springing forth just as Tula released a fireball. It skidded against the barrier's surface before streaking into the mass of goborrins, earning a squeal of surprise from the Magister. Beside her, Andriun's face morphed from surprise to delight. Of course; he hadn't seen what the Hymnflute could do.

The two of them sprang forward to join Zaide and Lark inside the barrier and Zaide let it drop so they could, sucking in as much air as his lungs could hope to hold before he launched it again. Behind him, Lark cracked the last lock and the other Desheni crowded around her to help their comrade from his cage. All five of the hunters sent Zaide glances of reverence, bordering on awe.

The princess didn't offer them time to gawk. "Retreat over the hills, back the way we came!" she ordered, pointing with one of her knives. The tip of it was bent strangely from whatever she'd done to open the locks.

Andriun said something to the hunters in his own tongue and they all turned as Lark took the lead. Together, the group fled with the shield around them, but the goborrins pursued. Individually, they might have outrun them, but they had to stay close to stay within the Hymnflute's barrier, and the weary hunters slowed them down. Zaide dared not let the shield fall, but he flinched every time he heard weapons bounce off the barrier. That he heard them bounce off *air* was strange beyond reason, yet the prickle of frustration that ran up his left arm reminded him strange had become his way of life.

He stayed at the back of the group, the Spectrum Blade still in his grasp. The Hymnflute only needed one hand to play, a merciful piece of fortune he'd not appreciated before now. He tried to keep the shield steady as Lark chose the direction they went. Northwest, away from the camp, toward the village's lake.

Water. He recalled Andriun's magic and cast a look over his shoulder. Not all the goborrins followed them. Some had vanished, and he liked their odds better for now. If Andriun could summon ice to hold them, they could finish them off, even tired as they were.

As long as those missing didn't come after them with reinforcements.

"This way!" Andriun pointed with his spear and changed the party's direction. They cut straight north now, and Zaide assumed that meant he'd had the same thought. If they could get to the water, they'd have an advantage.

At the top of the next hill, a faint sliver of white gleamed in the distance. They were close. The lake was just ahead. Zaide could keep playing that long. They would make it that far. He allowed relief to wash tension from his shoulders.

His foot hit a stone and tore it loose from the earth. His leg twisted as he fell to the earth with a crack. The Spectrum Blade dug into the ground and tore free of his grasp as he rolled.

The shield fell and the goborrins howled in response. Panic clawed at Zaide's chest as they sprang for him.

The beast in the lead landed on Andriun's spear.

Lark skidded to a halt and turned back.

Zaide tried to push himself up. Pain knifed through his leg and he fell back to the dirt with a shout, then sucked in a breath through his teeth. Lark reached for him, but he thrust the Hymnflute into her hands. "Shield," he managed, the single word strangled.

Worry pinched her brow, but she was the only other person who knew the melody. She raised the Hymnflute to her lips and stepped back, giving room for the others to aid him.

Tula landed at his side next. She wedged an arm under his and helped him rise. The stabbing pain in his leg subsided to a throbbing ache as he raised it, removing pressure from the injury. One of the Desheni hunters they'd freed appeared at his other side.

"My sword," Zaide said. He looked back and flexed his fingers, as if that alone could summon the Spectrum Blade to his grasp.

Andriun twirled his spear, driving back the goborrins as the shield sprang to life again. The barrier thrust the pig-faced monsters farther from the group. He turned, regarding the Hymnflute with a new respect. "Why are we running?"

"Uh, so we don't get chopped up and eaten by those things?" Tula pointed at a goborrin as the beast slammed its chipped sword against the shield.

Zaide grimaced as he hopped on one foot, turning with his escort so he could retrieve the Spectrum Blade from the dirt. They helped him closer. The sword pinged with concern the moment his hand closed on it.

"No, I mean, why do we run if we have a shield?" Andriun pointed over his shoulder, at the same goborrin Tula had drawn to his attention. "There are many of us now, we can take turns. We listen to the song, watch how it is played. We can walk from here to the lake's edge, where the uncured ham can be drowned."

"Uncured ham?" Zaide struggled to keep his balance as he sheathed the blade. Tula's arm around his ribs helped, but the familiarity of the touch left him uncomfortable.

"It is supposed to be an insult," Andriun explained. "I do not suggest that we eat them."

"Yeah, that doesn't sound sanitary," Tula agreed.

Lark gave them such a death glare, they all fell silent and let the air be filled by the frustrated howls of goborrins and the sweet notes of the shielding song.

Their advance was slower after Zaide's injury, but the lake

grew nearer and a few of the goborrins peeled off instead of pursuing them with all the speed of a drowsy snail.

When the princess began to labor over the song, Andriun took a turn. His first notes were halting and the barrier trembled, giving rise to a new chorus of jeers from the goborrins that tailed them. He adjusted and the shield grew more stable.

Lark seized Zaide's arm from Tula and took the Magister's place. "Watch him play. You're next."

"I already know how the Hymnflute works," Tula protested.

"Oh, you've played it and know the song by heart?" The princess raised a brow.

Tula's mouth worked a moment before she shut it and turned her attention to Andriun's efforts.

The Desheni hunter on his other side traded places with one of the others. The rest of the Desheni walked in a group, speaking in low tones. The Hymnflute hid their words, though Zaide doubted he'd understand them, anyway. Still, he watched them from the corner of his eye as he hopped along, searching for signs the weary hunters might turn on them. He saw none.

"I'm sorry," Lark breathed as they climbed a more difficult slope.

Zaide struggled to keep his foot from touching the ground. "For what?"

She lowered her eyes. "If I hadn't given the Captured Spring back to Andriun, then..."

"Athradan would have found it and taken it either way," he said before she could find her words and go on. Hopping was hard; he was out of breath long before they reached the top. It took him a moment to continue.

Lark took it as an opportunity to speak. "But I should have anticipated the problem. I knew it was too valuable, yet I even offered to give it back, and now—"

"Now we'll just have to get it back." He bumped his toes against a stick and grunted at the pain from that single touch.

There was little alternative. If they didn't recover the artifact, he'd be unable to fight. He grimaced.

"Is it bad?" the princess asked, but the face he'd made hadn't been from pain.

He licked his lips and flinched at the mingled taste of sweat and dust. "Listen. The Molten Dagger—"

"I have it," she said.

Good. "You need it. Use the dagger. Give your knives to two of the hunters. I can't help you." And without the Spectrum Blade, cutting them down would be harder. If he was incapacitated, would the sword allow someone else to handle it until he recovered?

A strong sense of negativity flooded into him from the sword's place at his side.

He sighed in frustration. "If I'm your handler, you should have to follow my directions sometimes."

The princess stiffened beneath his arm. "I beg your pardon?"

"Not you."

Her eyes flicked to the sword's hilt, hovering between them.

"It won't let anyone else use it," he said to confirm. "Not even temporarily."

"It told you that?"

It may as well have. He started to say as much, but a thread of wariness touched him from the sword's apparent consciousness, and he glanced to his other side. The Desheni hunter helping him walk wore a guarded expression, one that made Zaide uncomfortable. He disguised his glance by looking past the man, searching for his other friends. "Does Tula still have a blade? That would equip three of the hunters." The Magister had swiftly grown adept at flinging fire around, something he supposed he'd have to worry about at some point. For now, it would be convenient.

"Four, if we make Andriun give up his spear and have him focus on his magic." Lark looked back, too, frowning at the sight of Tula holding the Hymnflute. The barrier hadn't shuddered when she took over, indicating she'd done a good job of paying attention to the song.

Zaide considered them for a moment, too, then made himself nod and look ahead. "That may be our best bet. That leaves just one of them unarmed."

"To help you walk?"

"I'd be fighting if I could." Zaide would have preferred to put himself at the front of the fight with the Spectrum Blade in his hand. Maker's mercy, what would happen if they didn't get the spring back from Athradan? He'd never broken any bones before and didn't know what it felt like. It could be a sprain, he thought, but either one could leave him unable to walk for weeks. Could something as desperate as war wait that long?

"I know you would." The look the princess gave him was more reprimanding than knowing.

Zaide forced himself to smile back.

Her eyes widened with surprise, then indignation clouded her face and a rosy shade of irritation bloomed in her cheeks.

Before she could give him an earful—his better ear was toward her, too—Andriun pointed ahead with his spear.

"Head for the beach," Andriun ordered. "Enter the water."

Of course. Goborrins couldn't swim. If Zaide couldn't fight, the water was the safest place he could be. He nodded, but his eyes flicked to the Jadoran knife that still served as spearhead. "Andriun, your spear—"

"I heard. It does not leave my hands. I am capable, but not so capable that I can leave myself defenseless. Two hunters will accompany you in the water. They will keep you safe."

Zaide wanted to argue, but thought better of it.

Scarce moments later, they reached the water's edge and Lark stepped away, leaving him with the Desheni hunter for support. She thrust her silver knives into the webbed hands of two other hunters, who accepted them, but seemed uncertain. She produced the Molten Dagger from somewhere Zaide couldn't see.

Tula passed over her curved blade without halting the Hymnflute's song, and the remaining unarmed Desheni kicked off her boots and moved to Zaide's side.

"Into the water." The woman pulled him toward the shallows. He didn't have time to remove his boots.

They were no more than waist deep before the Hymnflute's barrier fell.

A dozen bellows of delight went up from goborrin throats.

"Brace yourselves," Andriun shouted as he stepped backwards into the water.

Zaide didn't know how he could brace for anything, but he let the two Desheni pull him into the waves.

Startled, he looked down at the lake. Lakes weren't supposed to have waves, yet they lapped toward the shore with growing strength until suddenly, everything lurched so hard that Zaide thought he'd be ill.

The goborrins had begun a rush down the slope, but now they paused, realizing their mistake.

Andriun spread his arms, and the water answered his call.

CHAPTER TWENTY-THREE

THE WAVE ROSE until Andriun stood in its shadow, his arms wide, welcoming attack.

Some twenty feet away, the goborrins milled, some snorting and licking their noses, others drawing back. They eyed the others as if they were hungry and their opponents were a meal. Perhaps they were. Andriun would not pretend to know what goborrins ate.

He met their eyes, willed them to strike first.

Tula did, instead. "Let's go!" the Magister shouted as she swung her arms forward and brought her hands together. Fire burst from her hands and poured across the open space. Goborrins roared as the flames engulfed them, their squalls so like those of wild boars that Andriun fought back a shudder.

He spun with his spear extended and the motion directed the water forward. Instead of crashing past his companions, the water arced overhead and slammed into the goborrins, extinguishing Tula's flames. Fat plumes of steam spewed into the sky.

"Hey!" the Magister cried. She glared at him, her hands upraised, golden dragon marks shining on her arms.

Andriun ignored her. He swung the spear, directing the surge of water to solidify around the arms and legs of the monsters as they flailed. Ice crackled and hardened, but they were stronger than he expected, and several broke free. They crashed forward, but they came alone while the rest struggled in ice.

Despite their unfamiliar weapons, the three hunters darted forward to strike.

Tula ran to the side, earning herself enough space to swing her arms and direct magic again.

Andriun moved, too. He did not have to use his spear to move the water or form ice, but the magic answered more readily when his movements flowed like water. Tula's flames filled the air with the scent of burning flesh and the screams of dying beasts. Metal rang as the hunters he'd grown up with met the swords and axes of unfamiliar opponents. All the noise was upsetting and unsettling, but the water around his ankles was a soothing constant.

Water flowed back toward the lake as ice melted. He gathered it around his feet and spun it into a whip, cracking it across the slope. The goborrins were taller than the hunters and the water struck their upturned snouts. More than one stumbled, earning the opening his hunters needed.

The princess moved with them, her golden hair flowing behind her like a banner. At first, he had worried about the dangers of letting the princess fight. They had focused on running from encounters since they first met, but she was stronger than he anticipated, competent with the black glass dagger in her hand and just as courageous as Zaide.

Or perhaps that was as foolish as Zaide. Andriun glanced back to confirm he still floated alongside the hunters sent into the water. He felt bad to exclude him; Zaide was their most capable fighter, but he could not fight while injured. If he were not restricted to the water, Andriun suspected he would still try.

Zaide's attention was on the fight, a mix of frustration and concern on his face, but he remained in the lake.

Subtly, so gently none of them would feel what he was doing,

Andriun pushed against the water and moved them farther from the shore. Then he looked back and smothered a curse when he found a goborrin only inches from his face.

The monster roared and collapsed, clawing at Andriun's shoulder as it went down.

Lark stood behind it. She jerked the Molten Dagger back and shot him a frown. "Eyes forward."

Andriun did not know what to say, so he said nothing at all and gathered the water again. This time, he picked one enemy and drove lances of ice into its side, piercing the gap between plates of crude armor. His hunters advanced on the goborrins still trapped in ice and dispatched them, one after another, before they could escape. Together, Lark, Tula, and Andriun dispatched the rest.

It was only when the last one fell that he realized how weak they had all become. Their group was comprised of excellent fighters and powerful mages, armed with remarkable weapons. Yet they had struggled to destroy even a tiny fraction of the army camped on his father's doorstep. Travel had been hard, their pace brutal.

The water had saved them, allowing Andriun to trap two thirds of the goborrins that pursued them so they could face them with more reasonable odds. Had they not reached it, or had more goborrins followed, he was not sure the ending would have been the same.

"Pile up the dead and I'll burn them," Tula said, though she was breathless.

"No. Pile them and leave them. They will be a warning." Andriun strode toward the trees as he spoke. He collected a large, sturdy stick and carried it back toward the bodies.

The Magister gave it a dubious look. "What's that for?"

"Ah, a pike. To mount a head?" He pantomimed staking the ground and mounting one of the goborrin heads on it.

Lark made a sound of disgust. "We are not doing that. Leave the bodies. The goborrins who find them will know what it means. We need to get farther north, away from the rest. They'll send a scout after us eventually."

Andriun sighed and cast his stick aside. She was right. "We will find somewhere to rest, to camp. I will tend to Zaide's injury to the best of my ability."

"How are you planning to do that?" Zaide asked as he splashed to shore with the aid of the two hunters beside him. "You got some special healing skills you've been holding out on us?"

"Well, yes," Andriun said, "though I do not think they are what you mean. I am a healer because I know the medicine of my people. We do not cure everything with the Captured Spring. I know herbs, and I know how to care for wounds."

"Hopefully you know how to fix broken bones fast, then." Zaide winced as the hunters helped him back onto dry land.

Without a thought, Andriun made a dragging motion with one hand. Water fell from their garments.

Zaide blinked in surprise. "I don't remember you being that adept."

"I have had much time since I was exiled from my home, and little to fill it with." It was more explanation than Andriun cared to give in front of the hunters, but he figured it was polite to provide something. "I have had much time for practice."

For the first time, one of the male hunters addressed him. "Did you know we were captive in that camp?"

The question was not an accusation, but Andriun suspected it was more than curiosity or hope. "No," he admitted. "We approached with the intent of determining how many goborrins were near enough to attack the village. When we saw you, we could not leave without first seeing you go free."

"There are a number of goborrin camps in the mountains," the princess added. "If we find out how many, I may be able to petition my father for aid."

"Or we can ask Jadora," Tula put in.

Andriun wished they had not spoken at all. The hunter's eyes narrowed and for a moment, Andriun feared they had been part of the trap.

"You seek to aid the Desheni?" the hunter asked, looking between them.

"Of course," Lark said. "Don't you?"

Then the man exhaled and lowered his head.

Relief flowed over Andriun as smoothly as water.

"I am Adghadan," the hunter offered, more for the princess's benefit than anything. Andriun already knew who he was. "My party departed from our village two weeks ago. We stumbled across the goborrin camp in the forest."

"Adghadan?" Zaide repeated. "That's not going to work. Adghadan, Athradan, Andriun... That's too many A-D-N names. One of you needs to use something else."

"Zaide," Lark snapped.

The hunter did not seem offended. "You may call me Ghad, if you wish."

Tula shook her head. "No, I've been thinking of Gadranus as Gad for three weeks now. I'll get confused."

This time, a crinkle creased the hunter's brow.

Andriun grimaced. "You are all being very rude."

"You're making things difficult by having all these same-sounding names," Zaide replied.

"What do you suggest, then?" Adghadan asked, tone flat and clearly humoring them.

Tula tapped a finger against her chin. "Well, you could be Desheni Hunter One, that could be Hunter Two..."

"All right, now you are being rude," Zaide said.

The Magister harrumphed. "Have you got better ideas, then?"

At last, the princess stepped between the two and held up her hands to order both of them to silence. "Do you have a family name, Adghadan?"

The hunter frowned at her. "Ikan."

"May we call you by that name?"

He nodded, and Andriun breathed a sigh of relief. He should have asked for her diplomatic intervention sooner.

Ikan, as he was now known, gestured to the other Desheni men from his group. "This is Dak, and this is Belan. Family names, to spare you confusion," he added dryly before gesturing to the two women. "The others are Tanna and Leine. Those are not family names. Will they give you difficulty?"

"Not at all," Tula said with a smile.

Andriun scarcely kept himself from rolling his eyes. "You said your party left the village two weeks ago and you found the goborrin camp then. What led to your capture?"

The expressions of all five hunters darkened.

"We saw Athradan in their midst," Tanna said. "We thought he had been captured, or that he was in danger."

"So you know whose side he's on," Zaide said.

The look Ikan gave him was less than appreciative. "I had my doubts when I saw Andriun on the slope with strangers. Especially..." He trailed off, his mouth working a moment. What he wanted to say was obvious.

Zaide spared him the struggle by offering a smile that was almost genuine. "Yeah. I've been getting that a lot."

"I would imagine you have," Ikan said flatly.

Tanna shifted forward, her face and voice serene, perhaps to blunt the severity of her husband's words. "But a lot has happened. We know you are not your father's son, Andriun."

She meant it kindly, but Andriun still inwardly flinched. For much of his life, he had longed for Athradan's approval. Sometimes, he had been fortunate enough to gain it. That approval meant less now. He could not condone his father's choices or actions and could never support the man's apparent cooperation with their enemy, but part of him still felt as if he was suspended in Athradan's shadow, slowly growing toward the day the role of Shaman would be passed to him. To become a worthy replacement for his father had long been a desire. Now, though, he was uncertain how to feel.

Lark spared him from having to offer thanks. She held herself so regally, no one could ever doubt her identity. "I imagine you've pieced some things together by now," she said as she looked between Tanna and Ikan, "but I will offer further information. I am Dasienna, daughter of King Sendassian. Zaide wields the Spectrum Blade on my behalf and answers to me."

"Sometimes," Zaide muttered.

She shot him a glare, but regained her equanimity fast enough. "We travel with Tula, the new Magister of Jadora."

"Are they supposed to know that?" Tula asked with a hand cupped around her mouth. She earned herself a glare, too.

Lark went on. "We came seeking the Paragon of Water, as we need his blessing for the Spectrum Blade's power to be restored. He refused to assist us."

"Athradan has changed," Ikan admitted.

"Time changes us all," Andriun replied. It had come to change him faster than he desired. "But time is not on our side. Come. We must move north. We will round the lake and decide what we must do when we reach the far end." That would be far enough removed from the goborrin camp that the monsters would be unlikely to follow, and with the absence of ice around the lake after he and Zaide destroyed the colossal ice beast inside the cavern, there were no Tricen or other foul spirits to be found.

Come to think of it, much of the strange magic that had plagued his people had disappeared after Zaide took the Captured Spring and the cavern collapsed. Andriun had not considered that the massive, tree-like ice titan could have been what spawned the ice creatures that roamed the frigid nights. All he knew was his time in exile had been peaceful, and summer had grown warm again, without the influence of ice magic and the frozen lake.

The group followed without complaint as he stepped over a goborrin's corpse and trudged northward, his hand wrapped tight around his spear. That was something else he'd have to see to, once they found someplace to settle. For now, he set an easy pace, mindful of how fast Zaide could travel with one of the hunters on either side.

Murmurs of conversation reached his ears, small talk between his friends and his people, and the ease with which they spoke stirred a strange sadness in Andriun's chest. In years past, his people had often traveled to Ganede. He had gone with the trade parties plenty of times in the years that straddled the gap between childhood and manhood, but it was not until this moment, filled with friendly camaraderie between the hunters and the outsiders, that he realized he had missed those trips.

No, it was worse than that; he had come to resent the way his father isolated their people.

It will change, he told himself firmly. Everything would change, and he had begun to think that change would be soon.

Behind them, a low cadence of drumbeats confirmed his fear.

They could not move fast, but stopping too soon struck him as dangerous. The sun had settled low on the horizon by the time they reached a suitable resting place at the northwestern edge of the lake. The sound of drums had faded, though not so long ago as Andriun hoped. They could take a good night's sleep, but likely no more.

"Help him sit," he ordered as he put down his spear and opened a pouch at his belt.

Zaide had hobbled along with assistance all day without complaint, though exhaustion had etched lines into his face and left dark smudges beneath his eyes. Despite that, he still managed a thank-you as Tula and Belan helped him sink to the ground.

Andriun regretted that he had not stopped to tend to his friend's injury sooner, but the goborrin drums had hounded him, putting an itch between his shoulder blades that would not be pacified with a scratch. He chose a few tiny packets of herbs from his collection and knelt by Zaide's foot.

"Hope you got some magic in there," the broken-born joked, though his voice was strained.

Andriun wished he did. "Only herbs, but they will help. There are some for a poultice and some for you to drink. They will assist with the pain. Tula, will you start a fire?"

"Oh, I'm good at that," the Magister said cheerily. Her enthusiasm was far from comforting, but he let her take the hunters to gather what was needed to heat water for the herbal tea.

Lark and Tanna stayed behind, the latter occupying herself with the arrangement of stones for a fire pit while the princess knelt by Zaide's side.

Zaide gritted his teeth and sucked in a breath as Andriun removed his boot. There was considerable swelling. Yes, they should have stopped sooner.

"Are you able to move your toes?" Andriun asked, observing the way Lark stroked their friend's arm. The princess was something of a puzzle. She went to great lengths to make herself unapproachable, but she struck him as a tender soul wrapped in thorns of her own design.

"Not without it hurting a whole lot," Zaide said with his jaw clenched. But his toes did move inside his good woolen socks.

Tentatively, Andriun probed the injury. "Do you experience numbness? Or is there a specific sort of pain?"

"I feel everything, and everything hurts. Aches like a bad tooth." Zaide winced whenever Andriun pressed on it, but that was a good sign.

"I do not believe it is broken," Andriun said as he concluded his inspection and drew a tiny wooden bowl from one of his bags. "I will make a poultice for this."

Lark cast the things in his hands a suspicious glance. "Out of what?"

"Ah... I do not know your name for it. Ours means knitbone."

Which made Zaide frown, of course. "I thought you said it's not broken."

"I do not believe it is," Andriun repeated. "But knitbone will help with the bruising and swelling, and I will fashion you a brace." Out of what, he did not know. He did not have anywhere to get bandages, nor did he have anything from which he could make a comfortable splint. Sticks would do, but how good they would feel, he was not sure.

He collected a few decent straight branches from trees nearby. Tula and the others returned with firewood while he gathered them, and the fire crackled soothingly when he made his way back to sit and strip their bark. The princess already had water heating in a metal cup for Zaide's restorative tea to be brewed.

Ikan stayed by the campfire only long enough to exchange quiet words with his wife, then departed between the trees. There was anger in his step, but Andriun did not believe it was directed toward them. Everyone in the camp had to be frustrated, and everyone had different ways of handling that emotion. He tried to keep a tight rein on his own feelings. He still did not regret the choices he had made, even if they had shattered his life, but he was forced to admit—at least privately, to himself—that they had grown into an uncomfortably weighty burden.

Burden or not, though, he could not dwell on it. He noticed the way the other Desheni around the campfire glanced his way. They were troubled, hesitant, hoping for a leader they could trust. In spite of his choices, they wanted that leader to be him.

He could not disappoint them. Not with camps of goborrins close enough to crush his people. Yet all he could think of now was how easily his plan had been dashed by trying to view just one. They still did not know how many of the monsters roamed the north, and now he feared the goborrins—or the broken-born commanding them—would carry word back to his father.

A difficult place to be, Andriun conceded.

Maker guide me, he thought as he pushed herbs into the cup. *I am lost.*

"Where is he going?" Lark asked quietly when Ikan did not return.

Tanna circled the camp while the others rested, scanning trees the way Andriun had done. "To search for good stone."

The princess's brow furrowed, but Andriun knew what it meant. He did not know when they had discussed it, or even if they had; Ikan was the leader of the hunting party, and so Ikan's decisions for the party were final. Andriun would not complain.

It was a quiet vote of confidence, of support, a signal the Desheni they rescued had decided to join their cause.

He pushed the cup toward Lark, entrusting her with Zaide's care while he stood and untied the Jadoran long knife from the end of the staff he had cut with his friend's help, back in the mountains.

Lark took the cup, but looked at the blade in Andriun's hand with an unspoken question in her eyes.

Tanna pointed out a well-shaped and low-hanging branch, and he nodded.

"Tomorrow, we will face my father," Andriun said. "But tonight, we make spears."

CHAPTER TWENTY-FOUR

WHEN ZAIDE WAS THIRTEEN, his foster father, Verlin, had fallen from a tree while hunting. The Elder had made it clear how fortunate he'd been to have sustained no more than a broken leg, and a mild break, at that. He'd been off his leg for weeks. Zaide had taken as many of the man's responsibilities as he was able, though he recognized now that what he *had* done had been far too much to ask of a child.

They were fortunate the neighbors had been so caring. With their help, he'd hunted for the family, chopped firewood, tended repairs to the cottage, and still found time for all the drills and practice he'd taken for himself, back when he believed he might be selected in the Spring Choosing. Verlin had watched and guided from the sidelines, leaning on a wooden crutch as he shared directions and made suggestions, encouraging Zaide every step of the way.

Now, as Zaide practiced moving with a crutch of his own, he doubted his ability to do even that much for his friends.

"I think he needs two," Tula said after watching him circle the campfire twice. Lark stood behind her with her chin cradled in one hand.

His ankle felt better after a solid night of sleep, but he

suspected that had more to do with the willow bark in that bitter tea Andriun made. The injury had been splinted with sticks and wrapped with a knitbone poultice thick beneath the cloth, which he suspected had been cut from someone's spare clothes. He didn't recognize the strips of pale cotton as anything anyone had worn, and he silently prayed it wasn't made from someone's unmentionables. That would have been too embarrassing to bear.

"I think you're right," Lark said when he stopped. "Can we get another?"

The Magister nodded and wandered off between the trees. It had taken them some time to find a branch in the appropriate shape and size, and it would likely take longer now, since Tula would have to venture past the trees she'd already searched. Zaide tried to be appreciative of the rest that expedition would offer him. Slowly, he hobbled back to the fireside and sat.

Andriun and the other Desheni sat there, tying stone blades to spear shafts, making extra spearheads and weaving strips of bark into rope with a single-minded determination.

Zaide wished he could join them, but they worked so stoically that he felt unwelcome. He tried to remind himself that it wasn't about him; this was Andriun's fight, the Desheni's fight, and he would only get in their way. He'd help in other ways.

"Give me your knife," he said to Lark as she settled nearby.

She eyed him oddly. "Why?"

"So I can sharpen it." Which one he meant was obvious.

Lark considered the offer for a moment and he almost thought she meant to refuse, but eventually, she drew the blunted blade from its sheath at her thigh and passed it to him, hilt-first.

Zaide took it with care. The damage was not as bad as he'd first expected, though the edge on one side was definitely warped. He dug his whetstone from his bag, silently thanking whichever of the Jadoran guardswomen had the foresight to include it with his things. He'd hone his long knife before they moved on, too.

"I shouldn't be trusted with weapons," Lark said softly. "Maybe there's a reason the blade rejected me."

"Yeah, we both know that's not true and you're just feeling sorry for yourself. You should quit that, because I'm feeling a lot sorrier than you are right now, and you don't want to get me started." He brushed his thumb across the blade's edge, testing to see how dull it was and then tilting the knife to judge the angle of its bevel. This brought back memories, too, of all the nights he'd watched Verlin sharpen his good carving knives.

The princess regarded him in silence for a long time, then drew up her knees. "How do you always do that?"

"Do what?"

"Smile and joke without anything ever getting to you." She shook her head. "I wish I had half the courage you do."

"I don't feel very courageous," Zaide said. "Just stupid for tripping in the forest. My foster father would be ashamed of me. After all the work he put into teaching me how to get around in the woods, I went and did this." He waved a hand at his bandaged ankle.

She shrugged. "People have accidental injuries all the time."

"Yeah, but you have to admit it's a pretty bad thing to have happen to whoever is carrying this thing." He pointed to the Spectrum Blade at his side. The sword hadn't given him any more impressions or feelings since he'd considered passing it off to someone else. Now, he thought at it, envisioned himself giving it some sort of invisible nudge, but he didn't know what he was trying to push against, and no response came. He reached for the whetstone. "Get me some water for this, would you?"

Lark obliged, then settled to watch as he took her knife across the stone with steady, even strokes. "We'll get the Captured Spring back," she promised. "We'll get it today."

He kept his hands steady, mindful of the angle of the blade

against the stone. "I hope so. Imagine me limping around, trying to fight Gadranus and put an end to the Rise."

She appeared more troubled than amused. "We'll heal you. We have to."

"Maybe we could just cut it off. Save some time. Give me a wooden leg so I don't have to wait for anything broken to mend." He offered a smile, lest she take him seriously.

Lark almost cracked a smile of her own. "Or a peg, like a merchant I once saw in Amrochan."

"I'll keep a knife stuck in it, just to startle everyone." He turned her knife and gestured, as if he meant to poke his calf.

That stole a laugh, and she grasped his hands to force the knife back, as if she thought he really would.

Something weighed on him, and Zaide glanced up to see Andriun studying them with a neutral gaze. He sobered.

"We are ready," Andriun said without preamble. "Gather your things."

Lark's newfound cheer evaporated in an instant and she slipped away to collect the few belongings she'd unpacked. At some point, Tula had given the Vale Hymnflute back to the princess, and she slung the strap for its carrying harness over her shoulder so it dangled at her hip. She left her knife in Zaide's hands, so he returned to sharpening it.

"How do you expect this is going to go?" he asked as he worked. He didn't have anything to pack, aside from the whetstone he was using. It would be easy enough to slide back into his bag when he was done.

Andriun slid his own bag of supplies onto his shoulder. "We will confront my father before the whole village. Ikan and the others will support my claims during the confrontation. I do not expect it will go well, but either he will concede, or we will force him to do so." He paused, and his eyes traveled to the bandaging on Zaide's foot. He'd checked it that morning, so there was no reason to pay it any mind, but its existence seemed to trouble him. "We will recover the spring, one way or another."

And until they did, Zaide would be out of commission. The possibility of the meeting going so poorly that goborrins might end up being involved crossed his mind, but he refrained from laying that burden on top of those his friend already carried. Injury was awkward and frustrating, but Andriun had to face his own father. How would that feel, if the roles were reversed? Zaide fought back a frown at the thought.

They could be reversed. He'd never allowed himself to consider it until the moment they'd encountered that small group of broken-born in the mountains. No one knew where Zaide's father had gone; he assumed the man was long dead, but what if he wasn't? What if he'd abandoned his family in Kolmar on purpose, answered a call to some other cause? What if Zaide did have to confront him? The possibility left him cold, and his hands grew still with the knife.

Andriun sighed. "We will get it," he said, the words a promise Zaide hadn't expected. The hunter had interpreted his solemnity as something other than what it was. Not that Zaide could fault him for that. Lark knew of his desire to learn his father's fate, but he'd spoken little of it otherwise. Andriun had no way to know the darkness of his thoughts.

"Hey, look, I found a stick!" Tula announced triumphantly as she hopped down the slope. She slowed to a stop beside the fire and looked between the two of them, belatedly realizing she'd interrupted something. Her lips pursed and for a moment, Zaide thought she might inquire what was going on, but she set her eyes on Andriun's bags and the new spear in his hand and brightened, instead. "Oh, are we heading out now? Good thing I got another crutch for Zaide, then." She gave it a swing.

Zaide ducked and the stick scarcely missed the top of his head. "I'll need more bandages if you don't watch what you're doing."

"Oh, sorry." She tip-toed over to lay the second crutch beside him. "Do you need help getting up?"

He shook his head. "I'm going to finish this while the rest of you break camp."

"Well, give a shout if you need help getting up. Are we done with the fire now?" Tula snapped her fingers and the flames extinguished, leaving behind the faintest plume of smoke.

"We were not," Andriun said.

"Oh. Well, I guess you are now." Tula grinned at him. "I'll get my bags."

Andriun turned his head to watch as she scurried over to where she'd left her things the night before. "She can be exasperating."

"So can the princess," Zaide said.

"But they both like you well enough."

"Sometimes." Often, he doubted Lark did more than tolerate him. Now and then, in the shining moments where he was able to elicit a smile or laugh, he thought she might classify him as a friend, but it was unlike the easy, bantering friendship he had with Andriun. Or even with Tula. Zaide readily admitted he and the Magister had gotten off to a poor start, but he'd warmed to her over their travels. Her peppy, positive attitude was infectious and reminded him of himself, in a way. He'd never acted like that, of course, but her outward spirit was a strong reflection of how he'd felt inside when he thought of leaving Kolmar to serve as part of the garrison. It was hopeful, innocent. With all that had happened, the world needed more of that.

"All right," Zaide sighed as he deemed the blade good enough. He was the last one sitting, so he returned the whetstone to his bag and reached for one of the crutches. "Let's get moving."

Andriun started forward as if to offer aid, but seemed to think better of it. Zaide didn't want help, anyway. He didn't want to be a burden to the group, slow them down or hinder their movements. The makeshift crutches helped, though it didn't take long for him to pause and dig through his bags to find something to use to pad the tops. What little spare clothing he had looked awkward, twisted around the tops of the sticks, but they proved much more comfortable against the undersides of his arms as he walked. He leaned on them more than he wanted; if either crutch had a handhold, he could have used his arms to brace himself.

The Desheni hunters followed Andriun, for the most part. Ikan had positioned himself at the back of their group, one of the stone-tipped spears in his hands. His expression was about as friendly as that spearhead, but strangely, Zaide didn't worry about the man being at his back. He had a determination about him—something he'd seen in Andriun, and in Lark—that convinced him they were on the same side.

The princess didn't seem to share his conclusion. She hung close to Zaide, casting suspicious glances over her shoulder now and then. Ikan didn't seem to notice—or if he did, he didn't care.

Ahead, Tula walked close by Andriun's side, her notepad out and ready. She asked questions as they traveled and Andriun answered all of them, though he seemed to grow more tired as she wrung information out of him.

"My father will not expect us from the north," Andriun explained as they walked. Tula had started by asking for his interpretation of events, which eventually grew to asking about his plan for what was to come. She wrote less now, perhaps knowing having their intentions on paper could work against them, but she kept her pencil poised.

"Does that make coming from the north better, or worse?" Her fingers twitched; now and then, she scrawled something. Zaide couldn't see it clearly from his place in the group, but he thought it was a drawing instead of notes.

"It depends on if we are seen ahead of time." Andriun offered her a smile that was a shade too stiff to be sincere.

Zaide tried to puzzle out the plan on his own. "North of the village is a flat field," he murmured to Lark. "We'll have to cross that without being seen or attacked." In the winter, with the cover of snow, escaping across that expanse had been easier. The dark, too, had helped hide their retreat. Maybe they would have been wiser to try an approach during the night.

"That doesn't seem possible," Lark said.

"You remember much for having been there just once before now," Ikan observed. Until now, the man had spoken little.

Zaide found it hard to look back. He couldn't rotate easily on crutches, so he tried to smile over his shoulder. "It was a memorable visit."

"I recall." His expression did not change. "I still do not know what led Andriun to help you."

At the front of the group, Andriun was still explaining things to Tula, oblivious to the fact he was under discussion. Zaide gazed at the two of them, wishing they'd had more time to talk to the Desheni hunters who accompanied them now. All they'd done was run, then camp. Somehow, he thought Andriun might do a better job of explaining. "He believed me."

"He gave you the spring?" Ikan asked.

"No. He gave her the spring." Zaide tilted his head toward Lark. "I was just the delivery boy."

Ikan turned his gaze to Lark, his eyes dark and thoughtful. "So this is it, then. This is our last stand."

"This is the Rise," Lark said, confused.

"Yes," the hunter agreed. "And the end of all we know."

From anyone else, Zaide might have taken that as a sign of hopelessness, but Ikun's tone was calm and flat. It was the same way one might relay a simple piece of information, free of fear, full of knowledge.

"Your people's histories tell you that?" Zaide asked.

"The Oracle has told us that."

Andriun stopped in the middle of the game trail they followed through the woods. "What was that?" He turned and locked eyes with the hunter.

Ikan was taller, older, yet he averted his eyes as if ashamed. "The word came after you departed. At least, that was when it came to us. We don't know when your father heard. Some of our people were concerned by your banishment, afraid of what awaited us without a Shaman to replace him. That was when he told us. He said it did not matter, for this Rise would be the last."

A sense of something came from the Spectrum Blade. Zaide leaned against one of the crutches as he tried to decipher it. Amusement? He hadn't thought anything particularly amusing. *Are you listening to everyone around us? You hear what's being said?* he thought at it.

He was not surprised when the sensation vanished and the blade fell silent.

You have to be, he told it. *I just don't know how you're listening.* Was it through his ears, or its own? No; that didn't make sense. Swords had no ears.

A tingle of amusement returned.

Of course.

"This makes sense, given my father's decision not to fight," Andriun said. "But you are here. If you take this knowledge as fact, why have you joined me? Knowing I will fight? Knowing this battle is pointless?"

This time, it was Tanna who spoke. "That you fight is why we have joined you."

Ikan nodded. "Athradan has decided to surrender. But all he has told us was this will be the end. He never said that Shadow won."

For a time, the scratch of Tula's pencil in her notebook was the only sound.

"The last Rise," Lark breathed at last, her voice soft, dreamy. "Could you imagine? All these centuries of battle, slowly losing territory and people, losing lives... If this was the end..."

"No more Goborrins," Zaide said.

"And no more cruel emperors trying to swallow the world," Ikan added.

It sounded too good to be true.

The princess looked to Andriun. "Do you really think it's possible?"

"Your Highness, I do not believe there is any alternative. We will fight, and we will win." Andriun gave a resolute nod and motioned for their procession to continue.

The hunters said no more and Lark walked with a pensive look on her face, though the storms in her eyes were a little lighter than before.

They all walked with an eager step, save Zaide, whose turning thoughts dragged like his splinted foot when it caught in dead leaves.

There was an alternative. He wouldn't speak it, but he knew they all knew it. For they could replenish the blade, face Gadranus, and win—or they could be struck down and shattered as easily as glass.

CHAPTER TWENTY-FIVE

ANDRIUN HESITATED at the edge of the northern forest. The field waited ahead and the clear afternoon sky arched over it, making the village—and the apparent army that waited beside it—seem small.

"Fish guts," Andriun muttered.

His party stood in a row alongside him, Desheni hunters to one side and the rest of them to the other. He still was not sure how to think of their hodgepodge group. A Desheni, a Jadoran, an Amrochan, and a broken-born. Andriun could not imagine a stranger mix. That he considered himself a part of their group, and not part of Ikan's group, should have told him something.

"So what do we do now?" Lark asked. She shaded her eyes and squinted at what waited ahead. The line in the distance shifted constantly, rippling like heat waves rising from stone.

Belan and Leine tapped the ends of their spears against the ground. The tapping cadence made the back of Andriun's neck prickle, but he did not feel he had the authority to tell them to stop, whether or not they looked to him for guidance.

Why did they follow him? He understood their reasoning, but he did not understand the choice. They could have fled, could have gone west or south, escaped and started their own village elsewhere. They were young, too young to have offspring yet. They could have traveled to warmer waters, to where the Desheni had first come ashore, to where their tails would be safe from the choice between cutting or freezing.

Instead, they followed him to what waited across the field. To war with his father, to what had to be certain death.

Zaide thumped one of his sticks against the ground. "Well, we don't gain anything by standing here. Let's go get the Captured Spring, then we'll worry about the sword."

Always so confident, so reckless. Andriun both admired and rued his nonchalance.

Tula shrugged and hefted her bags. Her notebook had disappeared into her voluminous pockets, but he expected he would see it again before the day was over. The Magister strode forward as if the line of opponents on the other end of the field did not matter.

In a way, Andriun supposed they did not. Zaide was right; they gained nothing from hesitation. Yet he did not know if those lined up beyond the field were Desheni or goborrins, or perhaps neither—it was just as possible that they were broken-born.

Then do they threaten us, or the village? The thought came unbidden and Andriun squeezed his eyes closed. It did not matter, he reminded himself. One way or another, they had to break that line and locate his father.

Zaide started forward after Tula. Ikan signaled the other hunters forward. They moved, leaving Andriun and the princess side by side.

"Is there a plan?" Lark asked.

"I do not believe so." Andriun twisted his hands around his spear, then gestured for her to precede him.

She shrugged and strode into the grass. "Impulsiveness always works for Zaide. Let's hope his luck carries us through."

"Maker preserve us," he murmured, although not quietly

enough, for the princess chuckled and replied so flatly, it made his blood cool.

"If we're lucky, He won't."

Slowly, Andriun started forward. They walked abreast, a band of nine against what resolved into dozens. The faces that waited on the other side of the field were Desheni. The sight gave him relief. No monsters. No sign of his father's betrayal. There was still hope for what he had to say.

He expected resistance, perhaps even combat, and braced himself in preparation.

Instead, as they came closer, the faces of the Desheni hunters that ringed the village morphed into looks of consternation.

Andriun drew breath to speak.

Ikan spoke first. "You face north, when the threat lies in another direction. Have we gone so soft in our years of peace?"

A number of hunters exchanged worried looks.

"The Shaman warned us of danger from the north," one said, although he avoided meeting Ikan's eyes. "Then you come in such company—"

Ikan scoffed and flicked a hand in a curt gesture of dismissal. From anyone ranked lower, it would have been an offense. "Where was the Shaman when the monsters to the south held us captive? Me, my wife, my hunting party? Where was Athradan when we needed protection?"

Andriun stepped forward then and swallowed hard. He had to tread carefully. He had overextended the mercy of his people enough times already. "I know what I have done. I know you are here to reject me, but do not reject them. I have seen what is out there. I have seen what they could do. I could not leave any of our people trapped by the enemy, nor could I bear the thought of leaving them without aid when they were weakened from capture."

A few turned their attention toward Zaide. He bore their scrutiny unflinchingly, and that his hands remained on his crutches and did not go near his sword seemed to put a few at ease. Only the Desheni held weapons, and Andriun himself let his spear rest against his shoulder, as neutral a hold as he could manage without letting it fall to the ground.

"We will see they're taken care of," the self-appointed leader of the villagers said. He motioned for space to be made to let Ikan and the other hunters through.

Ikan shook his head. "I will not enter until I have spoken with Athradan."

Worry touched a few faces.

"The Shaman cannot see you now," someone said. Not their leader, this time.

Andriun scanned the line, lingering on each person there. People he knew. People he had once trusted. How much did they know?

"Why? Because he's not here? Or because he's afraid?" Ikan spat the last word.

Tanna put a hand to his arm to soothe him.

For a moment, no one knew what to say.

So, then. It was time for him to speak. Andriun curled a hand around his spear and stepped forward. The way his people flinched hurt, but he showed no suffering. "You do not understand the situation which we have fled. You do not know the conditions under which my uncle's hunting party was found."

Lark's head turned almost imperceptibly, and yet that subtle movement was more than enough to express her displeasure at this information being revealed.

Andriun meant to say more, perhaps include something to relieve her ire, but Ikan interrupted, his eyes ablaze. For all that Tanna tried, he would not settle. "Athradan will answer me," Ikan snarled. "He will answer for what he has done, for he knew where I was imprisoned, and he walked away! What Shaman turns his back on his people? On his own brother? How far have we fallen that his exiled son must be the one to honor our blood ties?"

"Blood ties mean nothing in the face of betrayal," someone shouted.

Andriun allowed himself a resigned smile. He had not seen who spoke, but they did not know how well they made his point for him. "Precisely. That is why I am here. I was willing to accept the choice of our elders when my father declared me a traitor. But if I have betrayed our people, it is only by honoring the king and delivering the Captured Spring to the princess's hands, so the Spectrum Blade could be recovered."

A few uncertain frowns answered him and Andriun hesitated. They knew he had helped claim the spring from its hiding place, that he had given it away, that he had endangered their children. But beyond that, he had never questioned what they might have been told. Did they not know the blade had been the reason behind the quest?

"I used to believe I was wrong," Andriun continued slowly. "I believed that my father showed wisdom I did not understand, when he refused to aid Her Highness. I believed my exile was not only so I might serve penance, but so I might meditate on what I had done wrong. But Princess Dasienna honored our sacrifice, our struggle, and returned what was ours when her need was fulfilled."

"And Athradan's excuses are weak," Ikan put in. "It is summer, my friends. Summer! Our children are safe. They were always safe. What has threatened them? Not frostbite, but goborrins."

"He led goborrins against our home," one of the villagers protested.

"Who? Andriun?" Ikan scoffed. "Goborrins imprisoned my hunting party, but it was not by their own choice. I know who commands them through this forest, and that is why I was held within their camp. Goborrins are monsters, mindless, weak, and it was by my own brother's command that I was imprisoned!"

A hush fell.

"Enough!"

Andriun's hands tightened around his spear as the row of familiar faces parted and he saw his father approach.

"Be careful," Lark murmured beside him.

"I know what I am doing." What he must do. His father had left him little choice. Andriun shifted to stand sideways as he brought his spear around one-handed and pointed it at his father's chest. A rush of whispers and nervous breaths flowed from the Desheni watching him as he adopted the centuries-old pose of rejection.

Athradan stilled on the path. For a moment, he stared. Then he extended a hand to one side, palm flat toward the earth. Water welled forth from the ground and swelled in fat droplets that broke from their stems and rushed upward to his palm. He closed his hand around it and it hardened into a lance of ice.

The display left Andriun disgusted. Through all the years since he had taken his place as Shaman, Athradan had sworn he bore no magic. To see him flaunt it now only proved him a liar to the rest of their people, and doubt decorated the expressions of many who watched. How many had known before? How many were shocked by the discovery their leader had lied? Andriun did not know, and knowing others may have been in on the secret only incensed him more.

"You have failed your people as Shaman," Andriun said. "You have failed the king as Paragon. And by refusing to stand against Gadranus in the Rise, you have failed the Maker by rejecting your commission. If you will not stand beneath the mantle of Paragon, then I will."

The Shaman's lip peeled back. "You would threaten my life before all our people?"

He did not want to kill his father. He did not even want to fight. But people backed away, clearing space between them, preparing for violence—and yet doing nothing to stop it. Andriun kept his spear level. "If that is what I must do, then so be it."

"You are a fool," Athradan spat.

Before Andriun could respond, his father launched the ice lance toward his head. It flew with unexpected force and accuracy, but he was ready, and spun to strike the ice out of the air. He struck it with the shaft of his spear and it exploded into snowflakes. The white motes swirled around his head and he waved a hand to clear the air. The ice answered, flowing away on the wind, just in time for a second attack.

Shouts rose from the crowd as Andriun deflected another lance. This one splintered and fell away as shards. He had reacted too strongly the first time; he could not afford to impede his own sight.

"You betray our home! You betray our people!" Athradan flung lance after lance, giving Andriun no time to plan or retaliate. All he could do was shatter each piece of ice. All the while, his father moved forward, pressing him farther back into the north meadow, angling them toward the lake.

"You betray my authority and my trust!" Athradan swung both arms, launching two jagged spears of ice at once.

Andriun sidestepped. He broke one. The other hurtled past his shoulder and crashed into the lake. He glanced back. Instead of fading, the ripples grew, and he knew he had made a mistake. He reached for the water with his senses and summoned his magic. The water slipped beyond his grasp and he bit back a curse. He was strong, but his father was stronger than he had ever imagined. Why had he hidden such power for all this time? He tried again, backing closer to the water and extending a hand toward its surface. It responded, but not to his call. In the center of the ripples, a small swell began to rise.

"Remember, as life is choked out of you," Athradan said as he advanced. "This is what you chose."

The Shaman lifted his hands and from the water, there rose a creature like nothing Andriun had ever seen.

CHAPTER TWENTY-SIX

WATER ROSE and rose until it towered over the meadow in a
pillar. Zaide tried to look, but the sun was to the west and it
glinted, blinding, behind the column. He shaded his eyes in time
to see the pillar split.

His heart lurched and he spun to seize Lark. "Look out!"

Dozens of writhing tentacles lashed out across the lake's
shore as he all but flung the princess aside. She hit the ground
hard as one of the gray-blue tentacles wrapped itself around his
good leg. It tore him from his crutches and dragged him across
the earth toward the water. His fingers dug in around clumps of
grass, but he found no purchase. Gritting his teeth, Zaide swept
the Spectrum Blade from its sheath. It flashed as he struck the
creature, severing the tentacle and leaving searing light at the
end of it and the stump it left behind.

Behind him, Ikan and the rest of his hunting party roared.
They surged forward in unison as a half-dozen tentacles coiled
around Andriun's torso and legs to fling him into the air.

Water surged from the lake to catch him and Zaide pumped a
fist in victory. He didn't know how Athradan had kept the water
from answering before, but somehow, his friend had regained
control.

Zaide rolled onto his stomach and tried to get to his knees, using the Spectrum Blade for support. He barely made it before another tentacle wrapped around his injured ankle and hauled him back. Pain shot up his leg; it was all he could do to contain a scream. He gripped his sword with both hands and stabbed downward, but the creature's arms writhed as if it anticipated every move.

A burst of flame lashed against the tendrils and a strange shriek came from the water, drowning the cries of the Desheni as they retreated into the village. Zaide gasped for breath as it released him. He wouldn't have long before it came at him again. He craned his neck to look for his crutches, sparing a nod of thanks for Tula as she helped Lark to her feet. The forked branch Tula had found before they left the forest lay some fifteen feet away. He dragged himself to his knees again and crawled toward it, shedding his travel bags as he went. If he could get up, find some way to balance on one foot, he might be able to fight.

More tentacles surged out of the water. They raced across the earth, only to be speared by Ikan and the other hunters. The limbs writhed like earthworms as they pegged them to the ground and did not let go.

"It does not have to be this way!" Andriun shouted. He still held his stone-tipped spear, but he wielded columns of ice like javelins and pinned tentacles down the same way the hunters had done. Athradan still advanced on him. The shaman gestured with both hands, beckoning the monster toward the shore.

Something heaved in the water. A mass broke through the ripples, a shimmering gray-blue monster with iridescent green shades sliding across its skin. It rolled and lurched, heaving higher, exposing eyes—too many eyes—and a mouth full of too-human teeth that gnashed at the air.

"Maker's mercy," Zaide breathed. He reached his crutch just as another tentacle cracked down against his back. He sprawled flat on the earth, but clung to both the branch and the Spectrum

Blade. He couldn't keep the thing from wrapping around him and dragging him into the air, and it lifted him so fast, his head spun when he looked down.

The sound of Lark's voice saying his name rushed away from his ears and he clenched his jaw as he scrambled for a plan. He couldn't walk. Couldn't fight with practiced sword forms. But if the monster carried him close enough, maybe he wouldn't have to. Zaide breathed as deep as he could with that coil tightening around his ribs and willed himself not to look down.

The monster's head rolled upward, dozens of black eyes blinking at him. If he'd had Lark's crossbow, he would have fired a bolt into every one of them.

Below, ice crunched and crackled and people screamed, but Andriun's shout of frustration was impossible to miss.

Zaide looked down without thinking. His stomach dropped, but he spotted Andriun a second later, rising into the air with a handful of tentacles holding him fast.

"It's not too late for you to surrender," Athradan called from below.

Andriun spat in response. The Shaman snarled in anger.

Zaide's hand curled around the hilt of his Jadoran long knife. "Catch!" he shouted.

His friend glanced up as if surprised to see him, then paled. "Do not throw that at—"

Before he could finish, Zaide flung the blade. It flipped end over end before slamming point-first into one of the monster's limbs, yielding a screech. It all but released Andriun and he swung upside down, suspended by his ankle.

"That is not helping!" Andriun shouted, though he rocked to gain momentum. The beast's injured tentacle twisted back on itself, searching for the knife. Andriun found the hilt first and jerked it free, slicing the tentacle off in the process.

The whole monster lurched and Zaide used the shift in angle to chop through another tendril. "What is this thing?" he shouted.

"Do you think I know?" Andriun yelled back. He bent upward to stab the tentacle that wrapped around his ankle. The beast released him and he crashed into the deep water below. The beast's human-like teeth gnashed at the sky as it bellowed, tentacles thrashing in the water, seeking its prey.

Zaide tried to reposition himself so he could aim his sword at the monster's face. Or, what he assumed it was its face. It was hard to tell with all those eyes. He considered trying to cut the thing, to see if it would drop him, then thought better of it. Andriun was trapped underwater, surrounded by thrashing tentacles, but Andriun had gills. If he went under, he'd just drown.

A flash of blue broke through the surface of the murky water, followed by a glint of steel. Andriun struck hard and fast with Zaide's knife, but for every tentacle he severed, a new one was quick to appear.

More tentacles struck the ground below. Tanna and Belan drove them back with spears, while Ikan advanced toward the Shaman. He shouted something, the roar of thrashing limbs in the water too overwhelming for Zaide to make it out. From the way the other hunters leaped into motion at the sound, cutting tentacles and pressing forward, he thought it was a command.

But only the Desheni answered. Zaide's eyes swept the shore, searching for Tula and the princess. They'd been there a moment ago. His stomach turned and he strained to see something other than churning water below. Before he could see anything, the creature that held him lurched, and whatever sickness had abated came rushing back as the beast swung him back and forth through the air. It pursued Andriun toward the shore, he realized a second later. Andriun pushed back against it with his magic, drawing up a surging wave to force the monster back out into the lake.

It rolled over. Zaide rolled with it, and his eyes widened as the water rushed toward his face.

He sliced through the tentacle that held him and crashed into the waves with the severed limb still wrapped around his chest.

The water stung on impact. The force jarred his leg, but somehow, he held his breath. The murkiness stung his eyes. As if to help, the Spectrum Blade's glow intensified in the water. All around him was a torrent of twisting, thrashing tendrils, and it was a miracle none of them found him as he fought his way to the surface. He crossed into the air and sucked in as much as his lungs could hold.

The thing should have come after him. It didn't. Instead, it churned back toward the edge of the lake.

Zaide tossed his head to flip his hair out of his face, then stretched his free hand forward. Swimming with the Spectrum Blade in hand was awkward, but the sword hummed, eager for battle. It was both invigorating and disheartening. Would it have been as eager if they fought the Shaman himself, instead of whatever this was?

Not that we can fight like this. He clawed at one of the creature's slick arms as it slid past, struggling to find something to hold. It slipped away, but at least that meant it hadn't pulled him under. Another kick with his good leg—his injured leg hurt too much when he tried to use it to propel himself—put him closer to the monster's head, though progress was painfully slow, especially since it was moving.

It slammed a dozen of its tentacles onto the shore, burrowing the ends into the earth to pull itself forward. The Desheni hunters stabbed and cut, but it ignored their spears this time. Its countless eyes swiveled in their wrinkled sockets to train themselves on Andriun. All the while, the Shaman's arms worked in the air, beckoning. Summoning.

Controlling.

His gestures weren't just magic, they were orders for the monster to move. Or maybe that was magic? Zaide didn't have any; he didn't know. What he *did* have was a sword in his hand, and he knew how to use that. He lunged at the next tentacle that swung past, his movements made sluggish by the water. The Spectrum Blade pierced it, and instead of slicing, he twisted.

The monster squalled and slammed that arm back into the water. Zaide almost lost his grip, but when it pulled its tentacle back up, he came with it. Its eyes bulged and swiveled toward him as it lifted him higher, then closer, its maw opening wide.

Zaide jerked the Spectrum Blade sideways, tearing it free of the monster's flesh, and dropped toward the creature's face, sword down.

The blade flashed as it struck and bit deep into one of the creature's countless eyes. The creature's scream threatened to make his ears bleed, but Zaide held fast, driving the blade deeper as vibrations coursed up his arms. Light scorched the blue-gray flesh around the point of impact, threading outward across its face and into its lipless mouth. Something black oozed from around the sword and he didn't know if it was blood or ink, but the beast didn't give him time to wonder.

It heaved sideways to plunge him underwater, tentacles coiling around his legs so he wouldn't be able to escape.

The sword flashed as the force of the water ripped it from the monster's face. Zaide struggled to turn the blade to hack through the tendrils that bound his legs, but the water fought him and he settled for sawing against it and leaving bands of light behind. The harder he sawed, the tighter it squeezed, and it wasn't long before black began to encroach on his vision.

Come on, he growled in his head, willing the blade to cut faster, but his limbs were growing heavy. He let the last of the air from his lungs, hoping it would buy him a few more moments.

One let go. His grip faltered. The Spectrum Blade's colors flickered, shifting, swirling in brightening patterns of alarm.

Abruptly, the second tentacle released and something slid around his ribs and dragged him upwards. Somehow, he kept hold of his sword.

His head broke the surface. Zaide tried to breathe, but his lungs were heavy and no relief came. He lurched toward the shore, dragged by something. Someone. He couldn't see. Couldn't breathe.

Then his back hit the ground. A wide webbed hand flattened over his nose and mouth and pulled. Heat and pressure blossomed in his chest and Zaide arched against the pain. That blue hand pulled farther, farther, drawing with it a fat snake of lake water. His chest spasmed and he sucked in a breath by reflex. Black and gray spots swirled in his vision and he coughed.

More air came. More. Each breath came punctuated with coughing.

Andriun rolled him over and slapped his back. "I may have set a bad example," he said between thumps. "You, my friend, do not have gills."

Zaide couldn't find words for a witty reply. He coughed again and Andriun plastered a hand over his mouth. For a moment, Zaide thought he was trying to get him to be quiet. Then a strange, dragging sensation in his chest made his stomach heave, and his friend pulled more water from his throat. Suddenly, the air came easier. He panted, but raised a hand in thanks.

An instant later, a tentacle larger than the ones he'd seen before slammed down beside him.

"Time to move," Andriun said. He took Zaide by the arm and dragged him to his feet.

Zaide hopped twice and then hurried forward with his friend's help. Behind them, the monster dragged itself to the water's edge, a massive, hulking mass of flesh peppered with eyes and split by not one bare-toothed mouth, but two.

"You sure you don't know what that is?" Zaide gasped as he looked back.

"I know it was not in the lake before now, and I know it is about to not be in the lake at all, so move!"

Lark and Tula stood at the edge of the village ahead. A long line of Desheni threaded its way up the mountain path as they fled.

Zaide's stomach sank. "The goborrin camp."

"Ikan has gone ahead to stop them," Andriun said.

"Your uncle." Zaide supposed they should have guessed from the similarity in their names. "Were you planning on telling us he was the Shaman's brother and could start a big fight, or...?"

"I have started enough of a fight on my own." The ground shook as another massive tentacle struck the earth, and Andriun winced.

Lark stepped forward to meet them.

"Look, he kept the sword!" Andriun grinned.

The princess did not appear amused. She took Zaide's face in her hands to examine him. "Are you all right? We thought you'd drowned!"

"I think I did. Kind of." His throat was raw and his voice came out rough, but that he was moving and talking seemed to be enough to offer her some relief.

She ran a hand through his wet hair to sweep it back from his face. "We have to keep moving. Athradan is commanding that thing, somehow. We need to steer it away from the village and get it somewhere it'll be harder for it to fight."

"I don't think that's going to happen." With how the ground trembled under their feet, he suspected it was more than strong enough to topple trees, and the last thing Zaide wanted to do was give it tree trunks to use as weapons.

Tula bounced on her toes. "The goborrins! We'll take it to the camp!"

"So they can team up against us?" Zaide asked incredulously.

Lark's eyes lit up. "No, she's right. Remember the spider? In Kolmar?"

"I wish I could forget," he grumbled.

"The goborrins fought it," she said. "We'll lead this thing around the village and toward the goborrin camp and bait them into fighting each other."

Zaide glanced between the girls, then turned to Andriun. "Do you think Athradan will fall for it?"

"He will believe the goborrins are on his side. And they may be." Andriun didn't frown, but his doubt was obvious. "At this point, anything may be worth a try."

Which was a polite way to say they'd given up on any semblance of a plan. Zaide nodded. "I need a crutch."

"Didn't you have one when you went out into the water?" Tula asked, rising on tip-toe to look past his shoulder. Her forehead crinkled with disappointment. The one he'd lost had been the one she found.

"I didn't lose it on purpose," he said, wanting to smooth things over.

Her shoulders slumped, but she nodded. "I'll find something." She trotted off into the village before anyone could say anything.

The rest of them stared after her.

"Should, ah... should we have told her to hurry?" Andriun asked.

"I should hope she knows that already." Lark dipped under Zaide's other arm, eyeing the Spectrum Blade as it dangled dangerously from his hand. "Come on. She'll find us. Hopefully before that thing does."

Zaide looked back. The whatever-it-was writhed as it dragged itself across the field and toward the village. "Yeah, I think I liked the giant Tricen better." He hopped forward and they both stumbled.

"The what?" Lark asked.

"I think my father made it," Andriun said helpfully. "Perhaps he made this too. Perhaps I will get monster-making powers when I am Shaman. Then they can fight on our side."

"First we have to live long enough for you to become Shaman." Zaide moved as fast as he could. After a few steps, they settled into a steady rhythm and fled through the village together.

They were halfway through when Tula popped out of a house. "I found a stick!" She held a cane triumphantly overhead.

A thunderous crash announced the arrival of the beast. Wood cracked and shattered as it launched itself on top of a building. Tentacles slithered down the street, stretching toward them.

Zaide hissed.

"Yes, that's how we all feel," Lark said as she slipped away and ran to meet Tula. She snatched the cane from the Magister's hand and flung it in Zaide's direction before she grabbed Tula by the arm. "Don't try to fight it! Just keep running!"

The cane clattered to the ground a short distance away. For an instant, Zaide felt a surge of indignation at the idea they would run ahead and leave him behind while he was injured. Then Lark's knives came out, and Tula sprinted toward the surging mass of slimy arms. They weren't running; they meant to buy him time.

"So much for getting it around the village." Zaide hopped faster, leaning on Andriun as little as possible until he could get to the cane. He let go as soon as he could and swiped it from the ground. "All right, let's go!"

Andriun hesitated. "Do you know how to—"

"I said, let's go!" A splash of heat washed over Zaide's back, accompanied by a whoop from Tula. He did not want to see the state of the village when this was over. Somehow, things always ended up destroyed after they passed through.

Not your fault, he told himself as he adjusted his grip on the cane and hurried toward the slope. His leg was throbbing. They needed the spring. *Saving the world is just messy, that's all.*

The moment the thought crossed his mind, he snorted. Was that what they were doing? With monsters destroying cities at every turn?

Lark shouted something ahead of another crash. Zaide spun back to see what was happening, but she was already right there.

"Hello again," she gasped as she slowed to a jog. He turned

and they ran together, her pace adjusted to match his. "It seems we're back to running."

"That's what we do best." Not that the cane was a suitable replacement for a crutch.

"Well, we'll all be very fit when this is over, won't we?"

Zaide grinned. "Your Highness, if you keep saying things like that, everyone will figure out you have a sense of humor."

Despite the situation, the smile she gave him was sincere.

"Flirting later, running now!" Andriun shouted as he ran ahead, dashing the cheer from her face.

"I'm not—that wasn't—" Lark sputtered.

"Later," Zaide said. Behind them, another fireball exploded.

She bit back her protests and pushed on through the crashes and thuds, though she refused to run far ahead.

Before long, Tula trotted up beside him, gasping for breath. "Oh, you're going to need to run faster than that. I made it really angry."

"I can't imagine how you did that." He glanced at the Spectrum Blade, still held tight in his left hand, its surface churning like never before.

The Magister beamed. "It's my special talent. I make people angry when I'm trying to help."

"I noticed."

"Hey!" She pouted.

"Fight later," Lark shouted.

They crested the slope and the sounds of battle greeted them. Zaide's heart sank.

At least a hundred goborrins crowded the path, more spilling from the woods to join them. Dozens of Desheni wielding spears clustered together to fend them off. Andriun had already joined them and bounded forward with broad gestures, building walls of ice to keep the monsters away from the villagers who split up and fled into the hills. Among the small groups of fighting hunters, Ikan's band roamed, barking orders.

Lark stumbled to a stop. "They'll be destroyed," she cried.

Zaide tried to push forward faster. "Then we'll have to save them. Get the Desheni refugees organized. Take them through the woods. Follow the path we took when we were escaping, get them on the road south."

The princess nodded and hurried ahead.

"I'll help, too," Tula exclaimed.

"Stay right with her," Zaide said. "She needs help holding those monsters back."

She slapped her hands together before her. "All right! Fire time."

"Not too much fire," he warned as she ran to join the fight.

She waved a hand, dismissing his fear and making it worse at the same time.

He released a long, slow exhale. "Should have sent her to Andriun." But it was too late to change anything now. He evaluated the patterns in which the goborrins moved and adjusted his path. As long as he led with the left and kept his weight on his good foot, he could fight.

If he went down, it would be a disaster.

"No pressure at all, right?" he asked the sword as he raised it.

Its light flickered and a small hum tingled in his fingers. The sensation that accompanied it was new. Support. Encouragement. He paused to give the sword a strange look and the feeling evaporated in an instant.

"Uh, thank you?" He tilted the blade, but it gave no further response, and he didn't have time to think about it more. A wave of startled squalls went up from the goborrins, and he turned back toward the village as the first writhing tentacles crested the hill.

CHAPTER TWENTY-SEVEN

 Ikan roared as he drove another goborrin to the ground. He tore his spear free and wheeled to find another target. He fought with such ferocity, yet also with finesse. Andriun could only hope to match his skill someday. No matter how often they had sparred together, he had never come close.

"I would not go so far as to call it a plan," Andriun said, skirting the issue neatly as he drew another wall of ice from the ground. They were difficult to raise, but thick enough to slow down the goborrins. He did his best to wall off the part of the forest where his people had fled. From the corner of his eye, he had seen Tula and the princess go after them, and so he worried less than before. Tula had feigned ignorance of her power every time they stopped to rest, behaving as if she did not know how to light or maintain a simple campfire, but the way she flung blasts of fire from her fingertips betrayed her prowess as Magister. If she was with his people, then they would be all right.

If only he could say the same for himself.

"Here it comes!" Zaide shouted.

Andriun spun as the creature his father had drawn from the lake came into view, wriggling tentacles first. He did not know what came next and he froze on the path, a spear in one hand and Zaide's long knife in the other.

Somehow, Zaide kept going. He limped along with that cane, but he stayed in motion, his face showing none of the fear that twisted Andriun's stomach into knots.

Maker's mercy, how was he supposed to be Shaman? How was he supposed to take care of his people when he did not know what to *do*?

A tendril lashed forward to seize Zaide's cane. He lopped it off and continued, though he turned to walk backwards—a questionable choice, even without the injury. Andriun started forward to help, but something snared the back of his collar and dragged him backwards. He spun with the knife ready and pulled his strike at the last second.

His father released him and drew back a step. He raised the ceremonial trident that represented his role and took a battle stance.

"What—How did you—" Andriun looked over his shoulder, then yelped as the trident plunged past his face.

"Your choices grieve me, but they are your own," Athradan snarled. "My mistake was not killing you the first time!"

Those hateful words cut deep, but Andriun had no time to hurt. He retreated a step and prepared to fight.

He caught the next plunge of the trident with the pole of his spear and steered it toward the ground. With his left hand, he lunged in with the knife. It cut through the thick hide sleeve of his father's coat, but if it drew blood, he could not see.

Athradan backhanded him across the face and knocked him back.

He shook his head to dull the sting. He did not want to hurt his father, just render him unable to fight. Not that he wanted to fight at all. "Think of what you are doing. Please." He deflected another stab. "I am your son! Does that mean nothing to you?"

His father's response came in the form of ice bursting from the ground in jagged spires.

Andriun hissed and leaped back. He shattered them with a wave of his hand and the trident almost snared his arm. The magic was a distraction, a risk he could not afford. He moved back farther.

"Watch out!" Ikan roared.

A second later, a tentacle swept along the ground.

He leaped over it and it struck Athradan's legs by mistake. The Shaman fell with a shout. Andriun dropped his spear and lunged forward to seize the trident from his hand.

His father would not let go. "You will never be Paragon," he snarled through clenched teeth.

The tentacle came back around and lashed toward his head. Ikan intercepted it, piercing it with a spear and heaving it to the side, but it twisted back on itself and dragged him forward with it. The coil closed around him and dragged him toward one of the beast's mouths.

Andriun pulled harder. "Neither will you." He twisted and wrenched the trident free.

Ice crackled and swelled on the ground around the Shaman. "You still dare to defy your father?"

"No." Andriun lunged down with the knife. His father flinched as he slammed it into the ground through the shoulder of Athradan's coat, pinning him to the ground. "I no longer know who you are." He froze the ground around the blade to hold it fast, then spun to go to Ikan's aid.

Behind him, Athradan roared with anger, the sound growing faint as Andriun ran.

Zaide stood at the monster's feet—Andriun did not know what else to call the tentacles that supported its weight—with the Spectrum Blade raised, somehow fending off strikes without losing his balance. He teetered on his uninjured foot and Andriun could have cursed. His father had to have the Captured Spring with him. Why hadn't he stopped to take it? He started to turn back, but the monster turned enough for Andriun to see his uncle holding fast to his spear as it wedged the creature's mouth open. If the spear snapped, it would surely bite him in two.

This time, he did curse. "It has to wait," he told himself, as if verbalizing it made abandoning something so precious as the artifact more acceptable. He gripped the trident in both hands and bolted forward to leap between tentacles and drive it into one of the monster's eyes.

"Yes!" Zaide shouted over the monster's screams. The sound came in duotone, one cry from either mouth. "That's exactly it! We need to blind it, so it can't see the goborrins!"

Blind it? Andriun drew a breath to berate his friend for such a nonsensical idea, then he saw the way the monster thrashed. Its tentacles dragged along the ground, striking not only at Zaide, but anywhere the monster thought he might move. Somehow, through all of it, it kept from hitting the goborrins that ran through the forest. Those same tentacles had swiped his father off his feet, but only by mistake, when they had been trying to hit him instead.

Perhaps blinding it was not such a strange idea.

Andriun gathered what power he could. Water still dripped off the creature; he gathered it to twist it into tiny needles of ice before launching them back at the beast. A few hit their targets before the monster saw what he was doing and squeezed most of its eyes closed.

"It's not working!" Zaide shouted, as if Andriun had not noticed.

"I know! We need..." he grasped at the air as if it might provide the answer that eluded him. Something faster. Harder to deflect. Something to steal all its vision at once. "Tula!" He exclaimed.

Zaide turned as if to question, but Andriun had already bolted for the forest. He had seen them go that direction, helping his people to safety. Goborrins had gone after them. He only hoped the girls had been able to defend the fleeing Desheni on their own.

The goborrins had left clear tracks. Andriun flew past them, crashing through the undergrowth in a desperate attempt to catch up with wherever they had gone. He could not see them, but he heard them, and it was not long before he saw the tops of goborrin heads between the trees at the bottom of the slope.

"Tula!" Andriun shouted. He still saw nothing but the pig-like monsters, but even if their attention was all he drew, surely that would lead him to her. More than one of the brutes looked his way. He continued down the slope anyway, waving his arms and shouting for the Magister. "Tula! Zaide needs you!"

They should have sent Tula after that monster first. The Magister's power was in opposition to the Shaman's, but not always to a deficit. The beast was out of water now, out of its element, susceptible to her flames.

A goborrin launched itself at Andriun from behind a tree. He skidded to a stop and shouted as he pulled water from the ground in a spear of ice. The goborrin impaled itself upon it, squalling like a stoat on the end of a spear. Andriun panted. It had been a split-second decision. The Paragon's trident was still in his hand. He could have reacted with it, could have used it to drive the beast into a tree and let it skewer itself against it, the way they hunted boar in the mountains. He had used it already to strike the tentacled beast, and thin smears of an inky substance still coated its tines. Why had he shied away from using it now?

Because it is not yours, he chided himself gently as he resumed a zig-zagging path through the woods, darting around trees and dodging goborrins. *You are not Shaman. You are not Paragon. Do not forget your place.*

A skirmish on a nearby hillside caught his eye. A cluster of goborrins pressed toward a wall. Someone was cornered.

He gripped the trident tighter in his webbed hands. He was not the Paragon, but he was a hunter.

He would not leave his people undefended.

The goborrins didn't see him coming. He launched in with

magic, tearing spikes of ice from the earth below the beasts. Howls of surprise and pain rose into the air, along with a human exclamation, not of pain, but surprise and delight.

"Andriun!" Lark shouted over the noise. He just saw her, a flash of golden hair between the fleshy, half-armored bodies of goborrins.

He drew deep, catching water underground and ripping it upward to create two crude shields to force the goborrin hordes apart.

The princess was there, backed against a stony outcropping with Tula beside her.

"Tula," Andriun gasped. He had begun to feel light-headed; the more he used it, the more his magic took from him. But he could not give up, and he steeled himself as he strode forward between the barriers of ice. "Zaide needs your magic. Fire to blind the monster."

The Magister's brows shot up, then drew together in deep worry. "What about them?"

It was then that he saw what they defended so fiercely. A split in the stone, an entry to a cavern. The Desheni had gone inside and a few now stood with spears pointed outward. They had dug themselves in like badgers in a den. They would not be ousted soon.

"Go," he said as one of the ice shields began to crack. "This is my place. Not yours."

Tula started to run, then paused after a step to look back at the princess.

Andriun angled the trident's pole behind Lark and pushed her forward, too. "Go."

Lark gave a nod and hurried past the shields of ice.

Just after Tula passed them, they shattered.

Andriun intercepted a goborrin's sword with the trident and twisted hard. The trident slid up to snare the monster's arm. That twisted, too, and the crack that followed was enough to make his skin crawl.

With his free hand, he drew water up for another shield, protecting his flank as he fought. A few twists and stabs drove the goborrins back, but before long, he found himself pushed into the mouth of the cavern.

He smirked at the advantage they had unwittingly given him, then dropped below the thrust of a goborrin blade to lay a hand against the cool stone floor. Spears of ice shot out from every side of the opening, criss-crossing across the gap to form a barrier thicker than any shield he could have made. He pulled back, inch by inch, working more and more ice into the seal, until his grasp of power faltered and he fell to one knee, gasping for breath.

Only then did he notice the soft wash of light, the cool glow of a Desheni-made lantern as it flowed over his back and cast a diffuse shadow against the barrier of ice.

The Desheni behind him said nothing, but the air was thick with a sense of hesitation and something else.

Awe, he thought, yet that made no sense. He stared at his own shadow as he worked to catch his breath and silently prayed the ice would hold.

Weapons hammered against the far side of his ice in a dull echo, but the shield was too thick for him to see any signs of what they were doing. For a time, that thump was all he heard. Then, at last, a hesitant voice filled the cave. "Athradan?"

Andriun's heart twisted in his chest and he made himself rise. Slowly, he turned to face them. He expected disappointment. Anger. Instead, confusion adorned most faces when they saw him—and in a few rare instances, hope.

"He has fallen into shadow," he replied. His throat grew tight as he spoke, threatening to cut off his words. He made himself swallow. "But it will not take us."

A tremor shook the ground and behind him, the ice began to crack.

A hush fell over the Desheni as they worked their way farther into the cavern.

Andriun remained at the entryway and held the trident ready.

~

"Stay up," Zaide breathed. He tried to hold his balance, but the longer he fought, the more he swayed.

The cane was gone. When he had to move, he used the Spectrum Blade for support, and its lack of complaint surprised him. Now and then, he thought he sensed worry under the hum of battle hunger. It was small, fleeting, but the idea the blade might be worried for him brought comfort. Maybe it shouldn't have. Maybe he should have been concerned that a sword would think or feel anything, even if it meant something favorable for him.

A roar alerted him to a goborrin's presence and he spun to go in low and stab the creature in the side before it could swing its axe for his chest. The Spectrum Blade flared and light seared through the monster, like it always did. The goborrin fell with the wound still glowing, but Zaide rocked on his good leg.

He couldn't keep fighting like this. Trying to fight at all was madness.

"But we don't have any choices right now, do we?" he asked through gritted teeth, unsure whether he was speaking to himself or the glowing blade in his hand.

"Move!" Ikan shouted from above.

Zaide tried to pivot, but the tentacled beast was right there. He hissed and struck hard. The Spectrum Blade sank deep into one of the thicker arms it used to walk. The thing lurched and screeched, almost flinging Ikan from where he hung, still gripping his spear with both hands.

A strange crackle filled the air. A second later, a fireball struck the side of the thing's head and it collapsed sideways. The ground shook as it landed and Zaide fell to the ground beside it.

Before he could so much as sit up, a thin tendril wrapped around his knee and hauled him into the air.

Another blast hit it. Zaide swung upside-down and strained to curl up enough to reach the tentacle with his sword.

He fell before he could. Instead of the ground, he landed on a writhing mass of tendrils and tumbled sideways.

Then he hit the ground. Pain jolted his leg and the Spectrum Blade flashed, concern tingling through his hand.

Lark appeared beside him an instant later, the sharper of her silver knives dripping black. "Are you all right?"

"Never better," Zaide managed as he got his good leg underneath himself and struggled to rise.

Lark caught his arm and helped him up. They'd barely straightened before he lurched forward to deflect a goborrin attack. Before, the thrashing tentacles had kept the beasts at bay, and the monster had avoided moving any closer to them. Now, they came closer together—the goborrins seeking Zaide and Lark, the tentacle-beast struggling to escape the new onslaught of magic.

A thump behind them made Lark spin away, her knives in hand, but a second later, Ikan ducked in to seize Zaide's arm. "Your Highness, go!"

Lark almost protested, but a thrashing tentacle sweeping past the top of her head changed her mind. She bolted up the forest path without looking back.

"I had it," Zaide lied as the hunter turned to drag him along. Another gout of flame drove the monster's squeals higher in pitch. The shrill double ringing bounced around inside his skull.

"Of course," Ikan replied flatly. He wasn't much like his nephew, Zaide decided. Andriun had a sense of humor.

They found a rhythm after a moment and ran together in a way that reminded Zaide of the three-legged races they sometimes held during summer festivities back home. Smoke thickened around them as Tula's magic took its toll. Instead of running away, they made a wide circuit around the creature from the lake. Goborrins still came at them from every angle, but with increasing frequency, the lashing tentacles struck goborrins and knocked them flat.

They'd almost completed their circle when they rounded a tree and Zaide almost gutted himself on his own knife.

Athradan slashed at him with the Jadoran blade, but Ikan spun him backwards and out of the way.

Zaide was not going to be deterred. Instead of retreating, he dug his sword against the ground and launched himself forward. His sword snapped up and lashed toward the Paragon's hand.

Athradan's eyes widened and he withdrew, the strike scarcely missing contact with his blade.

Ikan swept in from the other side, plunging a fist toward his brother's head. His knuckles cracked against a sheet of ice instead.

"Duck!" Lark's voice rang between the trees.

Without thinking, Zaide dropped to the ground.

One of the monster's arms swung past, slamming into the Shaman. Athradan's face twisted with alarm as it coiled around him. He drove the Jadoran long knife into the tentacle, but it only wrapped tighter as it drew him into the cloud of smoke.

The monster's cries grew as it flailed, gray-blue tendrils thrashing against the ground.

Above it all rose one harsh, panicked scream, and the monster's limbs went limp.

CHAPTER TWENTY-EIGHT

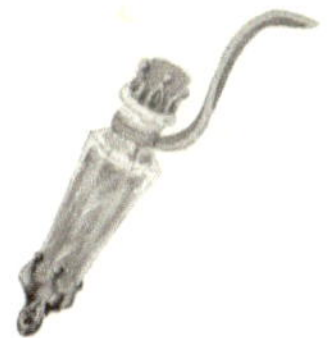

Andriun tilted his head and listened, but the forest beyond his ice wall had grown silent. Cracks marred the surface of the smooth barrier he had erected as reinforcement, but the goborrins no longer hammered against it. Had something else drawn their attention? Or were they waiting outside, setting some sort of trap?

"The cave is sealed," someone said. A scout, having returned from the far reaches of the cavern. That information was troubling. All the Desheni children and elderly stood behind him, interspersed with a few men and women bearing spears who had offered what defense they could. Most of the hunters were elsewhere, fighting goborrins. Fighting whatever that monster was that his father had drawn from the lake.

Andriun bit his lower lip in frustration. They could not hide in a cave forever, no matter how safe it had been to seal themselves off. But they could not venture out, either, not knowing what lay beyond. He was weary, but his magic had not left him yet. He could still summon ice, fortify what he had put between them and the monsters that threatened them, protect his people a little longer. He had to.

He was the only one who still could.

A woman gasped.

Cold light swelled beside him, bathing his face in a blue more vibrant than his skin. Andriun looked down at himself, at the rippling light that so reminded him of sun through the water as it flowed across his shoulder and half his chest.

Realization hit him so hard, it chased the breath from his lungs.

The jewel in his father's trident glowed blue like the clear tropic seas, fueled by the magic of the water trapped inside its shell.

Andriun squeezed his eyes closed.

He had known this would come, that his father would perish, that his symbol of power would wake to bestow that strength on someone else.

He had hoped it would not be today.

One of the elders stepped forward, one hand extended toward the trident. "The Paragon has fallen," she said, her voice steady and tinged with only the smallest hint of sadness.

Andriun pushed the trident toward her, his head bowed.

"I cannot take this from you," she murmured. "The light covers you. You are chosen."

He kept his head down. "I am not worthy."

"That is for the Maker to decide." She touched the trident gently, pushed it upright in his hand, and slid her fingers down to close around his. She squeezed his hand tight, strengthening his grip on the trident. The metal beneath his fingers was cool, reminiscent of his ice magic.

He tried to let go. She would not let him. "I am not fit to lead."

The elder's mouth tightened, a hint of disapproval in her eyes. "That will be discussed."

Andriun made himself nod. There was nothing else to do. The light still shone, flowing over his form, yet the light meant nothing except that he held the trident and he had been accepted. Until the elders approved him as Paragon—even if they did not recognize him as Shaman—he had no power, no authority. The light would persist until that ceremony, when the waters would be used as part of his blessing. Would that even happen, if he was not fit to lead them?

The elder patted his face. "We will discuss all this when we return to our village. Right now, there is nothing to do."

He knew she was right, but it was no comfort. "I will make a hole in the ice and see what is happening outside."

A nod of understanding was all he got. No smiles, no approval, no questions of what came next. Andriun had not expected much, but in the swirl of conflicting feelings that rushed through him now, he could not help wishing for more guidance.

But there would be no more. He knew that, accepted it, but still felt an ache deep in his chest. His father was dead. He did not know how it had happened or who had done it. He did not wish to know. There was no denying it, though, and that the last words shared between them had been threats would weigh heavy on him for years to come.

Slowly, he pressed a hand to the ice. It would be a small hole, just big enough for a glimpse outside. Melted water trickled down the slab of ice until a hole through which he could see had formed. He leaned close, grateful for the grounding cold against his face.

Beyond the barrier he had created, there was nothing. No goborrins in the mouth of the cavern. None in the woods beyond.

Nothing.

"They have gone," he said as he drew back. "I will open the way. Be prepared for danger." But he already knew it had passed. He could not explain it, but the moment the trident's jewel had begun to glow, it brought a sense of finality beyond knowledge of his father's death. Part of him knew the two were related, that he had been right about his father's connection to the goborrin camps and the dangers that lurked outside the Desheni village. It did not make it easier to deal with now.

The ice crumbled beneath his touch. It was slush by the time it hit the floor, and only moments later, it reduced itself to water that trickled out of the cavern and down the hillside. No goborrins remained, little more than footprints left to show they had been there in the first place. Andriun strode forward to survey the valley, but there was little to see.

His eyes traveled west, to where smoke hung between the trees and drifted upward in a lazy haze. Tula had gone that way. Between the smoke and the silence, he assumed that meant her efforts against the many-limbed beast from the water had been successful.

Someone stepped up behind him. He did not know who, but he assumed it was one of the elders. "What was that creature?" he asked without looking. "That my father drew from the waters?"

The man at his back made a sound of displeasure. "Who can say? We don't question the shadow. We don't wish to know it."

To that, Andriun nodded in agreement. He trudged a short distance down the slope, giving his people more space to decide how they wanted to exit and whether or not they wanted to follow him. He supposed they would have to decide that in more ways than one, though he had long since resigned himself to being an outcast. It changed little. The Desheni would persist, with or without him. In time, a new Paragon would be chosen, and his mistakes and misdeeds would be little more than a footnote in Tula's history books.

People trickled from the cave a few at a time, small clusters of families or friends. Two things he no longer held among the Desheni. Andriun struggled not to look, lest the reminder be too much. His father, gone. He knew it, understood it, accepted it, yet it still did not feel real. Had his uncle survived? Or Ikan's wife? He would not know until he pressed back toward the main conflict, but he waited to walk until people no longer stepped from the cave.

In the daylight, the glow of the trident's jewel was lessened. It no longer cast caustics across him, but it held a luminance that could not be explained by sunlight alone. He ran a fingertip across that jewel, wondering at the water inside. It had been captured from the birthplace of water, stored inside to reflect the Paragon's power and responsibilities. That it reflected a change in the Paragon's power was convenience, or perhaps a planned reminder.

Andriun froze. A reminder of water.

The Captured Spring.

He bit his tongue to hold in an oath, mindful of all the little fin-shaped ears nearby, and ran two steps forward before he realized he needed to justify himself. He turned back, searching the faces nearby, settling on a cluster of elders. "My father held the Captured Spring. I must go. I must see what has happened and see if it can still be retrieved."

The elders nodded. Understanding, but not approval. Someday he would hate that neutrality. Right now, he didn't have time. He clutched the trident and ran.

Near the road, the bodies of goborrins littered the forest. Andriun wove between them as he made for the place where he had last seen his father, scanning the corpses as he went. Dozens of goborrins, but not a single Desheni lay among them. It made no sense until he spotted his uncle. Ikan stood in the center of a ring of hunters on the ground, all of them weary and most of them bloodied, but everyone was alive. Ikan himself was covered in both red blood and black, but the tiny vial that gleamed in his hand was unmistakable.

Andriun flattened a hand against his chest in relief. "You found it."

Several hunters looked up, surprise twisting their faces when they saw the trident in his hand. Ikan looked at it, too, but did not seem surprised at all. "How many injured in your group?" The question was blunt, matter-of-fact, and very much like the uncle Andriun had always known.

"None." He was glad to answer honestly.

Ikan nodded. Finally, the first sign of approval from someone in his former clan. "Good. We are finished. Take it to your friend." He stoppered the vial and tossed it Andriun's way, as if it were little more than a trinket.

Andriun snatched it out of the air. "My friend? Zaide?" He turned in place to search the trees, but he saw no one else nearby.

"Down the slope." Ikan pointed. "Hold your nose."

The warning was strange until Andriun made it halfway down the slope to the village with the Captured Spring in his hand. When the village came into view, so did the dead beast, and the odor hit him so hard he almost retched.

"Sulphur," Tula called with a smile, as if it might stop his gagging.

Andriun covered his nose, but there was no avoiding the stench. "It smells like death." He supposed that assessment wasn't wrong, either. The massive thing lay deflated, marred with blackened spots where Tula's flames had made short work of it.

"Yeah, I guess it didn't react too well to the fire." The Magister tapped a finger against her lips as she looked it over. "Someone's going to have to clean this up. Zaide told me I can't just burn it all to ash."

The idea of a new fire mage wielding that much power was mildly unsettling. "Are you capable of that?"

"I'd rather not give her a chance to find out," Zaide said. He sat on the ground, as bloodied as Ikan and ten times as weary, but he managed to lounge in a way that made him look comfortable. Lark sat to his left and the Spectrum Blade lay on the grass to his right, its colors subdued. Oddly, the blue in it brightened as Andriun drew near.

Instead of pointing it out, Andriun raised the Captured Spring. "I've brought you something."

The princess gave her head a toss, the way she always did when she was irritated. "It's about time. Your uncle retrieved it from that thing, but he said Zaide would have to wait his turn. After everything he did to try to stop it, you'd think his turn should have been first."

"My uncle is protective of our village." Andriun would not allow them to fault the man for that. Not after the way Ikan had stood against his father and chosen to back Andriun's cause on his own. "And the spring has been out of our hands for some time. Forgive him for his concerns, for they are borne out of love."

Lark waved a hand and turned her face away. She would not back down in her opinion, it seemed. Yet Andriun thought she had warmed to him since their first meeting. Perhaps it would only take time for her to think favorably of his uncle.

Andriun knelt to check Zaide's ankle before he passed the spring to his friend. The tiny vial held only a few drops of blue liquid, but it would suffice. One taste was all it took, and the vial would restore itself over time. He just had to hope its power would not be needed again soon.

"Thank you," Zaide said, infinitely more grateful than the princess by his side. He took his taste, then capped the vial and passed it back. It only took a moment for its restorative properties to kick in, and Andriun saw the relief blossom in his friend as the pain he had carried began to subside. A sag to his shoulders, a steadiness to his breath, an easing of the lines in his forehead and around his eyes. Andriun was a healer, and those were signs he was trained to look for.

"Good?" he asked.

"Soon," Zaide replied with a weary smile.

Andriun could think of nothing else to say, so he nodded back and sat down on the other side of the Spectrum Blade. The colors definitely shifted when he was near. Or was it the trident the sword was reacting to? He glanced up at the gem. It seemed no brighter, but its glow had never stopped.

Zaide looked at it, too. "Guess that's the one from your father's hut, huh?"

"Yes." Andriun tried to make himself smile. He could not. "I was always under the impression it was purely ceremonial. Decorative. A reminder of his role as Paragon. I knew there was water captured in the jewel. I did not know it would do anything like this."

"Does that mean you are Paragon now?" Lark asked.

"Yes. And no." Explaining the intricacies of the matter would take longer than Andriun had energy for, so instead, he shrugged. The intricacies were not important, anyway. "I must be recognized first. There is a small ceremony. A transfer of power. I am capable of doing it on my own, I believe, because being unable to could leave us without a Paragon. The Maker would not have allowed for such a weakness in the chain. But to take that action without the elders would be a grave insult to my people."

The princess pursed her lips, then gave a nod. "Your people have dealt with enough already."

He flattened one webbed hand against his chest. "I am grateful for your understanding."

All Zaide did was shrug and lay back on the grass with his hands behind his head. "We've done the hard part. The sword gets blessed soon, one way or another. I trust you."

That statement was small, but in the wake of everything he had suffered, it touched Andriun in a way that startled even him. He fumbled over how to reply without it sounding too vulnerable or too dismissive. Before he got there, a soft rasp of breath broke his concentration.

Snoring.

"Stupid man, fighting on an injured leg," Lark muttered, though there was a hint of fondness in her words as she smoothed Zaide's tangled hair back from his face.

The pain was gone, Andriun concluded.

Zaide was already asleep.

CHAPTER TWENTY-NINE

THE DESHENI WERE SUBDUED when they filtered down from the hills and meandered back to their village. Some stopped to marvel at the tentacled creature that lay flat against the mountainside, which had continued to deflate. It was now so flat that Zaide thought it resembled an empty sack, give or take a few mouths or tentacles. Most of the Desheni passed it by, though, their shoulders heavy and their faces long as they saw the wreckage left in the monster's wake.

From the lake to where it lay defeated, the monster had carved a clear path. The houses in the way were gone, others damaged or partially destroyed. Zaide understood their pain better than most. He'd felt the same as he sat on the hill and looked down at the burned-out remnants of Kolmar. It was possible to rebuild, but no one turned their thoughts to such things when facing a loss.

After a time, Tula appeared by Zaide's side. "Is he still down there?"

"Right in the middle." He pointed, though his friend's position in the ruined village had not changed since the last time someone asked. Andriun had gone with the village elders as soon as they'd come to him, calling council. Zaide had been asleep then—he hadn't meant to fall asleep, of course—but Lark had been sure to rudely shake him awake so they could see Andriun off.

The elders now sat in a ring in the center of the village. The golden light of the setting sun made them cast long shadows. The longest belonged to Ikan, who rose from the circle now and then to walk around it and gesture. Angrily gesture, Zaide thought, but he was unsure. Andriun sat in the middle of the ring and never moved.

"Do you think they're being nice to him?" Tula asked, more quietly.

Lark snorted. "Unlikely."

"It looks more like they're sentencing him." At least he wasn't unarmed for it. Zaide thought that silver thing on the ground at Andriun's side was the trident he'd reappeared with, but he couldn't be sure. He touched two fingers to the Spectrum Blade on the ground beside him without thinking.

A small tingle of questioning rolled up his arm at the touch.

"Nothing," he murmured.

The princess cast him a strange look. "Nothing what?"

"The sword." He still hadn't managed to explain what its awareness felt like. How much would it change after Andriun helped restore his part of its power?

"I wish I could talk to swords," Tula sighed. A dreamy wistfulness took her face for a moment, then she gasped and clapped her hands together. "That reminds me! Look what I found."

Zaide blinked as she drew his missing long knife from a pocket in her coat. "You found it!"

"Uh, yeah, I just said that." She presented it flat on her palms. "I even wiped it off, because it was kind of disgusting. Don't lose it. I think you'd hurt someone's feelings if you lost it before you even got to use it."

An unwelcome reminder of its purpose. "I think I'm glad I

haven't had to use it." He returned the blade to its sheath, then glanced over his shoulder.

"I haven't seen any of the broken-born in the forest," Lark said. "And the number of goborrins was lower than I expected. I think they may have gone elsewhere."

"So this was just a base for them to rally before going somewhere else." Zaide fought back a sigh. They could have come from ships, or they could have come across the mountains. Had Beshnai been attacked? Word would have traveled to Amrochan first, while the cities across the Allied Kingdoms petitioned Sendassian for aid. He thought of the woman in Beshnai who had helped him find a ride. The farmer who had given it to him. The letters she'd never received from her son. He rubbed his brow.

Lark rested a hand on his shoulder. "We'll fix it. We're close, now."

Zaide hoped she was right.

Eventually, the scene below changed. The elders moved in close, forming a tight knot of people around Andriun, who remained seated. They huddled there for some time. Tula had meandered off again, but she resurfaced before the huddle ended and stood in the middle of the road, watching. Her notebook had made its appearance. Documenting the rise of the next Paragon, perhaps.

Was rise the right word to use? Zaide didn't know. Given that was the term they used for the return of Gadranus, he thought it unlikely. Maybe there were better terms. Recognition, or awakening. Something with a more positive story behind it.

Not that anything behind any of the ascensions had been positive. The Kolmari Elder's death was something Zaide still had not come to terms with, and Jadora was still in shambles.

He ran a hand down the length of the Spectrum Blade. "Do you ever feel like instead of fixing things, we just make everything worse?"

"Sometimes," Lark said. "But that's when I remind myself

that all this isn't our doing." She waved a hand at the village below, then broadened the gesture to include the corpse of the Shaman's monster.

"It wouldn't have happened if we hadn't come here."

"Perhaps not, but it didn't happen because of us. Athradan had plenty of opportunities to aid us. This was his choice, not ours." She sounded indifferent, but the lines at the corners of her eyes betrayed her worry.

"You don't really believe that," Zaide said.

She considered that for a time, then offered a weak smile. "But I want to."

"Something's happening," Tula called in a sing-song voice.

The circle of elders had expanded again. This time, they took turns striding forward. What they did when they reached Andriun was impossible to make out from a distance, but when all had taken their turns, the circle broke and everyone wandered away. Slowly, Andriun took the trident and rose.

Tula squinted. "That didn't look good."

"But it'll mean he's the Paragon now. They can't really deny him that." At least, Zaide didn't think they could. He took the Spectrum Blade and pushed himself up from the ground. Lark stood, too, and together, they waited for their friend to climb the hill.

When Andriun came near, they saw what the ordeal had been about. He wore a heavy necklace over his coat, adorned with all sorts of oddities. Bits of shells and horn, colorful stone beads, and bright coins. He touched it when he caught them looking at it. "Blessings," he said as explanation. "One from each elder in my home village. To remind me where I have come from, and to remind me to consider their decisions in the past when I must make new ones."

"So they accepted you?" Zaide asked.

Andriun hesitated, then tapped the end of the trident against the ground beside his boot. "I... have not been refused. For now, this is the most I can hope for."

"But you're the Paragon?" Lark inspected his necklace again, as if it might hold the answer.

"I am the Paragon of Water. That cannot be denied, for a power greater than any elder has chosen it. But I am not Shaman, and I do not lead my people. Adghadan—I am sorry, my uncle, Ikan—he will lead the northern Desheni. I have been given a quest by the elders, Ikan included. I am to prove myself, and if I succeed, then I shall take his place."

"What kind of quest?" Tula had crept up behind him, her notebook at the ready.

Andriun eyed it with disdain. "To do what my father refused, and see Gadranus utterly destroyed."

"What a coincidence," Lark said. "We're off to do that very thing."

And Zaide was glad to know Andriun would be with them along the way. He tilted his sword so it caught the light. "So, do you want to, ah..."

"Such is part of my quest, is it not?" Andriun held out both hands.

Zaide started to pass it over, then paused. "Is that a good idea? You know it bites, right?"

"So does a dog, should you disturb its slumber."

He couldn't argue with that. "Fair enough." Still, he concentrated on the sword as he extended it for Andriun to take, thinking stern thoughts toward the notion of misbehavior. A sense of annoyance ran up his arm first, followed by a notion of offense. He snorted.

Lark glanced from the sword to his face. "What?"

"I told it to be nice. It doesn't appreciate it." Zaide wasn't sure that was the best way to describe it, especially since the princess's eyebrows climbed, but it was as close as he could get.

"I do not doubt that the sword is nice. It is just selectively nice, based on its current needs." Andriun mustered a smile as he leaned his trident against his shoulder and took the blade by the hilt. He held it awkwardly, the weapon unfamiliar in his grasp, but he kept it horizontal and raised his other hand beneath it.

Zaide let go, fighting an odd mix of disappointment and consternation. "Nothing happened."

"I considered shouting and making a scene just to frighten you, but I did not think it was appropriate behavior for the new Paragon." Andriun spread his hand wide beneath the blade. Water collected there, seemingly of its own accord, pooling in his palm and spreading to fill the cup of his webbed fingers.

"Oh, I definitely think that would have been appropriate," Tula said.

The princess sighed. "Of course you do."

Andriun cleared his throat. "I am going to do my best to do this correctly the first time. If you do not mind, I would appreciate a moment of quiet."

Zaide shut his mouth and lowered his hands, though he didn't know what to do with them. He'd grown used to resting his hand against the sword's hilt when that happened. It was strange not to have it at his fingertips.

The water in the palm of Andriun's hand rippled and swelled as he brought it up beneath the blade. By the time it touched the steel, it was more of a bubble. It flowed around the blade's edges to engulf it, and soft, pale waves of light began to ripple down the blade. He murmured something as he drew the water to the hilt and let it settle there, though the words were unfamiliar. His own tongue, perhaps, or something far older, passed down from the elders for moments such as this.

Slowly, he drew the water down the length of the blade. As he did, a strange sensation of coldness swept through Zaide, making him shudder.

Lark eyed him, but said nothing. Each time the sword did something strange to him, her gaze grew a little more shrouded. He did not know how to allay her fears—or even if he should. Maybe he should have been worried.

Andriun didn't notice the interaction. He continued to the tip of the sword, then tilted his hand to draw the water back toward the hilt. This time, as the blade emerged from the sphere of water, a radiant blue light swelled in its surface. It intensified, though not in the same searing, flashing way Tula's blessing had led it to brighten. Nor was it piercing in the way Resia's blessing had been. This was softer, more comforting.

Fitting, Zaide thought, for a healer.

The water met the sword's hilt. "It is done," Andriun announced. He dropped the ball of water. Instead of splashing against the ground, it burst into snowflakes.

Tula gasped and clapped in delight. "You're so good with your power! I wish you could teach me."

He grinned. "You do not appear to be challenged." He turned the sword to offer the hilt back to Zaide. "Tell me, does it feel different?"

Zaide flexed his fingers and reached for the sword. He didn't know what to expect. A jolt? A stronger presence? He touched a fingertip to the pommel, then slid his hand up to the grip.

Instead of a change, he felt nothing at all.

Or maybe that is a change. He drew the sword back so he could inspect the swirls of color on its surface. It was no more sluggish than it usually was between battles, yet something still struck him as odd.

"Zaide?" Lark prompted.

He set his jaw and slid the sword into its sheath. "I thought it would feel stronger. It doesn't feel like much has changed."

The others remained silent.

He tolerated it for as long as he could, then shook his head. "So we need to decide what we do next. The sword is blessed. Do we go find Gadranus?" The shadowy thing they'd faced beneath the forest's temple still troubled him when he tried to sleep, but he kept that to himself.

"Do we know where he is?" Andriun asked.

The way Lark bit her lower lip and averted her eyes wasn't promising.

Tula looped a few odd doodles on her page, then lowered her notebook. "Does anyone? All we really know for sure is that he's somewhere to the east, out in the Shattered Lands. Right?"

"Unless he's moving with his armies. He meant to take Amrochan. He could be there now, for all we know," Lark said.

Zaide doubted it, but doubt alone wasn't helpful.

Andriun nodded, as if that had given him everything he needed to know. "Then we go south."

The princess's nose crinkled. "South? We've just come from Jadora. Going back does us no good."

"The Desheni are going south," he said.

Tula gasped softly and raised her notebook again. "What for?"

"Well, you have seen the village." Andriun gestured to the wreckage at the foot of the hill. "And you have seen the goborrin camps in the forest. So has my uncle. He leads them now. If he is also to keep them safe, he must take them somewhere it is possible to do so."

"What about the birthplace of water?" Zaide asked. He hadn't found the place welcoming, but the Desheni were meant to protect it.

"They have asked me to seal it away. None will be able to enter without the Paragon of Water. If all goes as we hope, that will be me. If not, then when all is settled and the next Paragon takes power, my people will return to fulfill their duties." Andriun smiled, though sadly.

Lark shook her head. "But what's to the south? The desert?"

"Farther." Andriun gestured to indicate much farther. "My people will pass through the bay and take to the seas. They will swim far to the south, to where we first emerged and took to the land, before we were tasked with the Paragon's duties."

"All the way to the tropics?" Tula eyed his outfit. It was lighter than what he'd worn through the mountain peaks and into the depths of the birthplace of water, but it was still far heavier than what would be appropriate for a summer anywhere south of where they were now.

This time, Andriun grinned. "Yes. You did not think we always lived wrapped in furs, did you? Look at me. We are pitiful by Desheni standards. There is no blubber left on me, or any of the people in my village."

"Blubber," Zaide repeated.

"Which is why Jadoran women are such a novelty," Andriun said. "They are all so... Long. Slender and muscular. No roundness."

"I have roundness," Tula protested.

He gave her a speculative frown.

"Enough," Lark snapped, the often-present storm back in her deep blue eyes. "You want us to go south with your people. They leave by way of the sea. Then what? What about us?"

Andriun answered as calmly as if he hadn't taken them along on an absurd tangent. "We will hire a ship and travel to Nimultis. We will speak with the Oracle. If anyone knows where Gadranus can be found and what we must do to strike him down, it will be her."

Zaide would have preferred to head for Amrochan, but a soft tingle brushed his senses and stilled his tongue before he could speak. He hovered a hand over the Spectrum Blade. "That's what we should do?"

For the first time in clear memory, the sword gave a deliberate response. Confirmation. Approval.

"Yes," Andriun said, a touch annoyed. "I just said this, did I not?"

The princess shook her head. "I'm not sure this is the best idea. It takes us away from the mainland, away from the action. It could put us farther behind than ever before."

Another prickle from the sword. Urgency and insistence. Zaide brushed a finger down the hilt. "Or we could comb the entirety of Amroch and still not find him. Maybe he is in

Amrochan. But maybe he's still in the Shattered Lands, like Tula said. We know nothing about that place."

Beneath his touch, the sword thrummed with a sense of pleased agreement.

"And it could be a trap," Tula added.

Lark considered it for a time, then sighed. "Then I guess we have no choice."

Reluctant as though it was, her acquiescence seemed to satisfy Andriun, for he smiled. "My uncle will lead our people to the south at dawn. We will rest in what remains of the village and depart with them in the morning."

The princess gave a nod, though it was more surrender and less agreement. She said nothing else as she turned to make her way to the village.

Zaide gazed after her. The sword was pleased, but he took the sense Lark only relented because she was outnumbered. How was he supposed to navigate the task of being her Bladebearer if nothing he did made her happy?

"Personally, I'm glad we'll be traveling all together," Tula said as she put away her notebook. It would likely emerge from her pockets again before she reached the village's edge. "I have so many things to ask your elders. If their oral histories are as comprehensive as you say, they'll likely know things about Jadoran history, too. That's good for my job, right?"

"If you say so." Andriun motioned for her to follow him as they set off after the princess.

Zaide lingered on the hillside. Part of him hoped for guidance, but the sword had gone quiet again. The lack of its presence left him uncomfortable. He didn't know what it was or how to explain it, but in the wake of Andriun's blessing, he was sure that something about the sword was wrong.

CHAPTER THIRTY

WITH THE ENTIRETY of the Desheni village traveling alongside them, movement was not fast. Zaide tempered his expectations as they trudged along. He should have been grateful; slow travel meant time to rest and recuperate from all they'd experienced.

They hadn't gone far before he took the time to cut a piece of wood from a tree that had been downed in a storm. It required a great deal of effort to hack it loose; the Spectrum Blade didn't cut through the wide log as easily as it cut goborrin flesh or slender saplings, but it was sharper than his Jadoran long knife, and the Spectrum Blade never seemed to need sharpening. It hadn't fussed about being used for such a trivial matter, but once he had his block, he didn't touch the blade again.

When night fell, he sat cross-legged near a campfire while a handful of Desheni cooked meals for everyone. The fragrance was tantalizing after so many dry rations. He savored it while he picked at the little block with the small folding knife he'd found in his bag. The blade wasn't substantial enough to be useful for fighting, but for wood carving, it seemed to do just fine.

After a while, Andriun joined him. "What is that?"

"A project," Zaide replied unhelpfully. His friend only stared, obviously expecting more of an explanation. Eventually, he relented. "I'll be a year older in the fall. I don't think we'll be done with this war before then."

Andriun gave a slow nod. "And that is... related to wood carving? Somehow?"

"It's a Kolmari tradition." Zaide stopped himself and lowered his hands. He'd felt defensiveness creeping into his words. He didn't have to be that way with Andriun. Of everyone Zaide had met, Andriun had most readily accepted him as Kolmari instead of broken-born.

He didn't have to explain anything else. Andriun nodded decisively. "Ah. For coming of age."

"Yeah. I should have started it a lot sooner, to tell you the truth. I should have had repairs on my cottage finished. I should have picked what I wanted to do with the rest of my life and been given a plot of land. The carving comes first, to know I understand all the fine intricacies of Kolmari craftsmanship. Then I'd start a courtship, and I'd build a house with my own hands for me and my wife to move into when we marry." Zaide turned the block over in his hand as he spoke, examining the shape he'd roughly scratched into its surface. When he said it like that, it sounded ridiculous.

Andriun stroked his chin. "Kolmari traditions seem complicated."

Zaide lowered his knife. "Aren't you the ones with tail-cutting rituals and stuff?"

"I am not sure I would call that a tradition, so much as a necessity." The hunter grinned and touched a hand to his neck, where the chain for the Captured Spring hung. "Besides, it may not be so necessary now. Ikan is not certain the Desheni will return to the north when the Rise has ended. Defending the birthplace of water is the Paragon's duty. The rest of them need not be there for the Paragon to meet expectations."

"And you closed it off, right?" Zaide hadn't seen him sneak off, but if he traveled with them now, he must have done it.

Andriun nodded to confirm the suspicion. "I went in the

night. I did not have to go far. My power is different now. When I touched the river that flows from that mountain, I was able to give it commands, so it was not necessary to travel."

"Convenient," Zaide said.

The hunter shrugged. "Perhaps."

Slowly, Zaide returned to carving. "What about you, though? You have traditions to mark the different stages of life, right?"

"Few," Andriun admitted. "Most traditions are rituals performed when rank passes from one to another. Otherwise, there are only two. The day a youth becomes a hunter, and the day a young man's bride is chosen."

"Chosen?" Zaide raised a brow. "Like when you propose, or?"

"The Desheni men do not propose. When a young man has proven himself, the elders will select his bride. She is given to him, and there is none of this troublesome courtship you Kolmari deal with." Andriun couldn't contain his grin.

Zaide lowered his knife again. "You don't get to pick your own wife? What if you hate her?"

"Why would they do that? The elders are not cruel. By the time one is old enough for a bride to be chosen, he will have befriended any number of matches. The elders know who you get along with. They watch everything. Besides, the bride and groom both have the opportunity to say no." Andriun shrugged. "To me, it does not matter much. I am not old enough for a wife."

"How old do you have to be?"

"It is different for all of us. For myself, the concern is perhaps not age, so much as... ah, a profound lack of maturity. This may have been influenced by my assistance in obtaining certain things without permission." One webbed hand flattened over the Captured Spring, then Andriun grinned again.

Zaide snorted softly. "You seem happy about it."

"Perhaps I am. I am older than you. Older than Tula, and

older than the princess. But my people live longer than Jadorans, Amrochans, or you. I am still young."

The choice of words struck Zaide as diplomatic, failing to identify him as either Kolmari or broken-born. "Still time for adventure?"

Andriun shrugged as if he couldn't help the statement's truth.

Zaide had to force himself to smile. "Most Kolmari marry by the time they're twenty. The longer I'm out here, the more I think I'll be lucky to even live that long."

"Well. For the sake of your traditions, I will hope you do."

"Thank you." Zaide shifted and snapped his knife closed. "Are you going to tell me why you really came over here, now?" He had no doubt it had nothing to do with his wood carving.

The way Andriun flinched told him he was right. "My uncle has a request."

Which Zaide was almost certain not to like. "Which is?"

"He wishes to fight you."

Zaide froze.

"Wait. No." Andriun held up a hand, palm out. "I have said that poorly. Let me try again."

"Please do."

Andriun cleared his throat. "My uncle has determined you to be a capable fighter. He wishes to test your skill for himself, so that he may see if there is room for him to teach you new things. You see, many Desheni hunters are capable fighters, but my uncle is unique. He carries a spear, but his specialty is a sword and shield."

That was decidedly less threatening. "Sword and shield doesn't seem like it would work well with..." Zaide flexed his hand, unsure if the commentary on the webbing the Desheni sported there was appropriate.

"Perhaps it does not. Or perhaps it does. I do not know, because I like my spear. And, uh, this thing." Andriun motioned toward the trident on his back.

"Trident," Zaide said.

Andriun frowned. "I know what it is called."

"Why didn't you say it, then?"

"Did you forget what this is called?" The hunter flexed one hand and pointed at his webbing with the other.

Zaide gave him a blank stare.

"Just because you know something does not make it comfortable to speak of, would you agree? I know what the trident is. What it represents means it is not a comfortable subject for me. I will improve with that, over time." Andriun sighed, then straightened. "The burden of responsibility is an unpleasant one, but you know this. You bear your own. Tell me, will you honor my uncle's request?"

He did bear his own. Zaide touched the pommel of the Spectrum Blade and willed it to share its opinion of a sparring match. No answer came. Discouraged, he put away his knife and the block of wood. "I guess so."

"Good." Andriun sounded genuinely pleased. "Come. I wish to see this happen."

Zaide bit back a remark that was more pithy than his friend deserved. He should be grateful; he'd hoped to find some opportunity to train with someone more experienced than he. From what he'd seen against the goborrins and the bizarre, many-tentacled creature they'd left slain on the mountainside, Ikan fit that description better than most.

When they reached Ikan, the man stood to receive them. "You've accepted," he remarked as he looked Zaide over. He didn't seem surprised, but pleased. "I will fetch my weapons."

"Looking forward to it," Zaide lied as he waited for the new Shaman to do just that. He wanted to practice. He wanted to spar. But he couldn't seem to shed the notion that something was amiss, and that sleep would have been a wiser choice.

～

For days, Zaide and Ikan sparred whenever their procession halted for rest. Andriun had not exaggerated. Ikan was exceptional in combat, and fought in ways Zaide had never seen. By the end of their third match, he'd given Zaide his shield. Before the fourth began, he'd fashioned a replacement for himself out of wood. It was a poor replacement for the worn metal shield Zaide now carried, but Ikan insisted Zaide would need it more. With the sense of wrongness that had plagued him since before they departed the ruined village, Zaide felt inclined to agree.

The party moved slowly with the entirety of that village accompanying them. More than once, he'd considered asking Lark if they should break away and move ahead, but Andriun was busy getting instruction from the village elders and Tula was busy writing essays on their oral histories. Lark remained alone most of the time, but now and then, she walked with Tanna or stood with the Desheni woman to watch Zaide and Ikan fight. All of them were occupied with something that seemed generally important, so he willed the itch between his shoulder blades to vanish.

On the sixth day after their departure, the itch refused to abate and he spent most of the morning restless. By noon, he understood why.

"People?" Tula asked in a whisper.

Zaide was just as concerned. The road between Ganede and Beshnai had been all but empty when he'd traveled it alone. Now, a steady flow of people moved north in small bands.

"The ships," he whispered back.

Beside him, Lark gave a grim nod. She moved ahead to speak with Ikan, their voices low but their glances to the south weighted with meaning.

Andriun fell in step beside Zaide. Instead of the princess and his uncle, he focused on the faces of those who filtered past them on the wide dirt road. "It has been some time since I was allowed to come this way, but I do not remember so many people."

"What else is around the Ellean sea?" Zaide asked. "Ganede and Jadora are at the mouth of the bay, but otherwise?"

Andriun tilted his head, thinking. "Estkel is in the marshy river mouths. It is nearer to Jadora, truly, but the road that circles the sea is easier to navigate. Then there is Sast, but no one can walk there."

Zaide only sort of recalled the island settlement. They were so unwelcoming, they weren't worth thinking about at all. "So more would be headed to Estkel. Maybe trying to loop all the way around to Jadora." Unless Estkel was under siege, too. Jadora's well-being hung in the back of his mind, a shadow over everything else. It pained him to think about it, but he didn't see how the desert city could mount a proper defense so soon after the siege from the inside.

"Estkel is too easy to cut off," Tula said. "No one seeking shelter would go there."

"So everyone's headed to Beshnai." How long had they been going? The people passing them were worn, fear-stricken, and eyed the traveling Desheni with concern. Yet no one tried to stop them. Zaide puzzled over that as another small group shuffled by, their heads down and their eyes focused on the dirt under their feet. There was one clear difference Zaide saw. The majority of the Desheni carried spears. Those fleeing were unarmed.

He glanced ahead. Their party was slowing. Ikan had stopped someone on the road to speak with, his face hard. Maybe that answered some questions. With a warrior that fierce heading their group, how could anyone think they were anything other than soldiers?

Zaide watched, but their faces told him nothing. He shifted his attention to Lark. Part of him wanted to approach her, to ask direction and work out a plan. Her face was unreadable, just like Ikan, but the familiarity they shared made her more approachable.

She caught him looking and turned so he could not see her face.

He hadn't done anything wrong, but it still made him feel sheepish. He rubbed the back of his neck. "So what do we do now?" This time, he glanced to Andriun. In spite of their friendship and frequent joking, he struck Zaide as the sort of person he ought to defer to. Maybe it was the presence of that trident leaning against his shoulder.

"Wait for instructions," Andriun said, calm and steady. He didn't seem older as Paragon, but he did strike Zaide as different. Wiser, maybe, in a way Tula wasn't. Or perhaps that was the way Andriun had been all along. "They will come."

Zaide would have preferred to take his sword and charge ahead, but Lark remained with the leader of the Desheni, and he didn't feel as if he could leave her behind. It had been easy, back when they'd first met, when she'd gotten on his nerves and he'd abandoned her in Kolmar's temple. It was strange how his feelings had changed. Now, he couldn't picture their team without her.

"We need a name," he said absently.

"A name?" Tula repeated. "For what?"

"Our team." He mustered a smile. "We're together until the end now, right? Until we see this through?"

"That is my intent." Andriun drummed his fingertips against the trident's pole. "I suppose we are a team."

Tula gasped and squeezed her hands to fists before her chest, much like an excited child. "There have been teams before, right? Is there a name for us? Like, a traditional one?" She bounced on her toes until Andriun put a hand on her head and pushed her heels down flat.

"No. There are just the Paragons. And the Bladebearer." Andriun glanced toward Lark, a thoughtful frown on his face.

Did he doubt the princess's place in their group? Or was it him? The way the role of Bladebearer came tacked on the end made him suspect it had more to do with the latter. Zaide cleared his throat. "I already know I'm a bit of an exception. The Bladebearer is usually someone from Amroch's royal family, right?"

Andriun started to speak, then shut his mouth and gave a slow nod. It took a while for him to add words to his answers. "As far as I know, the royal family was given the throne for that exact reason. So they could stand as leaders, and so they held the authority to summon the Paragons and retrieve the Spectrum Blade at any time it may be needed."

"Then it should have gone to her," Zaide concluded. It wasn't new information. They'd already been over that.

"One would expect it to pass to the next member of that bloodline. I cannot imagine what made the blade choose you. Which, I mean no insult by that," Andriun added the last quickly, a glint of apology in his dark eyes. "It is just..."

"Odd," Tula finished for him.

Zaide found himself agreeing, but the princess had turned, and she and Ikan moved toward them in unison.

"Your suspicions were well-founded," Ikan announced when he grew near. He did not speak loudly, but his voice was strong and his words carried anyway. Around them, Desheni grew still and waited to hear what information he'd gleaned.

Lark presented it, instead. "Ganede is under attack, but Elsanna may be thanked for disrupting whatever they intended. When some of the ships in the bay failed to unload at either port, Elsanna sent guardswomen to investigate and determine whether the ships should be directed to Jadora or Ganede. They found goborrins."

Tula almost beamed. "She's doing a good job."

"She has a lot of experience," Zaide said. "So, they're fighting on ships?"

"They have tried to seize the ships or run them aground, but the effort has been fruitless. The goborrins are making landfall, though a few at a time instead of all at once."

Now Tula's face fell. "They won't be able to defend Jadora and save Ganede at the same time."

"No," Ikan agreed. "Those fleeing Ganede have said the guardswomen have joined with their own guard force to encourage residents to evacuate. They will need more than mere swords to drive back the enemy now."

"Then they will have spears," Andriun said.

His uncle nodded. "I cannot spare many. I must protect our people. But I will send what I can, and you will lead them. Right now, the Paragon's power is the greatest thing the Desheni can offer as aid."

"So we're going ahead?" Tula asked.

"Immediately." Lark looked at Zaide as if she had more to say, but she shut her mouth tight and tilted her head to order him to move.

He answered by gripping the Spectrum Blade's hilt and turning toward the south. "If we hurry, we can make it in a day."

"Then let's pray the defensive forces can hold out that long." Lark's expression remained determined, but Zaide thought he saw a ghost of uncertainty in the tiny lines at the corners of her eyes.

He'd ask about their team later.

CHAPTER THIRTY-ONE

WHEN THEY CRESTED the last hill and Ganede came into view, the first thing Zaide saw was the smoke. He fought back thoughts of the other battlefields he'd seen. Jadora, Kolmar, Amrochan. They'd all been shrouded in smoke. No matter where he went, he found the same sort of destruction.

Tula stepped forward and planted her hands against her hips. "Well, it's a good thing we're bringing the Paragon of Water."

Andriun's brow furrowed. "What?"

"I'll bet you're a lot more effective than those powder extinguishers the librarians keep around." The Magister pantomimed dumping water on flames and punctuated the act with a hiss.

Lark interrupted by planting both hands on her shoulders and steering her down the road. "Keep moving. We'll be there soon."

There was something else she didn't say, but Zaide heard it in her tone. *They need us.* He only hoped she was right.

It seemed preposterous to think their tiny band could turn the tide of war, but he'd seen it several times already. Yet from where they stood, he couldn't see the state of things or plan for the battle ahead. All he knew was the goborrins were using fire, like they always did, and the Spectrum Blade was ready. It thrummed softly at his side, radiating a strange sort of energy through his hip. It spread down his leg and up his ribs, soaking into him, setting his senses on edge.

Andriun shared a few words of instruction with the Desheni hunters who traveled alongside them and they gave a sound of assent before the whole group continued down the sloping landscape. None of the hunters were familiar, and Andriun had not introduced any of them, but they had all volunteered and fixed their eyes on the battle ahead with a stoicism Zaide admired.

They trekked past a steadily growing stream of people fleeing the city. Zaide itched to draw his sword, but he moved faster with it sheathed.

Near the city's edge, Lark waved for them to halt. "Who else has been thinking of strategy on the way down?"

Warmth creeped up Zaide's neck. He should have been. He hadn't.

"We need to find a way to identify the ships bearing goborrins and prevent them from reaching the shore," Andriun said.

Tula nodded. "If we can identify them, then I can set the ships on fire."

"And I could push them farther out to sea, I suppose, but it does not look as if that is the best use of my power." Andriun's brows drew together as he gazed across the city. It was dusk, and fire rose from many of Ganede's wooden buildings. The blaze was spreading fast.

"You need to focus on putting out fires," Lark said. "Take your hunters to defend you. Fire would be dangerous in the city, so Tula, if those are too big for you to extinguish, you need to be on the beach. When ships make landfall and goborrins emerge, set them aflame. Go."

The Magister gave a single nod, then bounded toward the

city, her red hair streaming behind her in a strange mirroring of the flames that reached for the sky.

Andriun shared the orders with the Desheni and they peeled off in a different direction, headed for the largest blaze.

"What about me?" Zaide asked.

"You're my bodyguard," Lark said.

"Bodyguard?" He tried not to sputter. "But I can do better than that, I can—"

"You can do better than defending the princess and future queen of Amroch?" She quirked a brow, challenging him.

Zaide bit his tongue.

"Stay close to me. We're going to find whoever is in charge down there and let them know we're here to help." She gave her head a flick, the swish of her ponytail betraying her annoyance.

Let her be annoyed. Zaide fought back a scowl as he fell in step behind her and reached for his sword. Goborrins flowed through the streets, chasing people and skirmishing with guards. They'd have to approach those first to gain directions, and he wouldn't be caught without his weapon in hand.

The Spectrum Blade whispered as it slid from its sheath, the soft rasp something like music in his better ear. He savored it. The sword shone with swirling colors, rippling and flowing in patterns that reminded him of sunlight falling through the trees.

It flashed as Lark led him into the thick of the battle. A goborrin saw him and charged, but he was ready and met its strike so hard, sparks flew from his blade. The beast's crude sword screeched as it slid down the Spectrum Blade's razor-sharp edge. The sword's light intensified as Zaide flung the other weapon off and lunged in for a stab. The light spread from the point of impact, lancing across the monster's body as it screamed and fell.

A wave of cheers went up around him. The guards knew what the sword was, knew what he represented.

Maybe they would be enough to turn the tide after all.

"Who leads the defense?" Lark had to shout to make herself heard over the noise of battle.

Zaide didn't hear the guard's answer. Somewhere nearby, a chorus of shouts rose, followed by a crash and intense sizzle. Plumes of steam poured into the air. Andriun was already at work.

Goborrins fled the clouds of vapor. Zaide intercepted them, cutting them down one by one. These were the small goborrins, those that formed the numbers outside Amrochan, weaker than the massive brutes he'd first seen in Kolmar. The difference made sense now; the strongest had been sent to occupy the temple and the forest around it, what he now recognized as a vain attempt to keep them from retrieving the Spectrum Blade.

They'd been right to fear it. The sword sparked and shone as he dispatched monster after monster. It cut more easily than ever, imbued with Andriun's powers, yet something buzzed in the back of his head, warning him of something he couldn't quite grasp.

The sword was remarkable. The most powerful blade ever forged. Yet it bore a sense of anticipation, something yet to come. *Not enough,* the tingle in his hand whispered. He understood the sword's signals better and better, and in that moment, he agreed.

It wasn't enough.

He didn't know why he knew, but he knew there was something lacking. Was it him? Or was it the blade? Something hovered at the edge of what he had done, what he could do, begging him to find it.

Near the edge of the city, fire arced overhead and plunged down toward the bay. The cries that followed this time were not human. They drew him onward, past Lark and the guard she spoke with, pulling him toward the shore.

The princess snared his collar as he moved past. "Where do you think you're going?"

"We have to stop the ships," he said, though the jolt of her grasp made him stop and shake his head. He wanted to follow directions, meet her expectations and earn respect. What made him so eager to defy her now? In his hand, the Spectrum Blade vibrated as if it had been struck. It traveled up his arm like a shiver and formed a whine in his head.

You? He squeezed the hilt as if it might make the sound stop. It only intensified. Pulling. Pleading.

"Tula's in charge of the ships." Lark's voice could have cut steel. "Were you listening? Valla is here."

Zaide glanced up each of the streets around them. "Where?"

"Commanding the guardswomen. She'll be with Ganede's commander. If we find her, we can put together a better plan." Lark pointed toward the shore, where Zaide assumed the guardswoman had last been seen.

Blessedly, moving that direction made the Spectrum Blade grow still. He didn't know whether the quiver had been an actual movement or just a sense the sword gave him through their connection, but it didn't matter.

They'd not gone far before Valla came into view, her knives flashing in the firelight, but it wasn't goborrins she fought.

Instead, her blades clashed against a sword in the hands of a man with white hair.

They were equally matched, every blow met with a counter, but behind them, a new ship ran aground and spilled goborrins onto the sand.

"Zaide," Lark prompted.

He was already moving. Instead of the goborrins, he advanced on the man Valla faced. A spark of dread flickered on the guardswoman's face. Then she recognized him and her brows rose in a mixture of surprise and relief.

Alerted to his presence, the broken-born spun, but he wasn't ready and Zaide brought the Spectrum Blade down hard. It flashed as it struck the man's half-raised sword and the broken-born stumbled backwards. Zaide pressed in, hitting harder, raining a steady cadence of blows on the man until he fell to his knees.

Valla dealt the last strike.

A wave of disappointment crashed through him, not quite his own. He'd made it his fight, but he hadn't wanted to kill the man. The sword in his hand hummed with frustration over what it perceived as a slight, while Zaide pushed back against it with his thoughts. *He's a person, remember? We don't kill those!*

The indignation that prickled up his left arm was argumentative. He didn't have to hear anything to understand what it meant.

We kill when it's them. It's what we were made for.

That he knew the blade meant both of them, and not just itself, made him shudder.

"Thank the Maker for your timing!" Valla said, though she'd already turned to engage the first of the goborrins. Farther down the beach, Tula worked to stop another ship as long oars dragged it up onto the sand.

"It would have been better if we'd had more luck up north." Zaide took his shield from his back as he joined the guardswoman. He'd all but forgotten it in his haste to answer the sword's thirst for battle, but Ikan had given it to him, and he wouldn't let it go to waste.

She smirked. "Late is better than not at all, which is what we expected." The next wave of goborrins came and she lunged in with her blades like a whirlwind. She struck hard and fast, moving on before each monster hit the ground.

Zaide couldn't hope to match her speed, but he made up for it with accuracy. Every blow he landed was fatal, light searing in the wounds he left behind. They dispatched the first wave, then the second. Before the third emerged, flames exploded against the side of the grounded ship with such force that it lurched.

"Look out!" Zaide darted forward to catch Valla's arm and drag her back. The ship groaned as it rocked sideways and tipped onto the sand, landing right where she'd been, its masts cracking against the earth.

Her breath left her in a long rasp. "I'll forgive you for touching me," she conceded before she darted for the next ship.

"You're welcome." Zaide didn't know why he bothered. She was already out of earshot, spinning into the next attack. He adjusted his grip on his shield, grateful for the straps that held it to his arm as he'd pulled her to safety, then followed.

Ahead, Tula lobbed a fireball toward a ship in the bay, but the flames fell short and extinguished in the water. She kicked the sand and shouted something, though Zaide couldn't make it out. Judging by the look on her face, he was glad he couldn't.

"Zaide!" Lark's voice rang high, calling him back.

He twirled to face her, but she was pointing the other direction, toward a massive ship that had just crawled into sight. It turned toward the coast, the sheer size of it enough to drop his heart to his knees.

Torches or lanterns illuminated the ship's deck at regular intervals, the light glinting off the armor and weapons of so many goborrins, the twinkles resembled stars in the sky.

"Maker's mercy," he breathed.

Low, pounding drumbeats began on the ship and echoed out across the bay—not the beats of mimicked drumbird calls that he'd grown used to hearing in the forest, but the steady throb of war drums that shook his very bones.

That one ship was enough goborrins to overrun the city, no matter who was on their side. Zaide gritted his teeth and wheeled to face the princess. "Get Andriun down here!"

She fled into the city with a handful of guards on her heels.

Instead of gaping at the coming warship, Zaide turned and ran. He cut toward the water, where the sand was harder. He moved faster there, hindered only by the moments where the very edge of the waves made him stumble and splash. "Tula!" he shouted as he rounded the tipped-over goborrin vessel. Monsters had begun to come out a hole on the deck, but he ignored them, scanning the shore for the Magister as he ran.

A burst of flame silhouetted her against a pack of goborrins.

Zaide's thighs already burned, but he pressed harder and launched himself into the battle.

The Spectrum Blade tore through a goborrin's side, ripped free, plunged into another. They toppled around him, leaving him standing on the sand with his chest heaving.

Tula turned to him with her mouth open, ready to speak, but he cut her short.

"Tula, we need you. The big ship—"

She raised a hand, sparing his breath. "I called for reinforcements. Show me. We'll take it out."

He turned to point with the Spectrum Blade. It flared and brightened when he leveled it toward the ship.

Tula hitched her sleeves up above her elbows and stormed that way, goborrins forgotten. They fell over themselves trying to reach her and Zaide stepped into the fray. There were only a few left. The first all but stumbled into his sword, another already on the ground after tripping over its fellows. Zaide dispatched them both with fast, clean strikes before he tore into the rest.

When the last one fell, he ran to catch up with the Magister. Golden dragons glowed on her arms, bright in the deepening dusk. Andriun stood beside her, none of his Desheni at his back, a grim set to his mouth.

"I am strong," he said when Zaide approached, "but I am uncertain I can do anything to stop this."

"You don't have to stop it," Zaide panted. "Just slow it down. Tula, can you reach that thing with fireballs?"

Her grimace said enough.

He exhaled hard. "Okay. New plan. Andriun, see if you can pull it closer."

"Closer?" Andriun exclaimed.

"For the fireballs, silly!" Tula fanned her hands to the side, embers shimmering around them.

Zaide nodded. "For the fireballs. And I'll be... I'll... Maker's mercy, what am I supposed to do?" He raised his shield arm to rake a hand through his hair, but it was awkward and didn't work quite as he'd planned.

"Watch our backs," Andriun said as he pointed the trident's tines toward the sea. Water bubbled just offshore. It rose in an unnatural swell and rolled outward, undulating across the bay. The warship didn't even rock.

Zaide glanced over his shoulder, but the shore around them remained free of goborrins. Farther up the coast, Valla and a pack of guards and guardswomen held them at bay. He turned farther, searching for Lark, but she was nowhere to be seen.

"Fish guts." Andriun grimaced, then steeled himself. Concentration pinched his eyes and twisted the corners of his mouth. "It is heavy."

Tula scoffed. "Of course it's heavy, it's a giant ship full of pigs!"

She cupped a hand and the embers clashed, igniting a fireball in her palm. She took a few steps back, then gave herself a running start before she pitched the fireball out to sea. It took a long, powerful arc, but still landed painfully short.

"Blast it all," she grumbled.

"That is the idea, yes, but that blasted nothing." Andriun shifted his stance and strained to move the water around the ship.

Tula stuck out her tongue.

The water swelled around the ship, lapping against its sides in unnatural ways, yet it rose no higher and moved no faster. Andriun's jaw tightened.

"Nothing?" Zaide asked.

"I am not accustomed to trying to move so much water at once," Andriun said. "It is larger than it looks from the shore."

"Just push harder!" Tula made a shoving gesture with both hands.

A low growl escaped Andriun's throat. "If you think you are able to do better, you are welcome to try."

Beyond the ship and its lights, something glimmered in the

dark. Zaide shaded his eyes to block out the goborrins and their lamps, though he couldn't escape the way it glinted on the seawater. "What is that?"

Andriun retracted the trident and squinted into the distance.

Above the waters of the bay, a small, golden-orange gleam lit the sky. It flickered with movement, growing rapidly larger, and Zaide realized what it was that hurtled toward them in the night.

The moment she reached the same conclusion, Tula let out a whoop.

Reinforcements had arrived on wings of molten fire.

CHAPTER THIRTY-TWO

THE DRAGON PLUNGED toward the ship with talons bared. Zaide expected he'd raze the ship with flames, but instead, he struck the mast so hard, it shattered. The beam crashed onto the deck below, crushing goborrins beneath it.

"What is that?" Andriun exclaimed.

"He's a dragon, silly." Tula hopped from one foot to the other, pumping her fist in the air. "I wasn't sure he'd hear me from this far away, but he did."

His eyes widened. "Hear you? Maker's mercy, *that* is Magister Vorkaris?"

Zaide couldn't help but snort. "You know, a lot of these detailed oral histories you've apparently got would have been real useful to share before now."

Vorkaris banked in the air and came at the ship from a different angle. This time, flame did pour from his maw, bathing the ship's inhabitants. Far from surrendering, the goborrins retaliated with spears thrown toward the dragon's wings.

Andriun muttered something in his own tongue.

"What was that?" Zaide asked.

"It means—oh, how do I say it?" Andriun grasped at the air. "To trap outside a net? To think creatively. I have an idea."

Before they could ask what it was, water surged up the sand. It rose to his waist and lifted him off his feet. A second surge took Tula. At first, she shrieked. Then, as the water carried her out from the beach and held her high above the surface, she relaxed.

Zaide watched them drift toward the ship. Why hadn't he thought of that? It was far easier to take the Magister to the ship than to take the ship to the Magister. Seconds later, her fireballs joined the dragon's new wave of flames. No matter how the goborrins threw their spears, they fell short of the dragon's wings.

"What are they doing?" Lark's voice made him start. He'd stopped paying attention to his surroundings, preoccupied with the sight ahead. Any of the goborrins already on the ground could have taken him by surprise.

"Destroying a ship," Zaide said, hoping she hadn't noticed his distraction.

If she had, he couldn't tell. She swept an arm west and pointed at the horizon. "We have a problem."

Zaide sucked in a breath. Another massive ship had coasted into the bay, this one angled toward the rockier coast. "Goborrins can't swim."

"Valla has a spyglass. They're already loading smaller vessels."

Now that he looked, Zaide saw the guardswoman near the rocks. She peered out at the ship, the spyglass in one hand and a knife in the other. He winced. "Tula and Andriun are out there. We can't reach them." Would Vorkaris hear him if he tried to call for help? He'd felt the dragon touch his mind before, but he didn't know how to think words at him.

Lark's lips tightened. For once, she didn't seem to know what to say. The silence was unlike her.

Zaide met her eyes and held them. He didn't know what he was supposed to do, but he willed her to muster her courage.

"Guess we're stopping this one on our own." He started off to join Valla by the rocks.

"What? How?" The princess's voice cracked as she tailed him. "Zaide, we don't have the power! We don't have any archers, we don't have warships, the Paragons are busy—"

He didn't look back. "There has to be a way." That burning sense of *something* returned. It hummed in his senses the way the sword did, something just beyond his reach, begging him to find it.

Valla scarcely turned her head at his approach. "By my count, it's at least two thousand."

"Two thousand?" The tiniest quaver tinted Lark's words. "We can't possibly hold them off."

Zaide's palm itched. He tightened and released his grip on the Spectrum Blade, but it didn't abate. If anything, the prickle grew stronger. "Then we stop them in the water."

Heat touched his fingers. A hum in his arm.

Doubt creased her brow. "How can we?"

The ship had slowed. Goborrins slung their rowboats against its sides, lowering them with ropes.

Swing.

Zaide twitched. The thought wasn't his, more than a feeling, almost a voice. "I don't know, I..."

"You'd better think of something fast," Valla said. She lowered the spyglass and fitted two fingers to her mouth. Her shrill whistle was enough to make them both cringe.

Across the slope, guardswomen emerged from clusters of combat and pressed toward their commander.

Swing, the whisper came again.

"I'm trying," Zaide snapped. He raised his sword arm before he knew what he was doing.

Lark gasped and scurried back, beyond his reach. "Zaide, what—"

Swing!

He stifled a roar and swung hard.

Light flared in the Spectrum Blade and raced down its length at the peak of his swing. It tore free of the blade's tip with such force, Zaide staggered backwards. The blinding pillar of light lanced across the ship, tearing through its hull and the goborrins within. The crack of wood and piglike shrieks filled the night as the light winked out, leaving a trail of glittering motes in the air.

Zaide stumbled as the force abated and the blade dimmed.

"Maker's mercy, Zaide! What was *that*?" Lark squeaked.

"I don't know." His voice shook. "It just—it said—"

"Whatever it was, you'd better do it again." Valla pointed into the bay, toward the burning ship the others still struggled to stop. It loomed toward the docks without cease, even as the Magisters pelted it with fire. Andriun had returned to shore and pushed against its hull with all the waves he could summon. It was not deterred.

Zaide set his jaw and jogged down the slope, hopping a dead goborrin's body on the way.

Andriun did not so much as look up when he arrived. "They are loading the boats."

"Then we'd better be ready to fight the ones that make it to land," Zaide said. "Let go."

His friend nodded and stepped back, his shoulders sagging with exhaustion.

Zaide exhaled hard. *Do it again,* he thought at the sword as he gripped the Spectrum Blade tight and braced himself for the impending blast of power. *Whatever that was, just do it again.*

A pang of doubt shot up his arm, followed by determination.

Just one more time!

He set his jaw and swung.

Light streaked from the hilt and raced up the sword's length. It shot across the bay in the same brilliant beacon, zigzagging across the hull of the burning ship.

Goborrins screamed and flame burst outward as wood collapsed.

Zaide bore the light downward, ripping a hole in the bottom

of the ship. It crunched and lurched as Andriun seized the opportunity to push forward, flooding the depths of the vessel faster than naturally possible, silencing the monsters within.

Behind them, a wave of cheers rose from the city as the light winked out and the sword went dark.

Andriun raised his trident overhead with a shout of triumph.

Dazed, Zaide blinked to clear the afterimage of the beam, his arm sagging as a thread of cold crawled through his hand and seeped into his bones. A sense of sadness brushed his awareness, then faded like a sigh on the wind.

His heart skipped a beat. "Wait." He tried to focus on the sword in his hand, its form obscured by the glow that lingered even when he closed his eyes. "Wait!"

Someone bowled into him from the side. "You did it!" Lark cried, wrapping her arms around his shoulders.

Zaide swayed on his feet, then fell to his knees. The Spectrum Blade drove tip-first into the sand. Its steel was dark. No colors swirled. No light. Oh, mercy, what had he done?

Guards and guardswomen flowed down from the city. The fires had dimmed and a number carried makeshift torches. Many paused to ensure the goborrins they passed were dead. The rest moved past, intercepting the tiny goborrin rowboats that tried to reach the docks or beach, slaying them with a renewed vigor. The stragglers stood no chance.

"I can't believe it," Lark slipped away, a hand to her chest. "I never imagined, I didn't know—"

A rush of wings drowned out her words and churned dry sand from the shore. Vorkaris eased into a landing, then dropped to his belly to let Tula slide from his back.

"That was amazing!" the Magister shouted as she launched herself forward with such force, she stumbled and almost fell. "How did you do that? What did you do?"

"I killed it," Zaide choked. He touched the sword's surface, almost hoping it would reject him. Anything to show he hadn't undone everything they fought for.

The steel was cold. Lifeless.

Tula slowed her approach. "What?"

The princess looked at the blade and all the elation drained from her face.

Beside them, the dragon gave a low, uncertain rumble as he pushed himself back to his feet. *Its strength is unbalanced.* The words were soft, muted, unlike the head-splitting way Vorkaris had spoken to them before. He had to be speaking to all of them; the whole group looked his way.

"What do you mean?" Lark asked, though the dread on her face said she already understood.

Five elements compose the blade's power. The elements used to forge it. Fire, water, earth... these remain, but its power over light has been extinguished.

Zaide's heart sank and his chest constricted. "I didn't know. It —something told me—"

It does not matter, the dragon said. *What matters is that I have found you, Your Highness. I did not think I would in time.*

The princess tore her attention from the sword. "In time for what?"

When we parted, we still sought answers. I have found them, and they are not good.

"What about answers for this?" Zaide jabbed a finger toward the Spectrum Blade.

"Peace," Andriun said with a soothing gesture. "We already knew this was possible. It does not change our plans. If light is what it lacks, then the Oracle will be the one to aid us."

Yes, Vorkaris rumbled. *Her guidance is precisely what you need. In more matters than you know.* His reptilian gaze settled on the princess with enough weight to make her shrink.

"What more can there be, Magister?" Andriun bowed his head with deference when he spoke, a gesture the dragon seemed to appreciate, though Vorkaris still gave his wings an uneasy ruffle.

I flew north to seek you in the wilds, but you had already gone. It is a miracle that I passed near enough for your mortal Magister to summon me. Now we must go to the Oracle with all urgency, for I cannot counsel you in this.

"Is the news truly so bad?" Lark asked.

I can hardly imagine worse.

"Then we'd better get on the ships right away." Tula turned toward the docks, then put her hands against her hips and let out a thoughtful hum.

Travel among strangers is no longer safe, the dragon said.

Zaide shoved himself up and tore the Spectrum Blade from the sand. He'd never realized how different it was to hold the artifact. It had never been a normal sword, not truly. "Then we go together, alone. We've done everything by ourselves this long. What's one more thing?"

I fear ships will not be fast enough for your needs.

"Yeah, well, we have a lot of needs not being met right now," Zaide snapped.

The dragon bared his teeth and growled.

"Enough, both of you." Lark stepped between them. "Magister Vorkaris, you came bearing news. Stop tormenting us, please. What have you discovered that sent you to find me with such urgency?"

Vorkaris snorted, small plumes of smoke coiling from his nostrils.

Zaide lowered his head and made himself scan the area instead. All around them, people circled. They marveled at the dragon, whispered over the Paragons and the princess, and more than one finger pointed his way. He returned the Spectrum Blade to its sheath, uncomfortable with anyone else seeing the way it had gone dark.

How much haste had he stolen from them? What trouble could he have spared if he'd let the dragon try to demolish the second ship on his own? He tried to push the thoughts from his head, but they wouldn't go. A dozen times or more, the way he acted without thought had landed them in trouble, but somehow, he'd never expected an impulsive choice could cost so much. He turned his eyes to his feet as the dragon spoke again.

We sought the identity of the false Magister. We have found it, but who he was matters little now. Elsanna believes he meant to kill you. I believe she is right.

"Tell me something I don't know," Lark muttered.

Zaide tilted his better ear toward Vorkaris, though rationally, he knew it would do nothing to help him hear the voice inside his head. A voice much like the one he'd heard before he unleashed that beam of light, he realized. It was harsher, unfriendly, but tangible inside his mind in a way his own thoughts were not.

Tell me I didn't silence you, he thought at the sword. *Please.*

The sword gave no reply.

Vorkaris drew himself up, his draconic face unchanging, but his tone sympathetic in a way that made the look in his golden eyes into pity. *We also know who sent him to seize Jadora and claim your life.*

She tossed up her hands, exasperated. "And that is?"

A sense of dread lodged itself in Zaide's stomach as the dragon's eyes narrowed.

Your father.

GLOSSARY

Addare – (uh-dare) – An oasis city on the western coast of Amroch.

Amroch – (AM-roke) – The Allied Kingdoms ruled by King Sendassian. Originally a number of smaller kingdoms, unified as an empire for defense purposes.

Amrochan – (am-ROW-kan) – The capital city of Amroch.

Andriun – (AN-dree-un) – The Desheni Shaman's son.

Aren – A soldier stationed at the garrison outside Kolmar. Friend of Zaide and Resia.

Arkosh – A well-respected Master Librarian and one of Tula's mentors.

Athradan – The Desheni Shaman and the Paragon of Water. Leader of the Desheni people.

Beshnai – (besh-NIGH) – An isolated city on the northern coast of Amroch.

Broken-born – People born in the western kingdoms destroyed by Gadranus. Many seek refuge in Amroch, but face difficulty integrating due to their history in the war.

Bugrak – (BUG-rack) – Small, flat-faced and ugly gray creatures. Hunt in packs and use primitive weapons.

Captured Spring – One of the three artifacts. A vial that contains a self-replenishing healing tonic.

Chithal – (chee-thal) – A large port city and trade hub

Dasienna – (das-EE-en-uh) – The princess. King Sendassian's daughter.

Desheni – (duh-SHEN-nee) – A settlement named after the race of aquatic people who live there. The Desheni people bear blue-tinged skin, fin-like ears, webbed fingers, and gills on their necks.

Elder – Kolmar's chief overseer and most skilled mage. Zaide and Resia's mentor. Also known as the Paragon of Forest.

Elsanna – (el-san-nuh) – Chief of the Magister's guardswomen.

Estkel – (est-KELL) – A marshy city at the edge of the Ellean Sea.

Gadranus – (guh-DRA-nuss) – Breaker of the Shattered Lands, leader of the army that threatens to destroy Amroch. According to legend, he has been cursed to be reborn a thousand times as a punishment for his misdeeds.

Ganede – (gan-NEED) – Jadora's sister city. A port of trade on one of the peninsulas that frame the Ellean Sea.

Goborrin – (guh-BOR-rin) – Bipedal man-like monsters with pig-like faces and tusks. The smallest of the goborrins are the size of an adult man.

Ikan – A high-ranking Desheni hunter and a relative of Andriun.

Jadora – (jah-DOR-ah) – Ganede's sister city. Referred to as The Watcher. A fortress atop a desert plateau.

Kolmar – (coal-mar) – A small forest village in the southwestern region of Amroch.

Lark – The name Dasienna uses while traveling to protect her identity.

Magister – The leader of the fortress city of Jadora. Also known as the Paragon of Fire.

Molten Dagger – One of the three artifacts. An obsidian dagger that appears to have veins of magma trapped within it. Contains fire magic.

Moros – The warden of Jadora's prison and Elsanna's sweetheart.

Murk – A soldier from the garrison outside Kolmar.

Paragons – Leaders entrusted with the protection of the three magic artifacts.

Parral – (puh-rawl) – A port city at the southernmost tip of Amroch.

GLOSSARY

Plain – A soldier from the garrison outside Kolmar.

Raddan – A lieutenant and medic in Amroch's army. Stationed at the garrison outside Kolmar.

Resia – (ree-see-uh) – Zaide's foster sister and the new Elder. Bears a strong magical bond with the forest and wields earth magic.

Salamander – Bipedal lizard-like creatures found in Jadora's caverns. They attack anyone they deem an intruder.

Sarma – Resia's mother and Zaide's foster mother.

Sast – A fortress outpost on an island in the Ellean sea. Unfriendly to visitors. Little is known about the city.

Sendassian – (sin-das-see-an) – King of Amroch.

Shaman – The leader of the Desheni. Entrusted with the protection of the Captured Spring.

Shattered Lands – The western kingdoms destroyed by Gadranus.

Spectrum Blade – The fourth artifact. A legendary weapon said to be the only thing that can strike down the cursed knight Gadranus.

Tinith – (ten-nith) – A marketplace large enough to be its own city.

Tula – (too-lah) – An apprentice librarian at the Great Library in Jadora. Fancies herself an archaeologist and adventurer.

Vale Hymnflute – One of the three artifacts. A set of wooden pan pipes that serves as anchor for Kolmar's Vale magic. It bears power over earth and wind.

Vale magic – A spiritual shield that lays over Kolmar's valley and protects the forest from evil.

Valla – (vah-lah) – A high-ranking Jadoran guardswoman. One of Elsanna's most trusted soldiers.

Verlin – Resia's father and Zaide's foster father.

Vorkaris – The Magister who sealed away the Molten Dagger. Also known as the Dragonster, according to Zaide.

Yithel – (yee-THEL) – A trade city along the river north of Amrochan.

Zaide – (zayd) – A broken-born refugee fostered in Kolmar after his mother's death. Accidentally involved in helping the princess recover the artifacts and saving Amroch.